THE WORM IN
EVERY HEART

BOOKS BY GEMMA FILES

KISSING CARRION

THE WORM IN
EVERY HEART

GEMMA FILES

PRIME BOOKS

PUBLICATION HISTORY: See afterword for full details. "Nigredo," "Sent Down," and "By The Mark," are original to this collection.

Published in the United States by **Prime Books**
an imprint of **Wildside Press**
www.primebooks.net

ISBN: 1-894815-76-9

CONTENTS

INTRODUCTION

by Nancy Kilpatrick

I first met Gemma Files in Toronto in the early 1990s. I'd been a fanatical purchaser of vampire books and had a vast collection of titles (which now exceeds 1700, God help me!). Vampire volumes had come into vogue by then, and since I'd managed to acquire just about everything written prior to that time, I was relegated to the fresh blood of newly published works. Every month I would watch the cash register tally up four or more hardcover titles, depleting my finances and overburdening my bookshelves. I frequently purchased from Bakka Books, which at that time was Toronto's only SF/F/H bookstore. John Rose, the owner, kept saying: "You must know Gemma. She's the other vampire collector."

So I'd heard about Gemma, but we never seemed to be browsing in Bakka on the same day of the night of the full moon. I'd also been informed by a discerning bookish pal Bob (Hadji) Knowlton about his friend Gemma: "You've got to meet this girl. She's brilliant, and she loves vampires." I didn't put the two Gemmas together until the day I received a call. Gemma and I chatted a while, and I invited her to visit and see my book collection, and all the other vampire memorabilia (read: junk!) I'd acquired over the years, like a piece of plaster from the Grand Theater in Derby where Dracula was first staged, a promotional keyring from Dracula's Wallpaper Warehouse in Ontario, the four foot tall Nosferatu punching bag . . .

Right from the get-go, I knew Gemma was, as Bob said, "Brilliant." This young thing was just wiggling out of journalism school. She was the precocious offspring of parents in the arts, which likely set her up for being highly educated, thoughtful, attracted to all things creative, a bit melancholy, and extremely well read in the wide world of books, not just those involving bloodsuckers and other demons of the night. She arrived at my door wearing her multi-colored Moroccan cap, serious but modern glasses, and carrying a huge backpack which she always seemed to be lugging around; we talked vampires for hours. Needless to say, I liked her immensely. Not only was it refreshing to chat with another vampirophile, but I found her open and honest and not fearful about plunging into free-rolling discussions involving the deeply existential and macabre subject matter I favor. I became a kind of loaning-library for books she hadn't yet read, and a minor sounding board for projects, of which she had plenty in mind, so we met regularly for a while, until life impinged—for me, that meant the ending of a marriage and a move to Montreal.

At the time I met Gemma, she had been writing regular columns, mainly on film, for one of Toronto's entertainment weeklies, *EYE Magazine*. Besides reading her published articles, she handed me bits of her fiction to peruse, and I always came away thinking the same thing about her work: "Brilliant". Clearly this girl was destined for great things. So it surprised me not when she catapulted out of the small press and began selling her short stories to major anthologies like the cleverly-conceived, Stephen Jones-edited *The Mammoth Book of Vampire Stories by Women*, and *Dark Terrors 6*. Ellen Datlow picked up her amazing tale "The Emperor's Old Bones" (originally published in *Northern Frights 5*, and which is included in this collection) for *Year's Best Horror and Fantasy* (13). Gemma also sold stories to television, and won the International Horror Guild Award for Best Short Fiction. If I'd put money where my thoughts were about Gemma's fate, I'd be rich now, but then who would have bet against me?

Gemma utilizes style and grace in her writing, and possesses an adventurous spirit that shows in her work. She kindly penned "Rose Sick" for *Seductive Spectres*, one of the erotic horror anthologies I edited under the nom de plume Amarantha Knight. I then invited her to submit another story for *Demon Sex*. That story, "Bottle of Smoke" (which you'll read in this collection), was picked up by *The Hunger*, the HBO TV series of erotic horror shows, and then she went on to sell the program four more of her fine tales!

Now Gemma is all grown up as a writer, teaching film at a university, happily collecting accolades for her work. I take some sort of maternal pride in her successes. I'm one of the people who knew-her-when, who has never had a doubt that she will reside among the stars one day. Her writing is layered and textured. Her imagination and the subject matter she explores are reminiscent of Caitlin Kiernan's work. At the same time, she chooses words with a cleverness and sensitivity that reminds me of Poppy Z. Brite's short fiction. She shares the immediacy and accessibility of Neil Gaiman's writing.

But don't misunderstand me: Gemma Files is no copycat. She is part of the new wave of wordsmiths that add class to darker fiction by the intelligent use of language, and elevate the fantastic back to its rightful place as literature, reconnecting to its classical roots: *Dracula, Frankenstein, The Picture of Dorian Grey*, anything by Poe. Those beautifully constructed works that still, after more than a century, leave us shivering and breathless because their authors understood the power of words, that syntax could rupture readers, and do what Franz Kafka said it should, "melt the frozen sea within". Under that broad umbrella of the resurrectionists of this terrifying genre, Gemma Files is unique. Her work may leave you breathless. It could awaken realms within. At times you might sit stunned, wondering at the richness of writing, reconnecting to the reasons you have always loved to read.

In *The Worm in Every Heart*, Gemma's eclectic second collection, time and space are spanned: "Nigredo" is set in Warsaw during WW2, when gods beget monsters; "Ring of Fire" features a madman who uses the 1857 mutiny in India to his advantage; "The Guided Tour" takes us hitchhiking through the bountiful US of A; "Year Zero" reveals unexpected fallout from the French Revolution; the protagonist of "Flare" is an unusual Toronto arsonist; "Bottle of Smoke" puts a female spin on a tale that could be from the Arabian Nights; "Fly-by-Night" pits a modern military medico against an ancient vampire; "In the Poor Girl Taken by Surprise" revamps a werewolf legend from Quebec; a 19th century Russian scientist creates life in "A Single Shadow Make", but who is man, who monster?; "The Land Beyond the Forest" indulges the recollections of an English vampire of noble birth; "The Kindly Ones" questions whether or not a mother from Scotland is capable of love; a centurion from ancient Rome captures the wrong British girl in "Sent Down"; "By the Mark" blends flora, poetry and witchy alienation; "The Emperor's Old Bones" reveals a dark Chinese custom; and "The Narrow World" shows how sex magick can go awry.

The Worm In Every Heart beckons readers to a literary danse macabre that spans the ages and swirls through the cultural mosaic. The grim melody of life's bleakness blends well with the dark harmonies offered in these stories. These are fatal rhythms, ones we're all familiar with; the Reaper's scythe keeps the time. And Gemma's work is timeless. Destined to last. You can bet on it.

Nancy Kilpatrick
Montreal—2004

NIGREDO

It's 1944, late September, and Kotzeleh's just about decided that God probably doesn't exist—that that's definitely the best way to think about it, at any rate. Since, otherwise, she'd be forced to conclude He meant all this deliberately, and find Him. And kill Him for it.

On the eastern bank of the Vistula, just visible from Warsaw's borders, the Red Army have taken Praga; it was their lure which incited the Home Army to rise back in August, when they seized two-thirds of the city within three days: 40,000 armed insurrectionists with 210,000 unarmed helpers. But the Russians just squat there still, waiting, as reinforcements led by S.S. Lieutenant-General Erich von dem Bach-Zelewski—6,000 of their own defectors amongst them—continue to force the rebels back into Stare Miasto, the Old Town . . . down into miles and miles of sewers where food is scarce, water polluted, dysentery rife.

Warsaw's is a history of invasion, as Lev the Rabbi tells Kotzeleh whenever they have enough free time for talk, and sometimes when they don't; the city has been occupied more often than not, by anyone within marching distance. The Swedes, the Russians, the Prussians, the French—and after the French came the Russians again, a fact (Kotzeleh occasionally thinks) that really should have told the Home Army's leaders something, within context.

"How far do these tunnels go down?" Kotzeleh asks Lev, absently. He shrugs.

"Five hundred years or more, maybe."

"Nu? So long?"

11

"They've got catacombs here, just like in Paris. Pits of bone from the Plague. Some of them even feed into crypts where the churches used to be."

"Before the bombs?"

He smiles. "Before this shithole was even a real city."

Kotzeleh accepts this concept without question. Above them, the grating shakes with each new howitzer-hit, sifting stalactites of fecal matter down into the scum they wade in; von dem Bach's ordinance uses shells almost a metre in diametre, able to penetrate two metres of concrete. At seventeen, Kotzeleh's world has shrunk to nothing more than a compendium of holes where things used to be: Buildings, synagogues, people. Solidity, permanence, they're things of the past; this is a New Age, as Tateh used to say.

"My little thorn," he'd called her. "Be a thorn in their sides, my Kotzeleh. Go down smiling. Go down *killing*."

Now she does her worst, which usually works. And when it doesn't . . .

After Warsaw finally does fall, which (as it happens) won't be all so very long from now—over and over and over again, in the long, dark century to come—Kotzeleh will map in dreams these tunnels which are her second birthright. Will wander them once more with knife and gun in hand, searching in vain for the secret step-parent who occupies them still. Somewhere.

Here in 1945, though, Kotzeleh's shoes squish when she walks. Their soles are sodden cardboard, cloth sides soaked through, filled from top to bottom with sewer-water slush. When she takes her stockings off, her toes are a mass of white blisters she can peel away one-handed. Seams of dirt map her long, gaunt legs from calf to thigh.

How long have you been down here, dumpling? the contact asked her, cautiously, the last time she bought guns from him. *It's Katarczyna, am I right?*

My name is Kotzeleh.

Kotzeleh. But seriously, dear—how long?

A month. Two, might be.

More like more.

As though time mattered, down here. Or up there.

*No one should be down here for MONTHS, let alone a—*But here he'd trailed off, eyes skittering from Kotzeleh's calm, blue-grey stare, leaving her to fill in the blank herself: A woman? A girl? So sweet, so pretty and educated, so

Aryan-looking, made for more than a stinking corpse-mouth hole full of people like you? Like me?

If Marek knew, he'd begun again, finally. Kotzeleh cut him off.

Marek's dead, she told him. Then: *Do you have bullets for us, or not?*

Now she sits and watches the rats squabble over their own dead, thinking: *That'll be us, before long.* Remembers how fast a man named Okun died from eating just one, then remembers the burnt-meat smell from the squad's last manhole foray—two down one after the other, bang and bang, the rest dancing and screaming as they found the oil-filmed water suddenly alight from Fat Chavah's dropped Molotov—and feels her mouth start to water. Bites her cheek 'till she tastes blood, then stops . . . because it tastes too good, and she doesn't have any left to spare.

Down here, the cleanest things they ever see are Nazis. And she's already killed five this week without finding even one whose boots were small enough to fit her peeling, bleeding, sewer-sodden feet.

* * *

It's a set routine, even now: Back and forth along this trackless warren of dark water and dripping pipes, with only an occasional thin fall of barred sun, klieg-lights or street-fires to tell their way by. Kotzeleh and her crew work blind more often than not, avoiding traps by touch, memory and luck alike, marking whatever fresh ones they've tripped with braille-subtle scratchings, chalkmark scrawls like scat or spoor. From Old Town right along the main sewer under Kracowskie Przedmiescie, and out again at Warecka; check each station 'till they find someone left alive, make report, then double back again down into the dark, the wet. The long and pungent miles of echoing silence.

"Hell has seven levels, did I ever tell you that?" Lev the Rabbi asks—in a gasping whisper—as they slip free from the tangled knot of rusty barbed wire blocking their path, once a perfectly useable shortcut between storm-drains. "They go down like a ladder, rung by rung: Gehenna, Sha'are Mawet, Sha'are Zalmawet, Be'er Shahat, Tiit Ha-Yawen, Abaddon, Sheol—but that's not all, no. Because below even that, even further, you have the sea of Genesis, of first Creation: Tohu Yi' Bohu."

A harsh name like salt on the lips, warm and rough and weirdly familiar. That uterine sea we all swim in at least once, forgotten long before we know to try and remember its safely rocking waves, its full and buoyant embrace.

Pure Kabbalistic crap, of course—mystical babble like half of everything else Lev spouts, most times seemingly at random. He cut his sidelocks back when the fighting started, so he's probably damned now, and knows it. Still, the gesture also put him long past the point where fear of potential pollution might stop him from chattering on to Kotzeleh about anything Torah-related that slips into his head, under any circumstances; Katarczyna Mendesh, the least Jewish-looking Jewess in Warsaw, barely raised with a sense of her own heritage that extends beyond a lingering taste for gefilte fish and matzoh-ball soup.

Old habits really do die hard, she thinks. Then: *A good enough way TO die, if you had to pick one.*

But at least Lev's monologues help pass the time, as the rest of the group have already come to appreciate; give them something to take their minds off the muck around them, if only for a moment. Distract them from fixating on the little nagging details like that something slimy which hangs, caught, in the middle of the wire-bale they've just dodged past—ragged, half-submerged, some long-gone child messenger's discarded coat, maybe. Or maybe . . .

. . . something more.

Dead from hunger, sickness, a bullet in the back left too long untreated. Or smothered and cooked bone-black by that thing the surface troops keep warning is on its way, von dem Bach's famous *Taifun-gerat*, the Nazi storm-starter: A portable engine made just small enough to seal over manholes, pumping gas down into all the relevant nooks and crannies; one brief touch of a match, one stray spurt from a flame-thrower's nozzle, and all the scurrying in the world won't save you from the blast.

Like roaches from a burning butcher's shop, Kotzeleh thinks, unable to stop herself. While Lev adds, at the same time—right in her ear, already stinging with potential lockjaw where a stray strand of wire must have nicked her lobe—

"Everything starts over at the bottom, you see. Like in alchemy. Albedo out of nigredo, the gold out of the dungheap. The Philosopher's Stone, pretty girl; true paradise, regained."

Kotzeleh squints hard against the dim light, sniffing long and loud. "This doesn't smell much like paradise," she says.

A laugh, impossibly dry: "No, it doesn't, does it?"

Up ahead, Fat Chavah gives a warning hiss—footsteps, jackboots, passing by above. Lev and Kotzeleh freeze, rooted in the murky eddy, feeling for their triggers. But it's a false alarm, "like always" . . .

Except when it isn't.

"Could be we just haven't gone down far enough yet," Lev suggests, finally—trying to sound like he's joking, probably. And failing.

* * *

A day later, loaded down with new-won weaponry and making straight for Home Army headquarters—Ochota, 80 Wawelska Street, the last Old Town building left both standing and occupied—Kotzeleh and her companions run straight into that same chatty contact who sold them bullets sloshing back the other way, a straggly crocodile of fellow refugees in tow. The sound of their guns cocking in the dark makes him jump and freeze, 'til he takes a hesitant half-step further into the light and realizes who's leading the pack.

Relaxing: "Oh, so it's you, dumpling."

And now with the charm.

"As you see," Kotzeleh says—stating the obvious, studiously bland. "You should tell your people to walk quieter from now on, if they don't want to run into company; there's two patrols a mile 'til you get to the suburbs."

"Ah, yes." The contact leans closer, lowers his voice, assuming an intimacy Kotzeleh finds vaguely grotesque. "And you know why, of course."

"To kill us."

"Partly." A beat. "They got Radoslaw this morning."

Radoslaw.

Colonel Jan Mazurkiewicz, the Home Army's highest-ranking "officer". Behind her, Kotzeleh hears Fat Chavah make a noise somewhere between a sob and a sigh; Lev sags sideways against the sewer wall for a second, but masters himself almost immediately. While Kotzeleh just stands there, her cold eyes half-lashed, daring the contact to frisk her (metaphorically) for any signs of normal human weakness: Staring down the future's foregone conclusion like it was just another open pipe-mouth full of stink and danger, just another black and empty barrel on another Nazi gun.

So this is the end, she thinks, feeling nothing. And notes, aloud, with an acid little nod to his sleeve—

"That must be why you took off your armband."

The contact shrugs, unfazed. "Wear the Home Army's insignia from now on, you might as well paint a target on your chest." He gestures at the hard-breathing crowd behind him like he's showing off what he bought for dinner. "*They* need me alive, dumpling, to get them past the barriers; they want me alive, because *they* want to live. Can you blame them?"

THEM, no. But—

"—you should go too, maybe," Lev puts in, suddenly. Adding, as Kotzeleh pins him with a glare: "Look, it only makes sense, nu? While you still can."

"I'm fine where I am."

"But you . . . " He trails off. "You could get word to somebody, that's all I'm thinking. Get them to send back reinforcements."

And if there's no one left to send, Rabbi? What then?

"Why don't you go yourself, if you're so eager?" she snaps.

And now it's Lev's turn to raise his brows and shrug, throwing an ironic glance the contact's way—his thoughts so clear that Kotzeleh can practically hear them in her head. *What, me, with the Protocols Of The Elders Of Zion tattooed on my face? To men like this, I'm not even Polish—but you, Kotzeleh, you. You, my dear . . .*

. . . can pass.

As she already has done, many times, and may well do a few more before the bullet hits the bone. Yet the injustice of it twists in her nonetheless, raising a flush under sewer-pale skin—the contact, smiling that bad-teeth corpse's smile at her, his offer a secret handshake, a shared sin, the same temptation she's had to guard against since bombs first began to fall. A siren song whose first verse always sounds like *leave the Jews behind and come along, sweetheart, you with your pretty blond hair and your straight little nose, so Aryan-pure you'd fool the Führer himself,* whose chorus always sounds like *just leave them to die down here like the rats they are, come along with us up into daylight, and survive . . .*

"You could live a long time," the contact tells her, smiling wider. "You're young yet, dumpling."

Kotzeleh takes one last look at him for reference, then tucks her gun away again; he isn't worth the effort, let alone the ammunition. Answering, simply—

"No. I'm not."

To which the contact frowns, mouth kiting up on one side, like he's bitten into something sour. But whatever comeback he's planning is derailed when—with an ugly, scraping CLANG—the manhole above them is suddenly prised up, popping free like a boil to reveal a knot of gaping Nazi faces.

The refugees flatten, shrieks rising. A woman grabs both her children with a hand across each one's mouth, hauling them backwards out of sight, as confusion—ever-infectious—rips through the crowd around her. Caught full in the spill of sunshine, Kotzeleh goes for her gun but somehow gets her knife instead; she turns to see the contact waving frantically upwards, yelling: *"Mein herren*, no, don't shoot! We—"

And: Is that really the trail of an "s", right there at the end? Kotzeleh will never know, not that it matters—her blade has already punched through his voicebox and out the other side before she even thinks to aim it, loosing a startlingly vivid pump of heart's blood twenty feet in the air to spatter some Nazi's cheek.

Because that's what you get for not wearing your armband, you "charming" bastard. You get to die after all, the same as everybody else, even dirty Christ-killers like Lev—

(and me)

Another refugee, male this time, swerves in mid-flight to punch her full in the mouth, *hard*. And spits, as he does it: "Crazy bitch!"

Kotzeleh grins, through pinkening teeth. "Crazy *Jew* bitch," she corrects, gently.

Then the shooting finally starts.

Machine-gun chatter magnified from a thousand reverberate curves, kicking up brown spray as Chavah, Lev and Kotzeleh dive one way, the refugees the other—hot whine ruffling the rat-tailed nape of Kotzeleh's neck as Lev fires past her, a lucky shot that erases half of one Nazi's face in a single bloodjet burst. And then down, down, further and faster, slipping and sliding on corroded metal, shit-slimed clumps of trash.

They pause near a grate, a rushing waterfall of sludge, hearts hammering; Kotzeleh puts her head between her knees to clear it, and raises it again to an unfamiliar sound. Some odd sort of rhythmic, mechanical grunting that reaches them only sporadically, sandwiched between fresh volleys.

"They should be chasing us," Lev murmurs, to himself. Then, watching Fat Chavah sniff and Kotzeleh wrinkle her brow, still trying to place that ever-growing noise: "What is it you're smelling, you two?"

Fat Chavah: " . . . flowers?"
Gas.

* * *

Not even a hundred years since the Warsaw sewers' endless night; she *is* still so very young yet, after all. Or at least by her new tribe's reckoning.

Kotzeleh knows about monsters, then as now. The golem, the vampire, the dog-headed saint: She knows monsters are real, knows they exist. She's seen their work first-hand, and paid them back in kind for tear gas down the manholes and teenaged snipers bleeding out in the streets, rape and looting at will, doctors and nurses shot on sight, thousands herded into public parks and executed under manicured trees, in the genteel company of gazebos and swan-pools. 18,000 insurgents dead and 6,000 badly wounded, 15,000 marched away to camps as prisoners of war, 180,000 civilians killed outright—and 10,000 German dead balanced on the other end of the scale, 7,000 gone missing and 9,000 seriously injured, but never enough, never. Never.

No penance wipes this slate completely, even now. No ocean rift runs so wide or deep as to wash this stained hand clean again. It's permanent, like dye: No monster can ever change their nature, no monster can ever be forgiven. No more than anyone else—anyone equally guilty—ever can.

Not even her.

* * *

So: A soundless rush, some massive exhalation—one bright, hot gush of wind sweeping down on them from above, the *Taifun-gerat*'s pestilential breath. Fat Chavah turns, face crisping; a second later, she, Kotzeleh and Lev fall headlong through grate and floor alike as the walls collapse, the ceiling falls, the side of the pipe cracks open like a rusty iron scream. Down into the boiling mud with their hair and clothes on fire, shit-slimed ammonia stinging mist-thick in Kotzeleh's eyes . . . oh, it's just like a dream of Hell, all right: Her own, or someone else's.

And then there's nothing. A long slice of it, gas-burnt, gas-stinking.

"P- . . . pretty girl?"

(Not any more, most likely.)

But: Again, the same voice, weak but insistent—and Kotzeleh comes awake with a hand thrust hard where her gun should be, dust in her eyes and rocks in her hair, a rusty piece of metal half-piercing her palm: *Oy gevalt!* It hurts with a fierce, dull pain, though not strikingly more or less so than every other part of her body.

"Katarczyna, answer, I can't see you anywhere . . . answer me please, my little Kati . . . "

She coughs long and loud at that, a phlegmy clip-feed rattle. Correcting him, automatically—

"My name is Kotzeleh, Rabbi."

Somewhere nearby, Fat Chavah chokes hoarsely, weeping through the dust and flame. Kotzeleh reaches out wide with both hands, maimed and whole; she grabs Lev by the sleeve with her wounded one, Chavah by the flaking scruff of her burnt braids with the other, then fists down hard enough to make her scream inside and starts dragging them both forward through rubble and muck, crawling away from the fire inch by painstaking, pain-filled inch. Crawling towards . . . what?

"This tunnel was made to lead somewhere, obviously," Lev observes, ridiculously even-toned. Like some infernal tour-guide.

And: "Oh," Kotzeleh manages, blood clotting her sleeve fast to her wrist, "you *think*?"

Simply: "Yes."

(I mean, what's the alternative?)

Rising stink of burnt shit and mold, the post-blast silence ringing in their ears like distant earthquake rumble. Kotzeleh sets her shoulders at a determined angle, puts her head down and bears forward, pushing so hard her neck starts to ache and strain. Hears Lev kicking and punching at the walls beside her, feeling for any possible breach they can force themselves through. Chavah's whimpers dim. Everything narrows, boils away to purest effort, the way she likes it best.

And finally—after what seems like years, but probably only lasts bare minutes—the bricks do give way, tumbling all of them into somewhere new.

Lev is first to look up, which seems fitting; first to gape 'round at the arching, dripping, cavernous walls, so bright and dark with strange patterning. An ossuary jewel-box thrown open to the hot non-wind, shelves on shelves like narrow slate beds strewn with desiccated brown monk-skins, twinkling with dun shards of bone.

"One of your lost crypts?" Kotzeleh asks Lev.

"Seems so," he replies. And sloshes forward, squinting, while Chavah leans her burnt head against the nearest wall and vomits into her own hands—weirdly neat, like most things she does, regardless of her bulk. She heaves a few more times, reduced to bile, before slumping to trail her hands in the water, exhausted; if she's praying, she certainly knows enough (by now) to keep it to herself while Kotzeleh's still in close proximity.

Lev's running his hands over the facade to Kotzeleh's left, meanwhile, like he's reading a braille message through both burnt palms. And Kotzeleh just stands there, one hand on her knife-hilt, because it's not just losing a fresh layer of skin that's making her nerves crawl: Everywhere she looks, she can see them watching—empty eye-sockets, black and blank. Sprung jaws hanging, cracked teeth exposed in nude and lipless grins . . .

She clears her throat, rackingly, trying to form a thought that doesn't have to do with mummified Catholics. Managing, a swallow or so later—

"You think the Nazi slime had a good laugh, watching those fools back there scuttle? Jews versus the *Taifun-gerat*: Talk about a cheap show."

Lev doesn't turn. "Not so cheap, in the end. Probably didn't know it when they lit the match, but . . . "

(and here he gives a smile, oddly sweet and surprisingly sharp, familiar to Kotzeleh like her very own)

" . . . gas burns upwards."

And THERE's a comforting image.

But: "Come here," he tells her, veering off towards something new half-hid in shadow between two broken slabs of wall the blast must have knocked loose, much like his brains. "Look at this, would you?"

She feels her hand twitch before she can stop it, yearning to make a fist again, then thinks better of the idea; feels her whole arm spasm at the sting like a half-body wrench, a lopsided crucifixion. "Rabbi, we don't have the *time*—"

"Nu? Nothing but, surely, 'till the fire burns itself out." He crooks a finger, tempting. "Come on, Kotzeleh, indulge me. I want to show off my *shul* learning one last time, while I still have the chance." As she hesitates: "God would appreciate the gesture, I'm sure."

Kotzeleh breathes out through her nose, a single, calming huff. Finally—

"Your God wants a lot, Lev."

"But he's your God too, pretty girl. Isn't he?"

Well . . .

. . . remains to be proven, that.

Ikons and mosiacs stained by time, crawling with water-reflected light. And here between, out of this crack where the walls shivered apart, comes something extruding from the shallow, bricked-up cell hidden behind: A . . . box? A coffin?

Man-sized and lightly featured, rust-bleeding iron chased in bands of tarnished brass; the hinges have popped under heat, pressure, water-warping maybe, and its emptied shell gapes like a lesioned mouth, the whole inside of the thing embossed with crosses. As Kotzeleh peers closer, however, she finally realizes what she's looking at—it's one of those containers the Catholics routinely lock bits and pieces of their holiest holies inside, the better to prepare them for ritual display. Dust from the road to Egypt and splinters of the True Cross, broken femurs and nail-pierced palms; that severed tongue they keep in the Vatican's trea- sure-trove, black and slimy, wedged deep inside a skull made from glass and gold . . .

(relics)

. . . yes, that's the word. Which makes *this* a reliquary, though Kotzeleh can't ever remember having heard of—let alone having seen, in the so-called flesh—a reliquary big enough to hold somebody's whole body inside it.

On the wall above, meanwhile, just one flaking section of the nearest fresco: A monster's foreshortened face gaping down on coffin-box and supplicant/tourists alike, snouted, with teeth like tusks.

"What is that, anyway?" Kotzeleh demands. "A monkey? Some kind of . . . "

"A saint," Lev replies, still studying their find. Then adds, at her look: "Pretty girl—they've got their stories, same as us; it's rude not to listen at all, even when you know you'll have to kill them later on. Don't tell me you've never heard of Christopher, the Christ-bearer?"

Kotzeleh shrugs, a suppressed shiver. "Not like *that*."

The ikon stares, yellow eyes popping, as Lev traces a blackened trail of silver lettering around the reliquary's rim. Explaining, absently, while he does—

"It's the oldest form of the tale, you see: From back in the first millen- nium, when the Church was still organizing itself, agreeing on what was 'true' and what 'wasn't'. They don't debate things the way we do, after all—it's just one way or another, and anybody who takes the middle ground can stand there and burn. So.

"Used to be, before people drew accurate maps, Christians—and some Jews, too—believed a race of dog-faced people lived in darkest Africa. Big teeth, panting tongues . . . " He prods the painted rock with a gentle nail, to illustrate. "Cannibals, too, though that might not apply, since they couldn't possibly have thought ordinary men belonged to the same species as themselves—"

To which Kotzeleh nods, thinking: *And doesn't THAT sound familiar?*

(Never trust people who'd nail their own Messiah to a cross . . . oh, but wait, I forgot. That was *us*, wasn't it? Supposedly.)

That supposition alone being good enough, apparently, for everyone else involved to shift the blame squarely onto the shoulders of the Jews.

And now here they are, Lev and Chavah and she herself, squatting to soak their wounds in the shit of centuries because that same long-ago judgement has finally let loose a dragon on Europe, crushing and pruning and scorching all Warsaw alike—not *just* the ghetto, oh no, much as it may have begun there—to the bare earth with its hot, poisonous breath.

They call us vermin, she thinks. *But it's Christianity that's the true curse. All their talk of love and forgiveness—such garbage, in the end. Have you ever seen them leave a single thing upright and intact behind them, once they've decided it needed a laying on of hands?*

"St. Christopher the Cynophelus, who carried the Christ-child over water," Lev says, musingly. "Because the idea was that God's redemption could be given to anyone, if they only had enough faith. Even monsters."

SUCH garbage.

Behind Kotzeleh, Chavah has starting crying again; choking, anyway, which sounds pretty much the same. Her burnt head leaves marks where she leans it against the wall. While Kotzeleh fists her hurt hand hard, yet once more, at the scrape and bleed of Chavah's voice in her ears, forcing herself past an infectiously tempting rush of sympathy by putting her attention squarely elsewhere. Asking—

"What's the inscription say, anyway?"

Lev clicks tongue to teeth, backtracking, and lets his moving finger underline the words. "Home to Xawery, Crusader, Martyr . . . could be Martyr-*maker*, I'm reading it right . . . and Incorrupt. Contemplator for his sins, and ours. Keep him safe and secret, at your own souls' cost."

Kotzeleh glances around: Blood in the water, seeping like oil; skittering

THE WORM IN EVERY HEART

shadows on every side. She reaches for her knife, instinctively, as one seems to move a bit too fast and spider-like for comfort—but finds it right where she left it, sheathed in the hollow of her back between skin and waistband. Cold weight of metal, familiar like the pulse that hammers in her throat, sharp enough to scratch with every breath.

"Well, he's out of his box now," she points out. "Gone walking, I suppose; *Taifun-gerat* must have woken him up."

From Chavah, a hoarse whisper: "Kotzeleh, please . . . don't say *that*, don't say such things, *please* . . . "

"Why not? You think he can hear us?"

"Oh, Kotzeleh . . . "

"'Where his blood falls, lilies grow,'" Lev mutters, to himself, meanwhile. "But no, this Latin's so old—or might be it's some form I've never seen before, Slavic-crossed. Hungarian? Romanian, that'd work too—a Romance language, anyway—"

Chavah bends lower, cries harder, her tears making salty little circles in the sewer-water's scum; Kotzeleh shoots her a glance, before turning back to the shadows . . . shadows of gaping monk-corpse, of leering ikon-image, of fluttering, watery reflection, all of which suddenly seem somehow larger, and closer. Darker, too.

(As though that were really possible.)

"'Where he lets blood to *fall*, there lilies grow'—yes, I'm almost sure this time. That could be it."

"Lev," she starts, impatient—then stops, listening hard, as he just keeps on mouthing out the words in question, like he hasn't even heard her. Straining into the darkness above the raspy rise and fall of Chavah's breath, an incipient wail in every drawn lungful.

"'Where he *lets* blood.' Like a barber? Lilies are a holy flower, though, the kind you offer to saints, to the Virgin Mary . . . "

But: "Lev," Kotzeleh says again. Her hand moving, so much unasked it feels like someone else's, to take up its natural position on her knife's hidden hilt.

"Yes?"

"What do lilies smell like, exactly?"

Lev sniffs the air, frowning. Sniffs again. Frowns deeper.

"Like that," he replies, eventually.

* * *

23

Sometimes Kotzeleh wonders, even now, so long after: Who she might have become, instead of what. Some comfortable grandmother, a smiling Bubeh in flowered house-dress and sensible shoes, safely insulated from the past by as many layers of love as she could gather to herself; some elegant matron or spinster teacher in Krakow, in Paris, in New York, in Tel Aviv. Some apple-cheeked old lady, her gold hair faded to grey and her killer's bones hidden deep beneath wrinkles and varicose veins, beneath fat and frippery, beneath the instinctive (if inaccurate) assumptions of those who've never had to spit on the Torah in order to stay alive, to stand by and watch their neighbors lined up against the nearest wall. To clap and cheer as children are loaded onto trains bound for crematoria, or breathe the human tallow-soaked ashes from a burnt-out sewer pipe's back-blast . . .

What did you do in the War, Madam Mendesh? Oh, not Madam—very well, then. My apologies.

(So: Would that be Miss, instead? Or Missus?)

It must be nice to survive, she supposes—she, who always fancied herself a survivor, even when things were at their utter bleakest. If nothing else.

For Kotzeleh, however, the War goes on and on; there is no truce, no quarter, no V-Day to divide history into "before" and "after". Nothing but the same damnable darkness to fathom, ever and always, slow and painful as some diver lost far beyond his depth—hallucinations, pressure in the chest, that awful sinking feeling. An upside-down, mapless world full of (fellow) monsters.

For all of which, along with her many other sins, she knows—on some level—that she must surely have *God* to thank.

* * *

Lilies and blood, Lev's eyes on hers, Chavah's weeping. Then all at once, the fallen wall behind them cracks further, issuing five or so Germans in a spew of blackened bricks and melted mortar: Blinking, coughing, bloody like afterbirth. The straggly remains of some back-up platoon caught in the *Taifun-gerat*'s indiscriminate sweep, clutching their weapons so close you'd think they were substitutes for the crucifixes Hitler's already outlawed; a strange faith, but their own. And easier by far to pull the trigger than pray, Kotzeleh supposes, considering the usual outcome of either action—

Suddenly, she's locking eyes with Lev's gun-barrel rather than him, its sight drawing a careful bead on her forehead. "Down in the mud, Polack whore," Lev tells her, utterly matter-of-fact, as she gapes—then adds, to them: "You think I won't shoot, if I have to? Though I do hate to waste a hostage, especially one this juicy . . . "

Hidden behind a fresh fall of masonry, Fat Chavah kneels lower still, blinking her seared eyes furiously, hunting 'round for some-thing—anything—to use as a weapon. While Kotzeleh simply stands there doing her level best to look the kidnapped Christian, shivering shoulders hunched to hide where her hand is bound for, giving them the tearful blue eye through the dirty gilt fall of her hair. Thinking, all the while:

Oh, Rabbi, you idiot. Like the Mayor of Chelm, you're God's own fool.

What does he think this is, anyway—a mitzvah, some selfless act that'll get him back in the legendary G-d's good books? Sacrifice himself for Kotzeleh, to cover Chavah, so that when the Nazis kill him it'll provide enough distraction for them both to bring his murderers down in turn?

So slow: Seconds passing like centuries, as Kotzeleh's fingers find the knife, hilt-first. She quirks her mouth at Lev, signalling *It's all right, no more, you can stop now, NOW. Now, damn you. I said——*

(stop)

She can see his lips moving even from here, though, as the Germans shift, thumbing their safeties; that familiar invocation of last resort, clear as the prominent nose on his too-Hebraic face. *Hear, o Yisroel, the Lord our God, the Lord our God is one . . .*

And: *Not MY God, Rabbi,* Kotzeleh thinks, grimly. *Not by a long shot.*

A flash of the future now, its resonance echoing back over years, sharp as a turned thumb in a still-green wound. Because this is when she might have saved him, that's what she'll always let herself believe—right here, this very moment, had things only gone differently. But it's not like any of them will ever know, after all . . .

(Is it?)

One single moment: Here, then gone. Then Chavah slides her seeking palm across a hidden catch cunningly worked into the snaky tangle of demons crushed beneath St. Christopher's feet and jolts back, hearing it click; kicks up a dirty wave as she does so, making the Germans jump in turn. And *something* comes ripping through the wall to meet her, five leperous-white fingers catching her fast by the scalp, pulling her back through the too-small hole it's made—a scraping pop followed by a wrench, a crunch, by Chavah's body slumping headless into the murk, as the Germans open fire.

Lev falls, instantly pierced at the wrist, the knee, with one eye shot out and his hair full of blood, so cheerfully bright red it seems dyed; Kotzeleh lunges to slit the nearest German's throat as he does, some boy barely her own age wearing a uniform one size too small, then pivots to use his gun on the rest—white muzzle-fire blast and glare, hot whine of ricocheting bullets. Then dives deep, letting the shell-casings fall where they may, swimming through garbage to emerge at last, panting and dripping, by the chamber's door. Spits liquid waste and stands there for a moment, trying not to see where Lev's blood has already begun to surface . . .

Germans dead and dying, face-up or face-down; Kotzeleh watches them twitch, her joyless, skinned-back grin no more emotional than a dog's. Yet none of them should be able to talk, at this point—which is just what makes it so very strange, if not maybe far more than that, to realize someone *is* saying *something* from behind her, his voice husk-dry but patient as a snake under glass.

(*girl*)

Huge figure turned sidelong to line up with the first fissure's crack, dark on dark, like some Victorian silhouette portrait dressed in a rusty chain-mail gown, its eyes ravenous. Saint Xawery Martyr-maker in the livid flesh, crosses puffed raw on every visible surface like suppurating, Pope-blessed sores, watching her from that shadowed archway; Xawery, who must be kept safe and secret for all souls' sake, tipping Fat Chavah's severed head to his mouth and drinking hot blood from the open ruin of her shattered throat.

Red drools from his chops, slops to his wrists, pooling, gouting. And where it falls, whether on stone or water . . . or Chavah's abandoned hulk of flesh, for that matter . . .

(Oh no no no)

Those waxy flowers by his rotting boots? They *must* be lilies.

Girl, the Saint says, without really saying anything—that's what Kotzeleh *thinks* he says, at least, seeing how he's speaking Medieval Polish, unintelligible to her like Chaucer would be to any given Anglophile. But he improves so quickly it's as though he's plucking the right words from her brain, fingering through the folds, same as a common pickpocket. Taking what he wants and leaving the rest, making that his words clarify with only the smallest, most sibilant drag: Thus, and so—

"Girl," he says again, this time out loud. "What iss your name?"

Through a dust-dry mouth: "Kotzeleh."

"Kot-zssel-eh."

It means little thorn.

"Little Hebrew thorn," the monster says, gently, with a ruined smile. And Kotzeleh gasps, without meaning to, at the sound of him commenting so freely on what she's only just *thought*. There's a probing intelligence in those awful eyes, yet almost no sympathy; not as we understand the term, anyway.

Then: "Are you barren of God's bounty, little Ssephardesss? Can you ssee your own sshadow at noon-time? Does nothing grow where you sstand?"

Scripture, one assumes. A subject she's never excelled at.

"You kill well, Kotzsseleh-girl. For a peassant."

"I know."

"Of coursse you do."

Of course.

She risks a glance at Chavah's face, its burnt features gone slack and blood-loss pale; sees the Saint follow her eye-line, and begin to see a chance—the barest shadow of one, at least. That shattered section of wall the Germans came through, unguarded aside from their bodies. Guns floating stocks-up every few paces between her and potential escape, child's play to reach with a sudden rush . . .

(not to mention how this thing doesn't even know what a gun *is*, probably. For all he just saw her use one.)

"So why didn't you help me, then?" she demands. Xawery simply smiles, unpleasantly: So *many* of those teeth! And all of them so stained and jagged, like a box of broken bone-needles.

"I would never deprive a fellow warrior of enemiess," he tells her, mildy enough, smooth as milk in arsenic. And lets Chavah's emptied skull drop, at last, with only a tiny splash.

Kotzeleh lunges, grabs, fires without aiming. Makes the gap, squeezes through. Runs runs runs, into stinking darkness.

But even a scuttle carries for miles, in this echo-chamber. Which means she can already hear Xawery, following.

* * *

Words in her veins, like some mnemonic virus. She mouths them in her sleep now, whether or not she wants to—the Saint's confession playing dusk 'til dawn behind her shut eyelids, a flickering newsreel on endless loop. Remembers them as cold and wet and hollow, the same way they came that first time, as she fought her way up-current: Back towards the pipe she'd come from, back towards the manhole and the engine which covers it, with the reek of gas in front of her and the smell of lilies behind.

What iss it you kill for, Kotzsseleh? To live, only? Or doess your God require you to, even ass mine did?

Taking one corner after another, slipping on slimy stones, skinning her hands on the walls. The gas stings her eyes, but Kotzeleh runs on.

The Holy Land iss full of sstrange thingss indeed, ass I found when one came to me on the battlefield, offering ME ssurvival—at a price. But I never saw itss face, and when I woke in darknesss later, the hilt of my own ssword burnt my handss.

Through the first wall, past the bale of wire, that sad bundle inside it still smoking. Kotzeleh can hear the *Taifun-gerat* everywhere now, grinding-grating, like some horrible clockwork heart pumping out death.

Pray, they told me, to redeem this ssinful world. And sso have I prayed, almost consstantly, ssince they nailed me down in THAT. Yet I do not ssee that the world is much improved, for all my piety.

Loud, *loud*, almost deafening, and the gas so thick she can barely see, let alone run anymore. So Kotzeleh turns here instead, head swimming—and finds Xawery suddenly right up against her gun-barrel in a ragged blur of movement, peering down at her with those scarlet eyes whose sockets seem both hollow and painfully overfilled at once, like twin slit-pupilled blood-blisters.

"I never assked to become what I became," he tells her. "Only to sserve God in my way, ass Ssaint Chrisstopher did—Chrisstopher, who ate human flessh and prayed with a dog's tongue. Yet wass *he* ssaved."

And: "*No* one is saved," snarls Kotzeleh, feeling a great, grey wave of hopelessness roll up through her mouth. "No one. Not *one*."

(Not even those who deserve to be.)

She doesn't cry, though—she can't. That other one, Katarczyna; she could cry. But she's gone, and only Kotzeleh remains: Kotzeleh, her father's little thorn, hard and sere and bitter and barren. Sharp enough to pierce this empty-rinded world to its black, black heart.

Kotzeleh, unable to weep over Lev's stupid goodness, over her own realization that she actually did care for him—*now*, of all times, when there's nothing left that matters anyway. When it's too late for anything.

"No one is saved," she repeats again, quieter. "And monsters . . . are only monsters."

Monsters like you and I. Monster.

She feels her finger tighten on the trigger, and prays that the wave will be as fast as it seemed.

* * *

It doesn't end like this, however. Obviously.

* * *

Kotzeleh and Saint Xawery, caught in the typhoon's path. She smiles as the first blast perforates his midsection, loosing a flood of guts—but he just smiles *back* and hugs her to him, shrouding them both beneath what (at first view) looked like a mould-striped leather cloak, rather than a pair of folded, membraneous bat-wings.

He bites her, instinctively insulating himself with her blood, and she—helpless, hating, equally instinctively—

—bites him back.

So the *Taifun-gerat*'s wave passes over like the Angel of Death did in Egypt, engulfing but not consuming, shying from the same sign of blood which once kept Israel's firstborn safe. And they stand there joined, waves of thought passing between them in a bright, arterial circuit: Kotzeleh, still fighting, even as her limbs cool and stiffen; the Saint, cradling her, firm and fair as any father, his armor digging little crescent-shaped scars into her torso's hide. Musing, as he does—

Iss no one ssaved, truly? Not ever? But if I may be ssaved, so may you alsso, little Kotzsseleh. So may all we monssters . . . in time.

Years later, a whole new century, and she still can't make up her mind: Could it be that he *wanted* her to follow her better impulses, just like Lev did, even when she was so utterly sure she had none left? To *force* her to re-evolve back up out of the muck, and take her place in a Crusade so new it needed no Pope to sanction it?

Vampire against vampire, monster against monster. Kotzeleh against the world which made her what she is, living or dead: A hunter, a killer. A true knight of zealous, self-legitimized genocide.

Albedo from nigredo. This is the lowest point. So low, so deep, that the only thing left to do from here on in is . . . rise. Again.

Nigredo to albedo. The alchemical distillation process. Garbage into gold. Shit into salvation.

And: *Iss that what they're doing up there, do you think? Your enemiess, thesse oness who alsso bear the Crosss, though twissted to their own particular endss?*

Can they posssibly know they're creating gold ssuch as you?

Saint Xawery, Monster-Martyr, lays his latest victim down in the filthy water gently, as in a warm bath. Strokes her dazed eyes closed, with soft and tender touch. Thinking, while he does so—

Ah, little Ssephardesss, little Jew-girl. You'll make ssuch a fine, black joke to play on the upsside world.

But don't come back down here, daughter. Not ever. For God has given me this place for mine, and I will cede my share in it to no one . . .

(. . . not even you.)

The seventeen-year-old who once knew herself as Katarczyna Mendesh lies there in the clammy water of the Warsaw sewer, cursing the Saint and both their rotten Gods at once—all three or four, equally. She feels everything drain away.

And when night comes fresh once more, Kotzeleh wakes up for the last time, or the first: Swollen, filth-encrusted, thirsty with a brand new, deep red thirst. Again and again, and then yet again.

That night, and every night after.

RING OF FIRE

Late June, 1857:

"The sepoys themselves, strangely enough, have a phrase which describes my current state of mind to perfection: 'Sub lal hogea hai'—'Everything has become red.'"

* * *

Unlike most madmen, Desbarrats Grammar was debatably lucky enough to be gifted with an enduring understanding of the exact instant when his sanity had collapsed. The moment in question had occurred shortly after the retaking of Calcutta, during what his commanding officer had then referred to as "the mopping up", post-Indian Mutiny—a process of justice which, in keeping with the usual British reinterpretation of Biblical tradition, required considerably more for the price of an eye than payment in kind. Correspondingly, a method of retribution had to be improvised which would be both impressive and educative.

And this was how Grammar, then a mere twenty-two years of age, soon came to be standing next to a cannon across the mouth of which a lucklessly uprisen native soldier of the British Army had been strapped, briskly dropping his sword in one neat arc in order to visually indicate that the order to fire had been given—upon which the cannon bucked, swinging a bit to one side on the recoil, and enveloped him in a halo of molten blood before his attentive native second-in-command even had a chance to get him out of the way.

Grammar stood a moment, suitably frozen, only his eyebrows—still lightly sketched in gold—indicating that he had not been born with red hair.

His second-in-command asked him something, presumably in Urdu, which Grammar spoke quite well; his service in India had soon revealed an unpredictable facility for languages. But the man's voice, usually so clear and strong, had apparently dulled to a scanty murmur in the brief space between order and result. Grammar narrowed his eyes at him, straining to read his lips.

"Repeat that," he said.

The second-in-command did. No enlightenment ensued—until frustration brought him around the other side of Grammar's blood-soaked head.

" . . . thee, art thou hurt? Sahib, I have asked thee—"

Grammar nodded, slowly. He was beginning to form a theory, but knew it would have to wait some while yet to be confirmed.

"Keep by that shoulder, I pray thee," he replied, "that I might have the benefit of thy protection a little closer to hand, in the future. And bring on the next one."

Hours later, when the work was done, a physician reported that, yes, the cannon's concussion had blown out one of Grammar's eardrums, causing him to consequently lose all hearing on his right side. Grammar nodded again, thanked him, and left the tent—refusing, gracefully, the doctor's offer of a pan and cloth to wash himself with before he saw his commanding officer to ask that his duty be extended to finding and executing those remaining sepoys who had fled beyond Calcutta's limits.

Grammar wore his mask of sepoy's blood until it flaked and ran, until his own sweat washed the worst of it away. Only then did he accept a handful of rice from his second-in-command, with which to rub away the flies which had gorged themselves and died in his sanguine crown. Because he could not shave, he avoided mirrors; occasionally, however, the unexpected sight of his own stained face would waver momentarily in streams and puddles, or grin at him from the broad surface of a rain-soaked leaf. And he would pause, obscurely flattered to recognize—once again—how well this red dust suited him, redefining all those subtle undercurrents which had once swum invisible beneath his honest British skin. Reminding him of who—and what—he had always been, in truth as well as unvoiced dream.

This was the beginning of it.

The two mental games he had kept to for most of his life, Home-face and Acting-as-though-one-were-Away, had suddenly been discarded in favor of a third, less well- remembered play: Don't-Care Island. For madness had always lain dormant in him, the hidden loot in his genetic plum-pudding—generations of half-lies and after-the-fact explanations for inexplicable behavior, as when his grandfather had suddenly thrust his Aunt Myrtle's forehead down against a lamp during the playing of a game of cards, causing her hair to blaze up like a torch. Or unknown facts, like the layers of mutilated bird- and mouse-corpses which had, for so long, fertilized Strait Gate Hall's incomparable gardens. Now, due to a combination of circumstances no Grammar had ever faced before or ever would again, that madness had been given whip-hand.

And thus it remained.

It was perfectly easy to be mad in India, Grammar soon found, as long as one were British, with some rank, some breeding and—most importantly—some money to prop one up. After all, his madness made no particular outward show (at least, not in civilized circles); he did not rave, or make insane gestures. He did not shirk his duty—on the contrary, he embraced it whole-heartedly, always tasting the wind for any trace of slaughter. And this was because the smell of incipient tragedy whipped his madness into a fire that made his pulse pound like a singing, liquid drum. It made him grind against himself in a frenzy of excitement. And once, when the battle was safely done and his group had all had their way with a certain woman of the sepoys, it made him smile at her in such a warm and reassuring manner that she wept to see him, thinking him an angel—before cutting open her belly with his bayonet, and thrusting his penis inside the slippery bag of her bladder until both their groins were stiff with urine, blood and semen.

To you who listen, meanwhile: I do not tell you these things to make you hate Lieutenant Desbarrats Grammar, o my beloved, and neither do I tell you them to make you fear or pity him. I tell you only what is true.

* * *

July, 1857:

"Another body burning on the ghat this evening; as I stood to watch, there came a sudden flood of bats, as big as crows, flying over our heads. Beyond, the river was covered with odd-looking boats, and a copper-colored sky bent over all, vivid and still as some frieze from the Arabian Nights. (Memo: Romesh Singh reminds me that I have a riding engagement with the Misses Mill tomorrow.)"

* * *

Romesh Singh was Grammar's second-in-command; they had exchanged full names long before, at the outset of Grammar's posting, though Romesh Singh had never since been forward enough to ever suggest Grammar actually *use* his when addressing him. The Misses Mill, meanwhile, were called Ottilie and Sufferance: One tall, one not, both equally dishwater-plain and more than financially equipped to compete for the hand of Calcutta's most eligible potential bridegroom. Their coordinated flirtation, polished and hollow as an acrobatic troupe's routine, stirred nothing in Grammar beyond a dim contempt—as was, perhaps, only to be expected. But he was between atrocities at the moment, and in need of diversion.

"Were one to report today's weather accurately in one's correspondence," said the Miss Mill at Grammar's left hand (tall, therefore Ottilie)—her head swathed with soaked gauze under a big straw hat, hooped skirts well-spotted at the hem with mould—"no person at Home would ever believe one did not exaggerate."

"Especially since it is so very hot, one would not know how to spell the word large enough," the other—Sufferance, presumably—murmured.

Grammar made some slight noise in reply, vague enough to let either Miss consider it confirmation of her acuity.

It was mid-July, and the rains had just begun. Large stains rose like veins from the bases of pillars, while green ones spread darkly down from wherever water cascaded off the roofs of British-owned Calcutta's fine, white lime-coated buildings. The rooms grew high with blistered drawings, damp-cracked books, mildewed daguerrotypes. Silverfish were everywhere, and the cream of the Raj were already eating off of white marble tables covered to some depths by a frail, crackling layer of wings discarded by flying ants. The aforementioned heat, meanwhile—undiminished, even in the teeth of such humidity—had split the ivory frame of Grammar's only miniature of his mother, allowing white maggots to eat up the paint.

(I was there as well, of course, as an unseen extra darkness in the blur of their horses' shadow. It was my face that made the beasts shy an hour or so later, throwing both Misses to their respective injury and death.)

Down by the riverside, an age-bent man lay foetally curled in a palanquin sprawled almost directly across their chosen path—blanched and sallow beneath his tan, half-lidded eyes too full of blood to close, his friends and family hovering in patient attendance as death grew palpably nearer with every shallow gasp.

Grammar reined in. "What do they here?"

"He dies, sahib," Romesh Singh replied, shrugging.

Ottilie, generally a fraction quicker on the uptake than her sister, had already realized as much; gulping back bile behind one lace-gloved hand, she whimpered a genteel prayer, drawing Grammar's glance.

"Apparently," he agreed. Then, taking Ottlie's other hand—much to Sufferance's annoyance—and kicking his horse a step or two further on: "Suggest to this lot that he do it somewhere less obvious."

(Because it was only yet another scene of life under the Raj for all of them, o my beloved: A world of colorful shadows, glimpsed as from a great distance, as through the wrong end of binoculars—with no emotional response roused but that of the most casual interest as to whatever flat, exotic, meaningless vista might present itself next.)

Romesh Singh, ever compliant, barked some Urdu curses at the party, who drew back in quick and respectful silence—all but one woman in a red-and-gold sari, who hoisted the child on her hip a little higher and told it, beneath her breath:

"Be calm now, my darling, that thou dost not draw his gaze—only turn away in quiet, and think no more on what he is. Rhakshasa araha hai."

Grammar paused a moment, staring at her. His blue eyes dimmed to slits, so narrow they could only take proper stock of her flash by flash, a visual piece-meal: Red cloth draped loose over lithe brown skin, red dab of fixed bindi between her level black brows. Round curve of thigh flexing beneath red folds, enticingly graspable; flatter curve of belly stretched taut under the child's whimpering grip, inviting perforation. The whole of her lapped in red-tinged afternoon shadow and a sudden red wind that blew his own scarlet uniform jacket briefly open and shut, then open and shut again, rhythmless as a diseased heart's liquescent flap.

Through a rising hiss of arousal, he noticed—without even much anticipation—that his hand had already fallen, reflexively, to the hilt of his sword.

And Romesh Singh stirred uncomfortably in his saddle, sweat starting up on every limb, as he caught an improbable whiff of old blood—the death-inflected musk of British madness—from Grammar's clean blonde halo of hair.

"Sahib," he began, delicately.

Beside him, Ottilie Mill gave an equally well-modulated cough of pain. Suggesting, without rancor:

"You will bruise my hand if you continue to hold it so tightly, Lieutenant."

Grammar—abruptly remembering he and Romesh Singh were not, after all, free to act as though they were alone at this particular moment—nodded, politely, and let her go.

"My most sincere apologies," he told her, in English. And meant it.

(For she—and her sister as well, wide-eyed and silent behind the unfurled screen of her fan—were both so very little to him indeed that they deserved such meaningless courtesies.)

Then, switching back to Romesh Singh (and Urdu): "This . . . "

. . . indicating the woman, who stood stock-still before him, her eyes downcast . . .

" . . . has named me unfamiliarly, perhaps insultingly, as 'Rhakshasa'. Hast thou some idea of what she means by it?"

"No, sahib," replied Romesh Singh, his own eyes busy on the river's muddy bank—now thoroughly vacated, but for his countrywoman and her child.

"I do not think thou art being entirely truthful," Grammar said, sweetly. "But no matter, for I do not care enough to inquire further."

To the woman: "As for thee, let us not meet again; for I tell thee truly, if ever I behold thy face within these city walls, I will certainly rip thy child's head from its throat and wash my face in its blood."

He urged his horse on, gesturing to the Misses, who followed, gratefully—along with Romesh Singh, keeping his usual careful distance. The woman watched them go, hugging her child to her, and heard the distant cries of a pack of children playing age-old games with forced confinement and flame: A scorpion in the dust, under the pitiless sun; a sloppy circle smeared first with saffron, then further limned in lamp-oil; a spark, falling. Simple pleasures.

Up and down the river, meanwhile, servants waited on the green lawns of British estates, their only duty to push any bloated corpses which might come floating by a little further on, so as not to spoil the view.

Later that night, after the accident, I was to complete my role in the day's events by appearing to the surviving Miss Mill—Sufferance, cheated of her chance at precedence yet again—in the guise of her dead sister, naked and desirable. Her resultant suicide by hanging, from a peepul tree by the very stretch of riverside where she and Ottilie had listened (all uncomprehending, neither being particularly fluent in Hindi) as Desbarrats Grammar threatened to bathe in baby's blood, only lent the Lieutenant further social cachet, increasing his glamour as Calcutta's resident homme fatal—a turn of events which struck me, surprisingly enough, as not entirely to my liking. For though I am many things (all things to all people, as the phrase so aptly goes) I had never before thought myself vain.

It is from this point onward, then, that I enter into the narrative fully for the first time, o my beloved—making myself known, initially more through rumor than deed, but with an ever-increasing sense of proximity.

Any given human being is, under even the most reassuring of circumstances, a frail and awful thing: A far-too-crackable ivory nut stuffed full of addictive meat, a bag of scented blood, a walking fever. But since it is so patently in the nature of the British to haunt, as much before their own deaths as after them, I now understand just how predictably suited the mantle of my well-earned reputation was to fit Grammar, once mass opinion had mistakenly assigned it to him. The whims of a beautiful (and mortal) monster are, in their own way, often more fearful a threat than something inexplicable can ever be—especially for those unlucky enough to stand directly in his way.

We seemed fated to be namesakes, he and I. So, to seal this undeclared liaison, I began a series of elaborations on my usual theme—variations in the tone of red, involving our mutual chosen prey (unrepentant and uncaught sepoys, whores and beggars, low-caste Indians of all descriptions). The credit for which was inevitably laid directly at Grammar's increasingly bemused . . . and more than slightly flattered . . . door.

Obviously—though it was really then long past the time for such small pleasantries as introductions—a meeting was in order.

My plans towards this end were aided greatly by the nature of Grammar's next posting, which would send him upriver—to a tiny, jungle-bound village named Amsore, outside of which a last, lone outpost of sepoys was rumored to still be in hiding—and away from all the "civilized" influences which conspired to keep him sane.

The continuing presence of Romesh Singh, already more than half in worshipful lust with his chosen British "master", promised to be similarly useful, as he remained one of the few who did not fear Grammar enough to desert him. His potential impact on the situation could in no way be underestimated, since—the innate idiocy of his desires aside—he was a wholly upright Sikh, a career soldier, no prude, and (above all) no fool. He knew that wanting Grammar was both morbid and perverse on his part, but the freakish glamor of a berserker must always hold its own attractions, especially for a military man.

He was also the only person near Grammar who not only knew exactly what the woman had meant by calling him Rhakshasa . . . but might actually be counted upon—eventually—to tell him.

All people of Hind—educated as they are in the laws of dharma—know both of the Wheel, which pulls them up or throws them down, and of enlightenment, whose attainment offers them escape from it. But for the Rhakshasa, whose forms are as many as their hungers are simple—with whom I may, respectfully, stake my claim of kinship—there is no escape, and no need of one. There is no Wheel for us. Nothing changes. From the moment we elect to leave it, everything stays firmly tied to the same crooked track of appetite and deception.

Novelty, however brief, is the only thing we have left to welcome.

I had smelt Desbarrats Grammar coming from as far off as his landing at Calcutta-ghat, wading up through the river's muddy shallows, as the bearers struggled with his gear: A pale blaze of frustrated heat with nothing but itself for fuel, too quenchless for remorse. There was a hole inside of him that demanded either light, ever more light, or an equal and engulfing darkness. Romesh Singh still quietly offered him the former, which he spurned; it hurt Grammar's terrible British pride, I venture, to think the solution for his many sins could have been something so simple as love.

So he remained alone: A promise of sport, on my part.

And a possibility—however scant—of danger.

* * *

August, 1857:

"Some unidentifiably rancid stink seems to hang over everything I touch these days, always rising, though already thick enough to swim in.

38

This morning I woke feverish as ever, boots on and my clothes stuck fast to me, my own sweat so hot against my skin it made me wonder whether I had slept in blood. I am also running out of usable paper, a fact which does not disturb me overmuch, since I no longer know who I might possibly be writing this for."

* * *

Amsore had been one of the last places to succumb to the Mutiny, long after the boats at Cawnpore had drifted away on a bloody tide, and the well of the Bibighar was stopped with the beaten corpses of British women and children. But even as Amsore's settlers dithered in their punkah-shaded homes, a preparatory whisper had nevertheless gone up and down the nearby river's banks, borne on the dust from Meerut and running deeper than its own mud-sluggish current: A promise of support, of like-mindedness; of loyalty kept carefully unvoiced, and weapons kept hidden but ready. It was the old, old cry of the surreptitious sepoy-sympathizer, soon to become Grammar's adopted mantra: Sub lal hogea hai—"Everything has become red."

In this particular case, however, the signal had never been given time enough to go any further than that first glad acknowledgement. The Mutiny was a failure, a frenzied knot of rage without the necessary guidance to keep it from strangling itself in its haste to stem the "White Plague"'s spread. Calcutta fell again, its Black Hole found and emptied, and the few stragglers remaining fled—most straight into the British army's vengeful hands, some of them to Amsore . . . and beyond.

Into the jungle.

Outside of Amsore's limits, everything familiar falls abruptly away into a green abyss: Screaming monkeys, unseen eyes, filtered rays of feeble, leaf-washed sun. Snakes hang dappled and silent as vines, sectioned by their most muscular areas, and here and there—stumbling half-blind through an endless funnel of foliage—one trips headlong across knots of roots from which erupt bright, fleshy flowers, big enough to drink from. The Ramayana calls forests home to wind, darkness, hunger and great terrors—a poetic description, but not entirely inaccurate. Jungle-swallowed, one must eke out direction; one finds one's way with senses other than those most usually given or employed.

Outside Amsore, the trees hide miles of ripe, interlocking tracklessness:

Verdant ventriculation, sap-fed growth, a living maze. A wholly fitting provenance for lovers, or for madmen.

* * *

They found the camp at sunset, through a hazy glare of red already half-deepening to grey as twilight retook its nightly portion, adapting all it touched to darkness. Insects still hung thick around the ash-heap of a dampened fire, on which a brass pot full of half-cooked rice sat abandoned. Further still, a few hastily-improvised huts of mud and fallen wood vomited scraps of clothing or the odd rusty weapon, spoiled supplies and broken crockery. Detritus lay everywhere, the spoor of retreat, scattered and rank. Grammar's party—the bulk of them barefoot, and thus more likely to consider where they chose to step—picked their way carefully through it, stabbing at every heap and corner with their bayonets. Except themselves, nothing moved but those few small creatures one occasionally heard rustle in the grass, and—just above—three lone kites (barely visible, through a bald patch in the jungle's roof) which dipped and cawed in a slice of red-grey sky.

At the crotch of one overhanging tree's trunk, a wet, red, knotted rag of some not easily identifiable substance glittered. Under the tree was something else, equally red, but moaning; this proved—after Romesh Singh was so good as to kick it gingerly over—to be what remained of a man who had been partially flayed. It was a portion of his forcibly donated hide, apparently, that gave the tree its surreal extra coat.

"How long since is he dead?" Grammar called across the clearing, idly running his sword through a sack of dried beans that soon proved both soaked enough to rot, and full of maggots.

"He lives yet, sahib," Romesh Singh replied.

Mildly impressed by such resilience, Grammar stooped to examine the man, who lay gasping—long, low, shallow gulps of liquid air, the humid foretaste of approaching rainfall—but inert, a thin line of bloodshot ivory just showing under each eyelid. Using the flat of his blade, Grammar scraped lightly over the man's denuded chest, flicking the bright half-circle of raw flesh where his right nipple had once been back to full, painful life.

The man reared up with a scream, then back again. His eyes, all white around their irises, fell on Grammar—and immediately widened further in horrified recognition.

"Where are thy fellows, offal?" Grammar asked him.

The man coughed, wetly. At Grammar's nod, Romesh Singh kicked him lightly in the head, forcing him further sidelong into the mud. The man doubled up, vomiting earth mixed with blood on Grammar's boots. With a little moue of disgust, Grammar put one shiny black heel to the back of the man's neck, pinning him down, and leant again to rephrase his initial request, this time a bit more insistently. Adding:

"It will do thee no good to lie. Remember, thou hast some skin yet left to lose."

The man drew a fresh gulp of air, mixed with a fair chunk of his own waste.

"Thou . . . knowest," he managed, at last.

Grammar frowned.

"I fear," he said, "that thou art mistaken."

Even he, however, could see that the man was clearly far beyond dissembling.

Grammar looked to Romesh Singh. Behind them, someone gave a nervous little step backwards, crushing something not particularly loud, but obviously breakable.

"Thou knowest," the man repeated, dully.

"Then it can do no harm to tell me again."

The man spit, a weak, retching stream of pink, which Grammar easily avoided. His dying eyes took on a blank gleam of unsatisfied malice.

"Human tiger," he said. "Blood-drinker. Evil thing. Why dost thou return? Why bring thy lackies, when you needed none upon thy first visit? We were many; now my fellows are gone I know not where. And it was thee that brought us to this pass, white corpse-eating dog, thou mocking horror. It was thee."

(And here occurs a mystery you city-dwellers cannot hope to know, o my beloved, especially without the benefit of personal experience: The sheer, shocking speed with which light drains away when sunset has ended, here in the jungle's heart—in one bright gush, like blood from a slashed throat, leaving nothing behind but a certain stillness; the hush of drawn breath, or the barest of unvoiced sighs.)

On Grammar's deaf side, one of the company blurted, all unthinking: "Rhakshasa!"

Grammar did not hear it, of course—but caught Romesh Singh's brief little jerk of reaction from the corner of one eye, and whipped quickly around, following it to its trembling, rooted source. His pistol had already appeared in one hand, amusingly enough; primed, aimed and ready, almost before he had consciously thought to draw it.

"Who said that?" he asked.

No one answered. Undeterred, Grammar shifted only slightly, sighting down the barrel at the soldier he judged most clearly in range.

"You, I think," he said, coolly. And pulled the trigger.

Romesh Singh shut his eyes. There had been a bazaar boy the company had adopted, not long since—silent and tensile with near-starvation, good mainly for scouring pots, packing kits (but only when there was time to watch him do it, for he had never quite gotten over his early habits of casual thievery), and running those few small errands his shaky command of English would allow for. Grammar—stalking restlessly around camp, quietly ablaze with his usual nimbus of potential lunacy, as everyone took care to stay out of his way—had not even seemed to notice his existence, until the child made the understandable mistake of laughing at a whispered joke while still within Grammar's eyeshot. Without breaking stride, Grammar had swerved to scoop the boy up and carried him into the cooking tent, where he ground him face-first into an open cask of chili powder for some long moments, then dropped him. To stand, watching patiently, as the boy thrashed and huffed awhile at his feet—nose, eyes and throat all swollen shut, the rest a tight, red mask of burns—before suffocating on what later proved to be a flood of his own shocked mucus.

And he, Romesh Singh, had shut his eyes then as well, so as not to have to see Grammar's scarlet-coated back draw up all at once like a shaken snake, straightening with pleased arousal at the spectacle of his own cruelty.

(Thinking: *Oh.* Like a bell. *Oh,* a heart-beat's sharp-soft squeeze between rib and gut, tolling. *This is so wrong. I am so very wrong to even be here, with him.*)

Gunshot and thunder blended, signalling the torrent's arrival. And before this one (now forever nameless) soldier's corpse had fallen to earth, the rest of Grammar's company simply broke and ran in the face of Grammar's insanity—always no more than a reputable quirk, until it had finally turned their way.

The flayed man gave a laugh, drawing Grammar's second shot. The pistol jammed; Grammar swore and threw it after them, as the soldiers' shadows faded like ghosts under a curtain of warm monsoon rain, leaving officer and second-in-command alike behind, entirely at the forest's mercies.

Grammar snarled, a tiger's half-cough.

"Cowardly bastards," he said, in English. Adding, contemptuously: "'Rhakshasa', am I? Hardly an opinion worth dying over."

Romesh Singh, wisely enough, said nothing—his own eyes kept firmly shut—as a long, wet, green moment passed over them, darkening both their scarlet coats to rust.

Grammar laughed, and let the sheath drop away from his sword, falling point-down. It quivered by one foot, mud-supported, forgotten.

"Well, come then, my shadow," he told the curtain of underbrush before him (having, without even noticing, slid fluidly back into Urdu). "Or shall I haste to meet thee? For either way, you will find me as I find myself: Ready."

And still Romesh Singh stood, feeling the rain seep down through his clothes and lave his trembling body abruptly to life, every nerve set winking in the gloom like unseen stars above.

(Thinking only: *But now we are alone at last, thou and I. Together.*)

* * *

They were both wrong, of course. Grammar, all his impressively flaunted rage aside, was nothing near to ready—as Romesh Singh might have told him, had he cared to solicit a second opinion—and neither was alone, with or without the other.

For I was already here. As I always had been.

* * *

The rain, the mud, the dead and cooling bodies, the silent trees. I was present and accounted for in all of it at once, a speck of me everywhere the eye might care to light, pixilating slowly to fruition. In the very air itself, between every falling raindrop—sub-dust, sub-viri, void-breath on the back of the neck, a shadow on the face of the whole. I spread out around the carcass of the dead former sepoy like a stain, over the clearing's seared floor, so fragrant yet with ash; and ah, but that fire had burned brightly, for all it was only a heap of corpses doused in lamp-oil. Brown corpse melting to black, black rivulets twining like veins across the soaked earth, black snakes rising in their wake. A black river, abruptly, in full flood, lapping the British soldier's remains in as well with no visible distinction—rearing, seeping, clotting—knitting both together like some prescient scab, the kind that outlines itself before a wound has even been opened.

One hot whiff caught on the wind, a brief, intestinal stink: Eau de massacre. One sentient platelet left swimming in a sea of blood, shed and unshed alike.

Beyond the fire's sodden ring, Desbarrats Grammar had already slashed the first layer of leaves aside and forged on ahead into the jungle (bent on finding any kind of explanation for the night's work, or his sadly smirched reputation, that did not involve the word Rhakshasa), leaving Romesh Singh to plead vainly after him—sick to heart and increasingly cold, with his empty hands ineffectually raised against the drumming rain.

(For the bell tolled in him still, o my beloved—fluid, subterranean. Mateless, but crying for its mate. And this suited me so well I would have smiled to see it, had I but the lips to smile with—or the eyes to see.)

Such a lack, however, was easily remedied.

"Romesh Singh," I called him, softly. He turned.

Upright now, a loosely wavering column of matte black against the clearing's larger blackness—hollow, scarring, extruded from the space between all things—I drew myself in tight, and called Grammar's all-too-familiar face to me, simultaneously making myself both a spine to hold it up and a skull to hang it on. I let flesh drip over me, pore by pore.

Over the flesh, I drew skin; over the skin, blood.

Naked under the rain's caress, I opened Grammar's eyes—so blind, so pale, so very, very British, in the raw mask that was his truest reflection—and raised them, meeting Romesh Singh's.

"My good soldier," I said.

He swallowed, pupils wide, his dry throat grating tentatively back upon itself.

"Thou . . . " he began. "Thou art . . . "

"Oh, I." Stepping, cat-sure on Grammar's smooth-soled feet, to print the mud between us. "A wandering minstrel, I," I said. "A knight of air and darkness."

" . . . Rhakshasa," finished Romesh Singh.

He said it with a sigh, so soft the word was part of his exhalation. That fatal—that only—name. I nodded at the sound. To prove the truth of his assumption, I spread my hands—my fingers—on which the claws bend back so far they are not really claws at all, but twisting knives of sharpest horn.

"Shreds and patches," I said. "Dead man's fingernails."

And I peeled back Grammar's lips, to show how my teeth arced up from his narrow British jaw like some ill-timed jest, sharp and yellow as a carrion dog's.

Yet Romesh Singh held his ground, back straight, like the warrior he was.

(For we both knew Grammar was too far ahead now to hear him, even if he chose to call for help. But no man really wishes aid at such a moment, o my beloved—not when his longest-held dream finally stalks towards him on nude white feet, arms out, and smiling.)

"Let down thy hair, my brother," I suggested, "that I may feel its weight."

Lightly, surely, I laid my claws on either side of Romesh Singh's jaw and worked the muscles like hinges, pinching his lips open—and though I had hoped (if I could) to grant him a gentle exit, my hunger soon betrayed itself in their sharpness, rimming the corner of his mouth with blood.

He gasped, swallowing it.

"Be merciful to me," he whispered. "As . . . he would be."

Oh, loyal, loving, deluded man. A born victim, if ever there was one.

"Ah," I said, gently. "But we are the same, he and I. So I cannot promise you what he would never give."

A flash of moon, bisected, fell over us through the trees; the blood caught its light, sparking a hot copper flare of lust that made my own lips abruptly wet. To compensate, I licked his clean.

Our tongues touched.

This distracted him enough, hopefully, to make what followed only a brief (if, no doubt, rather unpleasant) surprise—as I suddenly forced the rest of my head through his mouth until his head cracked like a wishbone, rupturing his throat, making his face my collar, spraying teeth. Hugging him to me, *into* me, as I rooted for brains in the blind, red ruin of his skull.

I suppose I had foreseen—somewhat faintly, considering the Lieutenant's continuing capacity for unpredictable behavior—that the sound of this process would draw Grammar back to the clearing. Not that it mattered much either way, at this point, though forgoing a prolonged chase (wearing Romesh Singh's now-uninhabited skin, perhaps?) would certainly have saved me a little time. But just as the consumption of a long-desired object tends to erase whatever wait one may have had to put oneself through in order to attain it, so strategy must inevitably dim in appetite's shadow. Blood filled my eyes; I drank deep, and gave myself up to ecstasy.

Presently, however, I felt Grammar's blade graze the back of my neck—wing-sharp, a dragonfly's delicate needle—and knew my plans had not been laid in vain.

Popping Romesh Singh's remaining eye between my teeth (just in case, should intelligible conversation yet prove necessary), I turned—grinning—to show him his own face: Red from browline to Adam's apple, chin slicked with fresh overflow. And a jolt passed between us, starburst-quick—not one of shock, so much, as of recognition. The Lieutenant's prim British mouth crumpling like an insulted cat's, ludicrous with embarrassed amazement, to find his unsought namesake's pleasures were so very like his own.

The sword, however, did not waver.

I smiled at the sight—and swung Romesh Singh's carcass like a dancing partner, dipping it towards him, as if offering him a bite.

"You must be hungry," I said. "Please: Do not hesitate to indulge yourself."

Grammar snarled again (his sole response in such circumstances, it seems) and stabbed me through the throat; I flexed, and sucked him further in, immersing him up to his armpit. For one endless moment, too paralytic even for struggle, he felt my internal organs stroke him seductively, and gagged. At which point I interrupted his train of nausea in mid-heave, just as gorge met gullet, and assured myself of his complete attention by thrusting my own arm (up to the elbow) inside his armpit—cracking ribs, perforating lung, expelling a warm rush of half-digested food from the lower esophagus, all in quest of that wildly-fluttering knot of muscle he called a heart.

Grammar coughed, and went rigid. His eyes turned up. But it was not my intention to let him die quite so quickly, now that we had finally met.

My fingers closed fast around left and right ventricles, pumping him awake. Saying, solicitously:

"Oh, no. Be so good as to not leave me just yet, Lieutenant."

With an effort, Grammar forced his eyes to focus on me. A rictus pulled at his cheek. Words formed, along with a bright new bubble of blood.

"Do . . . your . . . worst," he replied, carefully. "I . . . don't care."

I gave him a wide, blank smile—and chanted, singsong:

"Don't-care didn't care. Don't-care was wild. Don't-care stole plum and pear, like any beggar's child."

Sucking him closer—the maw that had been me (and him as well, come to think of it) now covering almost all of him below the shoulder, sprouting a fine interior coat of teeth that pressed and teased, unable to resist sampling at the anticipated feast; here a shaven fingernail, there a beheaded nipple.

Looking down, I could see his genitals begin—all unnoticed, for once—to stiffen.

"But Don't-care was made to care," I continued, blithely. "Don't-care was hung. Don't-care was put in the pot, and boiled 'til he was done."

And I gave his heart another little squeeze, for emphasis.

Oh, yes, his Empire might well linger far into the next century. But he'd be going home much sooner—and not to London, either, where he might at least occasionally be able to buy someone to kill. Back to some dreary Suffolk estate, to take up the middle child's portion, dazzling idiots behind the hay-wains with a fading grab-bag of exotic memories, doomed to forever wear the mask of respectability. To marry, to breed, to be buried and rot. And all in a dim, small place that no longer held anything but potential boredom for him, where no one would know to stiffen at his scent, or whisper his name in fear as he passed by.

Well, we were in the jungle now. And the law of the jungle is universally understood: Eat, or be eaten.

"Have no fear, Lieutenant," I murmured. "For you may count yourself assured that, even if no else does, I will take care to always award you a place in my memory."

Grammar blinked, his eyes already red-lined and darkening, as the cilia slowly haemorrhaged. His mouth worked, but words failed him. I brought mine closer, in case a final sentence might yet be forthcoming.

Then he gave a gushing whoop, and laughed out loud, spattering our mutual visage with liquid viscera.

Whereupon—with no regrets to speak of—I bit the mad bastard in half.

* * *

And so at last we come to you, o my beloved—little raggamuffin, would-be tourist district date rapist. You, with your fresh-cut fade and precious Apache Indian concert tickets, with barely enough real Hindi under your belt to tell the demure Calcutta girl you once thought I was—when first we met, you all swagger and chatter, spinning yourself a man-sized noose of lies as you steered me towards this oh-so-deserted alley—a dirty joke. Here in this bright, drunken, filthy place, so full of neon and flies, this overhanging crush of shacks where one open window lets slip a lick of the latest Bollywood duet, another the drone of Johnny Cash falling down, down, down. The ring of fire, the endless Wheel, spinning.

You thought me merely a bumpkin to be robbed of her virginity, and yourself the true synthesis of Anglo-Indian culture, post-British Occupation. But I believe you now know better.

The Mutiny of 1857 marked one whole turn of the Wheel for India and Britain alike, replacing up most firmly with down; it gave the British (via the East India Company) a perfect excuse to stay in India, to seize control, to cut down the guilty and the "loyal" as well in their lust for gain. They imposed their own system of values on everything they met: Breaking apart clans, ransacking treasuries, erasing whole villages, disinheriting heirs because they were adopted rather than biological, and deeding the lands involved to a plump little Queen, more concerned with the state of her marriage than with exactly whose bleeding hands all these exotic gifts had been ripped from.

Soon enough, Army replaced Company—but nothing really changed. The British swept in like a tide of cockroaches, mating and killing as they willed, forcing themselves in at the top of our caste system in order to escape their own. They stayed until they had outworn their welcome a thousand times over, until those brought up in India—but still calling an England they had never even seen "Home"—were immune to even its most enticing charms. They maintained their stiff spines upright against heat and dust, forgetfulness, sensual excess and nonviolent protest, clinging to their Indian holdings even as the rest of their duskless Empire crumbled—slowly but surely—from within, until their provisional government here was nothing but a skeleton at the feast, last guest left at a singularly unpopular party, still busily stuffing food down its denuded jaws and protesting all the while (whining like a spoiled child, even as the bouncers edge it towards the door) that it is not sleepy, that it has hours yet to revel, wishes yet to make, and room for much, much more.

At last, however, the British did leave—freeing us to return to the long-postponed business of slaughtering each other over differences of race, creed, history. The Wheel had turned again, as it always will.

Yes, it burns, burns, burns, this ring of fire. It keeps on spinning. And I hope you find it hot enough for your liking, o my beloved, just as the Lieutenant and I do—and have, ever since that night in 1857, when his mad appetites mingled so very surely with my own immortal ones, along with his stringy white meat. That night, when I bit through him at one swallow—rind to pulp, red juice spurting, like an overripe piece of fruit—only to have the taste of him linger not only in my mouth but in every other part of me as well: Infected, infectious, infecting.

Before that night, I had no "true shape" to speak of. It was my curse, and my strength—this restless formlessness; this unstinting, innate empathy pulling me forward through the centuries, making every new thing I touched my potential refuge. This much, at least, has never altered. I can still be anything I choose, if I choose.

But now, whenever I relax my hold, I flow back—relentlessly—into *him.*

Namesake to namesake: The mask and the mirror. Desbarrats Grammar usurped my title, so I made him my prey; I consumed his flesh, and it engulfed me. What was an accidental mislabeling has become a complex truth. Here in the ring of fire, Lieutenant Grammar and I twine tight as mating heartworms, joined at the supernatural equivalent of DNA—the Mutiny that walks like whatever it chooses to. We catch and claw. And at last, almost two hundred years later—as the Wheel, in our case, fails to turn—between the two of us, each only half-there to begin with, something has finally evolved resembling a coordinated whole. Sub lal hogea hai, with a vengeance; so much so that neither of us—former occupier or former occupied—can truthfully tell where we once began, or where we now end.

For were we ever so very different, really?

Liars both. Madmen, cannibals. And monsters.

Ah, but I see you yet stir in my embrace—so slowly, so feebly. Your lips move. Do you wish to refute my words? To confirm them, perhaps?

Lean closer, then, o my beloved. Do not be shy, but do choose your side wisely. Lean closer, closer. And speak up, I pray thee—for I am still quite deaf in this one ear.

THE GUIDED TOUR

Hell eats its tourists.
—Andrew Vachss

Six cars had already passed me by without a second glance when Lester P. Budgell's green Oldsmobile finally lurched, hesitated and ground to a halt. Its passenger-side door opened to reveal a balding, paunchy man with a black string tie and a red and yellow checkered shirt. He had Elvis-length sideburns and tarnished silver caps on the wings of his collar. But I was tired. I had been walking along the highway since dawn. And I am also not as young as I used to be.

"Thank you," I said, taking his sweaty palm in my cold one.

"No problem, ma'am."

And then we were off, our tires spraying the blanched dust with dried tar.

As the scenery blurred and the sun sank below the rim of the windshield, torn by advancing clumps of cacti, he became talkative. I might have reminded him of his mother—it has happened before. He told me about his wife, his children and his job running a neighbourhood Piggly-Wiggly store in Arkansas, much of which flowed straight over me. I closed my eyes, took care to nod in the right places, and let my mind wander—something I find increasingly easy to do.

I went inside my head.

Inside my head is a beach that stretches farther than the eye can see in all directions but one. Beside the beach runs the sea. It is always night there, in my house made of driftwood by the cold sea's side. And sometimes, if I am not careful, the sea begins to rise. It rushes in through all the doors and windows of my house, filling its rooms with little silver fish and the bones of drowned men. Green, and slow, and dark, and deep. I sleep there, under the water, and I am at peace.

"Ma'am?"

I pulled myself back with a jerk. "I am sorry," I said.

"No problem," he repeated. "Just wondered what you were doing way out here all by yourself in the first place. Car break down?"

I shook my head. "No, a bus."

"Seniors' safari?"

"Excuse me?"

He blushed. "You know—trip for older folks, kinda a package deal? The, uh, guided tour?"

I smiled. He matched it, eager to make amends.

"The guided tour," I said. "Yes. Exactly."

Americans have a phrase for everything, as I have often noticed, though few of them ever fit. This particular one amused me. It was neat, easy, and—to a point—accurate. Too simple, of course.

Just like everything else.

"So your bus broke down, and then—?"

"They sent for a tow truck, but I could not afford to wait. So I asked for a refund." I smiled again, remembering. "They did not want to let me go, not out here, in the middle of the desert. But I can be—persuasive."

"I'll bet," he said, so softly he thought I couldn't hear him.

There was obviously more to him than met the eye. Whether it merited a closer examination, however, had yet to be decided.

"Why, hell," he exclaimed. "I clean forgot to introduce myself. Les Budgell, ma'am."

He waited.

"Vassila."

He frowned. "That's Russian, ain't it?"

Give or take a few miles, I thought. But I gave him the old lie, for convenience's sake: "Ukrainian. I still have relatives there."

And I might. Anything is possible.

Thankfully, he let it go at that.

Minutes passed. Another road sign flashed by, all white light like an empty mirror set to catch the moon, its words smeared to one big blur.

"Where were you in such a hurry to get to, though?"

I closed my eyes again. I find conversation wearying at the best of times, and this one was fast becoming like having someone rummaging inexpertly around in the back of your mind while he thought you weren't looking.

"Oh, everywhere," I said. "And nowhere. I am taking a—working holiday, so to speak. I want to see it all."

"What all?"

I shrugged. "America."

He laughed. "That might take some time, ma'am."

"It already has."

Being a nomad by nature, it took me many years of painstaking research to finally decide which country I wanted to become a citizen of. After all that rootless freedom, the idea of pledging my allegiance to any kind of flag was intoxicating. I came to America open-handed, all other options exhausted, like a true immigrant. Prepared for anything. Expecting it, in fact.

So far, I have not been too disappointed.

We were approaching the midpoint of our journey, that barren stretch where the bedrock breaks the soil and the houses fall away like a shed skin. Lights got further and further apart. Here and there, on the hills, I saw the fallen stars of night-blooming flowers twist towards the moonlight. Their scent was faint, but bitter.

And Lester P. Budgell began to look at me more often, with a kind of wistfulness.

At last, he cleared his throat.

"Older lady like you," he began, testing the ground for pitfalls. "Maybe you need someone looking out for you, all alone on a holiday trip. Your kids, maybe."

"I have no children."

"Husband, then? Friends?"

"All dead."

He liked that. Hunger jumped in his eyes, a fact he tried to conceal by immediately transferring his attention to the steering wheel.

"Road's a dangerous place, ma'am," he said.

"Oh yes," I replied. Almost as softly as he had. "I know."

With that, we reached either an impasse or an understanding. He stared out through the windshield at the dangerous road ahead, reduced by the night to a pair of headlights crawling over the asphalt miles. The car sped on, unhindered by questions, black tar unravelling under our wheels like a spool of funereal ribbon. And the moon looked down.

I shut my eyes one final time, and slept.

* * *

There was a distant explosion.

Some time later, I resurfaced to the dull thud and scrape of a shovel's blade on sand.

I lay in the back of the car. The hatch was up, obstructing the rear window. I stretched, rose, and stepped out for a better look, pausing only to check myself in the car door mirror.

As I thought. A neat bullet hole bisected my forehead.

Poor Lester. He had his routine down so pat—the "aw shucks, ma'am" country boy spiel was quite believable, and he obviously knew his territory and weaponry inside out. He had had practice. It would be interesting, in an academic kind of way, to try and spot how many similar graves dotted the surrounding hills. Not a lot of imagination to go with his initiative, however. He'd just fallen over a sweet deal and run with it ever since, because it worked too well to risk variation.

And here he was now, down on his polyester knees in the dirt, scratching out a shallow hole big enough for a large child. Or a small woman. His breath came in wheezy gasps as he threw each shovelful aside.

I stood and watched attentively for a few minutes before I tapped him on the shoulder.

"Hello, Mr. Budgell."

He shrieked and jumped to his feet, dropping the shovel.

"You're dead," he said.

"True," I conceded. "But you cannot really take credit for that."

He drew the gun without thinking about it, and shot me six times in the chest. Point-blank range. He kept shooting, even after he ran out of bullets.

I yawned.

Then I broke down the door to his head with a single blow, and went inside.

Lester P. Budgell's house took up his entire inner landscape, although a thicket of blasted trees moped around the front windows, shutting out the light. The house itself had many rooms, most filled with the leavings of his childhood—*Playboy* playmates whose faces had been erased with exacto-knives, a cat's head on a spindle set amongst a circle of pastel birthday candles, his older sister Alice's brassiere. As the upper levels grew gradually more modern, the souvenirs he kept there grew correspondingly more vocal. Some chambers had been sealed for years, and their inhabitants were extremely grateful when I let them go.

The upshot, boring as it seems, was that Lester had been picking up vagrants of both sexes and all ages along this strip of highway since he first got his real job as a travelling salesman. He would lie to them, charm them, take them out into the hills and eventually kill them. If they were female, he would shoot them in the head to preserve their attractiveness and then have sex with the bodies before he buried them. If not, he would hunt them on foot until he grew bored, shoot them in the knees and brain them with the shovel as they tried to crawl away. Two or three a trip, eight trips per year, ten years on the job And none of them had been missed yet.

"Puerile," I muttered.

Lester sobbed at my feet. His victims' memory-selves had found the kitchen, and were setting the house on fire. Nothing was exempt from the blaze. All that hard work, too.

It was long past time to be done with this cretin. I leaned forward.

Inside him, a wet red clock kept steady time. But inside me, a hard white clock had begun to tick again. I took his heart in mine and brought our pulses together, gradually speeding up. The buzz of gears filled his brain. A second hand spinning and spinning and spinning.

Then, as one, we struck.

* * *

The moon hid itself behind the next hill as I made my way from the grave Lester had meant for me but now filled himself, staring vacantly upwards at the starless sky. I dipped into a gully filled with nothing but dark, which refreshed me immensely. Rattlesnakes rustled as they fled the sound of my steps. They knew their place on the food-chain too well for self-deception, and I respected that. Unlike humans, they understood that when two predators meet they must both turn away at once and go in opposite directions. Or one will die.

I carried my shoes under my arm, feet bare for better traction, and the desert slipped by in even strides. Sand filled my tracks.

So, my friends. Who, or what, am I anyway?

My name, as I have said, is Vassila. When I was thirteen, I died of a sudden fever. I clearly remember the acrid smell of my own vomit dispersing, with one sharp retch, all the comfort and familiarity of the other smells in our tiny wagon, like the lard simmering in the brass lamp, or the bitter black tea they forced between my lips. I lay without crying, drenched in sweat and stale urine, my muscles pulled taut and trembling. My last memory was of my mother's hands—one passing over my cracked lips in silent benediction, the other offering me a tarnished cross to kiss.

The next time I died, it was from cold and starvation. I woke underground and climbed out just in time to see snow cover the trail of my caravan. The sun dazzled my weak eyes. I stumbled over the stones of my cairn as I struggled to follow, but frost settled deeper on me with each passing hour. My shroud cracked and fell away in rigid shards. My hair froze solid. My bare feet wore smooth on the wasteland, until bone gleamed through where the skin was thinnest. After fifty days, I could go no farther, so I fell on my face and died.

Later, the wolves found me.

The third time I died, I had settled in a tiny village along the foot of the Balkans. My new parents had found me on a high plateau and taken me in. She was a seamstress, he the local blacksmith. That winter was so harsh they could only raise a quarter of their expected crops. So when spring came, the Streltzy swept in like a killing wind and burned them out for failing to meet the Tsar's taxes. I was caught in the village square as I ran for shelter and passed from horse to horse. The last soldier to use me, sated, turned my head to the east and slit my throat. They rode over my body where it fell, dissolving into the sun.

When I could breathe again, I rose and walked away.

My education was over, at least the essential part of it. There was little, as I had discovered, that could hurt me—and nothing that could kill me. I aged, but slowly. Soon I learned to turn my enemies' power back upon them. I wandered. It was a long road, and the years went slowly. Many years, many deaths.

In Bruges they burned me as a witch. It took several months for my charred flesh to harden and heal.

In London I caught the Plague. Buboes swelled and burst inside my knees as I knelt to pray.

In Fiorenza, I drank poison and was thrown in the river. I woke to pallid

55

fish grazing at my face, and waded hip-deep in trash to the nearest bank.

In Bogota I was lynched. My boat overturned while crossing from Calais to Dover and no one survived, yet I alone survived. In Paris I fell from a hotel window, crushing bones that knit badly, and the limp lasted twenty years.

There were some suicides as well. The weight of centuries pressed on me with a sullen, constant ache I frequently longed to end. In Brussels I slit my wrists and drowned, Roman-style, in a soft pink bath. In Singapore I opened the gas mains wide, and waited. In Saskatoon I was too thorough. They buried me, and I had to lie quiet while my embalmed organs renewed themselves from scratch.

Then and there, I decided not to try again. The growing threat of cremation was something to consider. But this choice was not made entirely out of fear.

After so much time, I had begun to dream again.

So I bought a ticket to America.

I mounted the next hill, scaring the moon, which shot up into the sky once more to hang above the broad, glittering highway.

America is such a wonderful country, I thought. *So big. No borders to cross, no papers to show. Only the road. And the road goes on forever. Here I can be content, at last, no longer wondering what lies ahead or regretting what lies behind.*

And if there is one thing I have learned, it is that there will always be another car.

YEAR ZERO

And when I passed by thee, and saw thee polluted in thine own blood, I said unto thee when thou wast in thy blood, Live; yea, I said unto thee when thou wast in thy blood, Live.
         —Ezekiel 6:16.

At the very height of the French Revolution, after they killed the king and drank his blood, they started everything over: New calendar, new months, new history. Wind back the national clock and smash its guts to powder; wipe the slate clean, and crack it across your knee. A failed actor named Fabre d'Eglantine drew up the plans. He stretched each seven-day week to a ten-day decade, and recarved the months into a verdant litany of rural images: Fruit and flowers, wind and rain. The Guillotine's red flash, masked in a mist of blistering, lobster-baked heat.

The first year of this process was to be known as Year Zero. Everything that happened next would be counted from then on. And all that had happened before would be, very simply . . .

. . . gone.

* * *

Then: Paris, 1793. Thermidor, Year Three, just before the end of the Terror—

"Oh, la, Citizen. How you do blush."

I must wake up, Jean-Guy Sansterre thinks, slow and lax—the words

57

losing shape even as he forms them, like water dripping through an open mental hand, fingers splayed and helpless. *Rouse myself. Act. Fight . . .*

But feeling, instead, how his whole body settles inexorably into some arcane variety of sleep—limbs loose and heavy, head lolling back on dark red satin upholstery. Falling spine-first into the close, dim interior of the Chevalier du Prendegrace's coach, a languorous haze of drawn velvet curtains against which Jean-Guy lies helpless as some micro-organism trapped beneath the fringed, softly sloping convex lens of a partially lidded eye.

Outside, in the near distance, one can still hear the constant growl and retch of the Widow, the National Razor, the legendary Machine split the air from the Place De La Revolution—that excellent device patented by dapper Dr Guillotin, to cure forever the pains and ills of headaches, hang-overs, insomnia. The repetitive thud of body on board, head in basket. The jeers and jibes of the tricoteuses knitting under the gallows steps, their Phrygian caps nodding in time with the tread of the executioner's ritual path; self-elected keepers of the public conscience, these grim hags who have outlived their former oppressors again and again. These howling crowds of sans-culottes, the trouserless ones—all crying in unison for yet more injurious freedom, still more, ever more: A great, sanguinary river with neither source nor tide, let loose to flood the city streets with visible vengeance . . .

"Do you know what complex bodily mechanisms lie behind the work-ings of a simple blush, Citizen Sansterre?"

That slow voice, emerging—vaporous and languid as an audible curl of smoke—from the red half-darkness of the coach. Continuing, gently:

"I have made a sometime study of such matters; strictly amateur in nature, of course, yet as thorough an inquiry as my poor resources may afford me."

In the Chevalier's coach, Jean-Guy feels himself bend and blur like melting waxwork beneath the weight of his own hypnotized exhaus-tion—fall open on every level, like his own strong but useless arms, his nerveless, cord-cut legs—

"The blush spreads as the blood rises, showing itself most markedly at the skin's sheerest points—a map of veins, eminently traceable. Almost . . . readable."

So imperative, this urge to fly, to fight. And so, utterly—

—impossible.

"See, here and there, where landmarks evince themselves: Those knots of veins and arteries, delicately entwined, which wreathe the undersides of your wrists. Two more great vessels, hidden at the tongue's root. A long, humped one, outlining the shaft of that other boneless—organ—whose proper name we may not quote in mixed company."

Sitting. Sprawling, limp. And thinking:

I—must . . .

"And that, stirring now? In that same . . . unmentionable . . . area?"

. . . must—wake . . .

"Blood as well, my friend. Blood, which—as the old adage goes—will always tell."

But: *This is all a dream*, Jean-Guy reminds himself, momentarily surprised by his own coherence. *I have somehow fallen asleep on duty, which is bad, though hardly unforgivable—and because I did so while thinking on the ci-devant Chevalier du Prendegrace, that traitor Dumouriez's master, I have spun out this strange fantasy.*

For Prendegrace cannot be here, after all; he will have fled before Jean-Guy's agents, like any other hunted lordling. And, knowing this—

Knowing this, I will wake soon, and fulfill the mission set me by the Committee For Public Safety: catch Dumouriez, air out this nest of silken vipers. And all will be as I remember.

At the same time, meanwhile, the Chevalier (or his phantom—for can he really actually be there, dream or no?) smiles down at Jean-Guy through the gathering crimson shade, all sharp—and tender—amusement. A slight, lithe figure, dressed likewise all in red, his hereditary elegance undercut by a distressingly plebian thread of more-than-usually poor hygiene: lurid velvet coat topped by an immaculately-tied but obviously dingy cravat; silken stockings, offhandedly worn and faded, above the buckled shoes with their neat cork heels. Dark rims to his longish finger-nails—dirt, or something else, so long-dried it's turned black.

His too-white skin has a stink, faintly charnel. Acrid in Jean-Guy's acquiescent, narrowed nostrils.

"You carry a surplus of blood, Citizen, by the skin-map's evidence," the Chevalier seems to say, gently. "And thus might, if only in the name of politeness, consider willing some small portion of that overflowing store . . . to me."

"Can't you ever speak clearly, you damnable aristo?" Jean-Guy demands, hoarsely.

And: "Perhaps not," comes the murmuring reply. "Though, now I think on it . . . I cannot say I've ever tried."

Bending down, dipping his sleek, powdered head, this living ghost of an exterminated generation; licking his thin white lips while Jean-Guy lies still beneath him, boneless, helpless. So soft, all over—in every place—

—but one.

* * *

So: Now, 1815. Paris again, late September—an old calendar for a brand-new Empire—in the Row of the Armed Man, near dusk . . .

. . . where the Giradoux family's lawyer meets Jean-Guy, key in hand, by the door of what was once Edouard Dumouriez's house.

Over the decade since Jean-Guy last walked this part of Paris, Napoleon's civil engineers have straightened out most of the overhanging tangle of back-alleys into a many-spoked wheel of pleasant, tree-lined boulevards and well-paved—if bleakly functional—streets. The Row of the Armed Man, however, still looks much the same as always: A narrow path of cracked flagstones held together with gravel and mortar, stinking of discarded offal and dried urine, bounded on either side by crooked doorways or smoke-darkened signs reading Butcher, Candle-maker, Notary Public.

And in the midst of it all, Dumouriez's house, towering shadowy and slant above the rest—three shaky floors' worth of rooms left empty, in a city where unoccupied living space is fought over like a franc left lying in the mud.

"The rabble do avoid it," the lawyer agrees, readily. Adding, with a facile little shrug: "Rumor brands the place as . . . haunted."

And the unspoken addendum to said addendum, familiar as though Jean-Guy had formed the statement himself—

—*though I, of course, do not ascribe to the same theory . . . being, as I am, a rational man living in this rational and enlightened state of Nouvelle France, an age without kings, without tyrants . . .*

With Jean-Guy adding, mentally, in return: *For we were all such reasonable men, once upon a time. And the Revolution, our lovely daughter, sprung full-blown from that same reason—a bare-breasted Athena clawing her way up to daylight, through the bloody ruin of Zeus' shattered skull.*

The Giradoux lawyer wears a suit of black velvet, sober yet festive, and carries a small satin mask; his hair has been pulled back and powdered in the "antique fashion" of twelve scant years past. And at his throat, partially hidden in the fold of his cloak's collar, Jean-Guy can glimpse the sharp red edge of a scarlet satin ribbon knotted—oh so very neatly—just beneath his jugular vein.

"I see you've come dressed for some amusement, M'sieu."

The lawyer colors slightly, as if caught unaware in some dubious action.

"Merely a social engagement," he replies. "A Bal des Morts. You've heard the term?"

"Not that I recall."

"Where the dead go to dance, M'sieu Sansterre."

Ah, indeed.

Back home in Martinique, where Jean-Guy has kept himself carefully hidden these ten years past and more, the "Thermidorean reaction" which attended news of the Terror's end—Jacobin arch-fiend Maximilien Robespierre first shot, then guillotined; his Committee for Public Safety disbanded; slavery reinstated, and all things thus restored to their natural rank and place—soon gave rise to a brief but intense period of public celebration on those vividly colored shores. There was dancing to all hours, Free Black and Creole French alike, with everything fashionable done temporarily a la victime—a thin white shift or cravat-less blouse, suitable for making a sacrifice of one's-self on the patriotic altar in style; the hair swept up, exposing the neck for maximum accessibility; a ribbon tied where the good Widow, were she still on hand to do so, might be expected to leave her red and silent, horizontal kiss . . .

At the Bal des Morts, participants' dance-cards were filled according to their own left-over notoriety; for who in their family might have actually gone to good Dr Guillotin's Machine, or who their family might have had a hand in sending there. Aping executed and executioners alike, they dressed as corpses and preened like resurrected royalty, bobbing and spinning in a sluggish stream of old blood—trash caught in frenzied motion against the gutter's grate, at the end of a hard night's deluge.

The roll-call of the tumbrils: Aristocrats, collaborators, traitors and Tyrannists, even the merely argumentative or simply ignorant—one poor woman calling her children in to dinner, only to find herself arrested on suspicion of sedition because her son's name happened to be (like that of the deposed king) Louis. And in the opposing camp, Jean-Guy's fellow Revolutionaries: Girondists, Extremists, Dantonists, Jacobins, patriots of all possible stamps and stripes—many of whom, by the end of it all, had already begun to fall under fatal suspicion themselves.

These, then, their inheritors and imitators . . . these remnants wrapped in party-going silk, spending their nights laying a thin skin of politeness, even enjoyment, over the unhealed temporal wounds of la Mere France.

Jean-Guy met the girl who would become his late wife at such an affair, and paid her bride-price a few scant weeks later. Vivienne, her name had been. An apricot-colored little thing, sweet-natured and shy, her eyes almost blue; far less obviously du sang negre than he himself, even under the most—direct—scrutiny.

And it is only now, with her so long dead, that he can finally admit it was this difference of tone . . . rather than any true heart's affection . . . which was the primary motive of their union.

He glances down at a puddle near his boot, briefly considering how his own reflection sketches itself on the water's dim skin: A dark man in a dark frock-coat—older now, though no paler. Beneath his high, stiff silk hat, his light brown hair has been cropped almost to the skull to mask its obvious kink; under the hat-brim's shade, his French father's straight nose and hazel eyes seem awkwardly offset by the unexpected tint of his slave-born mother's teak-inflected complexion. His mixed-race parentage is writ large in every part of him, for those who care enough to look for it—the tell-tale taint of colonization, met and matched in flesh and bone. His skin still faintly scarred, as it were, by the rucked sheets of their marriage-bed.

Not that any money ever changed hands to legalize that relationship, Jean-Guy thinks. *Maman having been old Sansterre's property, at the time.*

This is a tiring line of thought to maintain, however . . . not to mention over-familiar. And there will be much to be done, before the Paris sun rises again.

"I wish you the joy of your Bal, M'sieu," Jean-Guy tells the lawyer. "And so, if it please you—my key?"

Proffering his palm and smiling, pleasantly. To which the lawyer replies, coloring again—

"Certainly, M'sieu."

—and hands it over. Adding, as Jean-Guy mounts the steps behind him:

"But you may find very little as you remember it, from those days when M'sieu Dumouriez had the top floor."

Jean-Guy pauses at the building's door, favoring the lawyer with one brief, backwards glance. And returns—

"That, one may only hope . . . M'sieu."

* * *

1793:

Jean-Guy wakes to twilight, to an empty street—that angry crowd which formerly assembled to rock and prison the Chevalier du Prendegrace's escaping coach apparently having passed on to some further, more distant business. He lies sprawled on a pile of trash behind the butcher's back door, head abuzz and stomach lurching; though whether the nausea in question results from his own physical weakness, the smell of the half-rotten mess of bones beneath him or the sound of the flies that cluster on their partially denuded surface, he truly cannot tell. But he wakes, also, to the voice of his best spy—the well-named La Hire—telling him he must open his eyes, lurch upright, rouse himself at last . . .

"May the Goddess of Reason herself strike me dead if we didn't think you lost forever, Citizen—murdered, maybe, or even arrested. Like all the other Committee members."

Much the same advice Jean-Guy remembers giving himself, not all so very long ago. Back when he lay enveloped in that dark red closeness between those drawn velvet curtains, caught and prone under the stale air's weight in damnably soft, firm grip of the Chevalier's upholstery.

But: "Citizen Sansterre!" A slap across the jaw, jerking his too-heavy head sharply to the left. "Are you tranced? I said, we couldn't find you."

Well . . . you've found me now, though. Haven't you—

—Citizen?

The Chevalier's murmuring voice, reduced to an echo in Jean-Guy's blood. His hidden stare, red-glass-masked, coming and going like heat lightning's horizon-flash behind Jean-Guy's aching eyes.

He shakes his head, still reeling from the sting of La Hire's hand. Forces himself to form words, repeating:

" . . . the Committee."

"Gone, Citizen. Scattered to the winds."

"Citizen . . . Robespierre?"

"Arrested, shot, jaw held on with a bandage. He'll kiss the Widow tomorrow—as will we, if we don't fly this stinking city with the Devil's own haste."

Gaining a weak grip upon La Hire's arm, Jean-Guy uses it to lever himself—shakily—upwards. His mouth feels swollen, lips and gums raw-abraded; new blood fresh and sticky at one corner, cud of old blood sour between his back teeth, at the painful root of his tongue. More blood pulls free as he rises, unsticking the left panel of his half-opened shirt from the nub of one nipple; as he takes a step forward, yet more blood still is found gluing him fast to his own breeches, stiff and brown, in that—

. . . unmentionable area . . .

And on one wrist, a light, crescent-shaped wound—bruised and inflamed, pink with half-healed infection. A painfully raised testimony to dream-dim memory: The Chevalier's rough little tongue pressed hard, cold as a dead cat's, against the thin skin above the uppermost vein.

I have set my mark upon you, Citizen.

Jean-Guy passes a hand across his brow, coughing, then brings it away wet—and red. Squints down, and finds himself inspecting a palm-full of blood-tinged sweat.

"Dumouriez," he asks La Hire, with difficulty. "Taken . . . also?"

"Hours ago."

"Show me . . . to his room."

* * *

And now, a momentary disclaimer: Let it be here stated, with as much clarity as possible, that Jean-Guy had never—hitherto—given much credence to those old wives' tales which held that aristos glutted their delicate hungers at the mob's expense, keeping themselves literally fat with infusions of carnal misery and poor men's meat. Pure rhetoric, surely; folk-tales turned metaphor, as quoted in Camille Desmoulins' incendiary pamphlets: "Church and nobility—vampires. Observe the color of their faces, and the pallor of your own."

Not that the Chevalier du Prendgrace's face, so imperfectly recalled, had borne even the slightest hint of color . . . healthy, or otherwise.

Not long after his return to Martinique, Jean-Guy had held some brief discourse with an English doctor named Gabriel Keynes—a man famous for spending the last ten years of his own life trying to identify the causes of (and potential cures for) that swampy bronze plague known as Yellow

Fever. Bolstered by a bottle or two of good claret and Keynes' personal promise of most complete discretion, Jean-Guy had unfolded to him the whole, distressing story of his encounter with the Chevalier: Shown him the mark on his wrist, the marks . . .

. . . elsewhere.

Those enduring wounds which, even now, would—on occasion—break open and bleed anew, as though at some unrecognizable signal; the invisible passage of their maker, perhaps, through the cracks between known and unknown areas of their mutual world's unwritten map?

As though we could really share the same world, ever, we two—such as I, and such as . . .

. . . *he* . . .

"What y'have here, Monsewer Sansterre," Keynes observed—touching the blister's surface but delicately, yet leaving behind a dent, along with a lingering, sinister ache—"is a continual pocket of sequestered blood. 'Tis that what we sawbones name haematoma: From the Latin haematomane, or 'drinker of blood'."

There was, the doctor explained, a species of bats in the Antipodes—even upon Jean-Guy's home island—whose very genus was labeled after the common term for those legendary un-dead monsters Desmoulins had once fixated upon. These bats possessed a saliva which, being composed mainly of anti-coagulant elements, aided them in the pursuit of their filthy addiction: A mixture of chemicals which, when smeared against an open wound, prolong—and even increase—the force and frequency of its bleeding. Adding, however:

"But I own I have never known of such a reaction left behind by the spittle of any *man* . . . even one whose family, as your former Jacobin compatriots might term it, is—no doubt—long-accustomed to the consumption of blood."

Which concludes, as it ensues, the entire role of science in this narrative.

* * *

And now, the parallel approach to Dumouriez' former apartment—past and present blending neatly together as Jean-Guy scales the rickety staircase towards that last, long-locked door, its hinges stiff with rust—

Stepping, in 1815, into a cramped and low-hung attic space clogged with antique furniture: Fine brocades, moth-eaten and dusty;

sway-backed Louis Quatorze chairs with splintered legs. Splintered armoires and dun-smoked walls, festooned with cobweb and scribbled with foul words.

On one particular wall, a faint stain hangs like spreading damp. The shadow of some immense, submerged, half-crucified grey bat.

Jean-Guy traces its contours, wonderingly. Remembering, in 1793 . . .

. . . a blood-stained pallet piled high with pale-eyed corpses left to rot beneath this same wall, this same great watermark: Its bright red darkness, splashed wet across fresh white plaster.

Oh, how Jean-Guy had stared at it—struck stupidly dumb with pure shock—while La Hire recounted the details his long day's sleep had stolen from him. Told him how, when the Committee's spies broke in at last, Dumouriez had merely looked up from his work with a queasy smile, interrupted in the very midst of dumping yet another body on top of the last. How he'd held a trowel clutched, incongruously, in one hand—which he'd then raised, still smiling . . .

. . . and used, sharp edge turned inward—even as they screamed at him to halt—to cut his own throat.

Under the stain's splayed wing, Jean-Guy closes his eyes and casts his mind back even further—right back to the beginning, before Thermidor finally stemmed the Revolutionary river's flood; before the Chevalier's coach, later found stripped and abandoned at the lip of a pit stuffed with severed heads and lime; before Dumouriez's suicide, or Jean-Guy and La Hire's frantic flight to Calais, and beyond—back to Martinique, where La Hire would serve as plantation-master on Old Sansterre's lands 'til the hour and the day of his own, entirely natural, demise. The very, very beginning.

Or: Jean-Guy's—necessarily limited—version of it, at any rate.

* * *

1793, then, once more. Five o'clock on that long-gone "August" day, and the afternoon sun has already begun to slant down over the Row of the Armed Man's ruined roofs—dripping from their streaming gutters in a dazzle of water and light, along with the last of the previous night's rainfall. Jean-Guy and La Hire sit together at what passes for a table by the open window of a street-side cafe, their tricolor badges momentarily absent from sashes and hats; they sip their coffee, thus disguised, and listen to today's tumbrils grind by through the stinking mist. Keeping a careful tandem eye, also, upon the uppermost windows of Dumouriez's house—refuge of a suspected traitor, and previously listed (before its recent conversion into a many-roomed, half-empty "Citizens' hotel") as part of the ancestral holdings of a certain M. le Chevalier du Prendegrace.

Jean-Guy to La Hire: "This Prendegrace—who is he?"

"A ci-devant aristo, what else? Like all the rest."

"Yes, to be sure; but besides."

La Hire shrugs. "Does it matter?"

Here, in that ill-fit building just across the way, other known aristo-crats—men, women and children bearing papers forged expertly enough to permit them to walk the streets of Paris, if not exit through its gates—have often been observed to enter, though rarely been observed to leave. Perhaps attracted by Prendegrace's reputation as "one of their own", they place their trust in his creature Dumouriez's promises of sanc-tuary, refuge, escape—and the very fact of their own absence, later on, seems to prove that trust has not been given in vain.

"The sewers," La Hire suggests. "They served us well enough during the old days, dodging Royallist scum through the Cordelliers' quarter . . . "

Jean-Guy scoffs. "A secret entrance, perhaps, in the cellar? Down to the river with the rest of the garbage, then to the far shore on some subterra-nean boat?"

"It's possible."

"So the malgre Church used to claim, concerning Christ's resurrection."

A guffaw. "Ah, but there's no need to be so bitter about that, Citizen. Is there? Since they've already paid so well, after all—those fat-arsed priests—for spreading such pernicious lies."

And: *Ah, yes,* Jean-Guy remembers thinking, as he nods in smiling agreement. *Paid in full, on the Widow's lap . . . just like the King and his Austrian whore, before them.*

Across the street, meanwhile, a far less elevated lady of ill-repute comes edging up through the Row proper, having apparently just failed to drum up any significant business amongst the crowds which line the Widow's bridal path. Spotting them both, she hikes her skirt to show Jean-Guy first the hem of her scarlet petticoat, then the similarly red-dyed tangle of hair at her crotch. La Hire glances over, draws a toothless grin, and snickers in reply; Jean-Guy affects to ignore her, and receives a rude gesture for his politesse. Determined to avoid the embarrassment of letting his own sudden spurt of anger show, he looks away, eyes flicking back towards the attic's windows—

—where he sees, framed between its moth-worn curtains, another woman's face appear: A porcelain-smooth girl's mask peering out from the darkness behind the cracked glass, grub-pale in the shadows of this supposedly unoccupied apartment. It hangs there, empty as a wax head from Citizen Curtuis' museum—that studio where images of decapitated friend and foe to France alike are modeled from casts taken by his "niece" Marie, the Grosholtz girl, who will one day abandon Curtuis to the mob he serves and marry another man for passage to England. Where she will set up her own museum, exhibiting the results of her skills under the fresh new name of Madame Tussaud.

That white face. Those dim-hued eyes. Features once contemptuously regal, now possessed of nothing but a dull and uncomplaining patience. The same wide stare which will meet Jean-Guy's, after the raid, from atop the grisly burden of Dumouriez's overcrowded pallet. That proud aristo, limbs flopped carelessly askew, her nude skin dappled—like that of every one of her fellow victims—

(like Jean-Guy's own brow now, in 1815, as he studies that invisible point on the wall where the stain of Dumouriez's escape once hung, dripping)

—with bloody sweat.

His "old complaint", he called it, during that brief evening's consultation with Dr Keynes. A cyclic, tidal flux, regular as breath, unwelcome as nightmare—constantly calling and re-calling a blush, or more, to his unwilling skin.

And he wonders, Jean-Guy, just as he wondered then: why look at all? Why bother to hide herself, if only to periodically brave the curtain and offer her unmistakable face to the hostile street outside?

But—

"You aristos," he remembers muttering while the Chevalier listened, courteously expressionless. "All, so . . . arrogant."

"Yes, Citizen."

"Like . . . that girl. The one . . . "

"At Dumouriez's window? Oh, no doubt."

" . . . but how . . . " Struggling manfully against his growing lassitude, determined to place the reference in context: "How . . . could you know . . . ?"

And the Chevalier, giving his version of La Hire's shrug, all sleek muscle under fine scarlet velvet—

"But I simply do, Citizen Sansterre."

Adding, in a whisper—a hum? That same hum, so close and quiet against the down of Jean-Guy's paralyzed cheek, which seems to vibrate through every secret part of him at once whenever the blood still kept sequestered beneath his copper-ruddy mixed-race flesh begins to . . . flow . . .

. . . *for who do you think it was who told her to look out, in the first place?*

* * *

In Martinique—with money and time at his disposal, and a safe distance put between himself and that Satanic, red-lined coach—Jean-Guy had eventually begun to make certain discreet inquiries into the long and secretive history of the family Prendegrace. Thus employed, he soon amassed a wealth of previously hidden information: facts impossible to locate during the Revolution, or even before.

Like picking at a half-healed scab, pain and relief in equal measure—and since, beyond obviously, he would never be fully healed, what did it matter just . . .

. . . what . . .

. . . Jean-Guy's enquiries managed to uncover?

Chevalier Joffroi d'Iver, first of his line, won his nobility on crusade under Richard Coeur-de-lion, for services rendered during the massacre at Acre. An old story: Reluctant to lose the glory of having captured three hundred Infidels in battle—though aware that retaining them would prevent any further advancement towards his true prize, the holy city of Jerusalem—the hot-blooded Plantagenet ordered each and every one of them decapitated on the spot. So scaffolds were built, burial pits dug, and heads and bodies sent tumbling in either direction for three whole days—while the swords of d'Iver and his companions swung ceaselessly, and a stream of fresh victims slipped in turn on the filth their predecessors had left behind.

And after their task was done, eyewitnesses record, these good Christian knights filled the pits with Greek fire—leaving the bodies to burn, as they rode away.

Much as, during your own famous Days of September, a familiar voice seems to murmur at Jean-Guy's ear, *three hundred and seventy-eight of those prisoners awaiting trial at the Conciergie were set upon by an angry horde of good patriots like yourself, and hacked limb from limb in the street.*

Eyes closed, Jean-Guy recalls a gaggle of women running by—red-handed, reeling drunk—with clusters of ears adorning their open, fichu-less bodices. Fellow Citizens clapping and cheering from the drawn-up benches as a man wrings the Princess de Lamballe's still-beating heart dry over a goblet, then takes a long swig of the result, toasting the health of the Revolution in pale aristo blood. All those guiding lights of Liberty: ugly Georges Danton, passionate Camille Desmoulins ...

... Maximilien Robespierre in his Incorruptible's coat of sea-green silk, nearsighted cat's eyes narrowed against the world through spectacles with smoked-glass lenses—the kind one might wear, even today, to protect oneself while observing an eclipse.

Le Famille Prend-de-grace, moving to block out the sun; a barren new planet, passing restless through a dark new sky. And their arms, taken at the same time—an axe argent et gules, over a carrion field, gules seulement.

A blood-stained weapon, suspended—with no visible means of support—above a field red with severed heads.

We could not have been more suited to each other, you and I. Could we—

—Citizen?

* * *

1793: Blood and filth, and the distant rumble of passing carts—the hot mist turns to sizzling rain, as new waves of stench eddy and shift around them. Dumouriez rounds the corner into the Row of the Armed Man, and La Hire and Jean-Guy exchange a telling glance: the plan of attack, as previously determined. La Hire will take the back way, past where the prostitute lurks, while Jean-Guy waits under a convenient awning—to keep his powder dry—until he hears their signal, using the time between to prime his pistol.

They give Dumouriez a few minutes' lead, then rise as one.

* * *

Crimson-stained sweat, memories swarming like maggots in his brain. Yet more on the clan Prendegrace, a red-tinged stream of sinister trivia—

Their motto: Nus souvienz le tous. "We remember everything."

Their hereditary post at court: Attendant on the king's bedchamber, a function discontinued sometime during the reign of Henri de Navarre, for historically obscure reasons.

The rumour: That during the massacre of Saint Barthelme's Night, one—usually unnamed—Prendegrace was observed pledging then-King Charles IX's honor with a handful of Protestant flesh.

Prendegrace. "Those who have received God's grace."

Receive.

Or—is it—*take* God's grace . . .

. . . for themselves?

Jean-Guy feels himself start to reel, and rams his fist against the apartment wall for support. Then feels it lurch and pulse in answer under his knuckles, as though his own hammering heart were buried beneath that yellowed plaster.

* * *

Pistol thrust beneath his coat's lapel, Jean-Guy steps towards Dumouriez's door—only to find his way blocked by a sudden influx of armed and shouting fellow Citizens. Yet another protest whipped up from general dissatisfaction and street-corner demagoguery, bound for nowhere in particular, less concerned with destruction than with noise and display; routine "patriotic" magic transforming empty space into chaos-bent rabble, with no legerdemain or invocation required.

Across the way, he spots La Hire crushed up against the candle-maker's door, but makes sure to let his gaze slip by without a hint of recognition as the stinking human tide . . . none of them probably feeling particularly favorable, at this very moment, toward any representative of the Committee who—as they keep on chanting—*have stole our blood to make their bread* . . .

(a convenient bit of symbolic symmetry, that)

. . . sweeps him rapidly back past the whore, the garbage, the cafe, the Row itself, and out into the cobbled street beyond.

Jean-Guy feels his ankle turn as it meets the gutter; he stumbles, then rights himself. Calling out, above the crowd's din—

"Citizens, I . . . " No answer. Louder: "Listen, Citizens—I have no quarrel with you; I have business in there . . . " And, louder still: "Citizens! *Let . . . me . . . pass!*"

But: No answer, again, from any of the nearest mob-members—neither that huge, obviously drunken man with the pike, trailing tricolor streamers, or those two women trying to fill their aprons with loose stones while ignoring the screaming babies strapped to their backs. Not even from that dazed young man who seems to have once—however mistakenly—thought himself to be their leader, now dragged hither and yon at the violent behest of his "followers" with his pale eyes rolling in their sockets, his gangly limbs barely still attached to his shaking body . . .

The price of easy oratory, Jean-Guy thinks, sourly. Cheap words, hasty actions; a whole desperate roster of very real ideals—and hungers—played on for the mere sake of a moment's notoriety, applause, power—

—our Revolution's ruin, in a nutshell.

And then . . .

. . . a shadow falls over him, soft and dark as the merest night-borne whisper—but one which will lie paradoxically heavy across his unsuspecting shoulders, nevertheless, for long years afterward. His destiny approaching through the mud, on muffled wheels.

A red-hung coach, nudging at him—almost silently—from behind.

Perfect.

He shoulders past the pikeman, between the women, drawing curses and blows; gives back a few of his own, as he clambers onto the coach's running-board and hooks its nearest door open. Rummages in his pocket for his tricolor badge, and brandishes it in the face of the coach's sole occupant, growling—

"I commandeer this coach in the name of the Committee for Public Safety!"

Sliding quick into the seat opposite as the padded door shuts suddenly, yet soundlessly, beside him. And that indistinct figure across from him leans forward, equally sudden—a mere red-on-white-on-red silhouette, in the curtained windows' dull glare—to murmur:

"The Committee? Why, my coach is yours, then . . . "

. . . Citizen.

Jean-Guy looks up, dazzled. And notices, at last, the Prendegrace arms which hang just above him, embroidered on the curtains' underside—silver on red, red on red, outlined in fire by the sun which filters weakly through their thick, enshrouding velvet weave.

* * *

1815. Jean-Guy feels new wetness trace its way down his arm, soaking the cuff of his sleeve red: His war-wound, broken open once more, in sympathetic proximity to . . . what? His own tattered scraps of memory, slipping and sliding like phlegm on glass? This foul, haunted house, where Dumouriez—like some Tropic trap-door spider—traded on his master's aristocratic name to entice the easiest fresh prey he could find into his web, then fattened them up (however briefly) before using them to slake M. le Chevalier's deviant familial appetites?

Blood, from wrist to palm, printing the wall afresh; blood in his throat from his tongue's bleeding base, painting his spittle red as he hawks and coughs—all civility lost, in a moment's spasm of pure revulsion—onto the dusty floor.

Spatter of blood on dust, like a ripe scarlet hieroglyphic: Liquid, horrid, infinitely malleable. Utterly . . . uninterpretable.

I have set my mark upon you, Citizen.

Blood at his collar, his nipple. His—

(—groin.)

My hook in your flesh. My winding reel.

Jean-Guy feels it tug him downward, into the maelstrom.

* * *

1793. The coach. Prendegrace sits right in front of Jean-Guy, a mere hand's grasp away, slight and lithe and damnably languid in his rich, red velvet; his hair is drawn back and side-curled, powdered so well that Jean-Guy can't even tell its original color, let alone use its decided lack of contrast to help him decipher the similarly-pallid features of the face it frames. Except to note that, as though in mocking imitation of Citizen Robespierre, the Chevalier too affects a pair of spectacles with smoked glass lenses . . .

. . . though, instead of sea-green, these small, blank squares glint a dim—yet unmistakable—shade of scarlet.

Play for time, Jean-Guy's brain tells him, meanwhile—imparting its usually good advice with uncharacteristic softness, as though (if it were to speak any louder) the Chevalier might somehow overhear it. *Pretend not to have recognized him. Then work your pistol free, slowly; fire a warning shot, and summon the good Citizens outside . . .*

. . . those same ones you slipped in here to avoid, in the first place . . .

. . . *to aid you in his arrest.*

Almost snorting aloud at the very idea, before he catches himself: That an agent of Jean-Guy's enviable size and bulk actually need fear the feeble defenses of a ci-devant fop like this one, with his frilled wrists and his neat, red-heeled shoes, their tarnished buckles dull and smeared—on the nearest side, at least—with something which almost looks like . . .

. . . blood?

Surely not.

And yet—

"You would be Citizen Sansterre, I think," the Chevalier observes, abruptly.

Name of God.

Recovering, Jean-Guy gives a stiff nod. "And you—the traitor, Prendegrace."

"And that would be a pistol you reach for, under your collar."

"It would."

A punch, a kick, a cry for help, the drawing forth of some secret weapon of his own: Jean-Guy braces himself, a match-ready fuse, tensed to the point of near-pain against any of the aforementioned. But the Chevalier merely nods as well, undeterred in the face of Jean-Guy's honest aggression—his very passivity itself a form of arrogance, a cool and languid aristocratic challenge to the progressively more hot and bothered plebian world around him. Then leans just a bit forward, at almost the same time: A paralytic blink of virtual non-movement, so subtle as to be hardly worth noting . . . for all that Jean-Guy now finds himself beginning—barely recognizing what he does, let alone why—to match it.

Leaning in, far too slow to stop himself, to arrest this fall in mid-plunge. Leaning in, as the Chevalier's red lenses dip, slipping inexorably downward to reveal a pale rim of brow, of lash, of eyesocket. And leaning in yet further, to see—below that—

—first one eye, then another: Pure but opaque, luridly empty. Eyes without whites (or irises, or pupils), the same blank scarlet tint—from lower lid to upper—as the spectacles which masked them.

Words in red darkness, pitched almost too low to hear; Jean-Guy must strain to catch them, leaning closer still. Places a trembling hand on the Chevalier's shoulder, to steady himself, and feels them thrum up through his palm, his arm, his chest, his wildly beating heart: A secret, interior embrace, intimate as plague, squeezing him between the ribs, between the thighs. And . . .

. . . deeper.

Before him, the Chevalier's own hand hovers, clean white palm turned patiently upward. Those long, black-rimmed nails. Those red words, tracing the myriad paths of blood. Suggesting, mildly—

Then you had best give it to me, Citizen—this pistol of yours. Had you not?

Because: That would be the right thing to do, really. All things considered.

Do you not think?

Yes.

For safety. For—safe-keeping.

. . . exactly that, yes.

Such sweet reason. Such deadly reasonableness.

Jean-Guy feels his mouth drop open as though to protest, but hears only the faint, wet pop of his jaw-hinges relaxing in an idiot yawn; watches, helpless, as he drops the pistol—butt-first—into the Chevalier's grip. Sees the Chevalier seem to blink, just slightly, in return: All-red no-stare blurred by only the most momentary flicker, milky and brief as some snake's nictitating membrane.

And—

"There, now," the Chevalier observes, aloud. "That . . . must suit us both . . . so much better."

Must it—not?

A half-formed heave, a last muffled attempt at a thrash, muscles knotted in on themselves like some mad stray cur's in the foam-flecked final stages of hydrophobia—and then, without warning, the Chevalier is on him. Their mouths seal together, parted lip to bared, bone-needle teeth: blood fills Jean-Guy's throat, greasing the way as the Chevalier locks fast to his fluttering tongue. His gums burn like ulcers. This is far less a kiss than a suddenly open wound, an artery slashed and left to spurt.

The pistol falls away, forgotten.

Venom spikes Jean-Guy's heart. He chokes down a numbing, stinging mouthful of cold that takes him to the brink of sleep and the edge of climax simultaneously as the Chevalier's astringent tongue rasps over the inflamed tissues of his mouth, harsh as a cat's. Finds himself grabbing this whippet-slim thing in his arms by the well-arranged hair, anchoring himself so it can grind them ever more firmly together, and feels a shower of loose powder fall around both their faces like dirty city snow; the Chevalier's ribbon has come undone, his neat-curled side-locks unraveling like kelp in an icy current. At the same instant, meanwhile, the nearest lapel of his lurid coat peels back—deft as some mountebank's trick—to reveal the cold white flesh beneath: No pulse visible beneath the one flat pectoral, nipple peak-hard but utterly colorless . . .

. . . oh yes, yes, yes . . .

Jean-Guy feels the Chevalier's hands—clawed now—scrabble at his fly's buttons, free him to slap upwards in this awful red gloom. Then sees him give one quick double thumb-flick across the groove, the distended, weeping velvet knob, and send fresh scarlet welling up along the urethral fold faster than Jean-Guy can cry out in surprised, horrified pain.

Name of death and the Devil!

The Chevalier gives a thin grin of delight at the sight of it. His mouth opens wide as a cat's in flamen, tasting the slaughterhouse-scented air. Nearly drooling.

People, Revolution, Supreme Being, please—

Lips skinning back. Fangs extending. His sleek head dipping low, as though in profane prayer . . .

. . . oh God, oh Jesus, no . . .

. . . to sip at it.

More muffled words rippling up somehow through the femoral knot of Jean-Guy's groin, even as he gulps bile, his whole righteous world dimming to one pin-prick point of impossible pain, of unspeakable and unnatural ecstasy—as he starts to reel, come blood, black out:

Ah, Citizen—do not leave me just yet. Not when—

—we are—

—so close—

—to meeting each other, once more.

* * *

In 1815, meanwhile—

—Jean-Guy looks up from the bloody smudge now spreading wide beneath his own splayed fingers to see—that same familiar swatch of wet and shining scarlet resurface, like a grotesque miracle, above his gaping face. Dumouriez's death-stain, grown somehow fresh again, as though the wall . . . the room, itself . . . were bleeding.

Plaster reddens, softens. Collapses inward, paradoxically, as the wall bulges outward. And Jean-Guy watches, frozen, as what lies beneath begins to extrude itself, at long last, through that vile, soaked ruin of chalk-dust, glue and hemoglobin alike—first one hand, then another, one shoulder, then its twin. The whole rest of the torso, still dressed in the same rotten velvet equipage, twisting its deft way out through the sodden, crumbling muck . . . grub-white neck rearing cobra-like, poised to strike . . . grub-white profile turning outward—its lank mane still clotted with calcified powder, its red-glazed glasses hung carelessly askew—to once more cast empty eyes Jean-Guy's way . . .

This awful revenant version of M. the former Chevalier du Prendegrace shakes his half-mummified head, studying Jean-Guy from under dusty lashes. He opens his mouth, delicately—pauses—then coughs out a fine white curl, and frowns at the way his long-dormant lungs wheeze.

Fastening his blank red gaze on Jean-Guy's own. Observing:

"How terribly you've changed, Citizen." A pause. "But then—that is the inevitable fate of the impermanent."

"The Devil," Jean-Guy whispers, forgetting his once-vaunted atheism.

"La, sir. You do me entirely too much honor."

The Chevalier steps forward, bringing a curled and ragged lip of wall along with him; Jean-Guy hears it tear as it comes, like a scab. The sound rings in his ears. He puts up both palms, weakly, as though a simple gesture might really be enough to stave off the—living?—culmination of a half-lifetime's nightmare visions.

The Chevalier notices, and gives that sly half-smile: teeth still white, still intact, yet jutting now from his fever-pink gums at slight angles, like a shark's . . . but could there really be *more* of them, after all these years? Crop upon crop, stacked up and waiting to be shed after his next feeding, the one which never came?

They almost seem to glow, translucent as milky glass. Waiting—

—to be filled.

"Of course, one does hear things, especially inside the walls," the Chevalier continues, brushing plaster away with small, fastidious strokes. "For example: That—excepting certain instances of regicide—your vaunted Revolution came to naught, after all. And that, since a Corsican general now rules an empire in the monarchy's place, old Terrorists such as yourself must therefore count themselves in desperate need of new . . . positions."

Upraised palms, wet—and red; his "complaint" come back in force, worse than the discards in Dumouriez's long-ago corpse-pile. Jean-Guy stands immersed in it, head swirling, skin one whole slick of cold sweat and hot blood admixed—and far more blood than sweat, all told. So much so, he must swallow it in mouthfuls, just to speak. His voice comes out garbled, sludgy, clotted.

"You . . . " he says, with difficulty. "*You* . . . did this . . . to me . . . "

"But of course, Citizen Sansterre; sent the girl to the window, tempted you within my reach, and set my mark upon you, as you well know. As I—"

—told you.

Or . . . do you not recall?

Sluiced and veritably streaming with it, inside and out: Palate, nipples, groin. That haematoma on his wrist's prickling underside, opening like a flower. The Chevalier's remembered kiss, licking his veins full of cold poison.

(*If I can't stop this bleeding, it'll be my death.*)

Numb-tongued: "As you did with Dumouriez."

"Exactly so."

Raising one clawed hand to touch Jean-Guy's face, just lightly—a glancing parody of comfort—and send Jean-Guy arching away, cursing, as the mere pressure of the Chevalier's fingers is enough to draw first a drip, then a gush, of fresh crimson.

"God damn your ci-devant eyes!"

"Yes, yes." Quieter: "But I *can* make this stop, you know."

I. And only I.

Seduction, then infection, then cure—for a price. Loyalty, 'till death . . .

. . . and—after?

How Prendegrace trapped Dumouriez, no doubt, once upon a long, long time past—or had Dumouriez simply offered himself up to worship at this thing's red-shod feet, without having to be enticed or duped into such an unequal Devil's bargain? Coming to Prendegrace's service gratefully, even gladly—as glad as he would be, eventually, to cut his own throat to save this creature's no-life, or spray fresh blood across a wet plaster wall to conceal the thing he'd hunted, pimped and died for, safely entombed within?

And for Jean-Guy, an equally limited range of choices: To bleed out all at once in a moment's sanguinary torrent and die now, or live as a tool the way Dumouriez did—and die later.

Minimally protected, perhaps even cherished; easily used, yet . . . just as easily . . .

. . . discarded.

"There can be benefits to such an arrangement," Prendegrace points out, softly.

"He sacrificed himself for you."

"As was required."

"As you demanded."

The Chevalier raises a delicate brow, sketched in discolored plaster. "I? I demand nothing, Citizen. Only accept—what's offered me."

"Because you aristos deign to do nothing for yourselves."

"Oh, no doubt. But then, that's why I chose you: For being so much more able than I, in every regard. Why I envied and coveted your strength, your vital idealism. Your . . . "

. . . life.

Jean-Guy feels the monster's gaze rove up and down, appraisingly—reading him, as it were, like—

Hoarse: "A . . . map."

The Chevalier sighs, and shakes his head.

"A pretty pastime, once. But your body no longer invites such pleasantries, more's the pity; you have grown somewhat more—opaque—with age, I think."

Taking one further step forward, as Jean-Guy recoils; watching Jean-Guy slip in his own blood, go down on one knee, hand scrabbling helplessly for purchase against that ragged hole where the wall once was.

"What *are* you?" he asks. Wincing, angrily, as he hears his own voice crack with an undignified mixture of hatred, fear—

(—longing?)

The Chevalier pauses, mid-step. And replies, after a long moment:

"Ah. Yet this would be the one question we none of us may answer, Citizen Sansterre—not even myself, who knows only that I was born this way, whatever way that might be . . . "

Leaning closer still. Whispering. Words dimming to blood-thrum, and lower, as the sentence draws to its long-sought, inevitable close—

" . . . just as you were born, like everyone else I meet in this terrible world of ours, to bear my mark—"

—or be my prey.

With Jean-Guy's sight narrowing to embrace nothing but those empty eyes, that mouth, those teeth: his disease made flesh, made terminal. His destiny, buried too deep to touch or think of, 'till it dug itself free once more.

But—

—I am not just this, damn you, he thinks, as though in equally silent, desperate reply—*not just your prey, your pawn, your tool. I was someone, grown and bred entirely apart from your influence: I had history, hopes, dreams. I loved my father, and hated his greed; loved my mother, and hated her enslavement. Loved and hated what I saw of them both in myself: My born freedom, my slave's skin. I allied myself with a Cause that talked of freedom, only to drown itself in blood. But I am more than that, more than anything that came out of that . . . more than just this one event, the worst—and most defining—moment of my life. This one encounter with . . .*

. . . you.

Stuck in the same yearning, dreadful moment through twelve whole years of real life—even when he was working his land, loving his wife, mourning her, mourning the children whose hope died with her. Running his father's plantation, adjudicating disputes, approving marriages, attending christenings; watching La Hire decline and fall, being drunk at his funeral, at the Bal, at his own wedding . . .

. . . only to be drawn back here, at last, like some recalcitrant cur to his hidden master's call. To be reclaimed, over near-incalculable distances of time and space, as though he were some piece of *property,* some *tool,* some merest creeping—

—slave.

Marked, as yours. By you. *For* you.

But—this was the entire point of "my" Revolution, Jean-Guy remembers, suddenly. *That all men were slaves, no matter their estate, so long as kings and their laws ruled unchecked. And that we should all, all of us, no matter how low or high—or mixed—our birth either rise up, take what was ours, live free . . .*

. . . or die.

Die quick. Die clean. Make your last stand now, Citizen, while you still have the strength to do it—

—or never.

"It occurs to me," the Chevalier says, slowly, "that . . . after all this . . . we still do not know each other's given name."

Whatever else, Jean-Guy promises himself, with one last coherent thought, *I will not allow myself to beg.*

A spark to oil, this last heart's flare: he turns for the door, lurching up, only to find the Chevalier upon him, bending him backwards by the hair.

Ah, do not leave me, Citizen.

But: "I will," Jean-Guy snarls, liquid, in return. And hears the Chevalier's laugh ring in his ear through a fresh gout of blood, distant as some underwater glass bell. That voice replying aloud, as well as—otherwise—

"Ohhhh . . . I think not."

I have set my mark upon you.

My mark. *Mine.*

That voice in his ear, his blood. That smell. His traitor's body, opening wide to its sanguine, siren's song. That unforgettable red halo of silent lassitude settling over him like a bell jar once more, sealing them together: Predator, prey, potential codependents.

This fatal Widow's kiss he's waited for, in vain, for oh so very long—Prendegrace's familiar poison, seeping into Jean-Guy's veins, his heart. Stopping him in his tracks.

All this—blood—

Blood, for all that blood shed. The Revolution's tide, finally stemmed with an offering made from his own body, his own—damned—

—soul.

Prendegrace raises red lips. He wipes them, pauses, coughs again—more wetly, this time. And asks, aloud:

"By your favor, Citizen . . . what year is this, exactly?"

"Year Zero," Jean-Guy whispers back.

And lets himself go.

FLARE

I rent a basement apartment in Chinatown. That was one of the terms of my contract. With my kind of hours—8:00 PM to 6:00 or so the next morning—I need a place to sleep undisturbed, insulated from noise or light. My bedroom is a sweaty concrete box with a single, carefully bricked-up window. On those rare occasions when I wake before sunset, I lie there and watch the tiny chinks between mortar and stone widen as the draft leaks in off Spadina, making the dust motes dance. I hear my landlord, Mr Pang, open his refrigerator door to check that none of the eggs has hatched while he was out. Outside, a crazy woman sorts garbage and sings.

Eventually, I get up. And go to work.

* * *

Sometimes I dream. Then the walls melt in a rush of sand and sickening heat: Dar es 'alaf, 1991. A radio blares Megadeath as we turn and run, choking on equal parts nerve gas and dope fumes. Screams rise, and crunching, while we tear at the wall of corpses around us with our bare hands, desperate to escape—

—the wave.

A wave of flame. Twenty, thirty, fifty feet high and tiger-bright, guttering milk-blank smoke. It sweeps down, implaccable. Over and around and through us. Until we're nothing but ash on the desert wind, blown high and wide, up into an endless sky.

It's always the same.

In the dream, I am never afraid.

In the dream, I *am* the fire.

* * *

At 8:30 PM this evening, the telephone hissed. I caught it up.

"Yes."

"Where you been?" Battaglia whined.

I assumed it was a rhetorical question. "You know my schedule."

"Yeah, well—Charlie wants to see you."

I snagged one black boot, scanning the room for its mate. "That much is obvious." Rummaging underneath the lip of my bed, I felt the edge of something vinyl, and dragged it free: Success. "When?"

"Right now."

"Then tell him I'll be late," I said, and hung up.

Five minutes to change my underwear and wriggle into my bodysuit, five more to the garage, three more on top of that to load my belt and kick-start my bike. Twenty-five minutes later, I braked in front of Myczyk Trash Removal.

Charlie was already inside, waiting for me.

* * *

I opened Charlie's office door without knocking, and found him in his usual spot—behind the desk. Battaglia leant against the left-hand corner, smoking nervously. I gave that game up ten years ago, myself, and have never regretted it since. A filthy habit.

Not to mention dangerous.

"Myczyk."

"Vosloo."

We looked each other over. A study in not unpleasant contrasts—big Polish-Italian gangster, little Korean-South African arsonist: Our cultural mosaic at work. And pretty nicely, in his case, except for that scar creasing the left corner of his mouth into a permanent sneer . . .

As if I really had time for that sort of thing, anyway.

"The Spiro job, Vosloo," Charlie said. "Been some complications."

Spiro Garments, corner of Church and Queen. Last night. Simple torch job.

"Such as?"

He settled back in his chair. "Such as the stiff in the cellar. Firemen got there first. Now the cops're in on it too, and the press looks hungry—bad publicity, Vosloo."

I folded my arms. "What can I say? PR's never been my area of expertise."

Charlie stretched—a predatory gesture. Then again, he could make pouring coffee look predatory. Sure impressed Battaglia, though; he almost dropped a new-lit Camel down the front of his shirt, then burned his fingers trying to catch it before it set his chest-hair on fire.

"Okay," Charlie concluded, at last. "We'll play it your way. Maybe you didn't know he was there. Maybe you did, but you got carried away. You're an artist, right? But here's the thing, baby—cops trace you, the egg ends up on *my* face." A pause. "Get it?"

"They won't trace me."

"Care to take a bet?"

He raised an eyebrow. I simply smiled.

"Why, Charlie. And I always thought you didn't like to lose."

Smoke hung in the air between us. When I left, my clothes would stink all night of Battaglia's cheap aftershave (Selsun Blue?), mixed with the lingering reek of struck, sulphur-headed wooden matches.

"Are we done threatening each other now?" I asked.

Charlie narrowed his eyes. "If I wanted to wish you harm, Vocloo, believe me—you'd be harmed already."

Cute turn of phrase. But I didn't want to disillusion him; life's a scary enough proposition, as it is.

"Fine, then. What *do* you want?"

He shrugged. "Look, I don't have time to deal with this crap—that's what I pay my lawyers for. I got a busy night ahead, and no time to play Sherlock Holmes Junior."

"So . . . ?"

"So—you do it *for* me. Or you kiss your commission goodbye."

I glanced over at Battaglia, who quickly looked away, took out a pocket knife, and started trimming his cuticles. I glanced back at Charlie, my own eyes narrowing. "We have a contract," I reminded him.

Charlie didn't answer.

"A contract," I repeated. "You shook on it, right in front of me."

Battaglia began whistling in mid-tune, something that could have been

"Camptown Races" on the world's worst day.

"Just remember that," I said. And left.

* * *

It happens all the time.

I saw a picture, once: Two legs sitting in front of a blank TV set, the skin of their upper thighs fried so crisp it had partially melted to the chair beneath. Nothing else. Just a big pile of ash and a black spot on the ceiling which—on closer examination—turned out to be rendered grease. Investigators later found a tooth, embedded deep in the off-centre of the TV's shattered screen.

They call it spontaneous human combustion.

I used to wonder how it would feel, back then. A stirring in the stomach, like really bad indigestion? A warm breath on the back of your neck? A fine red seed at the base of your spine, suddenly slapped awake, like some fire chakra primed to spark and bloom?

And then . . .

. . . the wave.

Like lava. Like the airless heart of a furnace. Like Ground Zero.

Like love.

* * *

"Maia Vosloo," Harry Orphan repeated. He rolled my name in his mouth, like a pickled egg. "Long time, lady. Never thought I'd see *you* here."

"In the Mood Ring?"

"Alive."

Harry and I had met at Dar 'es Alaf, before the wave. He'd been covering American women in action, or—as he put it—"The Babes Behind the Bombs." I was infantry, which hadn't interested him much until I'd pointed out that if he followed my platoon long enough he was sure to be in line for a few charred civilians, not to mention a nice, juicy prospective "Why Are We in Kuwait?" sob-piece.

Ah, the simple pleasures.

Harry tugged at his wispy beard. I knew what he saw: A tiny woman wrapped scalp to sole in black vinyl, goggles screwed down tight over the slits in her fetishistic full-face mask. A plastic zipper where my smile should be. I run a normal body temperature of one hundred and thirty degrees; in daylight, with my suit on, I can make thermometers explode.

Curiosity notwithstanding, Harry didn't ask about my clothes. Or where I'd been for the last five years. Or whether or not my discharge had been . . . honorable.

I thought I could trust him. For a while.

"Harry," I said, "I have a problem."

I sketched in the details, and watched his color fade.

"Oh, Maia. Oh, shit."

I went on, keeping my tone plausible. "You *know* me, Harry. Nothing if not professional. For murder, I charge extra—and I don't recall my fee being anything out of the ordinary." I paused. "I've been framed."

He gulped. "Well, what do you think *I* can do about it?"

"Just a bit of extracurricular research. Access to your terminal at work."

He bit his lip. "I don't know."

"If you can't help me, Harry," I said, softly, "I certainly understand."

Harry sighed. He bit his lip again, worrying at it. He brushed back his thinning curls with one visibly sweaty palm.

Hurry *up*, I thought.

"Tonight?" He asked, at last.

"That'd be nice."

He stood up. I joined him, pushing back my chair as he fumbled with his coat. "This place closes at one," he said. "What say we take a stroll?"

And out we went, across the asphalt, neon reflections running like rain beneath our feet.

* * *

I let Harry struggle with the door's lock for a full minute before I offered to help. "Thanks," he gasped, and stepped aside. I heard him breathing raggedly, over my left shoulder, as I stooped to examine it. Not exactly complex. I removed a hairpin from my kit—not one of those half-plastic Western ones with its ends tipped in resin, but a true *kanzashi* of solid, blue-honed steel—and thrust it between the tumblers, as far as it would go.

Then I stood up again, and kicked the door in.

Harry's editor's office was cramped, and smelt of mouldy pizza. I'd expected as much. The *Nova Express* was nobody's *New York Times*, just an underground rag with (fairly) new management that'd finally made the long plunge into a haze of recycled, high-yellow tabloid headlines: Two-headed feti, cannibalism, miracle cancer cures. They'd apid big bucks for Harry, though, mainly because he always knew just the right angle for a celebrity car crash, or a particularly gory industrial accident.

"What was the name of that building, again?"

"Spiro Garments," I repeated, absently. A faded centrefold hung above the filing cabinet; she looked vaguely familiar to me. Closer examination placed her as my third-to-last landlady, the one whose house I'd had to take out after she broke my lease.

"Uh huh." Tapping ensued, then stopped. Harry peered at the screen, pale yellow letters reversed and flashing across his lenses.

"That's weird," he said.

"What?"

He beckoned me over. A copy of the structure in question's original bill of sale appeared onscreen, signed by one Albert Spiro. Harry scrolled down to show a will, recording the warehouse's passage from Spiro—now dead—to one Giancarlo Stada."

"Stada—"

"—witnessed the first deed, and collected on the second," Harry agreed. "Now look at this."

More tapping.

Stada, I thought. I'd heard it before, though in what context eluded me.

"Bingo," Harry breathed.

Three articles, all set at Spiro Garments. Two were dated 1946. **SHOOT-OUT IN CHURCH, FIVE DEAD.** Ernst Vandecker had been arrested in the basement of St. Joseph of Arimathea's after killing most of his gang and a pair of cops. **AUSCHWEISS DIAMONDS STILL SOUGHT**, read the second. Vandecker's loot, for which he got a hundred and ten minimum with no parole, hadn't been found yet. The last piece was an obituary-sized announcement from 1952. St. Joseph's, bought by Stada, was going to be demolished to make way for a warehouse.

Stada.

Harry shook his head. "Dead end, Maia."

But Ulrich would know who he was.

"Maybe not," I said.

Then I heard footsteps.

Light, slow, and measured. Accompanied by a racing blur of heartbeats, a collective wheeze of imposed silence. Two, or more likely three. Probably armed. Definitely dangerous.

Outside the door.

"Get down," I hissed, pushing Harry under the desk.

"What the—?"

The first shot popped over my head with a hiss-crunch of breaking glass, defacing the centrefold behind me. I palmed a smoke grenade and pulled the pin, lobbing it hard through what was left of the editor's splintered name. The door bulged inward as it blew, and a boiling blue cloud filled the room. One gunman screamed as he caught some shrapnel in his leg and stumbled, snapping cartilege. Another shot erased the computer's blinking screen.

"Window!" Harry gasped, teeth phosphorescent in the glare.

I nodded.

He threw the chair against the glass, then struggled to rip away the wire grating beyond. I stepped forward into the heart of the smoke and paused, listening.

Just two men after all. One was already down, holding his knee. The other whirled, aiming for where my head should be. I kicked him in the stomach. He staggered, then lunged—

—to catch my glove.

His nails snagged it, ripping it.

Oh, nonononono.

"I really wouldn't do that, if I were you," I said, reasonably enough. He just snarled. I sighed, and shrugged.

"Have it your way, then."

And the rip grew wider, peeling back. Peeling *open* like the crack of an unlocked door. Still wider. Until, at last, the skin began to show.

"What the hell—?"

He flinched back, light spilling up at him.

Too late.

My hand tightened on his, flesh scalding at my touch. He gasped, too surprised to scream. Because something was coming, spiraling up inside me, spilling out around me. Ground zero for the wave, arched fifty feet high. Shimmering.

And hot.

Harry looked back, already half-thrust to safety, and froze—so I pivoted and kicked him the rest of the way through.

"Lady—" my hired gun said, or started to. But the dust motes burst aflame, all at once, and seared his throat to silence.

I put a finger to his lips.

"Sssh," I said. "It'll be over before you know it."

He threw up his hands, pleading, and the room went white.

* * *

It was raining steadily now. Police cars screamed by as I dragged Harry through the alley, clambering over piles of old magazines and split garbage bags. He paused, mouth open, at the curb to watch me scrape a crushed tomato from my bootheel, simultaneously suturing my rip (*fire in the hole, Vosloo; bank it quick*) with some electrician's tape from my backpack.

"Call a cab, Harry," I said without looking up.

No reply.

"Harry."

Harry licked his lips, and swallowed hard.

"You blew up my office," he said.

I straightened, glove firmly re-rigged. Much trial and error had determined the quickest way to button up and prevent secondary explosions. The effort was proving well worth the cost.

"What *are* you?" Harry asked.

My shadow spilled over his like dark wine. Our eyes met. He flinched.

I shrugged. "What I've always been, Harry."

Over his left shoulder the moon resurfaced briefly, a fish's dark belly breaking water. "What Dar es 'alaf made me. Saddam had gas bombs, so they issued us suits—but nobody really knew how they'd react under combat situations. They needed rats for the maze, and we were elected. It was a test. Operation Flare, they called it. And when that big wave finally came down, most of us melted down on impact to so much rubberized ash—but I rode the fucker all the way back home.

"Remember my platoon, Harry? Flax. Anderson. Doon. They're spread thin across a ten-mile blast zone, out in the middle of the desert somewhere, because they just didn't have what it takes to stare the fire down . . . whatever the hell that is. But me—"

I opened my eyes, only to find that the moon was gone. Inspected the tape: That famous Flare Effect once more safely throttled back to a hot little molecular shiver. Just an itch—which would eventually have to be scratched.

But not now. Not here under the rain-diffused streetlight with Harry trembling at my side.

"Me, I'm still here," I finished at last. "And I do as I damned well do."

* * *

It was 3:30 a.m. by the time we reached the Fallout Shelter. I prised the staff restroom window open, slipped inside, and settled down on the nearest toilet seat to wait. Harry stayed out under the sign, still shivering, hands thrust deep in his pockets. No complaints, no commentary, just a numb bemused kind of silence.

I can't really say I minded.

At 4:58, I finally heard the door open. I thought it best to let him finish before stepping from the stall.

"Ulrich," I said.

He wheeled, almost zipping up his testicles. "Christ Almighty!"

Not quite.

But seeing as his pants were back up, I thought we might as well get down to business.

"I need information, Ulrich."

He peered at me through watering eyes. "Why me?"

"Because you're my informant."

"Right," he muttered. "Okay, what about?"

"Ernst Vandecker, the 1946 haul. And a man named Stada."

Ulrich sniffed. "Old news, Flare. So why should I bother?"

I smiled. "Just for kicks?"

Ulrich gulped reflexively, hiding it behind one palm. "Right," he repeated. "Connect the dots, my favourite game. Okay." He paused, thinking.

I gave him his moment. Rain beat through the open window, washing the peeling paint below it clean.

"1946," said Ulrich. "Vandecker hits the joint. He's killed two cops, which makes him pretty much this week's big man on campus. People come to him for career advice—one of them a young punk named Stada. Stada comes up, trades secrets, and when he gets out he heads straight for Spiro Garments, where Alberto Spiro's running a load of stolen cars

90

through every week. He's independent, needs muscle to keep the big boys off his tail—and muscle Stada has."

"Fast worker," I commented.

"The fastest. Except for . . . well."

And he gave me that smile again—a secret kept back for extra savouring. But I didn't care enough to prompt him. And besides, if he liked it that much, he was sure to get there eventually.

"In 1958, Spiro makes a will. An accident follows. Now Stada has the business, he's built himself a little empire, which takes more muscle, not to mention more money. But when it comes to the crunch, he always finds just enough."

"Okay, let's take a giant step here," I interjected. "Vandecker told Stada where he hid the Auschweiss diamonds—somewhere in the foundations of St. Joseph's is my guess. By getting control of Spiro Garments, Stada got the haul."

"Smart, Vosloo. So: Stada's getting old now. He hires a young guy to do business for him. And when the kid gets restless—"

"—he pulls exactly the same move on Stada that Stada did on Spiro."

Ulrich nodded. "But he can't find Stada's loot, see? And the cops catch up with him."

"Which is where Vandecker comes in again."

"Exactly," Ulrich said. "The kid worms his way into Vandecker's cell, and offers to spring them both—for half the haul. Vandecker takes him up on it. They hit Spiro's, they find the diamonds, and Vandecker disappears, and the kid gets even better than Stada. But this year, Vandecker shows up again. Mistakenly fences a diamond to one of the kid's employees. And the kid figures maybe Vandecker held out on him." He paused for effect. "Maybe there were two hauls."

"Both hidden in Spiro Garments."

"Yep."

"Which I was contracted to burn—and where Vandecker would have to dig it up."

"Yep, again."

The bathroom was very small. It had no visible smoke detector. Only the window, flapping open. I felt the walls contract.

"Ulrich," I said softly. "Tell me this . . . *kid's* . . . name."

"Charlie Myczyk."

Which is what I thought.

"Excuse me a moment," I said, remounting the toilet.

I pushed out into the alley once more. Once past the ledge, rain fogged my goggles, rendering me almost blind, while my brain clicked a mile a minute, connecting the dots.

Charlie shadowing Vandecker, taking the loot and killing the old man, leaving his body in the same secret hiding place where the diamonds were hidden for so long. Then me, all unaware, torching the place on contract, and getting the blame for the bones in the ashes.

Very neat.

I felt around the corner for Harry's arm and shook him sharply.

"Harry, wake up."

No response. I shook him again, and listened closer. Still nothing.

Then I noticed the hilt of an icepick jutting from his neck.

I wheeled back to the window, locking eyes with a couple of bouncers just walking in—bench-pressed, Armani-clad, their twin stares flat under bad New Wave haircuts. Ulrich stood safe behind. Revenge was not an option, so I cut my losses and ran for the fire escape.

The sirens which had hovered shark-like in the distance ever since leaving the *Nova Express* suddenly intercepted me at the bottom. One squad car, one unmarked car, and something I hadn't seen since the bad old days: A matte-black Impala with a doctor-soldier double-date behind the wheel.

Military Intelligence.

Ulrich's Elvis-esque pompadour had already unravelled into a stew of greasy forelocks, obscuring his eyes as he climbed through the window. As the spooks got out of their cars he met them with a showman's flourish.

"The Flare, gentlemen," he said. "She's all yours."

Two pairs of shaded eyes flicked over me, already simultaneously fitting me for cuffs and a hospital gown. I got it then—Charlie had believed my boasts after all. Not able to take out his own trash unaided, he had called in the big boys—my erstwhile, purely accidental, patrons. Now they would collect on the government's investment. With interest.

"Private Vosloo," said the doctor. "I've read your file."

I'll bet you have.

"We'll take it from here," the soldier told Ulrich, and slapped a thick packet of bills into his hand. Ulrich just smiled past him, at me.

"Drop me a line sometime when you know how the Spiro job comes out, huh, Maia?" he said affably.

I ignored them all. The soldier asked me something as the cops frisked me, but his voice was static on an empty channel. I numbed my knees and fell unprotestingly backward into their waiting arms, allowing myself to be pushed inside the patrol car. By the time my mind began to work again I was already on my way to who knows where, hands limply cuffed in my lap. A grill separated me from the bulging nape of the driver's neck. His partner gazed out the fogging window, lighting a cigarette. A curl of fragrant smoke grazed my eyes.

Now.

And I brought my right foot down against the floor of the car so hard the boot-heel shattered, igniting the flare concealed within it.

The driver recoiled from the sudden rush of phosphorus-blue flames licking at his back, barely avoiding giving himself a concussion on the juncture of the roof. His partner dropped the cigarette into his lap. "Christ!" he exclaimed, scrabbling for it.

With this distraction as cover, I ducked, took the end of the electric tape in my teeth—

—and *pulled*, reopening the rip.

The radio spat out, "Red one, red two: Where's the fire?"

An apt choice of words.

Because I was starting to feel the rush, now. The glow—palm-centred, and spreading.

Finally managing to bat the errant cancer-stick well away from his crotch, the partner turned to face me, gun up. I put my hand to the grill, just over its muzzle, and smiled. Handcuffs sliding down my gauntlets like sweaty mercury, already going liquid. Beside him, the driver, radio in hand: "Sir, yeah, I think we have a situation here—"

Starting to go for the burn.

The gun smoked and softened, and the cop shrieked, dropping it. The driver turned white. The radio kept right on chattering: "Disengage and pull over, repeat, pull over. Do nothing to perforate Vosloo's protective shell. Patrolman. Patrolman. Red one. Red two, do you copy?"

"Ever wonder what it would've been like to make a drop from the Enola Gay, right at the moment of impact?" I asked the guy on the right, conversationally.

"I have kids," he managed, holding tight to what was left of his fingers.

"That's nice. Boys or girls?"

From the corner of my eye I saw the driver had finally got his gun free—so I punched right through the fiery hot spot in the grill, spraying his incredulous, half-turned face with glowing metal. The partner, making a remarkable mid-cringe recovery, lunged for the wheel, and I hit him across the face as I pulled my hand back through the grill. He fell sideways, gasping as his nose bled.

The car lurched over some kind of curb, jouncing badly, skidding across a divider and up onto an exit ramp. I glanced back into the rear-view mirror, and saw the Impala swerve to follow. The radio had already cut off, abruptly, in mid-blare.

That's right. No more time for talking, not now.

I sighed, letting my head loll back, right hand already at my throat, little finger snagged in the key of my zipper. With that flush boiling up through me like incipient fever, flesh hot as gangrene; veins like wires, laid bare and sparkling.

The Impala sped up, squad car jolting as they tried to run it off the road. Then metal screeched and dragged as the bumpers locked. We hurtled forward while the road curved out from under us, well away from the yawning chasm—

Just me, or is it getting hot in here?

The doctor leaned on the horn. The soldier unholstered his gun.

And I . . .

. . . let it rip.

* * *

I broke through the roof as it peeled away and hit the cliffside with far more force than I'd expected, missing a rock-borne head injury by a mere hair's breadth. By the sound of that grinding snap my left arm made on impact, I assumed it was probably broken; I also seemed to have either developed a permanent stitch in my side, or cracked several of the same side's ribs. The whole sole of my boot had ripped away, exposing scalded skin to the hissing rain: No tape, no coverage, about sixty seconds left until the next combustive blast. And . . . I had lost my goggles.

I lay limp for a moment, letting the mud seep around me, and felt my bones slowly begin to defuse. Because it was so nice there beneath the overhang, down amongst the trees' bare roots, where erosion had made everything soft and loose and cool and dark—soft enough to cradle, cool enough to soothe. Dark enough, almost, to actually put me *out*.

But the lit seed in my stomach told me otherwise, every time I took another blood-laced swallow of rain.

I pushed myself up by my good arm, stumbled, then stood—wavering a little—to watch the lovely orange storm below, Impala and squad car melting from the inside out, caught in the act like some pyrolangist's ultimate wet-dream. A chance updraft hit me full in the face, gusting my eyes shut, and I revelled in its reviving heat: Sparks singing my clotted hair, soot blackening my face. And still I stood fast, quite transfixed, drinking in the wave in all its complex, terrible, all-consuming glory.

But not afraid, no. Because, after all, the wave could never hurt *me*.

I know it far too well—too intimately—for that.

* * *

So now, I wait. I know that Charlie assumes I died in the crash—a scenario which Battaglia, yapping at his heels as usual, was no doubt all too eager to suggest. The sun is up and it hurts my eyes, naked without the protection of my goggles—just a pair of dark glasses and a triple layer of fresh electrician's tape, up here where I roost amongst the pigeons, above Charlie's penthouse balcony.

It took me an hour and a half to get back to Mr Pang's, and my supplies. An hour and a half of cold rain in my eyes, abraded skin on wet asphalt and sizzling sparks inside that wouldn't ever quite go out, always poised and waiting for the rain to let up just a little, even while I wended my way through Chinatown.

Soon enough, however, noon will come and Charlie will wake, pulling his incongruously gaudy velvet curtains aside to face the day. He'll step out onto the balcony in that checkered bathrobe of his, yawning and stretching—maybe praying, even. Who knows.

Which is when I'll slip down on him, silent and swift: The wave made shaky, igneous flesh. Ground Zero crashing in at last, consuming him, as it must us all.

And when only his bones are left, long after those bones are nothing but a fine, grey, rendered ash like that of a slow-burning cigarette, then I'll go home. And go to sleep.

Thinking: *All in all, a good night's work.*

BOTTLE OF SMOKE

You enter your Aunt Maris' garden through a hole in the wall, so draped as to be half-hidden by a fallow choke of dead trumpet vine. The grass is sere on the frozen ground, dry and uncut, still high enough to have to wade through. Your own breath, white and visible, blows back over your face like a veil in the wind, a gumbo of rotting herbs—coaxed forth from that half-moon-shaped flowerbed under the small back window—mingling with it. You smell basil, taste thyme. Dead marigolds. Desiccated rosemary. You smell and taste something that died here not too long ago, when the weather had already turned too cold to let it rot away quickly.

Inside your jacket, your breasts press painfully against the ribbing of your T-shirt. Because your maternity bra was not among those few things you grabbed as you made your escape from the hospital earlier today, they ride unrestrained, full and leaking; you cup one cartoonishly, mittened hand and arm beneath them, propping them up protectively, and use your other to dig with, scrabbling at the rigid dirt. You start to kneel, but something seeps down one thigh, quick and hot—blood? Fluid? So you rise again, bend carefully over. Try to ignore it.

Your stomach still bulges slightly—a pale swell, an empty gourd. If you only pressed hard enough, you think, you might be able to feel something rattling around inside it.

Perfectly fit to leave, according to hospital staff—despite the strenuous objections of Diehl, your (hopefully) soon-to-be ex-husband. A clean bill of health; no complications. Hale and hearty.

And hollow.

Eventually, you find the key to the kitchen door buried under a broken stone cupid's head rakishly set (ever so slightly askew) in a nodding circle of withered things that probably used to be pansies, right where your Aunt Maris' unexpected last note said it would be. The lawyer who read you her will passed it on to you, discreetly sealed inside a rough-woven, off-white envelope with an unfamiliar watermark, the pulp of its paper thick with cotton fibres. The note itself written in strong black ink, bordered with a faint, printed pattern of Arabic writing—a poem maybe, or a curse, or an advertisement for some hotel, but completely indecipherable to you, no matter its actual content—framing Aunt Maris' few choice words, a looping flow of script, as terse and stylish as herself:

They gave you my name. I give you my house, and everything in it, with this sole proviso: Use it as you see fit, but tell no one of your intentions. If you need it, find it. And use it.

And since you do, you have. And will.

You breathe on the lock, scrub at it clumsily, showering the mat with frost. Faint icy flowers flourish at every corner of the door's glass insert, a pale frenzy. At first, the key sticks; but as it turns at last, with a distressingly loud wrench, the first flurry of that snow they've all been telling you to expect—these three days running—finally blows over your shoulder, sending a few flakes up over the collar of your coat, across that feverish line of flesh which occasionally comes and goes between the otherwise impervious meeting of hat, sweater and bundled-up hair. They melt on contact, as though consumed by some inner infection.

Your nipples hurt. The mess between your thighs is cooling now, insistent. You want bed, bath, music, sleep. Dreams, even—preferably borne on a tide of Drambuie fumes, rendering them incoherent and easy to forget.

You step inside, into dusty silence, and let the blooming, colourless riot of the door's glass forest swing shut behind you, ice marbled like veins over the trunks of numberless suggested trees—hidden eyes, gleaming here and there, amongst the frail and subtle leaves.

* * *

1949. North Africa. Somewhere outside of Ain Korfa.

The woman's name, Maris has been assured, is Sufiya. *She makes bottles, Madame. Excuse me, Mademoiselle.* The ceilings of her hut are too low for Maris to stand upright; she enters sideways, slipping on sand. Curtains are everywhere, veils fine as smoke. Outside, two musicians perform—some kind of flute and a small drum bound with hide on either end, and a girl dancing with a cane held between her hands. *One thought you might take an interest, seeing as you collect them.*

So hot, and dry, and breathless, in the dimming light; everything turns flat and pulsing, as when you walk into a dark shop on a bright afternoon. The girl is reduced to a series of undulations, a bored mouth, the liquid sideways flash of an eye.

Wouldn't Maris rather stay outside, and ask her whether—for a modest fee (but then, all fees are modest, here)—she might be persuaded to do more than dance?

But here is Sufiya now, between the curtains, barely visible against a bank of convex and reflected light, her collection—her wrapped limbs gilded by a warped, bluish halo of glass. Smoking. Watching. Combing the tobacco's sweet exhalation back over her head in handfuls, like gaseous perfume. It lingers, heavy and enticing, more than possibly laced with something stronger.

Ya Ummi, foreigner. One hears you seek me.

There are faint blue tattoo marks between her brows, shards of mirror hanging from her long, dark hair, braided into it. More tattoos, stretched triangular by time and gravity, on her long, full, bare brown breasts. Maris feels a fresh clutch of interest, and lets the dancing girl slip away, forgotten. She takes her hat off, loosing her own pale braid like a sudden flood; Sufiya smiles at the sight, revealing flat, slightly discoloured teeth. Also bluish.

Again, the barest suggestion of addiction; there is a definite nervous edge to her Oriental langour. The inside of her bottom lip is tattooed as well, rimmed in faded purple.

Is her tongue? Will she show her?

You have money, one doesn't doubt, Sufiya says, putting her cigarette out in the sand at her feet. *Foreign lady.*

Maris smiles herself. *Much,* she replies.

Sufiya shrugs, fluid.

Then you may ask . . . what you will.

* * *

Your Aunt Maris, on your mother's side, for whom you were indeed named (much as your father might sometimes like to imply otherwise)—Aunt Maris, the family myth. Literally unmentionable. Few of her pictures survived the internal purge, but here is one: A snapshot, small and brown-tinted, taken in Tunis, the year that you were born. There, under the lone palm, one bright slice of darkness in a collective mass of shadow, straight-backed for her age, linen-suited. Her hair—pile on pile of it, gone quite colourless as bleached silk—is hidden, like yours, under her hat. But not against the weather.

Her eyes are black stones under incongruous ink-black brows, crinkled at the edges, long washed clean of anything but curiosity.

Your parents met and married late; both are old, comparatively speaking, and she was always older than either. A world traveller. Cosmopolitan. Serene and self-contained.

Self-*outed*, in fact, for longer than most people ever knew the closet was for more than keeping clothes in. But though she may well have had regrets, she had no visible shame.

Over thirty years ago, she took her inheritance and spoke the Deplorable Word, calling herself what she really was. The rest of your family threw her from them, genteelly erasing her—except for her name, which they deeded to you, instead.

Hoping to start over fresh, no doubt.

Your Aunt Maris, whose lifeblood flows unchecked in your veins, beats unchecked in your heart. And beats unchecked between your legs, hammer-hard, whenever some woman you find attractive passes close enough to steal the breath from your throat.

You thought of Aunt Maris the first time you read Garcia Lorca, the first time you dissected a foetal pig, the first time you had an orgasm with someone other than yourself.

Family reunions had not been barred to her—at least, not explicitly. You saw her there, twice from a distance, once accidentally close; she met your gaze across the proverbial crowded room, and followed you into a guest bathroom when you slipped away to splash some water on your suddenly flushed face. You glanced up from the sink and froze to see her behind you, reflected in the bathroom mirror. She just looked at you, carefully, almost studiously. With those empty eyes.

And you stared back, breathless.

So you thought of her opaque eyes, flat and bleak as some unmapped moral absence. You thought of her knived tongue, her soft white lips. You knit your thighs around the head of a girl you barely liked, whose name you can no longer even recall, and saw the bedroom lamp flare like a star. And you thought you would gladly cut your own heart from vent to vent for the chance to make your Aunt Maris feel the way this moron between your legs (Pamela? Patti?) was making you feel at that very moment.

Absences, especially unexplained ones, attract more than presences; you know that now. They breed infectious dreams which sink marrow-deep and wait there for a touch to reignite them—linger like figures drawn on glass, in condensation, invisible until someone else's breath brings them to life once more.

* * *

Sufiya and Maris share tea. Sufiya passes her bottle after bottle, smoothly shaped, almost invisible in the faded dusk. A lamp has come on in a nearby house, fierce and guttering, but it casts more shadow than light. Darkness washes over the both of them in waves, stirs in the bottles' warped depths, sluggish as caught smoke.

Sometimes one may keep oil in them, Sufiya says. *Or perfume.* She pauses, slyly. Watching to see how Maris will respond.

Or perfumed oil, Maris replies, deadpan.

Sufiya laughs, and drinks some more tea. She no longer bothers to pull her robes around her when she moves. The rest of her body is lush and burnished, faintly decorated everywhere one looks; her mirrored braids chime slightly, softly. Whatever her poison of preference, it leaves little physical trace.

Maris smiles. Carefully, she says: *In my country, we have a tale of how a ghost may be caught—in a bottle.*

Sufiya's eyes gleam.

Many things may be caught in bottles.

Spirits? Maris asks. (The pun does not occur to her until the word is already out.)

Sufiya grins. *Oh, certainly.*

Demons?

Perhaps.

Sufiya yawns and stretches, immodestly. Luxuriously. Everything peeling back at once.

Maris burns her tongue on an incautious swallow of tea, still quite hot.

Then bites it.

Have you heard tell of djinni, foreign lady? Sufiya asks.

* * *

You don't really know how Aunt Maris died, or when—your parents, typically, only told you about it because Maris' lawyer requested them to. Had there been any chance of reconciliation between you and Diehl, you think, they might actually have found some way to avoid mentioning it at all. But even they could see there would have been no point to such a deception, especially in light of recent events.

It had been a quarter past eleven, and you were in Diehl's car. Together. Which was strange in itself—but then, you were on your way to a family gathering (your family), and Diehl could hardly have afforded to show up without you, considering how much trouble he'd gone to in order to marry into it in the first place.

Moving out onto Yonge, just past the local Gap, you took a pull from your mutual Starbucks thermos, and saw Diehl shoot you a look.

"Yes?"

"That could make you a little edgy, don't you think?" he said. "Given your . . . condition."

"Scared of what I might do?"

"No!" he snapped, quick and definite, as though the very thought insulted you both.

You took another sip. "Ah," you said, sweetly. "And how about what *you* might do?"

And so you started to argue again, started to fight—first verbally, then physically. A genuine struggle, quick but vicious. Your thumbnail digging at his eye. His fist across your jaw. Your hand on the door handle, the door you thought you had locked. Securely.

He hit you, pushed you. The door opened. You fell out.

And what had been inside you at that moment, that tiny, subdividing swatch of cells and energy—he, she, whoever it had once had the potential to become—

—fell out, too.

* * *

101

Maris shakes her head. Her pale hair parts like a veil. Her lips part, urgent and intent. She leans forward, ready to breathe in Sufiya's words like a kiss.

No, she says. *So tell me of them. These djinni.*

Adding unnecessarily: *One will pay, of course.*

Sufiya nods, over the rim of her cup. *Yes,* she replies. *One will.*

* * *

Your Aunt Maris' house—now securely snowed in—lies crooked and quiet, a psychic sump. Its old pipes keep it hibernation-hot. The floors of some upstairs rooms are so uneven that you can put a marble down near the window, step back, watch it roll slowly out the door, and hear it bumping down the staircase to the front hall. Breathing is an extra effort; every new move comes complete with a constricted sigh or malformed gasp.

You drift from room to room as masala chai brews in the kitchen—black Darjeeling tea boiled with milk, cardamom, cinnamon, cloves, sugar, thick and warming.

The furniture is covered in sheets. Pebbled glass gleams on the windows, not just in the bathroom, but everywhere. Some stained glass, but all of it that weirdly "experimental" 1960s kind, done in shades of dark brown and murky green.

Down in the basement, which you give just a quick glance from the top of the steps, the windows seem to have been painted over entirely.

"Maris?" Diehl had said, when the lawyer's letter came. "That crazy old dyke? That hermit? Anything you get from her, you'd have to sandblast before you could take it out in public."

"*My* aunt," you reminded him. "Not yours. Throw away your own relatives, if you want to."

"If mine were like yours, you could count on it."

Diehl, who came to your mutual wedding day prepared to make the best of a bad bargain, only to find himself terribly deceived about how much either of you could really take of each other's personal foibles—dumb things like a basic lack of actual affection, or a growing inability to mask one's true sexual preference. Who only wanted respectability, and political power, and the money to buy both. Bank accounts, to draw upon in your family's name; children, to give his own name to. And he did try, you had to give him that. He kept his mouth shut, his affairs discreet, his smiles wide. He never even hit you—except, of course, for that one time.

Which turned out to be more than enough.

While, in your mind—day after day, year in, year out—you cheated on him with every woman you saw. Even the ones you knew he was probably cheating on you with.

Nothing in Aunt Maris' house works well, or for long. It's hard to find the light switches; the fixtures are empty, or the lightbulbs die with a little blue flicker and a contractive rustle of fused glass.

Unfamiliar with the house and woozy on pain pills, you blunder into a downstairs bathroom—so long unused that the bath is full of dust—just as the stove's archaic timer begins to chime.

You turn, knocking your knee hard against the toilet bowl. A bruise will bloom, likely purple-blue, the orchid shape of the red mark.

Later, sipping the chai, you find yourself sitting in what must have been Aunt Maris' library, tentatively admiring the damage. A scratchy disk of old Bessie Smith tunes is still cued up beneath the encrusted cover of her record player's turntable—"Blue Spirit Blues," with its jazzy death-march refrain.

Leaning back in a velvet-covered chair, you open your robe to your waist and transfer your attention from knee to nipples, which have once again become raw enough to need soothing. The hospital gave you some salve, expressly for that purpose—it looks something like toothpaste, smells like crushed-up Ivory soap (faux camellia with a faint tang of plastic) and stings like unholy hell.

You anoint the raw tips, carefully, but the stuff clusters and clings, still too thick to absorb without rubbing harder. And you sure don't want to do that.

So you reach for the nearest book instead, hoping to distract yourself while the salve's touch dims from its present slow burn to a mild tingle. But its spine is cracked—it opens on a bias, loosing a carefully-hidden cache of pornographic snapshots which scatter on the floor. Small, brown-tinted, like that one photo of Aunt Maris. From the same period, perhaps? No, even older.

Some have notations in Arabic, red ink on sepia. Written on the back of one, in Maris' familiar looping script, the words: *Sufiya, 1949.*

You turn this particular one over, and the image revealed makes you burn even harder, nipples elongating inappropriately under their caps of medicinal cream. A spark set to your hidden bud, like a match to a short, short fuse.

So much better to show than to tell, foreign lady—a voice whispers in your head, strangely faint, strangely near, not at all strangely unfamiliar—always. *Do you not think?*

And easier, too.

The woman—Sufiya, one assumes—tilts herself towards the camera, spreading her bald, engorged labia wide with tattooed hands, long-nailed fingers: An upraised flesh pomegranate, flecked and packed with blurred, shiny stuff that could be juice, could be scar tissue, could be an oddly enticing mixture of both. Smiling wide, with both pairs of purple-rimmed lips. The topmost point of her deep-set navel is pierced with a small, silver ring and threaded by the fine-linked chain that circles her gorgeously lax waist, half-hidden in its soft folds. More of that wet, indefinite sheen extends down her inner thighs, so tensed and gleaming you can almost smell them.

The back of someone's head rears towards her, seen from above. Its hair is a dark, braided, mirror-fringed mass that matches her own mane, almost exactly—as though she were offering herself to her own reflection. The nape of the neck shows through, similarly tattooed with something vaguely oval, vaguely dotted. A supernumary eye, staring back at the camera's own.

That blur between it and her—an exhaled plume of smoke?

The extended tip of a hungry tongue?

Who was taking these? you wonder. Maris? Then, annoyed with your own denseness: Well, who else?

You flip the photo back over again, and reach for another, free hand slipping under the closed portion of your robe. Excavating. Scooping upward, collecting lubrication, digging for the point of most resistance.

A slow, fluid, stop-motion fantasy strings itself together in front of you, images flickering through your fingers, figures snapping unexpectedly from position to position. Sufiya bending back, legs widening like a pulled wishbone, as the other person laps over her bare, split mound and up past the ring and chain, suckling at either breast, then forcing apart her lips, smearing her with her own juices from nose to chin.

Another woman? Yes, almost definitely. A long curve of spine uncoils as it spreads itself out over her, ending in a wide pair of hips, two soft and resilient cheeks, a subtle shade or two paler than Sufiya's own—ripe and reflective, lush with internal movement.

A somber image, hammered silver, cast in some ancient, concave mirror. It dips and writhes, wraithlike, up through a series of sheer and smoky veils that peel back like petals, trailing along its flanks and sides, cradling Sufiya's rapt body on a foamy, barely transparent wave. A tide that ebbs and flows in sudden rushes, hiding more than they reveal.

And always from the back. The face always hidden.

Sufiya is obviously moaning now, eyes rolled back, mouth squared over bluish teeth; her partner rummages through her spread stickiness with both hands, their exact location evocatively uncertain.

Obsessively, you map the various possibilities on yourself: Suck your middle finger, sliding it first past your streaming cleft and then lower still, broaching the anus's brown flower; wedge your slickened index to its haft inside your vagina, as you use your thumb's broad pad to flutter your clit's hood back and forth, a makeshift tongue grinding against its moist, jeweled hardness.

Your gaze turns upward, inward—pleasure growing slow and spreading, in small, circular waves—shock and aftershock knit tremor-close, nerves alight and aimless—your desire snarled in on itself like some half-burnt summer firework, a curled, self-immolating frenzy, haloing your groin with heat.

Dropping the last photos, you find your free hand drawn inexorably back to your aching, slippery, fiery nipples—to pull them ever harder, ever longer, first the left, then the right—finally teasing a thin spurt of milk from one, with a sudden, painfully satisfactory jolt.

Uh. Oh, Jesus.

Your lids flutter. The ceiling shakes and reels.

Sweet Lord Jesus.

A sickly-sweet stink of soap rises, rushing back over your spasming body in a volcanic cloud. The discarded photos fade to white, becoming empty screens, rear-projected. Spilling a pale, unfocused light that melts their contents whole.

Sweet . . .

And a fresh load of watery blood explodes down your legs as you ride your hand to climax, soaking the chair beneath you. Your toes curling, cramping. Gasping. Breathless.

Sweet . . .

Too busy making that thin, endless, whooping shriek you faintly hear in the background to mind just how ridiculous you must look, even if there were anybody else here to see.

Or care, for that matter.

. . . sweet . . . Maris.

You come until you black out, then sleep until you wake, newly drained and doubly emptied—sometime after midnight, if the clock on that nearby desk still reads right. And when you do wake, though you can't remember lighting the traditional post-coital cigarette, you find you have more than a bit of trouble trying to read the time at all.

Because the room is full of smoke.

* * *

Afterward, Maris reorders her clothing, tucking her braid away. Sufiya slips the rest of her jewelry back on, piece by jangling piece. She cleans her face with a dampened cloth, fastidiously wiping away all traces of their visitor, as Maris raises the recorked bottle, watching the darkness concentrated beneath its warped blue glass skin roil—like mercury—from the diffused heat of her hand.

Djinni are evil angels, Sufiya tells her, moving the cloth slowly over her cleavage. *Unclean spirits, infinitely powerful, infinitely malign. Like ghouls, but with no flesh—no way to feel the carnal impulse, except through the body of a human being. All-powerful as desert storms, they nevertheless envy the fragile strength of one's simple human desires.*

She pauses.

And it is in this way—that they may be trapped.

Maris, recalled to herself, sets the bottle down again and checks her camera for possible damage, tightening its lens cap against the wind-borne wave of sand that has already begun to blow in under Sufiya's drawn curtains. Idly, she asks: *Will these pictures come out, does one think? Or is your pet demon too shy to risk its soul in a foreigner's machine?*

Sufiya glances back at her, eyes narrowing. *One would not call it shy,* she says, finally.

Oh, no, Maris replies, hidden once more behind her tourist's mask of propriety. *Not after such a show as that.*

The two women look at each other. Now it is Sufiya's turn to lift—and offer—the bottle. She makes the movement silently, smoothly, as though it

THE WORM IN EVERY HEART

were part of some tiny ritual—pregnant with hermetic meaning, and just the faintest whiff of high style. Of simple showmanship.

Did what you see impress you? she asks. *This is nothing. Once confined to the bottle, the djinni bows entirely to its keeper's will. It wants flesh, and it takes it however it may, even briefly. It will be one's double, one's partner, one's fallow mirror image in all erotic matters, its actions limited only by the range of one's imagination.*

Maris nods. *Assuming such things have limits,* she replies.

Sufiya dips her head in mocking imitation, the faultless picture of "subservience". Her earrings swing togther with a musical rustle, metal on metal. Bright as hovering insects.

One cannot doubt you want this, foreign lady, she suggests, slyly. *Now that you have witnessed the—attractions—of its inhabitant for yourself.*

The darkness, coiling. Licking the bottle's sides.

Maris represses a shiver. Says, coldly: *Would one really sell such a treasure?*

Sufiya, shrugging. *If another cares to buy.*

And the price?

That part of the bargain . . . is not my affair.

True night outside, now. A fingernail paring of moon has already risen over the vanished horizon, slim and sharp.

The djinni catch us as well, of course, says Sufiya, slowly, perhaps more to herself than Maris. *They catch us—by allowing themselves to be caught.*

Maris laughs, briefly. Remarks, mainly to herself: *Like every other woman.*

But her eyes are drawn inexorably to the glass, to the darkness under it. She sees her own face stare back at her from inside the bottle—bluely elongated, tongue tip to upper lip, reflective. Almost seductive. Her own black eyes, no longer empty, but filled with an endless wealth of shadow.

Her stomach gripes; it seems to her, abruptly, that she has been hungry a long, long time—far longer, in fact, than she has ever been aware of.

Maris lays her nail against the bottle's cork, softly, and thinks of a lover who will never fail or leave her. A lover who knows her, and loves her, like herself. A perfect reflection, whose constant hunger exactly matches her own—always growing, deepening, evolving. Never satisfied. Never slaked.

She thinks: How much would I pay, to be finally full? For once?

No price could possibly be too high.

* * *

Upstairs in your aunt Maris' house is . . . .

Stuff. Nothing much. Nothing to get excited about.

. . . belonging to a dead woman. With your name.

Still, it's not like there's anything you can do about it.

So here you sit, ensconced in her private bath—a huge porcelain monstrosity on squat, grey gargoyle's feet, filled rim-high with water so hot it seems practically sterile—as you drink her Drambuie and use her handmade soap, each cake individually wrapped in wax paper, with whole chamomile flowers buried in its fragrant white flesh.

You pop another pain pill and chase it with more liqueur, feeling it take hold all at once, its normal force already alcohol-bolstered.

Pulling the plug with your toe, you dip your head underwater, riding a luxuriant swell of fatigue—knowing you shouldn't, and doing it anyway.

Aunt Maris' house seems to have that effect on you, generally. But you're already beginning not to mind, so much.

Especially now that the remains of your latest small miscarriage (hardly worthy of the name, given the sheer traumatic impact of your earlier adventures in haemorrhaging; more of an after-carriage, if anything) have been carefully washed away, and are rapidly disappearing—in a fine, red swirl—down the bathtub drain.

You close your eyes, feeling the pill begin to take hold. You think of Diehl. Of the last time you saw him—the time before the actual last time, in the car. At the hospital, you were always kept carefully separated; the doctors agreed it would be bad for you to have to see him, and he—surprisingly enough—agreed with the doctors. Poor, persecuted Diehl, coming home unexpectedly early from some badly scheduled appointment, only to walk in on you with your skirt hiked up and one hand down your pants, surrounded by a selection from his "secret" stash of emergency pornography.

Gaping at the sight of his supposedly orgasmically challenged wife, head thrown back and face contorted, in the throes of full-fledged, autoerotic ecstasy. His look an amazing mixture of prurient interest and utter betrayal, as though he'd just caught the Virgin Mary scribbling her name and number on some bathroom wall, only to realize his pen was out of ink.

"You bitch," was all he'd finally had to say, once he got his mouth working again. "Bitch. Fucking, lying, frigid bitch."

And: "Only with you," you replied, weirdly cheerful, as you raised the nearest copy of Mayfair.

The water is almost gone now, though the heat remains; you suppose you might as well lie here until it seeps away entirely, before getting out and into one of Maris' old flannel robes. Then a hair drier, if you can find one; a towel, if not. Bed, either way.

A slumberous flush seeps through your extremities, making all your still-sore private parts hum with sudden tension. You feel stretched, strafed, empty of everything but your own emptiness. Barely fit to haul yourself up by the tub's sides and stumble into Maris' room, where you collapse face down onto her unmade bed.

On the table at your elbow, a blue-glazed bottle—precariously placed—captures the last of the light from the hall, shining like some ill-shaped star.

* * *

Sufiya watches Maris' straight, pale back fade away down the dark street. Already, she feels a bereft wave of desire knotting inside her, pulling all her pain centres taut with longing. Her teeth ache. The many lines of her face, imperceptible in the hut's dim light, all spring out fresh and sharp. Her eyes have gone dry as stones.

Well, she says, aloud, in her own, her private language. *One is glad enough to be rid of you, my foulest sweetness, my awful mirror. One may even wish the foreign lady joy of you, and to die with a light heart.*

There can be, after all, too much of a good thing.

* * *

Much later in the early morning, you think you feel yourself begin to bleed again and turn over, your hand accidentally brushing the bottle from its unstable perch. It wobbles, falls. Shatters.

Scatters, in a frail blue litter of glass.

Something pale blinks, unseen, among the pieces.

You grope for the belt of Maris' robe, only to find it already open, twisted asunder by the hard, round mass of your—stomach?

You open your eyes, expecting darkness. But the air is full of a soft, bright kind of visual diffusion—a pointilism too lightless to see by, exactly, yet lit all the same and pulsing with things barely seen. Fragrance, ether, carbon, a mere outline, a full-body mist, a bubble of blue-tinged steam. A person-shaped smoke ring, surrounding and penetrating you, stroking you from inside and outside at the same delirious time.

Contractions beat up through your gut and pelvis, painless, rhythmic. Forcing your legs apart. Forcing something up, and out, between them.

You open your mouth and gasp, air-starved—the whole world gone drunken and concave with a transparent film of warp—as something long and pale pulls itself from your packed-full womb, with a wrenching heave, squirming up and over you, pinning you down.

You deflate on contact, with an internal sigh, far too fast to even wonder over. A dream, a nightmare, a life-long fantasy finally come true. The want made flesh.

Pale hair hanging down, its braid unravelling like a spider's skein. Dark eyes, staring down into yours. Those soft white lips. That knived tongue. Sharp blue teeth, parting.

"Maris," it says, softly. Naming you. Naming itself.

Maris.

Or something that knows her well enough to reproduce her to the least detail. Something so close as to bloody well make no never-mind.

You arch to meet it, mouth-first, breathing it in like something addictive, something impossible. Liquid aniseed. Scented flower water. Poison gas. And wherever it touches, nerves flick on like lightbulbs, incandescent.

This lovely *thing* . . .

. . . makes your veins glow and sing, an unstrung neon network. It runs taut, cool hands down your sweaty breasts, cupping and circling. Pinches both nipples at once, light but firm, just hard enough to draw a moan. Its caress is alchemical—all your post-miscarriage flab miraculously transmuted, in one swift move, to yearning, open curves. It kisses your throat, moves lower. Pulling at the nipples now, teasing them longer than you would ever dare to, unchecked by your helpless whimpers. It fastens its lips on one, teeth and all, then sucks with such sudden fierceness it makes you cringe, forcing the last of your milk out in a single, painfully sweet gush.

Licking down your quivering belly, rimming your navel, tongue cool as well. You shudder, spread wide, hips thrusting automatically up, splaying yourself in anticipation. And it doesn't disappoint you, plunging its thumbs inside, then sliding farther still—using them like a speculum, peeling the labial rind to get at the tender meath inside. Its rapt interest alone enough to make you grind your hips, oozing, juices welling up like sap. Giving away all your secrets.

The Maris-thing looks up, smiling. Whispering, "You should see what I'm seeing."

This open book of mirrors, running slick and silver as mercury.

Oh, no. Oh—*yes*.

It lowers its face and licks lightly up your swollen crevice, making you thrash from the cervix outward. Pries your lips open wider and drives its tongue in deep, circling your button. Takes your clit between its teeth, and bites down hard.

Yes, yes, yes.

It slips two more fingers in, smooth and easy; you feel yourself grip them like a velvet vice, rippling uncontrollably. A heartbeat clench. Flinching from the strength of your own response. Running like oil and water, like that fresh heat down the crack of your ass, that rush of sweat and juice together. Your thighs trembling, spasming, as it lifts one leg by the soft inner knee, studies the result.

Your whole cunt ticking like some wet, red-pink, tightly ravelled clock—your labia puffed first mauve, then purple, swollen so far they've turned nearly inside-out—your fluttering anus, poised to bloom at a touch. And the shiny bead of your clitoris, hot and hard, still quivering for more of that cold tongue. Finding it harder and harder—

Harder. *Harder!*

—to keep your proper shape.

The thing with your Aunt Maris' face sucks your clit back between its teeth once more and nips gently, grazing it, scraping it. Sucks soft. Sucks hard. Keeping right on sucking—until you groan, and grunt, and thrust your hips back and forth, your cunt flooding her fingers—until you come wildly, babbling, bursting like some ripe fruit.

Oh yes, you think incoherently. *Come in. Come home.*

Your muscles sagging. Your ruined womb gaping ever wider, wider. Your flesh spread out in silent welcome, an open invitation. Your hollowed heart, its for the taking.

Come back inside me now, now. Now!

And the unclean spirit enters.

* * *

Here is what will happen, days later, when Diehl has finally traced enough of your path from the hospital to guide the police to your Aunt Maris' house.

You will still be upstairs, in Maris' bed, a once-fresh stain gone dry enough to sketch a thick, red-brown outline of your legs and thighs against the rumpled sheets. Your body, nude and lax, will be smeared with blood and dust from this last, most terrible (and wonderful) haemorrhage.

When the paramedics peel back your eyelids—deftly, gently—they will find your eyes turned back in their sockets, pupils mere wavering pinpoints. Your flesh will be cool, your breathing shallow. On your otherwise slack mouth, a faint—but umistakeable—smile will linger.

Back at the hospital, with Diehl's permission, they will run all the tests they can think of. They will prove you definitely comatose, functionally brain-dead.

And pregnant.

The nurses Diehl hires will watch you swell, marveling at your body's resilience. All of them will remark on a curious perfume that clings to your flesh, whilst the more allergic ones will also routinely complain that some unknown person, with flagrant disregard for your safety and security, apparently seems to keep on choosing your room as the perfect place in which to break the hospital's no smoking policy.

Diehl, meanwhile, will attempt to exorcise his rage and disappointment by using his power of attorney over your holdings to buy—and demolish—Maris' empty house.

Weeks after the bulldozers have come and gone, he may well reach into a pocket for change, but find only some small shards of glass, instead: the remaining traces of that bottle he found on the floor of Maris' bedroom, after the ambulance had already taken you away—old, and rare, and blue, and broken.

And empty.

FLY-BY-NIGHT

Ex-Staff Sergeant (USMC) Sonia Kopek was sitting by the window when they brought the vampire in. It was 8:30, a typical Monday night at Douglas Bell Memorial—residents drugged and gibbering, new entries being booked, interns slipping on vomit between the front desk and the nearest supply cabinet. The vampire was naked, dripping wet, skin like ice, handsome. Had long hair, which struck Sonia a bit faggy, but whatever turns you on. One cop kept the vampire in an arm-lock, nunchuks tight around his free wrist, while the other signed the log-book. When he was done, he gave it to Maunderly. As his hand went by, the vampire snapped at the cop's knuckles with broken bone-needle teeth.

"Motherfucker!" the cop exclaimed.

The vampire's eyes burned, like irises on an autumn bonfire. Hot and acrid, with that faint blue tang of sex. Sane and insane alike shrank—hushed, scalded—from his gaze.

But none of them seemed to notice he cast no shadow.

Except for Sonia.

Thin, plain, wire-boned Sonia, huddled into her straitjacket like a rhesus monkey waiting for today's injection. Her thorn-crown hair stood straight up, mocking gravity. A half-moon gouged above her left cheek-bone added extra emphasis to her bruisey, all-pupil, blank Belladonna eyes. Craziness aside, they remained her sole ornament. Black glinting gems; cow-velvet stupid, Halidol blind.

Ah, che bella donna!

She snorted at the thought.

La pauvre ragazza 'e pozza, more like.

The cops threw the vampire to Essen and Grillo, who—smooth as tag-team wrestlers—let his momentum carry him back through the violent ward's doors before following.

"Evening, Sonia."

Dr. Tau.

Not too bad a guy, as shrink buttheads went, if a little green for his own good. He had new shoes on; alligator. They complained as he squatted, flipping to her chart, ballpoint poised. "We cut you loose last week, right? So what was it this time?"

Sonia cleared her throat, noisily.

"Cops say you threatened to blow up a restaurant. Feinberg's, on West? Told them you had a bomb or something." He waited. Then: "You really think you were going to get away with it, Sonia? Or did you just sit down and wait for them to bring you back here?"

Sonia grinned, an uneven scribble of teeth.

"It's hard to run with a grenade down your pants," she said.

Dr. Tau sighed.

"Okay—you're back on the Fourth, all right? No privileges. Tell the truth, you're damn lucky no one bothered to press charges once they found out you were a Section Eight." At the end of the hall, the vampire had begun to scream—a string of intricate curses, so refined they barely sounded like English. "Sonia. Sonia, you hear me?"

Sonia closed her eyes. She remembered a movie, from when she was twelve; Christopher Lee's beautiful black-and-white face, his eyes red stones. Chin slicked brown with blood. Then Zia Tatya, incensed by her son-in-law's blasphemous choice of family entertainment, running down the rules in mid-pirogi-dunk: "Such things exist, fool, and have no cure. Never trust a man whose eyebrows meet, whose palms are hairy, with red hair, born with a caul, a man with no shadow." Years later, in the sewers of Dar 'es Alaf, she'd come suddenly nose-to-nose with one more civilian the clean-up team had missed. A monobrowed boy barely her age, dead so long his puke had turned to dust.

Sonia?

With effort, she got her eyes open again.

"Perfectly, doc," she said.

* * *

The vampire sat propped up against the Quiet Room's wall, as far from the window as he could get. A hospital gown dimmed his luster somewhat, as did the mottling of bars the nearest streetlamp cast across his face. His hair, still wet, hung straight and red. No visible scars. An amber spray of freckles, inappropriate to his pallor, punctuated his left shoulderblade.

"I know what you are."

The vampire turned, hissing—his teeth naked in the dark.

Sonia stared back, unimpressed.

Essen was down the hall talking baseball, Grillo in the john. Four in the morning was Douglas Bell's dead hour, most patients having either screamed themselves to sleep or been clubbed into a good imitation of it. Long experience had taught her this much: Once glimpsed sprawled and snoring by the baseboard, Sonia became invisible. All she had to do was wait until the hall cleared, and she was free to roam unchecked.

"And what," said the vampire, "is it you think I am?"

A struck silver tuning fork of a voice. Sonia shrugged. "Hey, buddy—I'm crazy, remember? Pleasures few and far between—maybe I'm getting off on jerking your chain." She paused. "Probably just another hallucination, anyway."

"Humor me."

Blue fish-hook eyes, caught and twisting. Endless holes of sky.

What the fuck are you doing here, Sonia?

Essen shifted his considerable weight; her breath froze. But he stepped forward instead, slamming the rec room door behind him.

Okay.

She let her lungs thaw, and met the vampire gaze-on.

"Uno bevitore di sangui," she said, levelly.

No response.

Well, that was worth a couple of yucks, she thought. *Nothing much else on the old plate, so, hey.* When morning came the shrinks'd grill him, like any other nut. They might even brush elbows at lunch, both doped flat-line. Smile vacantly at each other, drool a bit, move on—

"You're Italian."

Sonia shook herself loose, with a jerk. "Oh, no shit," she snapped, reflexively. "I look like I'm from Utah?" The vampire didn't blink. After a moment, unwilling: "Half."

Now stop looking at me like that.

"And the other of some Slavic derivation, I venture."

Sonia glanced away. The moon was a quarter stuck in grey dough—birthday money-bread, waiting for a baker.

Are you my present?

"Sun'll be up soon," she said.

"Very."

While they were still mopping up in Kuwait City, a PFC in Sonia's platoon had pulled requisition duty and done it so well they kept him there a month and a half. Then somebody nailed him diverting stuff—shipping a bazooka back home to Harlem, part by part. The Section Eight quota'd been filled that week, so he got stockaded instead. But Sonia could get behind what he was doing; once you've been armed, walking the street empty-handed again don't really appeal. She'd stashed crates of willie pete eggs all over the Bronx, herself. Wrapped three deep in Glad garbage bags, and ready to go.

Just in case.

Because you never knew, right?

Ever.

She felt the vampire's eyes tangle in her hair, like bats.

"Okay, say it comes up. Then what?"

He paused, considering.

"I burn," he said, at last. "And you—watch."

Uh.

Then, seeing her wince: "But I take it you've done *that* before."

Sonia blinked.

June 25, 1991; the Antichrist's birthday, Grandpop always said.

They were up on the ridge that morning, north by northeast, following a tip on some Iraqi deserters supposedly seen at the outermost well. Handler and Koo walking point, Raycee behind. Horse bones to the left, picked clean, under a saffron bell of sky. Mortensen's radio was still leaking static, even set as low as it went; it'd been that way since orientation back in Saudi. He kept fumbling with it, knocking the receiver on his helmet. When the job at hand gets second place, everybody suffers (DI Turner's favourite phrase, his breath halfway up your windpipe like a pepperoni fart). Sonia was in mid turn, *Cut that shit out* on her lips, when Mortensen's foot met the mine.

Bright black string-man against the sand, stretched too thin to catch hold of. Too thin not to snap.

And Handler behind her, repeating: "Holy joe, Sarge. Holy joe. I mean, Jeeze."

Screaming.

Her cheeks were wet.

Something touched her mind then, softly. Something—red.

Now listen.

A clawed hand peeled memory flat and laid it aside, folding the moment back on itself. Flame and noise shrank; a line, a dot. Handler faded.

No more time for words.

Sonia recognized the vampire's words, cool now as clean sheets ona fevered forehead.

No—need.

O shadowless angel, reasonable beyond humanity.

A toilet flushed. Grillo would be back any moment, with Essen close after. The vampire drew his long legs back, clumsy, as the dark around him dimmed. Four square feet. Three.

Dawn shivered the window's frame.

Step down, thought Sonia. *Stay SAFE.*

The vampire bent from it, until bone grated and locked.

Another thought, most insistently: *Let this bastard BE.*

"I'm nuts," she muttered, stating the obvious. Then: "Mortensen's dead, man. It wasn't—I—couldn't do anything."

That's no excuse, the vampire's no-voice replied.

Sonia moaned.

Jesus Christ, get out of my HEAD—there's enough of us in here already.

But her thumbs pricked, crawling, under the jacket. Her lips went dry; mouth, groin, nipples set abruptly alight. Her limbs shook. Fistfuls of tiny red ants emerged from her brain's grey folds, each clamouring—in his voice—to be heard.

You came for a taste of power, the vampire not-said. *To sit where my shadow should be, and watch. I commend your honesty. But let me go, and I offer you everything. Simply that. Let me free, and I swear I'll come back for you. I'll make you sister to the moon, mother of snakes. You'll live forever.*

Handler, keening. Grillo knocking at the rec room door.

Only free me.

Where the vampire ran out of corner, smoke began to rise.

Please.

Sonia's heart shook, blue with eyes. She drew a breath—which came back out as a word:

Yes.

"Hey, Kopek!" Grillo yelled. "What—"

Sonia turned, and—

—figure it OUT, dick—

—rammed her head into the nearest fire alarm.

Double uh.

Glass sprayed. Essen came running, keys ready, as her knees hit the floor. Grillo knelt beside her. He turned her face up with one huge hand, almost gentle:

"Oh, Kopek, you crazy bitch."

Well, THAT's news.

The impact had broken her nose, again. It hurt, but no sweat; she'd felt worse. She opened her mouth to speak, coughed blood and snot instead. Everything inside her head turned suddenly liquid.

Clangaclangaclangaclanga—

Essen sniffed. "Fuck me," he said. "Smoke."

Inside his cell, the vampire was starting to char. He howled along with the alarm, tearing chunks from the walls. Padding flew. Sonia thrashed on the floor outside, keeping time.

Come on, come ON—

And the sun was a spilled lamp, everywhere at once.

Like napalm.

Grillo threw one leg over her knees, and held it there. Shouting to Essen: "I can't hold her much longer here, man—"

"Yeah, yeah." Essen fumbled with the keys, misread labels, swore. Supplies, furnace, front lobby, elevator—

—clangaclangaclangaclangaclang—

—Quiet Room.

The vampire's hair finally caught fire. He tore at it with both hands, skipping a whole octave.

"Essen!"

"Got it," Essen replied.

Truncheon out, he kicked the door open.

And Sonia and Grillo turned as one at the sound, to see—

(incoming)

—Essen blown back in one red blast, throat unravelling as he went. His

118

head hit Sonia's thigh, cracking the femur. Grillo, next in line, had time for a yelp; then two blood necklaces (jugular, carotid) broke at once across the wall behind him, dripping. Sonia gaped up, shading her eyes, from his suddenly slack palm. Her lips skinned back in a snarl of protest.

"The fuh—"

A sole syllable, choked at birth.

Poised for flight, the vampire—by the light of his own wings' blazing, studied her face. Behind her brow, his words.

The first rule, my little Sergeant: Leave nothing living.

Bones bells ringing.

Even mad as you are, you must see that.

Synaptic mortar rounds.

(incoming)

But you'll die out there, Sonia thought. Then, instantly reconnecting her own dots with impeccable non-linear logic: *Or maybe not—with my blood inside of you.*

Up and down, the stairwells sang with running feet. Suddenly sure she'd probably never know one way or the other, Sonia gulped, then stared.

You made—me a—promise. Shaky breath. "Motherfucker."

Blue eyes crinkled, half-amused.

So I did.

Sonia blinked. In that one second, she felt the last eight years drop away like a thought gone wrong; a flurry of sloughed skin. She was home, whole, happy. She'd never left. Married to Gio from down the street, womb full and kicking. Makeup perfect, home congenial, flesh unscarred except for a little acne. Sanity intact. Never split wide and left to bleed, under an empty sky. Never burnt and screaming. Never splayed in her own pain like a cow in razor-wire, black with flies, while faceless things stood by and laughed and laughed laughed *laughed*—

—but before she could react, dead man's fingernails dug as her pulse. Lifted her, effortlessly, ceilingward.

And squeezed.

Hail Mary the Lord is with thee blessed art thou amongst women and blessed is the fruit of thy womb Jesus—

Sonia's chest narrowed; became a vise, screwed beyond its limit.

"Did it never occur to you, though," the vampire said, "that I might have been—lying?"

And leaned down.

—*now and at the hour of our deaths*—

Smiling.

(IN)

IN THE POOR GIRL
TAKEN BY SURPRISE

"Aren't you a little slut, to eat the flesh and drink the blood of your own grand-mother?"

    —"Little Red Riding-Hood", traditional.

This is an old story. Most stories are. Anyone who says different is lying, or perhaps simply misinformed.

But thus, and even so:

Once upon a time, my darlings, these woods were full of wolves—yes, even here in the wilds of Upper Canada, where the light which seeps between evergreens and maple trees alike is as brown and stinging as though it comes filtered through a thousand mosquito wings at once. Here where the sky is clogged with bark and cobwebs, where black biting flies hover thick under the branches and each step stirs the pine-needle loam up like hay, or sodden grey-brown snow; here amongst the tangle of crab-apple trees and blackthorn bushes, where even the quietest footfall is enough to send little toads hopping clear, like brown clumps of dirt with tiny, jewelled eyes . . .

Even here in these dim and man-empty places, where things leap from tree to tree far overhead, just out of sight. Where under the mulch and muck of dead leaves a veritable feast of dust lies waiting—a fine, dun carpet of ground and yellowed bones.

Which is why, if you hear footsteps behind you as you make your way along the forest's paths, it may be best to stop and hide and wait—as quietly as possible—until they pass you by. And if you see something high in the leaves above, something that looks like eyes travelling fast through the darkness, it may be best to ignore it, even if one is sure it can only be swamp gas—though in truth, there are few real swamps nearby, unless that sump of downed maples and frozen mud you struggled your way through to get to The Poor Girl Taken By Surprise tonight counts as such.

For there are so many things in these woods left still uncounted, even now: Trees whose branches rise high as church-spires, a perfect shape for the keels of bewitched canoes to scrape themselves upon. Caves in which squat the dried-out corpses of savages, hunted beyond endurance and sick with strange diseases, who starved to death rather than allow themselves to be captured and corralled like animals; their hungry ghosts may yet be heard keening at twilight, ill-wishing any white man whose shadow dares to cross their doorstep. A lake that goes up and a cathedral that goes down and a woman dressed all in birch-bark walking, rustling, with her left hand clutched tightly to her chest—that dead-white skeleton hand whose touch to the unwary forehead means madness, whose touch to the unwary back means death . . .

Yet here we sit snug and warm and dry nonetheless, traders and settlers and immigrants bound for even more distant places alike, before this open, welcoming fire; here we may eat and drink our fill and go 'round the circle in turn, each of we travellers swapping a story for our place beneath this roof 'till morning. And I will be more than glad to add my own contribution to that roster, if only it should please you to bend your ear and listen.

Might it be that you have a place already set at your table for a poor old woman such as I, *Monsieur? Madame?* A place at your sideboard for a starving, childless widow, *mesdames et messieurs, s'il vous plait?*

Oh, no matter; I have walked far tonight, expecting to go yet farther, before I saw your sign and heard your merriment. But I am not yet so weak with hunger that I cannot seat myself.

* * *

Once upon a time, and a time it was . . .

. . . there were two sisters who lived all alone, with no mother and no father to care for them, in the very deepest and darkest part of the woods. They lived in the house of their grandmother, who was often away on long trips, but they were not lonely, these two; never so, not in each other's company. For they were used, from long experience, to making their own amusements.

And what brought this lopsided little family to the heart of the forest, *deux gamines* and one old woman, so far away from everything that is soft, feminine and civilized? Their property dated back to before the Plains of Abraham, before the French Revolution; granted land in perpetuity, as dowery and domain, 'till one of them might be inclined to sell or give it away—and if that sounds like a curse rather than a gift, then so be it. A not-so-self-imposed exile in the no longer-New World for reasons untold, or (at least) unspoken.

The name, *messieurs?* Ah, but our names have come to mean so very little here in this empty country of ours, have they not? Just as our definitions tend to . . . shift, down the centuries. *Tessedaluye, Tesse-dal'oeuil, Tete-de-l'oueil*—"head of the eye", no? Or perhaps a misapprehension never corrected: Head of something very, very different. *L'oueil, la luce, la loup* . . .

And so it was, after all: *Tete-du-loup*, "head of the wolf". Wolf's-head.

A strange name, certainly. And yet I know it as well as though it were—my own.

The savages who had occupied this particular plot of land began to shun it soon after the family first arrived to take possession of their new hunting-grounds. For they were ferocious hunters, these ones, male and female alike; from winter through spring, summer and fall, each season to its own sort of prey. In the old country, it had been whispered that the Tessedaluye kept their own calendar, and maybe even their own prayer-book too—had pledged themselves neither wholly to the Catholic nor the Hugenot faith, in those dark days after Catherine de'Medici and her brood split France limb from limb, twisting the wound so that it would never heal cleanly again. Which made them no sort of Christians at all, perhaps.

Or not *good* ones, at any rate.

And where was this house, you ask? Oh, not so very far from here at all. Not so very far that they were not often diverted by the light and noise of The Poor Girl Taken By Surprise which spilled towards them from across the lake, since they had never seen a public-house before, or travellers in such numbers: Music, laughter, the rumble of ox-carts, bright city-bought fabrics, men and women dancing like leaves in the wind. These things were mysteries and amazements to the two sisters, poor solitary bump-kins that they were!

For they knew many things, these girls, you see, though the ways of Man were not among them. How to trap a rabbit, and skin it. How to tell the track of stag from that of moose. How to cook a hedgehog under an earthenware bowl, peel its stinging quills free, and crack it for its tender meat. What parts of every creature may be dried for carrying, which must be hung awhile before they become palatable, which may be pickled, or otherwise preserved. And which parts are best eaten just as they are, raw and red and dripping, on the very spot where they were butchered.

The human animal, only, was one they had never hunted. Let alone . . .

. . . tasted.

* * *

Girls are curious creatures, a fact their grandmother was well acquainted with—fated to be wild in their season, just as she had been in hers. So even though she understood that her warnings would (in all prob-ability) go unheeded, she was constrained to voice them anyway.

Come close, my darlings, come closer; listen to me a while, before I go where I must. We do not meddle with those we do not know, yes? Therefore keep always to the safest path, the well-trod road of needles rather than the easier-seeming road of pins—back and forth to Grandmother's house, where you may pull the bobbin and the latch will go up, open the door and come in.

And perhaps you should have stayed behind, old woman, if you feared so for their safety; this is what you may be thinking, and not without cause. But we cannot always choose the way things happen. I have my habits and my instincts, just as they . . . did.

A cry from the back, now: You, sir, *repetez-vous?* Ah, *were they pretty,* of course. For the most important questions much be answered first, natu-rally.

Well. We all know the tale of Rose Red and Snow White, do we not? From which one may gather that one was coarse and the other fine, one dark and the other fair. One might have been considered pretty, even in this company. The other—

—the other, not so much.

It was winter by then, which made things harder. Winter settles hard upon us all in this inhospitable place, am I mistaken? For when the light grows thin and the nights long, there is very little to amuse one's self with, aside from sleep. Or hunting when the hunger takes you, which is often enough.

The people at the inn, also hungry—some of you here amongst them, no doubt—tried their hand at hunting as well. But when one does not know the territory, *c'est difficile.* The girls watched their distress mount, counting down the days to their grandmother's return, and I think that it must have seemed to them that without their aid the men and women of The Poor Girl Taken By Surprise must surely pine and die like bear-cubs woken too early, beaver kits trapped in an icebound lodge . . . for they were tender-hearted creatures, as all girls are. Yes, indeed.

Almost as much so as they were also born hunters, long-used to watching and waiting while prey struggled deeper and deeper into its own trap. To check for signs of struggle in the snow or drops of blood in the underbrush, for the uneven prints of some weakened thing, for whatever Nature herself might have selected—pre-ordained, in her own magnanimous way—for them to cull.

* * *

The Feast of Stephen, Saint Stephen's Day, has long been set aside for charity. So that was the day our two sisters set out for the inn across the lake, bearing gifts with which to barter their welcome: Furs they had cured themselves, berries and fruits they had stored, a goodly portion of meat left over from their own store-room.

How they must have smiled when they drew within sight of these doors, as the moon rose and the snow began to fall—a night much like this one, come to think! For inside was light, warmth and singing, pedlars with their wares spread out on tables, all manner of strange and interesting folk from all manner of places they had never dreamed on, let alone been. And how the inn's inhabitants must have smiled to see them coming, also: These two girls, unaccompanied, with their basket of goods and their gawky, gawping stares. Like veritable manna from Heaven.

I was far away by then, *mes amis*, following my quarry under a lead-colored snow-storm sky. Yet I do believe, nevertheless, that I can reckon the very moment during which my granddaughters' rash actions led them somewhere they had never wanted to be.

You at the back—yes, you: I have no doubt you thought my Sylvie "pretty", when you knew her. And my Perrinette, with her puppyish ways; you must have thought her a bad bargain in comparison, though well worth the price of such company. When you fed them both grog and gin, played your fiddles and dared them to dance with each other, dressed them up in your cheap whores' cast-offs and rouged their lips and cheeks to make them look more . . . appetizing? *Oui, madame, c'est veritable:* I know for fact that you were there that night as chief inciter, if not ring-leader, in those drunken revels. And how, you may well ask?

Let us say that if I wrinkle my nose just so, I can—without a doubt— —smell it on you.

Their only mistake—the "sin" that condemned them—was that they had never learned how men, too, prey on men, poor little ones. I had spared them that knowledge, foolishly, out of some vain hope of preserving their innocence; far too well, as it turns out. And for that I will no doubt have to make amends, in time.

This glittering mess-hall, this carbuncle, squatting over a field of shallow graves. This poisoned honeycomb, a nest to trap and drown flies in. This place where off-season travellers sometimes simply disappear, leaving nothing but their few sad treasures and a table or so of full bellies behind.

But you were surprised as well, I am sure, when—after the girls saw you, for the first time, in your true shapes—they let you see them, in theirs.

* * *

My Sylvie found a thin place in the ice with her paw as they broke from the inn, and sank like a stone to its bottom. But my poor Perrinette, hampered by her fine new clothing, was easily brought to ground. And though she snapped at you with her slavering jaws and tore at you with her clever, clawed hands, you shot her all the same: Put a ball in her brain, tore her limb from limb, flayed her wolf's skin away from the man-skin still lurking below, then dragged what was left of her back inside.

For there is much meat to be had from a wolf, if one knows where to make the cuts. Almost as much, in the end, as there is on a poor girl, taken by surprise.

* * *

Yes, it is a sad story indeed. And though you do not seem eager to hear the end of it, I will tell it to you all the same.

These woods were full of wolves when we first came here, but we drove them out, hunting them almost to their extinction. For they knew the truth of our nature, just as the savages did: We are the sort who do not care to share what is ours, not even with our closest kin. So when the wolves had fled we hunted savages, and because we hunted them, the savages dressed up like us and prayed to us, prayed to us not to eat them. We became their gods for a time, until they fled as well, to find themselves others. Or—perhaps—to seek out a place with none.

But we are not gods, and never have been. We are Wolf's-heads. Tessedaluye. We are . . .

. . . shall I really have to say the word aloud, my friends?

The primal sin of those like myself, *mes amis*, is that because we were once people who acted like beasts, we are forever cursed to be beasts who know they were once men. A wolf hunts in a pack, to eat, not to kill—it is a proponent of all those most wonderful, natural qualities: Liberty, loyalty, fraternity. But a *were*-wolf hunts to kill rather than eat, a creature whose unslaked hunger is only for blood and slaughter, defilement and degredation. It will prey even on its own family, for the bonds of kinship mean startlingly little to it; it can violate the families of others, and will, for much the same reason. The were-wolf likes to play, to torture, and takes a grim humor in its continual masquerade, the toothy animal face beneath the gentle human mask.

Perhaps this is because the oldest story behind the myth—one which those amongst us educated in the Classics may well recognize—is that of King Lykaon and his fifty sons; Lykaon, whose disgusting crimes caused the old god Zeus to flood the known world, washing it clean for future, less perverse occupants. Lykaon and his sons, who were transformed into wolves for profaning and denying the gods, for serving strangers human meat, for ravening the land they were supposed to protect like bandits rather than rulers. And since sometimes Lykaon's name is linked with that of Tantalus, perhaps it follows that the rule he broke was the one which warns us not to share in the eating of our own children, or others'. For to force or trick others into sharing the flesh of your own line is always an evil sort of victory over them, a potential spreading of moral contagion.

Later, in Arcadia, followers of the cult of Lykaian Zeus believed that each year, one of their number would be doomed to turn into a wolf. If that person could only live for a year without tasting human flesh, he or she would return to human form; if not, he or she would remain a wolf forever. But to be a man turned wolf makes the hunger for human flesh a dreadful, and constant, temptation . . .

Ah, yes. Perhaps you have felt it too, by now: That very different sort of greed, aching in all your bones, at the root of every tooth. That itch beneath the skin, just where you can never quite reach. That song in your blood which calls out to the rising moon, dinning in your ears like some evil tide.

For we are all were-wolves here, make no mistake. Every parent who beats and rapes their own child, every man driven to eat his fellow's flesh—like a savage, though they most-times have better reason for it—by seasonal extremity. He, she, I, you; all of us who break the social compact by treating each other as something . . . less than human.

And the cry, the cry, echoing down unchanged throughout the ages: *It is not so, nor was not so, and God forbid that it should be so!*

But it is so. Is it not?

And still: *Calme-toi.* How could I possibly hurt you, *m'sieu*—an old woman like myself? Look at me. Look.

Yes, just that way.

Sit. Stay. *Assayez-vous*, each and every one of you, before I am forced to let my—worser—nature slip.

. . . better.

Ah, and now I recall how when I was but a gay girl like my poor Perrinette, still foolish enough to risk myself for trifles, I wore nothing but scarlet velvet . . . scarlet, so the stains would not show so badly. You understand.

Yet how times change, and how they do not. How do they never.

But I do not blame you for her death, any of you—oh no, not I. How could I, and not count myself a hypocrite? For I, of all people, should know how very difficult it is to refuse fresh meat when it presents itself, especially out here in this bleak and denuded frontier landscape. Out here, where hunger rules.

After all, I, too, have been known to prey on the unwary, in my time. I, too, have followed close behind travelling families and used their love for one another to harry them to their doom. I, too, keep a cellar full of bones.

Yet I will give you this one thing for gift, *mesdames et messieurs* of The Poor Girl Taken By Surprise: This much, I will tell you for free. That there is more than one reason, traditionally, why a wolf who speaks—a wolf with human hands—should always be *burnt* rather than *eaten*.

You killed one of my children, and ate the other. But I do not begrudge you—since, in doing so, you have allowed yourselves to be eaten from inside-out by this same raging hunger that has always driven us, I and my kind, down all the long years before we came to this country, and after. In a way, you have *become* my children, my kin; Tessdaluye by nature, if not by name. And how could I harm my own kind, after all?

Well . . . easily enough, as I have explained already.

Nevertheless, I catch myself feeling generous, for now. For as a fellow hunter, I do so admire your arrangement here—this inn, sprung perpetu-ally open like a trap disguised as providence; this fine, new trick of letting the little pigs come to be served and watching them serve themselves up, in turn. A steady stream of travellers lodging once, then moving on, and never being seen again: Only tracks in the snow, covered over before the moon next rises, and (here and there, in the underbrush) the rustle of soft paws following. With nothing left behind but the hard, dark scat of some unseen thing, so concentrated it must surely eat nothing but meat.

Oh yes indeed, *ca marche, absolutement. Ca ira.*

But never forget whose sufferance you live by from this moment on, curs. As last of my line, I am first in the blood here—alpha and omega, the aleph and the zed. And so you will come to my call, heel at my command, because I am—

—ah, *ca phrase?*

"Top dog."

You may even call me grandmother, if you wish.

A SINGLE SHADOW MAKE

They dance together then 'til dawn
And a single shadow make.
                    —J.R.R. Tolkien

1.

The first thing I saw was your face. I recall it now, as I always will.

* * *

"Tu es tres beau, comme un ange d'argent," my cousin—Count Ivan—murmured to
me, in his execrable Russian aristocrat's French, and his choice of form alone told me
what would follow. But it was 1818, I was twenty-five already, and sorely needed
money if I was ever to reach my stated goal—the re-Creation of new life from death.

And: "Ah, mon ange blanc, mon ange tombe," Ivan moaned, much later that
same night. And at last, altering my Irish mother's suitably Heavenly—yet a
touch too . . . plebeian—choice of name (Michael) for something more to his own
taste, as he finally reached his climax: "Oh, Mikela, Mikela."

All of which I took with a not inconsiderable grain of salt, bemused to find myself
the object of such passion—having always personally judged my attributes more
freakish than anything else, seeing the "moon-bleached" hair Ivan extolled more as
bordering on albino, the "silver" eyes mere light grey, and as defiantly crossed as
any Siamese's. Quite unworthy of Ivan's intent, melancholy lust, all told.

But as I've said, he was rich, and I not. So, to bed—and after, to the bank.

* * *

A blank slate, empty of all but the most brute sensation, I lay there unprotesting on the slab in my first dazed shock of life. Then came feeling—your hands running up and down my limbs, checking reflexes, testing for damage. A tickle at my brow as your scalpel's blade traced my face's outline through the gauze. And when the veil was drawn away I blinked, eyes watering, as the light flooded in. I looked up—

—into your face.

You bent over me, tensed for certain failure. I gaped. And triumph leapt in your slant, rain-filled eyes, so vivid under those pale brows—in that pale, pale face. Ivory hair fell about you, released from its loosened bow. I saw you clearly.

You were the first thing I had ever seen, and the only thing I have ever seen since.

* * *

From earliest days on, my greatest fear has been that of death.

I was born and raised in Ireland, son of a Russian trader lost at sea and the frail, white-gilt Catholic woman whom I came to worship. One day, when I was perhaps ten, we went out riding past an ancient, beehive-shaped structure of crumbling grey stone and mortar—the proper term for which, she told me, was "a tomb".

"Where we go when we are dead?" I asked.

"Yes."

"Mother, what is 'dead'?"

"Sleeping, my darling. One day we must all go to sleep, never to wake again."

I frowned. "I couldn't sleep that long."

I didn't understand why she laughed at that.

Once inside, I picked up a stray skull and hefted it in curiousity, testing its weight. My mother cried out to me to replace it, for it had been laid there to rest until the Day of Judgement. It could not be separated from its owner except at the cost of his immortal soul. And all at once, I realized what she had meant: That this object was what lay inside my own head, under my face, housing my brain. Some day I would "go to sleep", and then the skin which covered me would creep away. My bones would collapse in a heap and be left here, grinning under a blue sky, covered in birds' droppings.

I let the skull fall with a crunch, and was violently ill.

Not long after that, a fever took hold. My life was feared for, and I too believed—wholeheartedly—that I would die. As I tossed in my soaking sheets, I prayed to everyone and anyone I could remember for another chance.

"Twenty more years, Lord. Ten, even. And I will make sure there is no more dying ever, no more of the long sleep. Then dreams will come true, and the world will be full of light."

Childish, yes. But it held the seed.

* * *

It was as I stared at you, entranced, that the top of the keep burst into flames. I regarded this with amazement, but no thought of danger. You, however, saw and reacted—pulling me to the floor with one quick yank. I screamed, learning pain, and fought to dislodge you, not understanding your intent. Burning beams had begun to rain from the roof. One grazed me.

From that moment on, I have feared fire. Fire can strip me of everything you gave me in an instant.

Whimpering, I allowed you to lead me away.

Behind us, the roof collapsed with a sigh of heat, flames engulfing the laboratory. You shut the door against these sights. You barred it.

And then you led me away to your cousin's room, where you put me to sleep in his bed.

* * *

From my tenth year on—until the day they struck my name from the medical register—I fought to keep my childhood vow. My aim, and the unashamed way I spoke of it (as well as my need for an ever-steady supply of dead flesh) conspired to keep me an outcast. In England I treated with those grim men known as Resurrectionists to meet my experiments' demands, which so outraged my peers that they revoked my license.

I was alone then, my mother having died some years before in a carriage accident, miscarrying my stepfather's child. So I took what money of hers was deemed mine, and went to Russia, the ancient lands of my father's blood.

And it was here . . . with Ivan's kind assistance . . . that I finally delivered upon my promise.

* * *

Later, I regained my new-found senses and went in search of you, groping unsteadily along the walls. Luckily, I did not have at all far to go—only across the hall to the adjoining chamber, a room so dark that I stumbled over the threshold before I even knew it was there. Only a chance grab at some handy draperies preventing me from falling. But since my motions thus disclosed you—sprawled half-clothed beneath your bed's curtains—I soon had more than enough light to see by.

My eyes swept you up and down, each pass adding new detail. Your sharp profile, blurred in a moony cloud of hair. The bleak enamel of your nails. One cyanose nipple, half-revealed under your shirt-sleeve's shadow. Those long, pale lines—from ankle to hip to out-flung arm and clenching fist, the whole of you sheened with a fine ivory fur—drew me in, hypnotized, like a languorous undertow. By the slow pulse at your throat, the line of fleece shadowing your stomach brought a silent groan to my lips. Before I could quite reason my actions through, I found myself reaching—as gently as possible—to trail a single finger down from throat to nipple, to navel, and beyond.

You turned in your sleep beneath my touch, sighing. And as I traced the curve of your jaw, I felt us both come to full attention.

* * *

On occasion, I felt my apparent lack of every other passion but for an over-whelming need to conquer death severely. It seemed as though my quest to reorder Nature had determined I be punished for daring to flout its rules—to wit, that each time another touched me (my pretty cousin, for example), I would be forever doomed to remain at best acquiescent—at worst, annoyed.

But I was still human. As that sweet flush settling over me like a prickly veil—seeping, with exquisite lack of haste, down through the pressing fathoms of fantasy—testified.

Uneasy at this unexpected sensation's power, I pried my eyes open and reached for the bedside candle.

Dulled with sleep, it took a second for me to realize that the figure looming over me was, in fact—

—my creation.

No beauty, no. But then, that quality had never been my main object, and while I'd still been piecing him together the difference between our sizes had seemed, similarly, no consideration. Upright, however, he seemed huge and oddly alien, as *though the arcane commingling of science and necromancy I had practiced to bring him to life had conjured up a demon: Skin dark and dry, hands lightly clawed, jaws pushing forward like a muzzle into a grim jawful of shark's teeth. His eyes were mismatched, too, I noticed only now—one grey, one blue.*

But what matter? They worked.

HE worked.

The sight of the candle-flame made him recoil, varicolored gaze gone wide and wounded. But like the child he truly was, his attention span was too short yet to hold such fear for long.

Abruptly oblivious to me, he stepped back, eyes casting around the room for whatever caught his fancy. I followed him at a wary distance, observing how he studied each item in turn.

"Plate," I said, as he stroked a gilded slice of Ivan's best china.

He turned too quickly, toppling, and the weight of him almost broke my hand.

Then, still clutching the thing in question, he offered it to me.

"Plate," I repeated.

"Paaaht."

Soon we were pointing at all sorts of things.

Finally, he put a finger to my own chest. After a moment's hesitation, some imp of the perverse made me answer:

"Mikela."

"Mi-ke-la," he replied, clearly.

We smiled at each other.

* * *

Which is all that I remember of my first night alive.

2.

My liaison with Ivan yielded the keep (one of his hereditary holdings) and enough money to live on while I completed my experiments. Unfortunately, it also—for a time—yielded HIM, playing understandable havoc with my powers of concentration. Barely a fortnight had passed, however, before he came storming into the laboratory with a letter in one hand, a drink in the other.

"Most intolerable! My father has arranged . . . " His voice shook at the horror of it: " . . . a marriage."

"I feel your loss already," I replied, making another notation.

He left swearing eternal fidelity, a claim so patently foolish it gave me no honest way of even acknowledging it, let alone matching it.

* * *

My life soon settled into a seductive routine of education—question and answer, enthusiasm and exploration, all framed by your careful supervision—and one day, my curiosity piqued by a word I had heard you use once too often without definition, I asked: "What is this *God*, Mikela?"

"They say God made the world."

"As you made me."

You laughed, shortly. "Not quite—God has no need of science. He simply thought the world, and so it was."

"Then God made you."

"If you believe so, yes."

"And you made me," I smiled. "So you are God."

You turned, and I noticed a line between your brows I had never seen there before. "No," you said. "I made you, that's true—but God made all men, I only one. So I can never be more than God's shadow—his pale, pale shadow."

"You are *my* God," I said, simply.

And you shook your head—but I do not think you really wanted to.

* * *

A month had already gone by when Ivan's letter finally arrived, the gist of which was that he would be arriving shortly, accompanied by the new Countess—Rebecca, his wife.

Elle est tres belle, et douce aussi, Ivan wrote. Adding, in a cramped hand: Mais c'est seulement toi j'adore, mon cousin.

He advised me to expect him at any time. That particular evening, however, I intended to spend instructing my creation in the basics of English literature. So I filed the letter away, and promptly forgot all about it.

* * *

You had told me many times by then never to go beyond the last field of our lands. When I was ready, you said—and you would decide when that was. It rankled, even from a God.

That night, I sat near the window, watching a string of birds flap slowly across the purple sky. The light was almost gone, and the book I held was making my eyes hurt. I saw the last field's fence against the red rim of the sinking sun. And something rose in me—something that could no longer be denied.

A minute later, I was on the ground, running quickly and silently. Had reached the fence. In one quick leap, had bridged it.

Once on the other side, however, I paused in mid-stride, unsure of my next action. Ahead and behind me stretched the road. Lulled by the cry of night-birds, the slither and skitter of small creatures in the long grass, I stood stock-still and breathed deeply. The dark air, tainted and singing, spread like wine through my veins.

I did not see the men until I was upon them, nor they me.

"Make way for the Count's carriage, fellow!" One of them ordered, impatiently. Behind him reared a conveyance drawn by four harnessed things that stamped and snorted in distress, making their master curse, as my scent reached them. At this further disturbance, an exquisitely-dressed young man leaned from the nearest window, glancing imperiously about for the cause of his discomfort.

"Monsieur Grushkin," he said to the first man, "remind me once again, if you would be so kind, what exactly it is that I pay you for?"

The man flushed. "By your leave, Count Ivan," he replied—and stepped toward me, drawing a cudgel from his belt. But this fresh threat drew no reaction at all, since at that same moment—over his shoulder—I had spotted . . . her.

As dark as you were fair, and frail, with a cloud of ringlets hiding her dark, dark eyes. She hovered close by young Count Ivan's side, peeping through the carriage window, and that slender hand with which she held the velvet curtain open was so pale each vein brought a faint blue blush to her nacreous skin. At the sight of her, my mouth dried out. My temples throbbed. And like a barb to my spine's base, a hook arching up through dark water, the hunger took root: Soul-deep, nameless, aching. A negative image, fleet as steam on glass, faint haloed trace of an object struck by lightning, beneath which lurked only the dimmest recollection of what had roused it.

Silver flesh in a darkened room, and the slick touch of you stirring—sleepily—in my palm.

And when Gruskin's men shone their lanterns in my face, as I blinked at them in mute surprise, their eyes seemed to widen as one. Rebecca saw as well, though from much too far away to mark my features, and fell back with a quick half-scream.

"Un monstre, pardieu!" Your cousin exclaimed, in equal parts horror and surprise. I did not feel the first blow, but the second stung me. I caught the man's hand in mine, before he could strike again, and squeezed it until I heard a crack. He sank to his knees, screaming which is when the others leapt upon me.

I turned then, and ran. But not fast enough.

* * *

Exactly half an hour since I'd climbed the steps to his room and found him gone, I looked up as he entered the study. Behind him, a trail of footprints made from mud and blood admixed smeared their way across the polished granite floor.

"And where have you been?" I demanded.

"Get me a mirror," he replied.

* * *

"A *mirror*," I repeated, and bared my teeth as I had in the face of the last man's torch. I saw your anger give way to fear, then—just a hint, but a surprisingly gratifying one. You passed me a frame worked with a swirl of silver crosses. I gazed into it for a long time, before raising my head again.

"Why did you not tell me," I asked, slowly, "that I am a monster?"

"Because you aren't," you snapped, voice a lash.

"And neither are you a God."

It was the first bitterness I had ever spoken. With that disposed of, I returned to the mirror.

"All in all," I said, "the truth is this—that when you made me, you made me very ugly."

"I *made* you," you said, stiffly. "Most people would be satisfied with that."

"Ah," I said. "But if you had created me in the way most people do, Mikela, then I would be beautiful indeed."

Then I turned the mirror towards you, showing you your own face, and at this you were silent.

* * *

I was certain I'd earned his hate, then, along with his rejection. And if I no longer held any authority over him, my position would soon become untenable. He might turn on me, hurt me physically, as easily as breathing. He might even kill me.

Where can one go from Divinity, after all—but down?

"Who told you you were . . . ugly?"

"A young man in a carriage." He rummaged for the name: "Count—Ivan."

"Ivan, here?"

"In the courtyard by now," my creation replied, seemingly somewhat bemused by my panic. "Do you fear I might frighten your guests a second time, if given the opportunity?"

I flushed. "What I FEAR is Ivan withdrawing his patronage, without which you could never have come into being and cannot be maintained any further than I could on my own income—perhaps a mile or so from where we stand, if our luck held. As things stand now, your lack of cooperation may very well doom us both." I paused. "Are you LISTENING to me?"

* * *

My right hand, unnoticed, had found the table. Under it lay the book I had been reading, its title outlined by my index finger. I reconsidered it.

"No," I mused. "I am not a monster. But I am not a man, either. Not the shadow of God." I looked at you. "I am your shadow."

And still you sat in silence.

"I want a name," I said.

"Choose one yourself, then," you returned. "But *quickly*."

I opened your copy of *Beowulf*, not quite at random, and pointed to a word.

"My name is Grendel," I said, and heard the walls give it back to me.

3.

"You cannot conceive how glad I am to finally make you acquaintance, Dr Kosowan," claimed Ivan's bride, and offered me her hand—which, like her cheeks, was both a bit too pale for comfort and yet flushed with traces of a more hectic tone. Leading me to suspect that my cousin might not have too long a wait before being able to resume his bachelor status (albeit while clothed in a far less colorful wardrobe).

"Madam," I replied. And kissed it.

"*I feel the lack much less than I thought I might, however,*" *she hastened to add,* "*since my husband's family has already told me so much about you.*"

"*Of that, dear lady, I have absolutely no doubt.*"

Ivan, who had spent most of our exchange lingering uneasily by the rack that held his grandfather's silver duelling pistols, snapped his fingers, causing a girl to appear at Rebecca's elbow. "Dovya, you will conduct your mistress to her chambers," he said. "The journey has doubtless fatigued her, and she will wish to rest."

At which Rebecca nodded, and left, without a further glance in my direction. But Ivan's smile faded as he turned back, only to see me heading for the opposite door.

"*You'll stay, surely—*"

"*Regrettably not,*" *I replied. "I have a matter in the old wing—work of a rather unstable nature—which requires my immediate attention. I'm sure you understand.*"

"*Of course I do,*" *he said. "* . . . *Mikela.*"

* * *

You found me in the gallery, a refuge I chose not only for its fascinating row of family portraits—each dark oil with its own little plaque, Kosowan name and date of birth—but because its shuttered window looked directly down on that of the Great Hall. Through it, I had watched your conversation with Rebecca—that delicate duel between light and dark, with Ivan looking on, drunken and faintly afraid.

It was true that I hated him a bit less now, having seen how hopelessly he fawned on you. But I cannot honestly say I liked him any better.

And what an idiot he must be, I thought for the thousandth time, not to see how much she cared for him—and how little you cared at all.

I stepped away from the window as you entered, pointing at the wall beside me.

"Your family," I said.

"Yes."

I pointed again. "Your father."

"Whom I never knew, yes."

I traced the gleam of paint to form a cheek, a jaw, a dark grey eye—and closed my own.

"You are not God," I began. "But you created me. As your father was created by God, yet created another—you." I opened my eyes. "So you are my father."

* * *

And he smiled, so happy to have found me another title at last. While I smiled back, so unaccountably, witlessly happy . . . to bear one.

In the weeks to come, Grendel listened again: He read what I gave him, wrote what I set him, did what I told him. But it felt far too good to be teaching him once more, because there was a hint of the old look in his intent gaze—that look I knew well, yet could never bring myself to call by name. A little like worship, but a little more like love: The kind of love you hold for some pretty but intimately disposable thing, made all the more keen for knowing it won't outlast the strain of your loving it. And with a pushing toward something unreachable behind it, as always—some nameless hurt that I could never diagnose, or salve.

Oh, how I hated how my heart clenched and thudded to see it.

4.

"You keep something up there in the old wing," Ivan began, one evening. "Something which fascinates you beyond all else. Do you deny it?"

Already drunk, he swayed uncomfortably close to my desk, another half-full glass of brandy sloshing in one hand.

I shrugged. "Why should I?"

"Then deny this, cousin: Amidst such fascination, I find you have no more time for me."

"My work requires—"

"Ah, yes." He turned away, eyes straying as if magnetized, back to the mounted duelling pistols. "Your holy work, which *I* pay for. Whatever it is."

"I've outlined my ambitions to you more than once, cousin."

"Who is he, Mikela?" Ivan asked.

I had no real reply for such an implication, not that it merited one.

Ivan sighed to himself. Then, softly: "I almost begin to think that you no longer love me."

"You are a married man now, Ivan," I reminded him.

He nodded, soddenly. "Et elle m'aime de trop, aussi . . . ma pauvre Rebecca."

Realizing that we had apparently reached the French-speaking portion of the evening, I rose.

"I should go—"

But before I could get any further, either by word or deed, I found that Ivan's hand had already knitted itself deep into my hair, yanking downward. I hissed with pain, as the rest of me was quickly forced to follow.

"Release me," I spat, fighting to keep my legs from buckling.

"Oh, I think not," Ivan returned, almost civil—yet the pressure, as he lowered himself into my former seat, only increased. "On this particular occasion, I believe that you will rather stay and play the good host for my sake, angelic Mikela—always remembering who first gave you that position, and why. Stay, and be . . . gracious."

So, realizing that cool reason would be manifestly useless in the face of such foolishness, I sank to my knees—unbuttoned him—

—*and was.*

* * *

And that was where I found myself: Lurking out in the darkness behind the window, as though I had no home to go to. For indeed, this pane of glass seemed to represent all that separated me from the rest of the human world—so easily shattered, so impossible to mend. With Ivan sprawled in your chair and you at prayer before him, his legs spread wide as your bright head rose and fell in his lap, panting as he thrust himself down your throat, eyes screwed shut.

The image rocked me back, like a knife-thrust to the stomach. That he would do this to Rebecca, given my feelings for him (and her), surprised me not at all. But that you would participate . . .

"And with him," I whispered. "Him!"

Watching you nurse him, however diffidently, I wanted to knock him aside—and feed myself to you in his place, an inch at a time, until you choked.

To know would surely kill her.

But even as I formed this thought, I saw the study door swing open—at Dovya's touch—to reveal Rebecca's stricken face.

After which came the details, unrolling like some sordid farce: Dovya shrieking, hands over her mouth. Ivan, recoiling in mid-throe to spray your hair as you fell to one side, coughing up the rest of his spend onto the expensive Parisian rug. Rebecca, jack-knifing to spit a stream of solid crimson into one hand. And as she swayed toward the window, white and gagging, I saw in one awful rush just how unwittingly right my last prediction had been.

She fell. I stepped to meet her, arms outstretched.

A wave of broken glass bound us together at last as I folded her to me, her blank, burst-blood-vessel red gaze assuring me she had—at least—been spared the horror of my tears as her last sight.

* * *

Ivan I left in the study, drinking himself into a stupor, but it was only after a lengthy search that I discovered Grendel's latest hiding-place. The closer I drew to the fabled old wing, the more I noticed a ceaseless muffled whine emenating from somewhere beyond the wall . . . the wall behind which, I knew, lay the abandoned ruins of my former laboratory.

I unbarred the door and opened it, darkness swallowing my light like a giant's open mouth. But as my eyes grew sharper, I heard the sound I'd followed peak and change into muffled sobs. And a stench grew, something I hadn't smelled since my nights in the local churchyard, collecting scraps from which to fashion my wretched "child."

Grendel sat there, cradling Rebecca's corpse and rocking in mourning, his back to the far wall. Setting my candle carefully down near the door, I knelt beside him.

"Give her to me, Grendel," I told him, quietly. "Let me bury her, for God's sake. Why did you take her, in the first place? She's dead; turberculosis would have soon seen to that, if the shock hadn't."

He stared at me, then whispered: "How can you be so heartless?"

"I think," I replied, slowly, "that I may well have been born that way."

We sat in silence, then, while he spent some long time studying the eerie way Rebecca's slack mouth seemed to smile, as though in sleep.

"I tried," he murmured to himself. "I am my father's son, and that must surely count for something. But I cannot, cannot—"

"Cannot what?"

Tears coursed from his mismatched eyes. "I cannot . . . make her breathe. Again."

The words caught me short.

"But you could."

Oh, yes: For this was to be the next step, the next temptation.

"Help me," Grendel pleaded. "Help me, Mikela."

And now it was my turn to look down at Rebecca, primarily to avoid the wet weight of his sorrowful gaze. Hearing, even as I did so, that traitor voice at the back of my brain begin its damnable litany yet once more: Telling me how she was still fresh, still young enough to be malleable, still resilient enough to withstand the physical strain of re-Birth . . .

But at that moment, from behind us—shattering this reverie—came the slow sound of mocking applause.

* * *

It was Ivan, of course—his flies still unbuttoned, brandy bottle in one hand, duelling pistol in the other. The which weapon he now aimed—with surprising accuracy—at your brow.

"My cousin," he said, "I find—just as I long suspected—that you have been deceiving me."

You fixed him with a silver glare—but your usual power over him seemed, for the moment, to have been suspended.

"You're drunk," you said.

Ivan smiled—a mirthless twist of the lips.

"Indisputably," he replied. "While you, lovely Mikela, are without doubt the coldest male bitch who ever slid between two sheets for money. Still, let all that by, my genius kinsman. Do introduce me to your new—acquaintance."

"You can't seriously think Grendel—and I—"

Ivan laughed, a wet half-snarl—and I realized he was weeping, silent and slow, eyes all but unfocussed with angry tears.

"Surely, I can think nothing else." Then, to me: "And I will thank you, *sir*, to stand away from my wife."

I lowered Rebecca to the ground, stroking her eyes respectfully closed, and rose to meet his hateful stare.

Quickly, you said: "Grendel is my creation, Ivan—the artificial man I once told you of, dead flesh raised from the dead once more imbrued with life, do you remember?" A thin smile, to match his own grimace. "He is what you invested in."

"Some paramour of yours," Ivan replied, tonelessly. "A whore for a whore—and a precious ugly one, at that."

But the pistol—now less sure of its immediate target—had begun to shift, restlessly, between us. And in his indecision, you saw our chance.

"Better a whore than a fool," you said.

Ivan convulsed, as if slapped, and put the pistol's muzzle to your temple.

"Cousin," he whispered, "I have played the fool for you too long."

But even as his finger tightened, I slipped behind him, and twisted his head from his shoulders with a single, cartileginous crack.

* * *

One thing I have always prided myself on, and not immodestly, is the knowledge that no living man can make me tremble. But violent death can still instantly reduce me to that half-Irish child who once tried to vomit his own mortality out upon the grass of some old Celtic tomb. And the sight of Grendel, his hands gloved with Ivan's blood, offering me that dripping thing which had once housed Ivan's (grantedly, rather limited) intelligence, was certainly traumatic enough to produce this same effect.

I fell back, mouth full of bile, and raised my crossed arms like a beaten beggar. "Please," I begged. "Please, take it away."

Grendel considered me, and I thought I saw a hint of pity in those patchwork eyes.

"The great doctor Mikela Kosowan," he said. "Brilliant surgeon, pioneer of a new, deathless age. Count Ivan's homme fatal. One question for you—only one: Why did you make me?"

And for a humiliatingly long moment, pinned under the gaze of my greatest achievement, I could think of no good answer.

" . . . to see if I could," I blurted, at last.

Grendel nodded.

"He loved you," he said, hefting Ivan's skull at me, while I shrank back, panting—practically stumbling over Rebecca's forgotten body, as I tried to shove myself even further into the laboratory's farthest corner. "Did you deserve it?"

"I don't KNOW. Oh, Grendel, please take that thing away, you can't comprehend how it terrifies me—"

"I can, and I do. But it doesn't matter."

Discarding the head, he stepped forward. And I shut my eyes, sure that the inevitable end of all my hubris was as sure as my next breath.

* * *

When I touched you, you spun in my grasp, sweat dulling your hair, eyes grey as the gleam of a blade. "I was wrong," you babbled. "I was wrong, I admit it."

"Wrong," I echoed.

"Yes, wrong. You didn't want or expect to be created. My ambition drove me on, as it always has, and I thought of no one's comfort but my own. I cheated you, cheated Ivan, cheated myself. I was wrong."

"No," I said. "*I* was."

You stopped, met my eyes for the first time in—how long? You frowned, uncertain.

"I don't understand."

"I was wrong, I admit it," I replied. "I should never have asked you for Rebecca. I didn't want her at all."

Your mouth came open, then—small teeth, very even. Pale lips over a warm, red heart.

"I never understood the hunger she gave me. I didn't know. I found the answer in no book you said I should read. All the knowledge in the world, you gave me, but not this one truth. I didn't want her, I never did."

"No," you said, almost a question, edging toward a statement.

"No," I said. "I wanted you."

And smiled. Your mouth stayed open.

"Always," I said, "right from the start. God, Father, Mikela. Your face was the first thing I ever saw, the only thing I've ever seen, and I had forgotten." I almost laughed at the ridiculousness of it. "Forgotten!"

And what I had forgotten had festered in me like an open wound, a mouth I could never feed, a void I could never fill. Until now—until that idiot, your cousin, showed me what neither of us had ever been able to see before.

"Oh no," I said, so softly. "I wanted Rebecca, once. But she was only your shadow."

I could drown in your eyes.

"Only your shadow," I breathed, and held your head still as my mouth came down.

And then, of course, you ran—not getting very far. And of course you fought, though you—of all people—must have known the futility of it. And after I caught you, I did have to hurt you a bit. But only a bit.

So when I finally came walking through the keep toward your room, holding you as I had held her in the laboratory, I was happier than I had ever been since those bright days before I knew there were really any others in this world I thought created by you for me alone.

For me and you alone.

4.

"Let me love you, Mikela. Let yourself be loved. We're both monsters, after all—and even though you made me for yourself, God made you for ME."

And at those words I recover my senses, only to find us already converging upon our inevitable coupling with all the voluptuous paralysis of a nightmare. Whispering lie back, lie quiet, let me do what I was born for. *Over which I can hear my own voice, moaning: No, Grendel, please—remember whatever I was to you, not what you'd have me be.* But I hold you down with ease for all your struggle, shirt ripping open under my claws, nuzzling chest and throat alike in passion's swirl. *With each black tongue-flicker a quick electric jolt clear to the root of me, I'm harder than I've ever been before, pierced with silver skewers of twisted delight.* Free to swallow you whole at last, delighted by your gasp of unexpected joy. *No one makes me do anything, cousin, you may have bought me but you do not own me . . . No, Grendel alone holds that title.* And revels in it. *Knowing me better than I know myself, he's big enough to hold me down and do everything I MUST want done to me, in my hearts of hearts—slowly, and with exquisite relish.* Expressly for your pleasure, which is to say my own. *To turn me over, gently, and—*

—ease myself in, connecting up and *Oh!* All the way through in one smooth rush *Oh, ah* To clip something deep inside *And I* Twist and hiss, jerking *Laid utterly open* Right to the tight silk heart of you, oh yes *Hot breath between my shoulderblades, pinning me flat* Right on through *The pain, prone and panting against my cousin's sheets, satin knotting like a kiss along the length of me* Pounding *My God, I'm so SMALL to him* My claws on your hips, teeth at your nape *And I'll die, my Christ, I'll die* Of pleasure *Grendel howling as I clamp down on him now* While from your own throat comes a sound no angel knows *Our mutual arc pulling taut at last* Fit to spasm and *Jet—*

—together.

* * *

At last, he slept. I waited until he was deep enough to shift in his sleep and slipped from my commandeered bed to the cold stone floor, where I sat, head in my hands, for what seemed a very long time. Then I bit my lips, and rose.

The keep seemed different to me now. Emptier. And as I passed through the study with its shattered window a light rain splattered against my naked skin, reminding me that there had been no time for clothing. But what did that matter, after all?

Nowhere I could run from Grendel would be far enough. Nothing I could do would dissuade him. I had built him well, entirely TOO well, and it had brought me down from the height of a Creator to the depths of the Pit.

But I knew what must be done.

I turned a corner and limped down the hall towards the forbidden door—once barred, then reopened. The rain fell through the laboratory's pierced roof, soaking me to the bone.

I took my notebooks and all the instruments I could find, wrapped them in cloth and paper, doused them with volatile chemicals, and set them alight with a single spark. Then, spreading the detritus of my short career around me in a ring, oblivious to the pain of my burnt fingers, I lay back on the floor looking up at the watery sky.

Nemesis, I thought, who punishes the proud. I have made my own Nemesis.

As a bolt of lightning cracked the sky to show the glow behind, I drew my last remaining souvenir of Godhood towards me.

"Poor Ivan," I heard myself whisper. "Je suis desole, mon gentil cousin, parcequ'il est ma faut vous etes mort."

I raised the scalpel. Calmly, with that deft touch so admired amongst my peers at the Medical School, I brought it down. Calmly, I slit my wrists, one after another.

After which I lay back again, gratefully, and let my life seep away.

* * *

I see your face before me now, as always. Ever since the moment of my birth. Ever since the moment I lifted away the overturned surgical table, after waiting for the ring of fire to burn itself out, and saw you lying there.

So pale.

But you were wrong, my creator—and your plan, as is often the case when one must think fast under pressure, was poorly laid.

I got there before the notebooks could fully burn. A little charred, yes. But legible.

Hear me now, wherever you are: I cannot let you go. I will not.

And I am a good pupil, also. Surely, you must give me that.

Sleep well, Mikela.

* * *

I sleep, just as Mother said I would. I dream I lie packed in ice while years pass, years upon years. I dream I am disinterred and wrapped in bandages, raised toward a shining globe, the charge surging through me as I writhe and scream—blind, but hardly senseless. Then I dream silence, cut only by the sound of the scalpel tracing my jaw. I open my eyes, and the first thing I see . . .

. . . is your face.

BEYOND THE FOREST

Carola woke coughing blood.

The moon was already up. New frost had settled at dusk, lending the rotting leaves around her a leprous sheen. Her teeth ached. As she raised her hand to block the light, she saw that insects had laid their eggs beneath her nails as she slept.

Die, she told them, and felt their tentative hum dim slowly to silence.

Carola stumbled to her feet. Rain had left her shroud stiff with mud, her joints swollen. To her left, a lark cried out. She turned, clumsily, her train tearing loose with a sound like burnt bones popping.

As she paused there in the moonlight, a brief thought touched the back of her neck once, and was gone:

There is something, something . . . I have forgotten.

But it slipped away before she could quite catch hold.

The lark cried again, and was silent.

Carola had been out of the black earth since late summer and all through the autumn, stumbling after a slippery rope of moonlight which fell, every so often, between the faded curtains of the leaves. But now the trees began to look like ice-slicked skeletons again, and the air was chill. She would have shivered, had she felt it.

Carola sniffed the wind.

It had an unfamiliar scent tonight. Something fleet, almost barren, which yet refused to dissipate on further consideration. Like candle-wax, left to drip in a dark place for longer than was really wise. Or a rust-pitted blade, unsheathed at last. Like old blood.

It stank of foxes run to earth.

It stank like rebirth.

And once more, the pull:

. . . something . . .

The gaunt moon broke over the highest leaves and hung there, half-eaten by its own topography. It cast a finger to the north.

Carola followed it, and found a city crouching there against the ridge. It was a sign, of sorts.

Well, then.

Gathering her shroud about her, she set her feet toward it, and let them have their will.

* * *

The city was in fact a town, and that only loosely: More like an inhabited boil, allowed to flourish—by the surgeon's disinterest—under the shadow of the knife. It lay heaped haphazardly together, a mess of gables, chimneys and uneven stoops. Stone, wood, shingles, slate and mud. Fear ate at every table.

The town was old. No one remembered its name. And no one could even dare to guess whether it predated the castle in whose shadow it squatted.

A long shadow. Very dark. And very cold.

* * *

Walking swiftly, Carola crossed the bridge without a backward glance. Stones slipped beneath her stride. Thorns, provoked by her presence, reached down to pluck at her hair. Her eyes were open, her thoughts absent.

Something.

In her mind, a door swung slowly open on a stone room, floor strewn with rushes. Its windows stood tall and narrow, empty against the wind. From the fireplace, a knot of driftwood spilled shifting light. And in front of it, an iron chair. A man, speaking:

We are noble, daughter. God's favored servants. Our acts are His will made flesh. A hard thing to serve, truly, but harder thing still to truly rule—to know, to will, to dare, and to keep silent.

His eyes were grey.

And you. To you, the hardest task of all . . .

She saw the cancer which was to kill him rising in his throat like a black tide.

. . . to marry well, or well as may be. And to rule, despite it.

The moon went out, like a lamp. And when Carola found she could see again, nothing remained but the blue-black road, the horizon, and a mouthful of salt.

* * *

Here under the mountain, the wolves were more than seasonal rumors. They ran two by two, remorseless, through ditch and over stile into the fallow farm beyond. A scarecrow watched them pass, withholding comment. Moments after, the first flakes of snow began to fall. The wolves killed quickly and fled, mouths full of meat, before the moon had time to blink at their efforts.

But they veered at the skirts of the forest, sensing something with whiter teeth than their own was already on its way.

* * *

As Carola reached the last tree, the hunger took her. It set her bones aflame and left her burning, jack-knifed into the dirt. She rolled and howled, scrabbling, beneath its weight. It ate her heart and mind in one gulp, then settled down to chew. She bit the loam and drooled earth, teeth black with rotten leaves. Her hair became knives, her eyes coals, and there was nothing to be done at all but suffer.

Then, as suddenly, it let her go.

She looked up from where she knelt, panting. Over the nearest fence, all grain had turned to mush, and webs obscured the farmhouse's open door.

She dragged herself upright, and went on.

Carola followed the farm's wall around to what had once been a garden. A few crab-apples still dangled, higher than it was worth the while to climb. Beneath the bark, a faint chitter of grubs. Beneath the earth, worms.

And under the trees, an old man.

He stood with his back to Carola, looking down at a raw little patch of earth. In one hand, he held flowers. And the sight of him made Carola pause in mid-step, confused, because—

—he was haloed. Head, arms, legs, and spine all ran with a light the dull folds of his clothes could muffle but not contain. It spilled over his collar, blazed against the sky. It set the tree's bark shimmering with his hair's heat. The wind licked his bouquet apart, petal by petal, and the man stared on, oblivious.

He smelled of ecstasy.

Carola's empty stomach clenched, and growled. She shifted from one foot to another. Something broke beneath her heel.

The old man turned, and saw her. Her face—or his recognition of it, rather—made him sway back a pace, knees buckling slightly. The flowers fell from his hand, scattering.

Carola's eyes met his, and held.

"You," he said. "Oh, yes. Oh, you."

She watched, too detached to be wary, as he fumbled with the neck of his shirt, ripping the ties apart. Beneath, a curve of throat exposed itself, sweet and slightly pulsing. She felt a note run through her at the sight, needle-sharp and thrumming; the first phrase of an old tune, once learned under duress, but never forgotten.

Carola felt her lips curl back, ready to sing.

The old man smiled up at her, bleary eyes half-frantic.

"You remember me," he said. "Remember?"

And a flush lit the skin over his jugular, drawing her close, warming her like a flame's stir under the screen of a quick-lit lantern.

She approached him on tip-toe—he was so much taller than she, after all, though drooping now toward her like a sapling in a high, cold wind. One hand went to his cheek, the other slipping to cup the base of his skull, and she felt her nails resharpen themselves at the touch of him. His warmth. His smell. The beat and tick of his breath. All of that. All. Until—

"Ah yes, my Lady, yes," he hissed as she bore him back, as she fastened on him without mercy (though none was asked for)—as fresh blood washed the old cud from her back teeth, and the moon irised shut in that one hot jet like a burning rose.

* * *

Slowly, then, her eyes cleared. She was full again, quite stuffed sane. And it came to her that she knew this corpse, this ruined, elderly thing; that he had once been captain of her wedding guard—back when he was young

THE WORM IN EVERY HEART

and fine, that was, before prolonged submersion in the night had left him too crazed to do anything but cry aloud for his own death, and hug it close enough to kiss when it finally deigned to answer his call.

Carola glanced down at the patch of earth he'd wept by—the *grave*, word coming easy to her tongue—and saw with utter clarity a small, black stone, hidden in a covey of rotten bracken laced with dead moss, twisted by the cold into a spiky crown stiff with old spiderwebs. Where its shadow fell, the grass withered. And on it, in deeply-cut letters etched with rain—was her name.

CAROLA DE GUILDHADE.

She crouched there in her shroud, atop the ex-captain, frozen by the sight of it.

TAKEN TOO SOON.

Abruptly, something blocked her throat, curdling as she tried to swallow. It took her a long moment to realize—

No, not death. Never death. Never again.

—it was a laugh.

Because it was all coming back now. Like a jet of bile. Hot and scalding and virulent. And it was everywhere, burning her right down to the core. If she scrubbed for a thousand years it would still cling to the bone, marrow-deep, just out of reach. No shred of peace left to ease the passage, only the squall and the tearing. Christ Jesus yes, it was all coming back now, everything.

And how could she have ever thought it worse to have forgotten?

Whereupon she let herself arch back, feeling all her vertebrae wrench together at once, as the howl twisted up from her cold guts through her still, still heart, and further.

Out in one rush, to scald the stars.

* * *

Most of the castle had fallen away with neglect and disuse over the years, until only the tower still remained stable, unhindered by any sense of its own mortality. From its peak, blue fire lit the walls of a five-walled room.

At length, a hand drew the drapes aside, and thrust a dagger through the frame to keep them open.

Then the room's sole occupant gathered up his cards, and sat down next to it. To wait.

* * *

Carola de Guildhade, Lady of Raum.

The land was hers, to rule and serve. And she was the land's. So it had been for every eldest child to bear her family's name, time and beyond—since Bastard William had first breached England's coast, with iron and fire and God's holy Word.

A cold place, this inheritance of hers: Distant and small, but subject only to God and king. Raum stayed strong, always, as its lord was strong. To rule as child was one thing. It was necessity, made custom by constant threat. Threat of war, or quick successions. Of witchcraft, plague and poison.

But to rule as woman—required a husband.

"You are the land," old Bede reminded her. The threshing fires cast a bloody shadow on his face, turning—for a flicker—his cataracts yellow.

"I know what I am," she said. Softly.

"The land is yours, and you are the land's. If it wither, you pine and die. This all men know." He put one hand to his chest, rummaging in his robes, as if in search of his heart. "But if you be fruitful—"

"Say then that I marry, priest," she said. "Say I bear children. To who, their fathering?"

So Bede brought out the letter of courtship, still warm from his skin, on clean parchment in a firm, red pen. From a knight of great name and little purse, with a hunger for speedy marriage. And three months later, mounted and jewelled, she had taken the flowery crown from Bede's hands and turned it a long moment in her own, as if she'd never seen one so close.

"Shrive me, priest," she said. "I go now to battle."

"Only to woman's true work, my daughter, as God deems both right and pleasant."

Behind her, a young castrato scuffed the earth nervously with the toe of his shoe. The clouds hung waiting, air sweet with bees.

"Priest," she said, at length. "I pray you, keep well."

And put on the crown.

And rode away.

Carola shook her head, sharply. The world fell back into place with a sigh.

But the land is dead, she thought. My people fear me as damnation. And I—do not recall—my marriage night.

To her right, from town, came a distant music. The moon was waning. Above the trees, the castle's battlements stood suddenly plain against the lightening sky. But the tower room shone brighter and the road ran to an open gate, agape and lockless in the gloom.

Carola, unaware of her own movements, took up her train.

Someone keeps a lamp for me, she thought. Someone knows I am woken.

And her smile unsheathed again, unbidden. Teeth white as salt.

He shall not go unanswered.

* * *

It was almost dawn. A flush grew in the sky's far corner. Purple, then plum. Then red.

Far below, golden thread began to rim the ragged crenellations.

* * *

Footsteps in the great hall. Skirts in hand, Carola passed the cracked and silent fireplace, leaving a trail of dust. Tapestries flapped in the wind. Behind the great chair, two ravens perched on a slain knight's skull still fought over his remaining eye. Owls rose, shrieking, from the rafters. Carola ignored them, setting foot instead to the tower steps.

One, then another, and so on—up, higher and higher, into the coming dawn. Until the clouds were level with her knees. Until her chest rasped and burnt. Until—

—a door sprang up before her.

She paused for a moment, pressing her throat.

No lock left to open with a touch. It merely hung, rust-slicked ring poised for pulling. Between jamb and wall lolled a strip of room, widening with each new breeze. And—inside that room—a light, pale as a lit tuber, flickering at the table's head. Five grey candles, of uneven size, bases melted together?

Behind her, a voice:

"No. Look closer, Lady."

And the candles shrivelled, twisted. Grew nails. Became, at last, a grisly trophy shivering at the light's core—a mummified hand, bleak with flame.

The Hand of Glory.

"It makes the living sleep," said the voice, amused by its own expertise.

Nearer now. "And, as I long suspected—the dead wake."

Almost within reach.

But Carola stood still, thinking: Let him come to me, if he dares.

"Oh, but I do."

And Carola spun—

—to find him, smiling, at her elbow.

* * *

Down in the valley, dawn broke now in earnest, chasing crows from the frozen shreds of the wolves' kill. Townspeople began, tentatively, to unbar their doors.

* * *

But Carola and her husband stood—still as only the dead can stand—at either end of the five-sided room, and watched each other closely. The room was hung with purple from roof to floor, windows lost under a weight of velvet soft enough to muffle the world's scream to a dull hum, thick enough to shut out even the sun. Against this backdrop, Carola's husband shone like leprosy, toying with his dagger. His eyes were green, like cut church glass; his teeth, porcelain.

"Well met, truly, after so long an absence." He said, bowing. "Will my Lady sit?"

Carola did not reply.

"It seems my Lady prefers to stand," her husband told the walls. "And to stare." A pause. "Am I so different, then?"

"Not at all."

His brows raised. "She speaks! An honor surely worth a few years of anticipation."

Carola swayed, abruptly, and sat. The curtains stirred at her movement, dust spilling, to wake a handful of moths nesting near their base.

"A—few—?"

The moths hovered, caught, about the Hand. Its corona picked golden scales from their wings.

"Fifty, to judge aright," he replied. "Your pardon."

At his gesture, the moths veered too far in, crisped and fell together, twitching.

"There was no need for that," Carola said.

Her husband merely smiled.

"Hunger without need," he said. "And power without conscience; yes. But a man must hold true to his own nature, must he not?" Softer: "Or a woman."

As he spoke, Carola found her teeth had begun to ache once more. She rubbed at the corner of her mouth, sensing a stain.

"You cheated me," she said, at length.

"I? Never."

Then, mildly:

"My Lady, you do me wrong. And let me be your mirror in this—a fair bargain, since I promise you'll have no other." He rose, gracefully. "You see your fields fallow and your people craven, and blame me for it. But look you—'tis *your* castle shunned, *your* name taken in vain and prayed against in hope of God's protection."

He gestured again, making the dead moths skitter in the Hand's shadow.

"*I* am entirely innocent in this matter. My only crime is to have kept your marriage bed warm while waiting, these many long years, on your late return."

Carola examined her hands, closely, in the wavering light. Saw—as if for the first time—the broken nails, black with grave-dirt and old flesh. Saw how the skin drowned in its own whiteness, eaten from within by immortality. She ran her tongue reflectively across her teeth, drawing blood.

And raised her head at last, voice level—

"You are noble."

"As you yourself."

"Had you—land of your own?"

A flicker, at the corner of one eye. Just a flicker.

"Once," he said. "But that was long ago."

"And did no one ever teach you our duty? To serve those who serve us, or be unworthy of their love and our estate?" She stood now, flayed toes digging the stone like claws. "All that I have, I owe to them. This I promised."

Nose to nose with him, her voice rose to a thin shriek: "And you—*you have made me break my word.*"

He held fast and met her, stare for stare.

"You were *born* to this, Lady," he said. "Dead or alive—hunter, to their prey. What matter whether they love or fear, so long as you rule?"

"To rule, yes. And to protect. From beasts such as you."

A red light came into her husband's smile.

"Listen now, and be silent," he said. "You are the merest shadow of what you were. You are dead. You are alone. Together, we might take this land and everything beyond—if we are quick, and discreet. We may even love each other, in the end. But leave me, knowing nothing, and fear will dog you forever. Your prey will turn on you, and hunt you back into the grave."

And he brought her face to his, coming even closer.

"You are nothing," he whispered. "You *have* nothing. Nothing but me."

Carola felt behind her, eyes on his, along the curtain and the wall beneath it. Felt until she found her hold—

"Well, then," she said. "Let us to our union—husband."

—and twisted aside, ripping the curtain open, flat to the wall as the sun came washing over him in a hot, gold wave. She held rigid, self-blinded, until his screams turned to gurgles.

By sunset, there was nothing left but ash.

* * *

Dark crept in near supper-time, leeching the sky of every color but black. A cold wind blew in from the marshes. Flakes of snow lit and tumbled on its wake, like spindrift. Under the trees, assignations of long standing were kept and made again. Here a fire burned, and naked men and women danced back to back, as a goat in human clothes marked time. Here the Unkind Court rode in their finery, lances garnished with skulls, to hunt a mourning thing forever across the land-scape of a thousand dreams. Here the wolves slunk anew from their lair, bound for yet another farm.

And here the captain's grieving woman, finding her husband dead by Carola's uprooted grave, cut her throat with the rusted blade of his pike.

Carola sat in state at the tower's top, ashes blowing about her feet. Behind her, the Hand of Glory still burned. She had turned her chair to face the open window.

And all this is mine, she thought. Everything.

(And nothing.)

The sky dimmed further. A lidless moon rose and stared, without pity, down upon Carola's victory. Carola stared back . . .

For whatever else befalls, I am still Raum.

. . . as a tear of blood, unheeded, made its slow way down her cheek.

SENT DOWN

. . . that this, too, was one of the dark places of the earth.
          —Jack Conrad.

Divius Arcturus Martialis' bladder woke him, without dignity, well before dawn. Inside the tent an exported slice of Rome lay dozing, all shifting armor-clink and sour-stale sweat: Torc-burnt necks hidden beneath tarnished Medusa-head breastplates, Legionnaires' badges muffled in sweat-stiff furs, hides, woolen cloaks. The ragged remains of a "cohort" cobbled together from Northumbrian numeri, Romano-Briton infantry recruits trained to fight their own in the service of an Empire too cheap to reinforce their own crude weaponry with more than a used gladius each—an Empire which once took their loyalty for granted, but now barely acknowledged their existence. *Arcturus'* cohort, for all that was worth; not much, nowadays, plainest of plain truth be told. Less, and less . . .

      . . . and less.

Outside, meanwhile, Northumbria itself still waited: Slate-grey on black punctuated by intermittent salt-white flare of scraped-bare quartz turf-bed, chalk cliffs grey with fresh snow, darkness still pooled in their open cracks like oil on weather-waxed hide. Wet mist eddying in on every side, erasing the lightening sky.

This godless, gods-full place. This land where even shadows cast shadows.

Arcturus barely had words enough to tell how he had come to hate it.

160

Pausing by the foot of his standard, he shifted his kilt to empty himself, and watched a contemptuous curl of steam rise from the resultant puddle. His stomach reminded him just how far the village they had last taken booty from now lay behind them, even as he tried to shock it silent with a quick, reflexive curse, a half-attempted prayer—

Mars Ultor, war's Avenger, succor me. Look favorably on your faithful servitor. Ancestors, hold me up. Make me able to do what I must, for my men. For my own name's sake.

Call and response, automatic as breath: *Roma Invicta, fraterni!*

(*Roma Aeterna, magistere!*)

But this was no Roma, nor they Romans, for all their rapt devotion to their conquerors' ideals. This was elsewhere, beyond Empire's reach, beyond even the shadow of the Wall itself. Roadless ruin and darkness. Trackless waste.

Arcturus felt the wet cold—everpresent, never-escapable—begin to seep up through his bones towards his heart, and shrugged his wolf-skins closer. He turned back for the fire-pit, veering to where the seer-girl lay tethered at its outermost edge: Pale and still, her fine-boned wrists and ankles strung with gut, under a smoky blanket of ash-blackened spindrift.

She had refused to tell her tribe's true name—or her own, for that matter. They had dragged her by her pale hair from a stone beehive in that last village, a skull-clogged dirt-trap full of blood-mess and hanging herbs that gave a heavy, fragrant smoke when Lucian—Arcturus' numericus second, native-born himself, though better-tamed than most—fired them with his torch, almost as an afterthought.

'Tis sacred, that's what, he had said, his patois-inflected Latin even harder than usual to understand, as he rooted through the debris with the butt of his spear. *A holy place for gods to speak through—through here, through . . .*

Pointing: *. . . her.*

Our gods? Arcturus had asked. Only to see Lucian give an all-purpose shrug, his blue-tattooed cheeks glistening in the herbs' light. And reply, without much (apparent) interest—

. . . gods.

The girl bore similar marks, as they all did—even Arcturus, for all that he kept his Legionnaire's SPQR hidden beneath one shoulderplate: Light wounds rubbed with ash or woad, a charcoaled thread sewn beneath the skin and left to heal, uncleaned; permanent grey-blue lines bracketing the line of the girl's nose, circling out over her nostrils to spiral beneath her eyes.

Those pale, pale eyes.

Arcturus reached down and shook her roughly, by one nude shoulder—cold white skin, dappled with dew. "Do you live yet, barbarian?" he asked, slitting her hands apart. "Come back to me now, before I take mind to do your body some injury."

A long shiver took her, from heels to head. She bent back, bow-taut: Damp skin flushing like a caught eel's, as her absent spirit poured back into her. Her "fetch", Lucian had termed it.

We've the corpse, but she goes out anyroad, coming to call. She's sent for by those she serves, and 'tis her fetch what answers.

Her daimon, you mean? Her soul? A stolid, minimal shrug. *Why call it 'fetch', if that's all?*

Lucian laughed, shortly. *Ask it tha'self, magistere. When it comes to FETCH thee.*

In Roma, as Arcturus remembered, the gods only spoke when spoken *to*. Oracular justification of policy. Reward for public service. Deities were twenty a sesterce, the Pantheon stuffed to bursting with them: Borrowed, stolen, made up fresh from scratch to suit every purpose under heaven.

This one, though—she might look young in the body, this one, but she was sworn to old gods indeed. He had seen them look from her eyes, and laugh at him; felt their hands on him directly, now and always, more intimate than rape. Their invisible touch steering him here and there . . . softer, and more full of febrile activity, than a dead dog's belly by any given paved, spear-straight, Roman-laid road's side.

It was no great mystery, to loose your soul and bid it do secret business. There were witches in Roma, too.

Opening her eyes, now, as she rubbed—weakly—at her bruise-banded wrists: Faint rim of bloodshot cilia, fire-caught iris pale as dirty snow. Whispering—

"She hears tha, Roman."

"Arcturus."

"A, Roman. Tha."

"Speak *true* Latin, slut," he ordered her, yet again, freeing her feet likewise. Then: "Did you see our path?"

"A, Roman. She sees."

"You'll show us where it leads, then—and truly, understand? Or I'll cut your cords."

"She shows tha, a. As She shows she."

"As . . . your goddess . . . shows *you*?"

"A, Roman. 'Tis lore-ful, this. She takes she out-body, into dream. Sends she down."

"Down where?"

The girl gave him a grin—bloody lip-twist, complete with rim of broken teeth. All at once, Arcturus wanted to shove his tongue between them and let her bite down, abrade him with every (currently) hidden part of her filthy body. Watched as she reached up under her sodden twill skirt and rummaged, then drew her hand out and sketched a spiral in her opposite palm: Wet red, dark against her dirty grey-white skin. Juice of her split fruit, her open wound.

He knew it should have repulsed him; knew it didn't. And tried, with all his strength—

(faintest of all faint hopes)

—never to allow himself to wonder, explicitly . . . why.

"Sent down," she repeated. "Where was, is, will be. She sends she. *Shows* she."

"And then *you* show *me*."

"A-true, Roman."

"Arcturus. My name, girl: Say it." She looked at him. "*Say* it."

"A . . . rrr . . ."

(a *ha*, you savage bitch)

" . . . rrrRoman."

He took her again that very night, as they'd both known he would, for all he'd sworn not to. Lucian kept guard, stirring the fire; the others watched hungrily, from a discreet distance. Arcturus and his nameless seer lay together in the shadow of a chalk-cliff, meanwhile—under the empty skeletal gaze of some flat, long-jawed, long-dead beast-fish: A shark from ancient times, doomed to forever swim the dead sea of this rock's rain-slimed face. Sharp grin agape, ribs scattered and splayed, spine unstrung like a harlot's snapped necklace . . .

She tried to slip away from him in the midst of it, to send herself down that wet red spiral, but he kept her anchored with his prick—dug deep enough to force her back, and clutched her to him as they arrived together. When they finally severed, he glanced down to see himself painted similarly red from glans to thatch, dripping; blood sleeked the insides of her thighs like open wings, a bird crushed in mid-flight. Lips, widespread, on a second, deeper mouth.

And oh, but this was an awful place he'd come to at the end of all his ambitions, full of cold and dread. A place where the gods were bloody as Tarsan Diana, secret as Mithras, strange as Isis and unknowable—in the end—as the Jew heretics' one-god. A place where the land melted and fell away to mist, where people melted and fell away with it. Where a blue-cheeked girl had only to cast him one glance under her too-pale lashes for him to feel himself surge like the sea against his leather kilt, like rot in an unclean wound.

Dragging him down into herself, part by part: The soles of her bare feet, rinded with callus. Her cracked, black-rimmed nails. Her sly, colorless eyes, washed empty with strange gods' thoughts. Her bloody, red-lipped core.

Witchery. Necromancy. The road to Hades, or whatever name this girl—and Lucian—had for their particular version of Hell eternal.

This much Arcturus still knew: In Greece, in Roma—here, even—the dead drank blood, always. No matter *where* you called them from.

* * *

A week earlier, then, back at the Wall: Arcturus and his Tribune, immersed to their waists in the mineral-green, stone-warmed main tank of their home-fort's cramped lavarium. A reward for good service, supposedly—though far less so in practice than in theory, what with extended field duty amongst barbarians seemingly having left Arcturus rendered permanently uncomfortable even in the midst of most "civilized" comforts. Still, the bath's waters did hide most of his worst scars, aside from those which swam pale and knotted as mating sea-snakes just beneath the surface.

"If the Tribune might care to bring such a tedious matter back to mind, momentarily," Arcturus had begun, eking his words out between grit teeth, "the fact does remain, however annoying and irrelevant—"

"—that 'your' numeri still haven't been paid." The Tribune barely bothered to meet Arcturus' eyes, gesturing instead at the nearest slave, who came running with scraper at the ready. "Yes, Centurion, I do recall it. But really: What would they do with good Roman coin, those savages? They barter with each other for everything they need. A pig here, a woman there . . . "

"Then buy them something to barter *with*, if you don't want them thinking they're Citizens anymore. Or would you prefer to prove the Empire only honors its promises when it stands to gain something by doing so?"

Brave words, albeit foolish. To which the Tribune merely gave a dry smile, replying:

"But it's that very lesson they must learn sometime, Arcturus. Is it not?" *Especially now.*

"Your feeling for them does you credit. Still, facts must be faced—where Caesar speaks, we answer. And Caesar wants us gone from here, at least for the moment."

"Do they know that?"

"Not unless you tell them. Which I . . . of course . . . order you not to." (*Typical.*)

Arcturus strove to keep his digust well-hid, though probably not as much so as might have been best to his advantage; the Tribune's shrewd glance seemed to grow ever-colder as the bath progressed through its ritual phases: Soaking, slathering, scraping—steamed and salted like vegetables for the cooking, in this hubristic coccoon of pseudo-Mediterranean heat. By the time Arcturus stepped back out into the usual Northumbrian light drizzle of oncreeping dusk, an artificially hot fog rose from his pores to greet the night; the joints of his carapace, smoking like an ill-banked fire wherever his wolf-skins didn't quite reach.

Lucian fell into lock-step beside him as he broached the hill, glancing down at the freshly-polished Medusa-head on his commanding officer's breastplate. Venturing, at last: "Some rare thing, she, wi' such teeth and snakes. Thy guardian, is't?"

"Guardian?"

"Ay, magistere—a spirit set to help an' hold thee, wherever men-place and gods-place cross over. Same as I was sent t'find, up hill wi' no food 'till I come back calling on animal-brother as my own guardian, when first I grew a man."

"And did you?"

A gap-toothed grin. "As all did, sure. Had to, we wanted ever shuck of our milk-names."

"Romans don't believe in spirits."

"What, then?"

"Ancestors. Familial duty, fides. Household lares and penates."

Arcturus touched the Medusa's fierce grimace with two equally hilt-callused fingers, lightly. "She's a monster, no Goddess—her eyes turn men to stone. A nightmare, to strike fear in our enemies' hearts."

"Ah. Lore-ful too, that."

Lucian sounded approving; the corners of his pale eyes seemed to have lifted slightly, though Arcturus most-times found it almost impossible to tell what his mouth might or might not actually be doing, under that drooping moustache. It reminded him, all at once, of a passage from Diodorus Siculus concerning the Gauls: Their savage impenetrability, slaughtering both themselves and everyone else they came across in the pious service of gods so anathemic-sacred their names were considered better forgotten than prayed to.

"When their enemies fall," Siculus had written, "they cut off their heads and fasten them about the necks of their horses; and turning over to their attendants the arms of their opponents, all covered with blood, they carry the heads off as booty, singing a paean over them and striking up a song of victory, and these first-fruits of victory they fasten by nails upon their houses, just as men do, in certain kinds of hunting, with the heads of wild beasts they have mastered.

"The heads of the most distinguished enemies they enbalm in cedar-oil and carefully preserve in a chest, and these they exhibit to strangers, gravely maintaining that in exchange for this head some one of their ancestors, or their father, or the man himself, refused the offer of a great sum of money. And some men among them, we are told, boast that they have not accepted an equal weight of gold for the head they show, displaying a barbarous sort of greatness of soul; for not to sell that which constitutes a witness and proof of one's valor is a noble thing . . . "

Arcturus wondered how many heads Lucian's father might have had, in his press—whether he would have wanted Arcturus' head there, or turned down good money for it, if asked. Not to mention how many Lucian would like to have kept in his own, were the rules of conduct for a soldier of the Empire only lax enough to allow him such trophies.

By the fire, his cohort sat swapping food and stories: Roast dog, rambling tales of dead men boiled back to life in gigantic silver cauldrons and hags riding sleepers like horses, sucking the breath from their mouths along with their dreams. Arcturus hovered nearby, impatient, while Lucian hunkered down calm as ever by his feet, cleaning his weapons; the talk ebbed back and forth, only half in Latin. The rest was that same impenetrable language of shrrs and clicks Arcturus had long sinced ceased striving to decipher, a bird-speech of near-whispers and mournful, sussurant, desolate cries—hungry as the sounds the dead must make, when you cut them a ditch for the requisite sacrifice's honey-laced blood to pour into.

I will never truly understand them, he found himself thinking, hardly for the first time. But the plain fact of it suddenly seemed to rattle inside his ribcage like a thrown stone under his armor, gallingly unsought: Alien now and always, no matter how he might damage his career by fighting for their best interests, his complicit Roman flesh forever marked by the thumbprints of their mutual oppressors. Doomed to remain nothing more or less than one more nameless grey shade on Pluto's riverbank, stranded 'till time's end just outside the circle of light and safety and acceptance . . .

But: Two of them were arguing about something, their raised voices once more abruptly comprehensible; Arcturus turned slightly, listening.

" . . . something as them will die for, thus well worth the taking: Cairn-gorms, might be, we follow pass-road under Wall back where it take us . . . "

"Nay, fool. Art cairn-*stones* they horde only, they up there; one for each corpse, fast as *those* kill each other."

To Lucian, under his breath: "Cairn-gorms?"

Lucian didn't look up. "White water-clear stones, magistere, the kind Tribune pays best for. Same's we find in the fay-hills sometimes, in graves of them come before—'fore Roma, 'fore us'n. Those as dyed their bones red wi' clay, so dead wouldn't come seeking blood from they still left alive."

"Diamonds?" No, for those came from Africa—white quartz, perhaps; equally precious, in some quarters. "The sort of treasure they'd kill to protect, in any event."

"Like as be." Another circuit of the gladius' blade, salve-skin in hand. "Or not."

Well.

(That'd be a fine bonus indeed to go with their marching orders, now Roma stood officially poised—sooner or later, but certainly, and without much regret—to toss all Britain aside like some worn-through sandal.)

"And who do they discuss, here—what tribe, exactly?" He asked Lucian, as casually as possible. "The Ericii?"

Without even a shred or irony: "Nay, magistere. Those as they have no Roman names, to speak of."

Nor need of any, Arcturus didn't doubt, since Roma's influence had ebbed so low. Once tribes had flocked to be re-titled, but some . . . like these . . . had never even seen a Roman, in the true flesh. Which left them unprepared against Roma-trained attackers, in their blissful pagan ignorance—and none too likely to complain of ill-treatment at the local garrison afterwards, either.

If Roma abandons us, he found himself thinking—such heresy! And yet the sky did not crack nor lightning fall, amongst the constant fine grey spray of mist—we'll just have to look out for ourselves.

The idea, however comfortless, was also oddly freeing: An uncharted road, leading nowhere in particular. Anywhere.

Everywhere.

"With no Roman ties, we'd be a mystery to them," he mused, aloud.

Lucian nodded, slightly. "Aye, magistere. Those are full of mysteries, they."

* * *

Loyalties and betrayals; they shifted without warning like Etna's sides during an eruption, like his family villa's garden tiles during an earthquake. To the Britons, Arcturus knew, abandoning or denying one's god was an offense worthy of triple death, burial at bog, being sunk nude and nameless beneath the peat's watery surface—and Caesar, living Roman godhead, had long been his primary deity of choice. But the world was changing, packed full of fresh new gods to choose from: Even crucified criminals might be worshipped, if only their adherents claimed miracles performed in their name. Executed proselytes-turned-terrorists, discredited philosophers and politicians, martyrs and dupes of all stripes or principles; oh, and monsters too, without question. For one man's monster is always another's god, and vice versa . . . in the very oldest, truest sense of that old, true, quintessentially Roman phrase.

Meanwhile, the cohort kept on moving upwards, always upwards—past lakes and bracken, past more chalk-faced cliffs, past inscriptions on water-slicked rocks which meant nothing to Arcturus, but mimicked perfectly the ones on his captive seer-girl's skin: Faint with age, cut aeons ago and faded abrasion-shallow. She made sure to point them out to anyone who'd look, smiling sly and silent, while the numeri around her blanched.

The fog kept on increasing, and the birds—ravens, particularly—seemed to watch them from a safe distance. None of the remaining cohort bothered to speak Latin anymore, and their barbarian words piled on top of Arcturus like stones; he pored over the lilt and hiss of them in his head, at nights, whenever the girl went slack beneath him again. But study brought no relief: Every morning, they woke to find yet more men fled in the night, blending back into the hills—some taking the heads of their more Romanized companions with them, when they went. As though they needed gifts to placate their nameless Goddess, to show they understood the true depth of their own former faithlessness.

According to Lucian, the Celts thought in threes, not twos: Black, white and grey. Always an overlap where rules reversed themselves, or ceased to apply.

"It's good, then."

"Ofttimes. But na always."

"Then it's bad."

"Na *always*, magistere."

Neither wholly good nor bad, but never neutral. Energy, forth and back, circular and widdershins. The Old Sow, birthing her farrow to eat them and throw them up again anew, irrigating the world with their blood . . . and her shit.

It simply IS.

These gods of theirs: Lucian's, the seer-girl's, the rest of the cohort's. Old and cold as these mud-glistening hills, their faces always hidden, names never spoken aloud—as much Mysteries as those played out in the same cthonic caves Arcturus' mater had frequented yearly, baring her throat and arse before Dionysian Bacchus in Ariadne-Semele's guise. Half-remembered smells from such revels still overtook him easily, even now; the drunken retch of fermented honey under cleaner tang of crushed grape-leaves, the stink-hot gush of warm sacrificial entrails into a sunken stone escharon where some more recent child-intiate waited, shivering, to be reborn into a fresh new world of divine provenance and ecstasy.

Symbols and patterns repeated everywhere, like dross from the same common mold. Mithras killed the bull, too, as Arcturus learned when he joined the Legion's ranks. Isis wore a cow's head. Zeus turned poor Io into a heifer and let Hera chase her across whole continents, all to preserve his godly reputation from (verifiable) charges of philandering. The tribes of

169

Judah killed bulls, Baal's emblem, to praise their One-God for wresting the land they squatted on from the Rain-bringer's descendants.

And Roma scooped the whole horde up, meanwhile—sat them alongside each other and warned them to behave themselves, if they didn't want to be forgotten. Offered worshippers for support, a fair enough bargain, especially in the face of looming extinction. Romans saw, and treated, "the gods" as mere constructs, political concepts discarded when no longer useful: I acknowledge your gods, therefore you acknowledge my gods, and thus we forge an agreement from which we may both benefit and build on. Simple, logical. Simply logic.

But the seer-girl's absent, silent She, capital S to her far more humble version—

(an aspect, at least, of the same Goddess whose title Lucian feared to speak aloud? Perhaps. Very *much* perhaps)

—was far too alien to be bargained with in this manner.

In the village, mid-raid—and dragging the girl stiff-legged behind him all the way, with one hand knit deep in the dirt-dreaded quills of her pale hair—Arcturus had dropped his crested helmet in the very heart of a set hut-fire before moving on, nodding at those numeri who noticed to do the same; his plan, as he well knew, had no hope of working unless those crouching safe back at the Wall truly considered the entire cohort lost like one of Hadrian's Pict-bound legions. Yet it had seemed predestined for success, if the ease of that first engagement was anything to reckon by: Every step of it marked off, without even the slightest variance. Lay a trail and secure a guide, someone young or weak enough to be biddable, though rich in all the "lore" Lucian and his brothers judged necessary for such a journey . . .

Then he'd dodged around the slump and crumble of her former home, only to be confronted with a double arm-span's-width spiral carved through the turf behind it, right down to the chalk below—white furred with grey-green, touched here and there with red: Ochre, old blood. Both.

From behind him, an unplanned gladial side-swipe rang the bell of Arcturus' greave as the nearest numericus stopped dead, gasping, at the very sight of it.

"She!"

Arcturus stared, frowned. "Who?"

"*She*, magistere!"

"Give over, fool: There's no one *here*, soldier . . . "

But: "She-only, Roman," the girl had murmured, her warm breath puffing the clammy skin of his wrist; none but she herself grinning up at him, ragged teeth like chips of dirty ice, for which he'd split her lip with a single back-hand—too late to snap the stricken numericus from his stupor, as it turned out. For that, that exact, drawn-breath moment, had been when the fog came rolling down, at last.

And when it had washed away once more, hours later—retreating in dirty white waves, like some phantom tide—

—he'd found that a good third of "his" cohort had gone, along with it.

* * *

"Where are we now, Lucian?"

"Doubtful, magistere—the hills are tricksy, here-a-ways, and I've no dealings with these tribes, me."

"Do you think she leads us truly?"

"Truly as she might, that one."

Nearby, the seer-girl slept with her usual slack opacity, nails furrowing her palms. Arcturus had "forgotten" to hobble her, a more and more frequent occurence; she showed no signs of running any longer, slinking instead at Arcturus' elbow, that inevitable smile crimping her lips with secret—humor? Anticipation? Longtime proximity had failed to render him any more able to decipher her accent, let alone read her moods.

She had ceased to bleed, however, he had finally noticed. Unless one counted her rock-cut feet, printing snow and soil alike where she stepped in fresh, savage rust.

"The men seem quiet." At one of those unreadable shrugs: "Morale? They talk to you, still; you must have formed *some* opinion, by now . . . "

Lucian gave him a sidelong glance, considering. Then answered, reluctantly—

"They think, magistere . . . that we are moving into the land of the dead."

(With the unspoken coda, so obvious it *needed* no voicing: *Their* land of the dead, of course. Not yours.)

For even in this topsy-turvy country, Hades—and Tartarus, and the rest—remained safely *down*, not up.

That next morning, he woke hearing traces of conversation on the wind, quickly cut off as though they'd been talking about him while he slept. The cohort avoided his eyes, almost to a man. The girl caught his gaze, and winked.

To Lucian: "It won't be long now."

"Aye, magistere. Na long, surely."

"And they'll be pleased enough to have those stones, after all."

"Oh, certain."

Up, and up, and up yet once more into the gathering fog, by faint and winding no-paths: Tracks carved from chalk likewise, spiralling widder-shins, which crumbled precariously away beneath their sandals while the girl just skipped ahead, fleet and sure as any mountain-goat. Then a pause to rest by some uncharted lake's eddying side, where a sudden fall of sunlight more surprising than thunder or lightning dazzled them all with its brilliance—grey turned silver with reflected fire, illuminating water-droplets on the weeds and bracken, his own breastplate and greaves, the company's rapt faces all upturned as one towards the girl where she squatted in the icy shallows . . .

White circlet of light erupting from her head, transforming her. Blur-ring her blue-cheeked profile into a luminous, featureless oval, like she was some—

(*Goddess*)

—made manifest, flesh-bound yet transcendent, here on the soggy earth beside him.

And: *Who can tell how the Gods appear?* His mater's long-lost voice, cooing at his mind's ear. *They are Gods, after all—capricious, spiteful, quick to tempt and judge. As we might be as well, in their position.*

Blank, featureless. And yet, somewhere—somehow—he knew that smile was still there.

It was this last which touched him, hard and sharp, to the very quick. And thus he found himself bolt upright in mid-swing, his fist connecting hard with her jaw; saw her fall and his kick blend, the girl doubling into herself with a hurt little gasp, like any assaulted animal. Stopped only when his heel found the pulse of her neck and balanced there, panting—a precarious perch, what with his movement clumsily arrested mid-consummation—while his sole itched like ants in a wound to bear down hard and end this whole abortion of a "campaign" outright, the best and most controllable way he knew how . . .

"Calm thee, magistere!" Lucian cried, hand on Arcturus's elbow. But Arcturus shook him off, snapping:

"You've led us astray, slut—there's no cache here, just sheep and rain. And what did I promise if you betrayed us, do you recall it? *Do* you?"

Quiet: "A, Roman."

"How I'd cut your cords, that's right, and snap your neck for you too, if you've dared to play me false—do you understand me *now*, you Latin-less whore, or should I spell it out yet clearer? Barbarian!"

"A, she hears tha, a-true. She knows—"

Arcturus snorted. "Oh yes, so I've heard—far too many times to count, let alone believe. Then let Her tell me if you can't, and quickly, before I leave you no tongue to tell Her tales with: *Where is what we're seeking?*"

Leaning close, almost close enough to taste her gamy breath, while the toe of his sandal shifted to dig in hard just below her voicebox. Close enough to see her pale eyes flicker to him with one last wet flash, the tail-end spark of her earlier accidental deification: Blank, cold, silver. Impenetrable as mercury.

(Unnatural creature!)

"Look behind tha, Roman."

Behind, where the fog was already rolling away to disclose a cave's open mouth: Cracked chalk lips set in lichen-clad stone, bracketted by the same blue spirals as either pair of her own. And inside, a dropping off, a falling away; gentle but fatal, downwards into darkness.

A slope whose tilt struck the same angle—exactly—as the seer-girl's bloodied grin.

Lucian, always prepared, had already lit his lamp. Now he stepped forward, lifting it, to show the others where best to make their entrance. They slipped inside one by one, leaving he, Arcturus and the girl alone together.

And: One must keep to one's *fides*, Arcturus found himself thinking, automatic as drill. When a cohort steps so bravely into the very inmost heart of their former error, the very least their commander may do is to not hang back—not to show fear or hesitance, but discipline and consistency. To set an example.

To be *Roman*, without dispute, even in the face of all that is not—can never be—Roma. Not even if it wants to.

(If it *does*, indeed.)

Behind them—forgotten, for the moment—the girl was levering herself, shakily, to her feet again; Lucian handed his lamp on to the last man in and turned back, frowning, to see why his *magistere* was so slow in joining them.

"Wilt come?" he asked, finally. "'Tis an old-folk stopping-place, that's what; where they as chasing we kennel their goods under Goddess's protection, so can't stay out here, no-wise, with suchlike out to track us. But down-a-ways, in cave-heart, that's where we'll doubtless find what waits thee—"

The man meant his words to be comforting, Arcturus supposed, though their construction was anything but. For all his fine sentiments, however, he found himself locked fast right where he was: Eyes on the cave, unable to pry them free long enough to answer. Frozen core-deep in the knowledge that places such as this, legendarily, had always been what the route to *his* Land of the Dead was supposed to look like.

With more confidence than he felt: "Yes. Of course."

Lucian gave an odd little mouth-twist at that, neither happy nor disappointed—took the girl's dirty hand in his own equally filthy paw, with quite unnecessary delicacy, then moved aside to let her through.

"Lead on," he told her, rather than ordered; the girl just nodded, face set, impassive as ever.

But oh, Arcturus knew, that was never the way to deal with her, or any of her kind—closer to Lucian than he would ever be, in the final, most depressing analysis. Her with her bent head, her empty face, her lying, broke-toothed mouth: The least trustworthy guide he ever could possibly have picked to put his faith in, here beyond Wall and camp alike, not to mention that straight-sketched road-to-be which had taken him—along with those he led—away from it . . .

But this place had no roads at all, not that such as he or his former masters could travel. And when no place is paved, then everywhere is road—a mapless marsh of false turf over cold, wasting depths, where anything can happen.

The girl looked back at him, once, over Lucian's shoulder—an obvious challenge, albeit unspoken: See how your tamed dog comes to my whistle? Much like you, sniffing up under my skirt at all hours; you, always grinding my face into the dirt even while you dig grave-deep between my legs, so as not to risk catching your own fear reflected there.

A-true, Roman?

Not her voice, surely, so clear and plausible, another mocking echo within the confines of his increasingly-haunted head. But, perhaps—

—Hers?

Impossible to deny, either way, leaving him only two potential courses of action to pursue or discard; Arcturus tapped gladius-hilt to steady himself, and found it unyielding as ever. For though the Gods might be silent, yet his blade stayed sharp, his resolve firm—he would not be beaten, not now. Not even here.

So he followed her in, and down.

* * *

And now, down here in the deep, the dark . . . here in the Place of Skulls, the Goddess's own Grove, where meat hangs headless to ripen for her hogs, and the fruit of her worshippers' efforts lies everywhere in irregular, dun-glint, empty-socketted piles . . .

Down here near a rock pool lined with the same stones they've travelled so far to find, careless wealth heaped high and calcite dripping white in folds around its rim, a cruel blind eye surrounded by stalagmites carved so that stroking their ridges produces a weird, rasping kind of music—oh, and by a veritable forest of heads on sticks, too: Three or four to a spear each, some fresh, some mummified, their jawbones left flapping by sinew in the cave's black no-wind. Some yet recognizable, also, for all that the only light revealing them comes from Lucian's lamp's pitiful, guttering flame.

Cairn-gorms and "grove-stones", an equal treasure, equally sacred: Both taken in battle, as honor to the Goddess. Run the one through your fingers and they click wetly, soft as old bones. Raise the other to your ear and they whisper, like shells.

Here is where she struck him down with one blow, almost as though mimicking his attack in kind: Her small, single hand like a hammer, heavy enough to crush two planks together and make a crucifixion of them. Where she turned on him in full warp-spasm, the hero-halo breaking from her head to rend the darkness around them with an awful, pallid haze, her neck-muscles puffed and rigid like ropes, veins writhing up and down her naked limbs. Where her face first took on the glare and rictus it still wears, so utterly *other*—that of an actor's mask, the Oracle at Delphi, a Bacchante in full frenzy.

Maiden become mother become crone, become all three in one, all one in three: Proserpine, Hecate, the Gorgon on the shield. She become She, at long, long last.

As Lucian drops to his knees, gladius still in hand but drooping slack, she runs her hands together up the blade, then cups them; black blood fills the bowl of her locked palms and fingers, smoking hot. And Lucian bows his head to drink it greedily, lapping it from the source, staining his mouth and chin—then looks back down at Arcturus where he lies crushed to earth and grins for the first time ever, showing his teeth, unrecognizable. Irredeemable.

One of *them*, once more . . . and happy, in a way no Roman can ever have known him, to be so.

And: Lucian, he thinks, the hurt of it twisting inside him, worse even than the pain of her touch. Lucian, secundus, my right hand in peace and war. My friend.

Was it nothing but a lie from the very beginning, just some pleasant trick Arcturus worked on himself, all unknowing? Convincing himself the same things *he* felt might be glimpsed, now and then, in the Briton's melancholy gaze?

. . . *like as be, magistere. Like as be.*

(Or not.)

It's only now, with this madwoman's grip making his eyes sweat blood, that Arcturus recalls a slander once bandied about concerning another seer-girl, the Oracle at Delphi: That she—maiden, mother or crone, whoever she might have been at the time—was nothing more than a toy for politicians' aims or Emperors' decrees, half-mad and mumbling under the influence, evoking only the refuse of an empty mind whenever she yawned her jaws wide to admit "the God". That there was no *God* at work in Delphi at all and never had been, just whispers in the dark, murmurs in the sibyl's smoke-drunk ear; theatre, a peep-show, a circus. All sound and fury, mere ritual entertainment, for the idiot crowd's delight.

Would it be better to be killed that way, in outright massacre at the behest of human lunatics? Or at the hands of zealots, in the service of their whore-carried Goddess?

Whichever way truth lies, though, it won't matter, soon enough. Soon he'll be only another shade lapping at the blood-trough, another fluttering ghost on the Styx's tide, at *best*. And at worst—

In the cairns behind him—those he can glimpse, at least—the skulls are split, scooped, emptied. Which evidence suggests they mean to do the same to him, no doubt, before rising to greet the sky next morning; that cold grey sky, mist-hung, screwed down tight as any sarcophagus-lid. A tent with curtains slid and sewn shut, both, to hide a horde of red and dreadful doings.

Lucian, back on his feet, seems to cast him a vaguely pitying glance while the others hover close to hand, their weapons at the ready. Tells him, quiet, as they watch and wait—

"As is owed must be paid, magistere, that's what; as She tells us, reckon, or thy own Gods tell thee. What we owe, in turnabout, for all *thee* owes Her."

So it's as he suspects: They turned against him long ago, "his" whole cohort, perhaps before this cursed journey's very outset. Always seeing him not as a leader, a companion, not even as a fellow soldier in the service of strange and distant lords, but as sacrifice only—a Year King to be indulged and protected, steered fate-wards, before being torn apart to irrigate this awful land with his heart's last, waning spurts.

Well, so be it, then—what can't be cured must be endured. Let it never be said a son of Roma could not rouse himself to die bravely, no matter the field of battle.

And yet: May only poison grow where my blood falls, he thinks, vindictively. May my bones breed discord, like dragons' teeth. May my death curse you all, to your sons' sons' sons, as much and as surely as this end you plan curses *me* to wander nameless, without surcease, beyond the reach of anything I've known, or loved, or lost . . .

But here she is above him, her stiff hair rayed to frame a face whose own rigidity has started to blur, to soften. To settle once more towards those features he can still recall pressed to his in ecstasy, when the merest touch of her was enough to make him jolt and start in (seemingly) endless hunger.

He remembers her palm with its red-sketched spiral, closing about him in the dusk. Remembers his own lust with the same sick wrench as a wound long-healed, but once green with infection—the kind that takes a red-hot knife to seal and aches forever-after, especially in rainy weather.

"Divius Arcturus," she addresses him, in perfect Latin—and hikes up her skirts, all unashamed, to show him that place he faithfully hoped never to have to see again.

"Admire your work, Centurion: Her blood and yours have mixed. Maiden to mother, by your seed and my command. You will leave some small thing of yourself behind with us, after all."

"You," he says, mouth dry, and stops; swallows spit, and tries again. "You . . . are . . . *her* Goddess."

That *smile.* "Oh yes." And then, leaning close, rot-soft: " . . . yours, too."

Followed by that same voice, so persuasive, inside his narrowing mind:

For She is ALL in all, Roman—do you not know it for fact, truly, even now? All darkness. All mothers.

(*All* Goddesses.)

A flash, a dazzle, then a sudden plunge back to dimness and obscure, threatening motion: Lucian and his brethren stepping closer as her halo douses, blades in hand. Arcturus tries to appeal to Her, helplessly—but the Goddess is gone, leaving only the girl to cup her stomach, stroke his lips with hers. And whisper, with her more natural, broken voice restored:

"A, tha. Sleep tha, now. She has tha, Roman. She sends tha down. Sleep now, and wait 'till She bid she call tha name . . . "

The seer-girl slips her cold hands around Arcturus's waist. Slowly, carefully, she pronounces his name afresh—and stumbles over it, exactly as he always knew she would.

"Arc-tu-rus, tha'rt she's now, she—and She. Tha'rt She-own now, Roman-no-more. A-true."

Oh, Mars Ultor, Roma Aeterna. Roma, and all the Gods of Roma. Where have you allowed me to be taken? Where, *where* have you—

—*sent*—

—me?

(For perhaps all gods are conspirators, in truth. Perhaps *none* of them wish us well . . . or no single one, any more so than any other.)

The seer-girl, smiling: "Tha'rt spiral-end now, brave kill-king, trained and made to die well from tha name-day on; so She knew, when first set eye on tha. And so tha'rt here at last, such long time counting—sent here, by Her, to she. Sent . . . "

. . . down.

(*Down*, Roman.)

Nowhere else.

As though, in the end, there were anywhere else to go—

(Not here, at any rate.)

He can feel her fingers on his, rough and gentle; feels her sleek his hair the way one calms a fearful sheep on the altar's steps, that very same mild mixture of affection and regret. Knows himself at once a Citizen amongst savages and an animal amongst the elect, the two states of being balanced exactly, like Justice's scales.

And when the lamp falls, when Arcturus's eyes shut, when her lips brush his forehead one last time—now, then, here, there, everywhere—

—comes only darkness.

THE KINDLY ONES

In the beginning, chaos. From this rose sky, Uranus, and earth, Gaea. And Gaea loved Uranus, giving him many children, but the eldest of them he called monsters and exiled to her deepest depths. So Gaea conspired with her youngest child, Chronos, planning revenge. One day, while Uranus slept, Chronos fell upon him with a sickle and castrated him, throwing his severed testicles into the sea. From Uranus's spilled seed came Aphrodite, the goddess of sexual love, whose beauty sowed similar discord between the children of Chronos until time's end.

Also fell three drops of Uranus's blood, from which sprang—other things.

But this is just a story.

* * *

Monday was slow. Rain began in the early morning, still going strong a little after dawn, when Mavis woke. She made herself a cup of tea and studied wallpaper samples until noon, setting aside one with a pattern of thin blue leaves on pearl grey. At three, there was the funeral. She was home by five, and ironed a blouse while watching the six-thirty news.

Soon after that, at dusk, they came.

* * *

It was very late in 1943, during the Blitz, when Mavis met her husband. She had come to London, ostensibly to work in a munitions factory, along with her three older sisters. But all of them knew the unspoken reason for their collective flight from Glasgow. They went because Scotland was an old place, and a cold place, and because none of them fancied ending up like their mother, who had coughed her life away in the upstairs bedroom of their lower-middle-class home only a few months before.

Clara joined the army and ended up in artillery—shooting down Jerry planes all day, jitterbugging with Allied soldiers all night. By VE Day she'd gained two children, but remained staunchly unmarried. The kids turned out bad—one drowned down a sluice-gate, the other an interior designer in Manchester (and we all knew what that meant). Joan, always the pretty one, drove her ambulance over an unexploded shell in 1944. And Ellie was a nun somewhere in Brussels, but her order didn't allow mail so Mavis let her slip away without much regret—such a stiff little nit at the best of times, Ellie.

It was cold that night, walking home. She'd just reached the edge of the bridge when the sirens went off—blackout. She heard the bombs whistling around her and froze solid. Then, out of nowhere, a man—jumping past, pulling her with him as he dove for the nearest cover. "Get down, girl, Christ alive!" And they'd tumbled into a ditch together and stayed there all night, her head glued to his chest, eyes screwed shut in his arms and feeling his heart against her cheek like a snare-drum.

Three weeks later, they were married.

Eileen soon followed, and the war's end, and the boat to Canada.

* * *

The doorbell rang.

It was 7:15 by the kitchen clock—one of Eileen's presents, an idiotic grinning sun fringed by bent tin rays. Definitely not an hour for visitors, even expected ones.

Mavis rose. As if on cue, her headache drove needle-deep behind her left eye and lodged there, twisting. She squinted against the light, trying to dull it, and moved stiffly down the steps. As she touched the doorknob, the bell rang again. Anger welled up, a jet of blood in her mouth.

"Coming!" she snarled, wrenching it open.

The rain had finally stopped, and the sidewalks lay slick and dark before her. Across the street, Arthur A. Perry Junior High School—square as ever but unusually silent against the sky. An indigo-tinted flood of shadow smeared its outline to a blur, the full moon lighting one corner briefly before a cloud put it out. Mr. Cioberti's willow creaked to her left, shifting in the wind with a wet slither of leaves.

The porch was empty.

"Bloody kids," Mavis muttered.

She stood still a moment, looking out. The swollen joints of her elbows had begun to ache again, and the damp didn't help. But the street slept on, nothing stirring beneath the surface of its uncanny calm. At length, she turned away.

A nice cup of tea, she thought. That'll set me right.

The kitchen clock read 1:18 when she opened the door, and saw them.

The man who'd saved her, that night in 1943, was Allie Hennenlotter—tall, handsome devil-may-care Allie. He gave her his name, a child and a fresh start in a new country. He also turned out to be just the kind of shiftless drunk Clara'd always said he was. Refusing a battlefield commission because he didn't want to leave his drinking budies behind, he dragged her out to Saskatchewan and parked her on his father's farm while he pursued a series of low-paying jobs he couldn't hold long enough to send her a quarter of what she and Eileen needed to live on.

Even so, it took her three years to leave him.

She fled to Toronto, losing him in the crowd. When her bruises had faded, she applied herself to the task at hand—raising her child right. Took a secretarial job, upgraded her skills through night classes, fended off intermittent offers of marriage or mistresshood with a bland kind of "company" charm that won few friends but made even fewer enemies. She didn't make much, but all of it went to Eileen, who never showed the slightest bit of gratitude. Not that she'd really expected her too—like father, like daughter.

They fought daily until Eileen was 16, when she ran away to Montreal, with some cockamamie idea of becoming a ballerina. The postcards, far and few between as they were, retained an ever more strained optimism. Still, Mavis wasn't a bit surprised when her friend Dorothy's son Kerry saw Eileen dancing topless in a downtown bar.

It proved there was some form of justics in the world.

After that, she marked all of Eileen's communications "return to sender".

* * *

"What—?" Mavis began, and stopped in mid-question.

They reared up in front of the stove, blotting out the kitchen light. One great mass of—no, three; three sloping, shrouded heads. They regarded her eyelessly, without judgement. And the rest all just fell away, a grey, jumbled torrent of something that looked a bit like gauze—stained and stiff-streaked with clotted slime—sweeping almost to her own feet.

Their shadow poured over her, stagnant and cold. She held her breath against the smell. The air grew stale and heavy with moisture, as if before a storm.

Then she screamed, almost as an afterthought, and fled.

They followed, keeping a polite distance. A dull, rustling noise trailed in their wake.

She slammed the downstairs bathroom door on it, and paused, panting.

Minutes passed. Mavis met her own eyes in the mirror and grew steadily calmer. No need to rummage for her pills—this was a dream. Those things simply were not there. Could not be.

Would not be, once she'd gotten a hold on herself.

"You have nothing to be afraid of," she told herself, as deliberately as she could. "There is a God. And there are no monsters."

Eventually, she opened the door and strode forth.

They parted to let her through, giving her a good head start.

* * *

"It was really inevitable, Mrs. Hennenlotter," that nice doctor—Evans?—but he'd looked a bit Jewish, really—had assured her. "Your daughter was hopelessly in debt, addicted and alone, but too proud to ask for help. Her note blamed no one. In fact, the last sentence merely expressed a hope that you not be too disappointed in her."

He went on to confirm the funeral arrangements—closed coffin, no reception, donations to Covenant House instead of flowers.

Mavis thanked him and walked home, passing an inordinate amount of baby carriages for that time of year.

* * *

At work, the girls got together on a card. WEEP A WHILE, THEN MOURN NO MORE/I KNOCK AT LAST ON GOD'S GREAT DOOR.

"If you ever need to talk, dear—" Dorothy said.

Mavis nodded, absently, scanning the room from the corner of one eye. She didn't have to look too far. They were leaning against the far wall, next to the office copier.

No one took any notice. But then, no one ever did.

Not the passengers on her daily bus rides here and home. Not the people she met while walking to the store each evening. Not the customers at the neighborhood McDonald's, to which she had finally fled in despair, unable to cook under the constant pressure of that blind, triple stare.

They never came any closer, and they never spoke.

After a week, she broke down, and began to talk to *them*.

* * *

The call had come so early in the morning that Mavis was utterly unable to place the noise until her telephone had already rung five times. She scooped up the receiver, jamming it between ear and shoulder, and hissed: "Yes?"

"Mum, it's me."

Like a kick to the stomach. All air rushed from her lungs, leaving her answerless.

"Mum, are you still there?"

Mavis gulped, trying to steady her voice. "What do you want, Eileen?" she asked, finally.

There was a pause. Mavis could hear her breathing, shallow, as if something were caught in her throat. Then, thickly:

"I have a question."

"Well?"

Another pause, this one so long Mavis suspected she'd hung up. But instead of the dial tone, Eileen said:

"Did you ever love me?"

The stupidity of it slapped Mavis fully awake. She was back in known territory now. Struggling up in bed, she snapped: "What a thing to say! Really, Eileen—are you drunk?"

"No, mother." But she did sound remote—submerged in some frozen sea of pain, with ice blocking her escape.

"That's a change, then. Did I ever love you? I only worked all my life to keep you in good clothes, and no thanks for it, either. If that's not love—"

"Is it, though?"

"Four o'clock in the morning's no time for riddles, Eileen."

"Then you didn't," Eileen said. "Thank you. I'd wondered."

"Now, you just hold on a—"

"No," came the reply. "No, I've held on too long, I think."

Mavis groped for words, but they fled the numb, measured tone of Eileen's voice as flame flees water—extinguished at a touch.

"I just wanted to get it all straight, before I did it," Eileen went on. "When you started sending everything back, I think I knew then. It just took me a while to make up my mind. Now I have." Pause. "I guess I should thank you."

The line hissed softly between them.

Mavis felt her pulse hammer against the silence, unable to break it. Not for Eileen. Not for anything.

"I hate you," Eileen said. "I've always hated you. Even if you said you loved me right now, I'd still hate you." Her voice broke. "So why—why—can't I stop caring—what you *think* of me?"

Then a click, and an empty hum.

It wasn't until nine the next morning the police came to tell her they'd found Eileen, hanging by a studded leather belt from the shower-curtain rail in her apartment.

It was a lovely day. Birds singing and everything.

* * *

"I want you to go away," Mavis told them.

They, as usual, said nothing.

She paced up and down, feeling the strain in her limbs with every step. Her hips cracked as she turned to face them again.

"Who are you? What do you want?"

One of them, bored, tilted its head slightly towards the window. The others remained level, the blackness beneath their cowls locked steady with her eyes.

"*Speak*, God damn you!" she screamed.

The room dimmed, and the air filled with dust. A kind of murky haze seemed to rise from her beloved furniture, making it look old and clumsy and precariously perched on the edge of decay.

"It's Eileen, isn't it?" she said. "Isn't it? You want me to say I'm sorry, don't you? Well, I'm not. She was just like her father, never finished what she started. Thought she was better than me, who had to work for my living, but she found out, didn't she? Nothing but a whore, she ended up, and that's the plain truth."

They watched. Waiting.

"And what do *you* know about any of it, anyway?"

Dust filled her nostrils, stinging her eyes. She blinked at them, coughing.

Suddenly, a dull pain rolled through her like a tide.

"All right," she whispered. "I am."

The distracted one's head whipped back, surprised.

"I am," she repeated, sure of it now. Then: "Oh, I *am*."

Tears clotted the dust on her cheeks, as the light faded even further.

For a moment, nothing happened.

And now they'll go, her mind chattered away somewhere in the distance. They'll go now. They'll go. They will.

Then a kiss of pleasure rippled through the room. She looked up, just as the tallest one bent to show her a wide, flat, sharp smile that split its face from side to earless side.

Mavis smiled back, uncertainly.

Won't they?

"You repent," the tallest one said, in a voice like wind along a gully filled with dead leaves, at the height of October. "Good."

The others nodded.

"Now we can begin," they replied.

And as they raised their hands, Mavis saw their fingers were knives.

* * *

After Uranus's downfall, Chronos went slowly mad. Obsessed with the idea his children would destroy him, as he had destroyed his own father, he ate the babies his sister/wife Rhea gave him as quickly as they were born. But she saved the last one, Zeus, and hid him until it was time for him to fulfill Chronos's fears by becoming the ruler of a new crop of gods.

Rhea knew Chronos's madness was the work of creatures he himself had created, by committing the world's first murder; the goddesses of revenge, known as the Furies. Their names were Alecto (who Perseveres in Anger), Maegara (the Jealous One) and Tisiphone (the Blood Avenger).

They were dreadful beings. To placate them, men sometimes called them the Eumenides, or Kindly Ones.

But this is just a story.

BY THE MARK

All naming is already murder.
—Lacan.

Hepzibah, she called herself, mouthing the syllables whenever she thought no one else was looking. *Hep-zi-bah.* A powerful name, with strength in every note of it; a witch's name. She whispered it in each night's darkness, dreaming of poisons.

Outside, across the great divide between schoolyard and backyard, she knew her garden lay empty, sere and withered, topsoil still bleak with frost. Snow festered, greying, on top of the trumpet-vine's dead tangle. Behind that, the fence; further, a sloping away. Down past graffiti in full seasonal bloom, down into the mud at the base of the bridge, into the shadows under the pass, where the "normal" kids fought and kissed and loudly threatened suicide.

Into the Ravine.

One month more until spring. Then the nightshade bushes on either side of the property line would be green, each leaf bitter with possibilities.

But here she sat in Wang's homeroom class, textbooks laid open on" desktop in front of her: Fifth Grade English like an endless boring string of Happiness-Is-To-Me, When-I-Grow-Up-I, My-Favorite- Whatever Journal exercises, Fifth Grade math like hieroglyphics in Martian. Real reading matter poking out from underneath, just barely visible whenever she squinted hard enough—*Perennials and Parasites, A City Garden Almanac;* roots and shoots, pale green print on pale cream paper, a leftover swatch of

187

glue from where she'd ripped the school library slip off the inside back cover still sticking its back pages together. She sat there scanning entries while Mr Wang reeled off roll-call behind her, desperately searching for something, anything she could recognize from that all-too-familiar tangle of weeds along the winding path she usually took home, wasting as much time as possible until Ravine finally turned to driveway and the house—

—"her" house—

—that place where she lived, on Janice and Doug's sufferance, reared itself up against the sky like a tumor, a purse-lipped mouth poised to pop open and swallow her whole.

"Diamond, Jennifer," Wang droned, meanwhile, back in the world nine people out of ten seemed to agree was real. "Edgecomb, Caroline. Garza, Shelby. Gilford, Darien. Goshawk . . . "

Daffodil (Narcissus pseudonarcissus); Looks like: Star-shaped bright yellow corona of petals around a bonnet-shaped bell, with long, tulip-like stem and leaves. Toxic part: Bulbs, which are often mistaken for onions. Symptoms: Nausea, gastroenteritis, vomiting, persistent emesis, diarrhoea, and convulsive trembling which may lead to fatality.

"Often mistaken for onions . . . " like the kind Doug insisted on in his micro-organic salad, maybe. So no one'd be likely to question her having them, even away from the kitchen. Even hidden somewhere in her room . . .

She frowned, tapping the textbook's covering page. "May lead," though; not good enough. Not nearly good enough, for what she had in mind.

"Herod, Kevin. Hu, Darlanne. Isaak, Stephanie."

Oleander (Nerium oleander); Looks like: Smallish, wide-spread pansylike blooms on thin, tough stems with floppy leaves; Toxic part: Entire plant, green or dried—when a branch of an oleander plant is used to skewer meat at a barbecue, the poison is transferred to the meat; Symptoms: Nausea, depression, lowered and irregular pulse, bloody diarrhoea, paralysis and possibly death.

Nausea, depression—nothing new there, she thought, with a black little lick of humor. But Jesus, wasn't there anything in here that didn't come naturally (ha, ha) attached to having to roll on the floor and shit yourself to death? Anything that just made you . . . God, she didn't know . . . fall asleep, sink into peaceful darkness, just drift off and never wake up?

Aside from those pills in Janice's cupboard, the ones she'd probably miss before you even could swallow 'em? A little voice asked, at the back of her mind. No, probably not. 'Cause that'd be *way* too easy.

And if she wanted easy, then why play around with plants and leaves and tubers at all? Why not just straddle the rough stones of the St. Clair East bridge, shut her eyes and let go, like any normal person?

Choose her spot, avoid the trees, and there wouldn't be anything to break her fall but gravity. A mercifully short plunge, brief downward rush of wind and queasy freedom, with maybe one short, sharp shock as her head met the rocks below . . .

"Jenkins, Jason. Jowaczyk, William. Lien, Elvis."

Deadly Nightshade (Atropa belladonna); Looks like: Drooping white bloom over broad, veiny laeves, berries couched in beds of wispy leaflets; Toxic part: Entire plant, especially bright black berries; Symptoms: Dry mouth and difficulty in swallowing and speaking, flushed dry skin, rapid heartbeat, dilated pupils and blurred vision, neurological disturbances including excitement, giddiness, delerium, headache, confusion and hallucinations. Repeated ingestion can lead to dependency and glaucoma.

Not exactly *deadly*, then, is it? She thought, annoyed—and raised her head right at the same time that Wang raised his voice, all eyes already skittering to check her reaction: "Heather Millstone."

(You mean *Hepzibah*. Don't you?)

"Present."

Name after name after name, a whole limping alphabet of them—the roster of her "peers". She watched Wang's chin wag through the remaining call-and-response, counting freckles: Two faint ones near the corner of his mouth, one closer to the centre—a lopsided, tri-eyed face. From upside-down, it almost looked like he was smiling.

Mr Wang paused, apparently out of breath; sweat rose off him in every direction—a stinky heat haze, like asphalt in summer. He wore the same pale blue pin-striped shirts every day, and you could usually mark what time it was by how far the matching yellow circle at either armpit had spread. Whenever he gestured, waves of cologne and old grease spread in the direction of his ire. She was vaguely aware of having spent the last few minutes experimenting with his voice, even as her conscious mind turned lightly to thoughts of suicide—turning it up, turning it down, letting the words stretch sideways like notes of music. Shrinking it to a breath, a hum . . .

" . . . Heather?"

Aware of his attention, finally, she looked up, met his eyes. And: "Yes," she replied, reflexively—knowing that usually worked, even though she hadn't been listening well enough to really know what she was agreeing to.

"Yes, what?"

"Yes—Mr Wang?"

An audible giggle, two desks to the right: Jenny Diamond, self-elected Queen of Normal, Ontario. They'd been friends, once upon a time—or maybe Jenny had just tolerated her, letting her run to keep up with the rest of the clique while simultaneously making sure she stayed pathetically unaware how precarious her status as token Jenny wannabe really was. The last to know, as ever.

"I said, you're up. Yesterday's journal entry?" Another pause. "Sometime this week might be nice, especially for the rest of the class."

Oh, I'm sure. *Especially* for them.

The particularly funny thing being, of course, that she actually had done the work in question (for once). Poem, any subject, any length. She could just see the corner of it poking from her binder, if she strained—an uneven totem-pole of assonant paragraphs, neat black pen rows on pale blue-lined sheets, whose first lines went like so:

> *Always a shut door between us*
> *Yet I clung fast*
> *out here on the volcano's rim*
> *For five more years or a hundred,*
> *Whichever came last;*
>
> *How tall this pain has grown.*
> *wavering, taking root*
> *At the split mouth of bone.*
> *Your love like lava, sealing my throat.*
> *Words, piling up like bones . . .*

"Well, Heather? You know the drill. Stand up . . . "

. . . and let's get started.

Students normally stood to read, displaying themselves in front of everybody else. The class listened, kept the snickers to a minimum, clapped when you were done. Big flourish. Good mark. Centre of attention, all that—

But. But, but, but.

Staring down at her own lap, caught short like some idiot fish half-hooked through the cornea. Staring at her poem, the binder's edge, one blue-jeaned leg, the other. The edge of her peasant shirt, only barely hiding the area between, where well-worn fabric slid first to blue, then pale, then white along the seam. Normally, that is.

Tomato-red flower blooming at the juncture now, spreading pinky-gross back along the track of her hidden zipper, her crotch's bleached denim ridge. Evidence that she had yet once more left the house at that particular time of the month unsupplied, probably because her mind was frankly elsewhere: Choking on the thought of how unexpectedly soon Doug might return home from his latest "buying trip", maybe. Spitting it out like an unchewed cud of cereal into her napkin . . .

And: "8:30," said Janice, grabbing her bowl; the chair, pulled out from under her, shrieked protest. "Up and at 'em, pie."

Muttered: "Whatever."

"What's that?"

"Nothing."

Janice turned, abruptly—a bad move, considering how you didn't ever want her full attention on you, not more than you could help. Best just to stay background noise, an optical illusion: The amazing vanishing kid, briefly glimpsed from room to room. Because backtalk inevitably set Janice thinking of stove burners set on one, or pepper rubbed in the nostrils—enough to hurt, bad, yet too little to leave a (permanent) mark.

"Seems to me there's been a bit too much nothing been said around here lately," Janice said. "Seems to me, somebody might want to keep that in mind." Pause. "Well?"

"Yes."

"Yes, what?"

The exchange woke another surf-curl wave of memory, washing her right on back to the moment at hand—homeroom, Mr Wang, her poem. The impossibility of movement, without flashing her shame to the room at large. Her breakfast placemat's pattern swum briefly before her eyes, just for a second: A laminated rose-garden under improbably blue skies. Here and there, wherever the lines blurred, faces peeped out—pale and wizened features, gingseng death-masks, leering back up at her like tubers left to dry.

Thinking: Yes. Yes, Mr Wang. Yes . . .

. . . Mom.

Her tiny store of delaying tactics worn through at last, she swallowed hard and felt the vise inside her throat snap shut—tight, and hot, and dry. Jenny's clique were snickering openly now; the rest of the class just leaned forward, mouths slack in anticipation of tears. Nothing quite as amusing as a post-pubertal monster hemmed in by pre-teens, after all: Face stretched and straining, eyes aflutter while a grown man impatiently panned for public apologies.

And: Oh yes, you're so right, I'm so sorry sir. Like anybody but him really gave a shit.

She stared down at her own feet, the one knee visible through a rip in her jeans, scabby from crouching in the back yard—head bent, intent, waiting for monk's-hood to flourish. Then looked up again to find herself suddenly risen, blood-spotted ass flapping free in the wind, face-to-surprised-face with Wang himself.

"Ask her," she meant to say, giving a pert flip of the head towards Jenny—but the words came out in a scream, and took her desk with them. A general flurry ensued: Much ducking, the desk hitting the nearest window dead centre, with a concussive thump. Cracks rayed.

By the time Wang had uncrouched himself, she was already gone.

* * *

> *So who knows?*
> *It is well-fed.*
> *And once it has tasted blood,*
> *Who knows*
> *What seeds this thing may sow?*
>
> *But when the door closes this time,*
> *I won't look back. Won't check*
> *To see how little time it took*
> *For me to be erased.*
> *No longer plead my case*
> *Or tear my hair,*
> *That black engine behind your stare*
> *Pulling me away into darkness:*
>
> *I'm nothing now but air.*
> *Not even fit to disappear.*

Two rats stuck together at the sewer-grate's mouth: Carcinogens sprayed right and left as they thrashed together, squealing. She sat watching on the far bank, her fresh-washed jeans clammy against her thighs, burning with pollution. A stream of waste cut the Ravine's heart in two uneven halves, like a diseased aeorta; here it shrank to a mere grey trickle over stones. A doll's face stared up at her from the nearest tangle of weeds—one eye gone, the other washed blind by the current.

God, please, please, God.

Not, of course, that she really put too much faith in that particular fable, any more than she truly "believed" any of the other mildly comforting stories she'd told herself over the years. Or maybe she did—but only at moments like these. Only when the stakes were high, and all other avenues of escape closed.

Make Wang not tell. Make Janice not be home when the school calls.

A bird sang suddenly, somewhere in the gathering dark.

Make Doug not come home. Not yet. Not ever.

It was cold.

Yeah, and why not ask for a smaller rack while you're at it, reality sneered back at her, from every visible angle.

Rustling in the bushes, now, on either side. Snide whispers. Giggling.

"Hey, Hea-ther . . . "

Just two weeks before, Mrs Diamond (Jenny's mother, the school nurse and that most contradictory of things, a nice adult), had maintained cheerily that all these girls would be jealous of her in a year—even, improbably enough, Jenny herself. In a year, they'd be desperate to have what she had, to be what they thought she was. The same Jenny who'd already decided it was real good fun to make sure an open box of Tampax somehow snuck onto her desk during Recess, or rifle through her bag at lunch and then leave one of her pads—oh so artistically arranged—where everybody could see it, snicker, make comments. A white-winged hunk of cotton squatting in the homeroom doorway like some flattened mouse: *Ooh, hey, guys. What'cha think THIS is, huh?*

(Well, we know who it prob'ly BELONGS to, at least . . .)

Snicker, snicker, snicker.

Dropping squashed packages of McDonald's ketchup in her binder, knowing they'll smear and dry like brown Crazy Glue all across her journal, her poems. *Just looked like the kinda thing you like, Heyyy-ther. Soh-REE.*

Didn't matter how many words she strung together, or how well—how many plants she could raise, catalogue, research or harvest, to what mysterious and potentially fatal purposes. In the world outside her own freakishly pubescent body, it was the Jenny Diamonds who had the real power—always had. Always.

But: Poor Mrs Diamond, bound and determined to put the best possible face on everything, however bleak. While she just sat there, thinking: Yeah, well. In a year, a thousand different things could happen. I could be DEAD in a year.

Or rather: Christ, I HOPE so.

"Yo, Heyyyy-ther . . . "

She levered up, made the stream's far side in one long-legged jump. Heard yelps rise behind her at the flicker of movement (*there she is, there she IS!*), and ducked headlong into the underbrush without a backwards glance, heading directly up: Up through the poison oak, up under the shifting grey-green shadows of trees, up where the hiking trail's woodchip-lined trail turned to mud and mush. Remembered the last time the clique had chased her down here, running her through the blackberry bushes 'till she was breathless with stinging scratches. Like she'd accidentally grabbed the Black Spot and just not known it; like she was marked with fluorescent paint, invisible to everyone but them. Like she was some kind of, what was that word—

—scapegoat?

Chosen ahead of time, like around kindergarten, to sink and drown under a steady tide of bullying, or picked on simply because she'd been unlucky enough to have grown boobs a year earlier than everybody else—to have them when they were still age-inappropriate enough to be weird instead of jealousy-bait, before they were prized collateral on instant cool. On top of every other unlucky Goddamn thing.

And then that older guy Paul—fifteen at least, a kept-back retard hanging with the Fives and playing Master Of The Universe 'cause everybody else didn't know any better—had caught up to her at last, shot out in front of everybody else to grab her by the sleeve and wrench, so the two of them went down in a heap together with her hair in the mud, and him on top. Grinning a wet, dumb smile as he stuck his hand down her shirt, like he was fishing for some kind of surprise gift-bag through a carny peep-hole.

"Heather, baby—man, that set feels nice. Just like a couple a' water-balloons."

"Get *off*—"

"Aw, you know you *want* it. Just be cool and go 'long, baby, everybody knows you're fifty pounds of slut in a five-pound bag . . . "

(They can, y'know—just *smell* it on you.)

She felt poison well in her heart, a cold black spurt; rolled and got on top of him all in one crazy lurch, using both fists to hammer his head down hard against the nearest hard thing: A root, a rock.

"Crazy mother b—"

He jumped back, bleeding, and the fear on his face was the most beautiful thing she'd ever seen.

But the rush of it drained away so fast.

* * *

If this was a movie, it only occurred to her now (as she pulled herself ever further upwards through the mucky treeline, her boots sopping-slippery with mud), then Jenny and her gang would later turn out to have cut the first girl to menstruate from the school herd every year. There'd be some conspiracy. These girls would disappear, never to be seen again—bleached bones under a swatch of weeds somewhere in the Ravine, after a terrifying midnight hunt . . .

But it wasn't a movie: Just life, nothing more or less. Considerably less interesting. Considerably more hurtful.

Further up the hill, the house's porch-light had come on. A car was pulling up outside—driver's side door painted with a coal-bright tiger, crouched and ready to pounce. The other was hidden from this angle; a voluptuous woman, censored by flowers.

God, you bastard.

The tiger opened. So did the front door.

She straightened, suddenly composed.

Tell you what, she thought. Make you a deal. You don't really have to make anything happen, okay? Just make me not care, when it does.

That's all.

A heartfelt prayer. Yet God, as usual, stayed silent.

And oh but she knew, so very very well, that her whole stupid life was an Afterschool Special cliche from top to bottom—her problems cliches too, each and every one of them. Plot twists so stale they all but gave off dust. Ludicrous. Laughable. Lame.

None of which made the pain any easier to take, if and—

(no, just when. When.)

—it came.

The rats, sated, had long since gone their ways. Janice was heading down the yard, already almost to the Ravine's lip. Beside her was a shadow in embroidered jeans, sizeable hand on equally sizeable hip. No visible means of escape.

Before her parents could start to call, therefore, she stood up. And waved.

* * *

"You decent?" Doug asked, pushing the door open; luckily, she was. This time.

She stood in front of the mirror, flossing carefully. One side, then the other, each tooth in turn. Wrap and pull. Up, down and all around, like a see-saw.

The dentist was a luxury. If she'd left it up to them, she wouldn't have a tooth left in her head.

Go away.

"Missed you at dinner, pie."

Right hand on her shoulder, heavy as a full vaccum-cleaner bag. The warped mirror bent his fingers back, blurring them together: One strange flipper.

"Ah elt ick," she said, mid-wrap.

"Put that down, babe. Let me look at you a while."

That's an order, she thought, bracing herself. Floss to the garbage, with a flick. She turned, eyes shaded, as if to some erratic light-source more apt to blind than to illuminate. He grinned back, eyes glued to her chest, watching it bounce with the movement.

"Jan told me you did some more growing up while I was gone this time," he said. "And I thought she was joking. My oh my."

A whiff of dope from down the hall; Van Morrison on the stereo. She could almost hear him now, soft and infinitely plausible, at least to a woman kite-high on Doug's own no-name brand of weed: *Just leave us two alone to get reacquainted a while, Jan—play Daddy, y'know. All that good crap.*

"'Course, I already saw you when I got back."

The cap was off the toothpaste. "Driving up, you mean."

Big grin. "Naaah, I mean last night. I was just off shopping, that's why I wasn't there at breakfast. But I saw you, all right. Was about three, so you were fast asleep, cute as a button, lyin' there in that big t-shirt . . . you sure you don't remember?"

She swallowed; the vise was back again. "No."

"Well, here I was watching you—and it being so long and all, I decided I'd give you a kiss. So I bend down, and you know what you did?" Pause for raection. None forthcoming, so: "Took my hand, and then you start—licking it, right? Like it was some old lollipop. Licking and licking." Still nothing. "Isn't that just the sweetest?"

"I'd never."

A shrug. "'Cept you did."

She finally spotted the cap, a red smudge wedged between divisions, halfway down the drain. Have to use the tweezers on that. "You're lying," she said, not looking up.

"Now, would I lie?"

Only every day of my life.

"I gotta go to bed. School."

But he caught her in mid-stride, backing the door shut; licorice on his breath, rank with time. Pinning both her hands as he reached high over her head for the nearest bottle of moisturizer. "Dad, please don't," she whispered. "Not anymore. Please, it hurts."

"But sweetie," he said, almost genuinely shocked. "You know I only do this for *you*, right? All part'a growing up."

Don't break you in NOW, it just hurts that much worse later on . . .

And then they were down on the floor, the tiles cold on her face. *Let me not care, let me not care.* His hands. Grunting. Distant shapes in the mirror, blurred and distorted beyond recognition.

Plus God, somewhere, laughing his nonexistent ass off.

* * *

She dreamed, later—for the first time since she was seven or so, that she could recall. The year it all started going to hell or she started noticing how bad it already was, whichever came first.

In the dream, she was wearing her long black dress—the one with the stiff Afghani embroidery, red and yellow with little round bits of mirror sewn across the bodice and down the front. A witch's dress. In real life it didn't fit anymore; she slept with it tucked inside her pillow-case, rough against her cheek in the darkness.

While *Hepzibah*, a voice called. *Hep-zi-bah.*

She brushed red hair from her eyes—thigh-long, bloody with a power that crackled through her fingers. The voice seemed to be coming from outside, in the backyard, or further: Yes, from the Ravine. She knelt down from the trumpet-vine's main knot, awaiting further instructions.

197

What do you want? The voice asked, finally.

Janice and Doug gone. And Wang. And Jenny Diamond. I don't want to have to go to school. I want people to leave me alone, or die.

As quick as she said it, the words bred and splintered. A thousand thousand shades of grey, but one true meaning: *I want them all to be as much afraid of me as I am of them.*

And it came to her, sitting there in the cool, impossible dirt of her impossible garden—all her carefully-tended poisons abloom at last, ripe and lush for plucking—that there might still be a way to unpick the thread between her and the world around her, even now. To give up all hope of love. To give up pain. To be free, free, free at last.

She felt it all collect, hard and hot, in a lump just below her sterum—a smooth black egg, finally about to hatch.

And: *This is the gift*, came that same whisper again—from inside, or outside? Or . . . everywhere? At once?

THIS is what you were marked for. To live.

Confirmation, finally, that the fantasy which had sustained her so far might actually be meant to be . . . more. Not fantasy at all. Truth, or truth-to-be.

Foreshadowing.

To OUT-live, Hepzibah. Everyone.

Repeating the words, tasting every inch of them, and wondering at the welcome, impossible weight of them: Live. *Out*-live.

(Everyone.)

After all, what did she owe anyone still left inside this shell she called her life? Really?

I always knew it, she thought, amazed at her own perceptiveness. That if I only didn't have to feel—then nobody could hurt me. Nobody.

Because: When you feel nothing, you can do . . .

. . . anything.

* * *

Later that night, after Doug and Janice had smoked and screwed themselves to sleep, she found their stash, their money, Doug's ridiculously "high-class" straight-razor. Turned it in her hands thoughtfully, thinking about what if this was America, what if the razor were a gun. Standing over them in the dark, watching them breathe and grumble until the weight of her shadow brought Doug up from sleep . . .

"Pie—" he'd begin. And:

"My name is Hepzibah," she'd answer. Then shoot him in the face.

Janice might even have time to scream, once.

Resurfacing in darkness, turning away. Musing how in a perfect world, a *movie* world, this ultimate revelation would have come to her just in time for the nightshade harvest, so she'd have already had time to gather and dry enough atropine-laced leaves to cut her parents' brownie-hash with dementia and blindness. But you couldn't always get what you wanted, as she knew all too well; daffodil bulbs stolen from the corner flower-shop and added to tomorrow's salad would simply have to do, in terms of a stop-gap. Not that she suspected either Doug or Janice would be in any ultra-big hurry to call the cops, anyway, especially over something like the famous disappearing kid having finally just . . . well . . .

. . . disappeared. For good.

Hepzibah slipped the razor in her jeans pocket and the pre-baggie'd weed down the back of her waistband, pulling her sweatshirt down to cover it. She paused by the hall closet to "choose" between her usual thin coat and Doug's thick sheepskin jacket, then paused again by the front door to dredge a single marvellously unfamiliar word up from the very bottom of herself, a new mantra, well worth saying over and over and over. Forever.

"No," she whispered, into the newfound night—an ornate and intact sound, utterly crackless. It pleased her so much that she made it again and again, in time with her own footsteps: Down the stairs, onto the pavement, 'round the corner. Gone.

A new poem growing, unstoppable, in every fresh beat of her tread.

> *But beyond their art still lies my heart*
> *Which no one knows, or owns.*
> *A porcelain frame for my secret name;*
> *An eggshell, crammed with broken bones.*

* * *

It would be thirteen more years and too many dreams of murder to count—fulfilled, unfulfilled, otherwise—before she finally made her first mistake.

THE EMPEROR'S OLD BONES

Oh, buying and selling . . . you know . . . life.
—Tom Stoppard, after J.G. Ballard.

One day in 1941, not long after the fall of Shanghai, my amah (our live-in Chinese maid of all work, who often doubled as my nurse) left me sleeping alone in the abandoned hulk of what had once been my family's home, went out, and never came back . . . a turn of events which didn't actually surprise me all that much, since my parents had done something rather similar only a few brief weeks before. I woke up without light or food, surrounded by useless luxury—the discarded detritus of Empire and family alike. And fifteen more days of boredom and starvation were to pass before I saw another living soul.

I was ten years old.

After the war was over, I learned that my parents had managed to bribe their way as far as the harbor, where they became separated in the crush while trying to board a ship back "Home". My mother died of dysentery in a camp outside of Hangkow; the ship went down halfway to Hong Kong, taking my father with it. What happened to my amah, I honestly don't know—though I do feel it only fair to mention that I never really tried to find out, either.

The house and I, meanwhile, stayed right where we were—uncared for, unclaimed—until Ellis Iseland broke in, and took everything she could carry.

Including me.

"So what's your handle, tai pan?" she asked, back at the dockside

200

garage she'd been squatting in, as she went through the pockets of my school uniform.

(It would be twenty more years before I realized that her own endlessly evocative name was just another bad joke—one some immigration official had played on her family, perhaps.)

"Timothy Darbersmere," I replied, weakly. Over her shoulder, I could see the frying pan still sitting on the table, steaming slightly, clogged with burnt rice. At that moment in time, I would have gladly drunk my own urine in order to be allowed to lick it out, no matter how badly I might hurt my tongue and fingers in doing so.

Her eyes followed mine—a calm flick of a glance, contemptuously knowing, arched eyebrows barely sketched in cinnamon.

"Not yet, kid," she said.

"I'm really very hungry, Ellis."

"I really believe you, Tim. But not yet." She took a pack of cigarettes from her sleeve, tapped one out, lit it. Sat back. Looked a me again, eyes narrowing contemplatively. The plume of smoke she blew was exactly the same non color as her slant, level, heavy-lidded gaze.

"Just to save time, by the way, here're the house rules," she said. "Long as you're with me, I eat first. Always."

"That's not fair."

"Probably not. But that's the way it's gonna be, 'cause I'm thinking for two, and I can't afford to be listening to my stomach instead of my gut." She took another drag. "Besides which, I'm bigger than you."

"My father says adults who threaten children are bullies."

"Yeah, well, that's some pretty impressive moralizing, coming from a mook who dumped his own kid to get out of Shanghai alive."

I couldn't say she wasn't right, and she knew it, so I just stared at her. She was exoticism personified—the first full-blown Yank I'd ever met, the first adult (Caucasian) woman I'd ever seen wearing trousers. Her flat, Midwestern accent lent a certain fascination to everything she said, however repulsive.

"People will do exactly whatever they think they can get away with, Tim," she told me, "for as long as they think they can get away with it. That's human nature. So don't get all high-hat about it, use it. Everything's got its uses—everything, and everybody."

"Even you, Ellis?"

"Especially me, Tim. As you will see."

201

* * *

It was Ellis, my diffident ally—the only person I have ever met who seemed capable of flourishing in any given situation—who taught me the basic rules of commerce: To always first assess things at their true value, then gauge exactly how much extra a person in desperate circumstances would be willing to pay for them. And her lessons have stood me in good stead, during all these intervening years. At the age of sixty-six, I remain not only still alive, but a rather rich man, to boot—import/export, antiques, some minor drug-smuggling intermittently punctuated (on the more creative side) by the publication of a string of slim, speculative novels. These last items have apparently garnered me some kind of cult following amongst fans of such fiction, most specifically—ironically enough—in the United States of America.

But time is an onion, as my third wife used to say: The more of it you peel away, searching for the hidden connections between action and reaction, the more it gives you something to cry over.

So now, thanks to the established temporal conventions of literature, we will slip fluidly from 1941 to 1999—to St Louis, Missouri, and the middle leg of my first-ever Stateside visit, as part of a tour in support of my recently-published childhood memoirs.

The last book signing was at four. Three hours later, I was already firmly ensconced in my comfortable suite at the downtown Four Seasons Hotel. Huang came by around eight, along with my room service trolley. He had a briefcase full of files and a sly, shy grin, which lit up his usually impassive face from somewhere deep inside.

"Racked up a lotta time on this one, Mr Darbersmere," he said, in his second-generation Cockney growl. "Spent a lotta your money, too."

"Mmm." I uncapped the tray. "Good thing my publisher gave me that advance, then, isn't it?"

"Yeah, good fing. But it don't matter much now."

He threw the files down on the table between us. I opened the top one and leafed delicately through, between mouthfuls. There were schedules, marriage and citizenship certificates, medical records. Police records, going back to 1953, with charges ranging from fraud to trafficking in stolen goods, and listed under several different aliases. Plus a sheaf of photos, all taken from a safe distance.

I tapped one.

"Is this her?"

Huang shrugged. "You tell me—you're the one 'oo knew 'er."

I took another bite, nodding absently. Thinking: Did I? Really? Ever?

As much as anyone, I suppose.

* * *

To get us out of Shanghai, Ellis traded a can of petrol for a spot on a farmer's truck coming back from the market—then cut our unlucky savior's throat with her straight razor outside the city limits, and sold his truck for a load of cigarettes, lipstick and nylons. This got us shelter on a floating whorehouse off the banks of the Yangtze, where she eventually hooked us up with a pirate trawler full of U.S. deserters and other assorted scum, whose captain proved to be some slippery variety of old friend.

The trawler took us up- and down-river, dodging the Japanese and preying on the weak, then trading the resultant loot to anyone else we came in contact with. We sold opium and penicillin to the warlords, maps and passports to the D.P.s, motor oil and dynamite to the Kuomintang, Allied and Japanese spies to each other. But our most profitable commodity, as ever, remained people—mainly because those we dealt with were always so endlessly eager to help set their own price.

I look at myself in the bathroom mirror now, tall and silver-haired—features still cleanly cut, yet somehow fragile, like Sir Laurence Olivier after the medical bills set in. At this morning's signing, a pale young woman with a bolt through her septum told me: "No offense, Mr. Darbersmere, but you're—like—a real babe. For an old guy."

I smiled, gently. And told her: "You should have seen me when I was twelve, my dear."

That was back in 1943, the year that Ellis sold me for the first time—or rented me out, rather, to the mayor of some tiny port village, who threatened to keep us docked until the next Japanese inspection. Ellis had done her best to convince him that we were just another boatload of Brits fleeing internment, even shucking her habitual male drag to reveal a surprisingly lush female figure and donning one of my mother's old dresses instead, much as it obviously disgusted her to do so. But all to no avail.

"You know I'd do it, Tim," she told me, impatiently pacing the trawler's deck, as a passing group of her crewmates whistled appreciatively from

203

shore. "Christ knows I've tried. But the fact is, he doesn't want me. He wants you."

I frowned. "Wants me?"

"To go with him, Tim. You know—grown-up stuff."

"Like you and Ho Tseng, last week, after the dance at Sister Chin's?"

"Yeah, sorta like that."

She plumped herself down on a tarpaulined crate full of dynamite—clearly labeled, in Cantonese, as "dried fruit"—and kicked off one of her borrowed high-heeled shoes, rubbing her foot morosely. Her cinnamon hair hung loose in the stinking wind, back-lit to a fine fever.

I felt her appraising stare play up and down me like a fine grey mist, and shivered.

"If I do this, will you owe me, Ellis?"

"You bet I will, kid."

"Always take me with you?"

There had been some brief talk of replacing me with Brian Thompson-Greenaway, another refugee, after I had mishandled a particularly choice assignment—protecting Ellis's private stash of American currency from fellow scavengers while she recuperated from a beating inflicted by an irate Japanese officer, into whom she'd accidentally bumped while ashore. Though she wisely put up no resistance—one of Ellis's more admirable skills involved her always knowing when it was in her best interest not to defend herself—the damage left her pissing blood for a week, and she had not been happy to discover her money gone once she was recovered enough to look for it.

She lit a new cigarette, shading her eyes against the flame of her Ronson.

"'Course," she said, sucking in smoke.

"Never leave me?"

"Sure, kid. Why not?"

From Ellis, I learned to love duplicity, to distrust everyone except those who have no loyalty and play no favorites. Lie to me, however badly, and you are virtually guaranteed my fullest attention.

I don't remember if I really believed her promises, even then. But I did what she asked anyway, without qualm or regret. She must have understood that I would do anything for her, no matter how morally suspect, if she only asked me politely enough.

In this one way, at least, I was still definitively British.

* * *

Afterward, I was ill for a long time—some sort of psychosomatic reaction to the visceral shock of my deflowering, I suppose. I lay in a bath of sweat on Ellis's hammock, under the trawler's one intact mosquito net. Sometimes I felt her sponge me with a rag dipped in rice wine, while singing to me—softly, along with the radio:

A faded postcard from exotic places . . . a cigarette that's marked with lipstick traces . . . oh, how the ghost of you clings . . .

And did I merely dream that once, at the very height of my sickness, she held me on her hip and hugged me close? That she actually slipped her jacket open and offered me her breast, so paradoxically soft and firm, its nipple almost as pale as the rest of her night-dweller's flesh?

That sweet swoon of ecstasy. That first hot stab of infantile desire. That unwitting link between recent childish violation and a desperate longing for adult consummation. I was far too young to know what I was doing, but she did. She had to. And since it served her purposes, she simply chose not to care.

Such complete amorality: It fascinates me. Looking back, I see it always has—like everything else about her, fetishized over the years into an inescapable pattern of hopeless attraction and inevitable abandonment.

My first wife's family fled the former Yugoslavia shortly before the end of the war; she had high cheekbones and pale eyes, set at a Baltic slant. My second wife had a wealth of long, slightly coarse hair, the color of unground cloves. My third wife told stories—ineptly, compulsively. All of them were, on average, at least five years my elder.

And sooner or later, all of them left me.

Oh, Ellis, I sometimes wonder whether anyone else alive remembers you as I do—or remembers you at all, given your well-cultivated talent for blending in, for getting by, for rendering yourself unremarkable. And I really don't know what I'll do if this woman Huang has found for me turns out not to be you. There's not much time left in which to start over, after all.

For either of us.

* * *

Last night, I called the number Huang's father gave me before I left London. The man on the other end of the line identified himself as the master chef of the Precious Dragon Shrine restaurant.

"Oh yes, tai pan Darbersmere," he said, when I mentioned my name. "I was indeed informed, by that respected personage who we both know, that you might honor my unworthiest of businesses with the request for some small service."

"One such as only your estimable self could provide."

"The tai pan flatters, as is his right. Which is the dish he wishes to order?"

"The Emperor's Old Bones."

A pause ensued—fairly long, as such things go. I could hear a Cantopop ballad filtering in, perhaps from somewhere in the kitchen, duelling for precedence with the more classical strains of a wailing erhu. The Precious Dragon Shrine's master chef drew a single long, low breath.

"Tai pan," he said, finally, "for such a meal . . . one must provide the meat oneself."

"Believe me, Grandfather, I am well aware of such considerations. You may be assured that the meat will be available, whenever you are ready to begin its cooking."

Another breath—shorter, this time. Calmer.

"Realizing that it has probably been a long time since anyone had requested this dish," I continued, "I am, of course, more than willing to raise the price our mutual friend has already set."

"Oh, no, tai pan."

"For your trouble."

"Tai pan, please. It is not necessary to insult me."

"I must assure you, Grandfather, that no such insult was intended."

A burst of scolding rose from the kitchen, silencing the ballad in mid-ecstatic lament. The master chef paused again. Then said:

"I will need at least three days' notice to prepare my staff."

I smiled. Replying, with a confidence which—I hoped—at least sounded genuine:

"Three days should be more than sufficient."

* * *

The very old woman (eighty-nine, at least) who may or may not have once called herself Ellis Iseland now lives quietly in a genteelly shabby area of St Louis, officially registered under the far less interesting name of Mrs.

Munro. Huang's pictures show a figure held carefully erect, yet helplessly shrunken in on itself—its once-straight spine softened by the onslaught of osteoporosis. Her face has gone loose around the jawline, skin powdery, hair a short, stiff grey crown of marcelled waves.

She dresses drably. Shapeless feminine weeds, widow-black. Her arthritic feet are wedged into Chinese slippers—a small touch of nostalgic irony? Both her snubbed cat's nose and the half-sneering set of her wrinkled mouth seem familiar, but her slanted eyes—the most important giveaway, their original non-color perhaps dimmed even further with age, from light smoke-grey to bone, ecru, white—are kept hidden beneath a thick-lensed pair of bifocal sunglasses, essential protection for someone whose sight may not last the rest of the year.

And though her medical files indicate that she is in the preliminary stages of lung and throat cancer, her trip a day to the local corner store always includes the purchase of at least one pack of cigarettes, the brand apparently unimportant, as long as it contains a sufficient portion of nicotine. She lights one right outside the front door, and has almost finished it by the time she rounds the corner of her block.

Her neighbors seem to think well of her. Their children wave as she goes by, cane in one hand, cigarette in the other. She nods acknowledgement, but does not wave back.

This familiar arrogance, seeping up unchecked through her last, most perfect disguise: the mask of age, which bestows a kind of retroactive innocence on even its most experienced victims. I have recently begun to take advantage of its charms myself, whenever it suits my fancy to do so.

I look at these pictures, again and again. I study her face, searching in vain for even the ruin of that cool, smooth, inventively untrustworthy operator who once held both my fortune and my heart in the palm of her mannishly large hand.

It was Ellis who first told me about The Emperor's Old Bones—and she is still the only person in the world with whom I would ever care to share that terrible meal, no matter what doing so might cost me.

If, indeed, I ever end up eating it at all.

* * *

"Yeah, I saw it done down in Hong Kong," Ellis told us, gesturing with her chopsticks. We sat behind a lacquered screen at the back of Sister Chin's, two nights before our scheduled rendezvous with the warlord Wao Ruyen, from whom Ellis had already accepted some mysteriously unspecified commission. I watched her eat—waiting my turn, as ever—while Brian Thompson-Greenaway (also present, much to my annoyance) sat in the corner and watched us both, openly ravenous.

"They take a carp, right—you know, those big fish some rich Chinks keep in fancy pools, out in the garden? Supposed to live hundreds of years, you believe all that 'Confucius says' hooey. So they take this carp and they fillet it, all over, so the flesh is hanging off it in strips. But they do it so well, so carefully, they keep the carp alive through the whole thing. It's sittin' there on a plate, twitching, eyes rollin' around. Get close enough, you can look right in through the ribcage and see the heart still beating."

She popped another piece of Mu Shu pork in her mouth, and smiled down at Brian, who gulped—apparently suddenly too queasy to either resent or envy her proximity to the food.

"Then they bring out this big pot full of boiling oil," she continued, "and they run hooks through the fish's gills and tail. so they can pick it up at both ends. And while it's floppin' around, tryin' to get free, they dip all those hangin' pieces of flesh in the oil—one side first, then the other, all nice and neat. Fish is probably in so much pain already it doesn't even notice. So it's still alive when they put it back down . . . alive, and cooked, and ready to eat."

"And then—they eat it."

"Sure do, Tim."

"Alive, I mean."

Brian now looked distinctly green. Ellis shot him another glance, openly amused by his lack of stamina, then turned back to me.

"Well yeah, that's kinda the whole point of the exercise. You keep the carp alive until you've eaten it, and all that long life just sorta transfers over to you."

"Like magic," I said. She nodded.

"Exactly. 'Cause that's exactly what it is."

I considered her statement for a moment.

"My father," I commented, at last, "always told us that magic was a load of bunk."

Ellis snorted. "And why does this not surprise me?" She asked, of nobody in particular. Then: "Fine, I'll bite. What do you think?"

"I think . . . " I said, slowly, " . . . that if it works . . . then who cares?"

She looked at me. Snorted again. And then—she actually laughed, an infectious, unmalicious laugh that seemed to belong to someone far younger, far less complicated. It made me gape to hear it. Using her chop-sticks, she plucked the last piece of pork deftly from her plate, and popped it into my open mouth.

"Tim," she said, "for a spoiled Limey brat, sometimes you're okay."

I swallowed the pork, without really tasting it. Before I could stop myself, I had already blurted out:

"I wish we were the same age, Ellis."

This time *she* stared. I felt a sudden blush turn my whole face crimson. Now it was Brian's turn to gape, amazed by my idiotic effrontery.

"Yeah, well, not me," she said. "I like it just fine with you bein' the kid, and me not."

"Why?"

She looked at me again. I blushed even more deeply, heat prickling at my hairline. Amazingly, however, no explosion followed. Ellis simply took another sip of her tea, and replied:

"'Cause the fact is, Tim, if you were my age—good-lookin' like you are, smart like you're gonna be—I could probably do some pretty stupid things over you."

* * *

Magic. Some might say it's become my stock in trade—as a writer, at least. Though the humble craft of buying and selling also involves a kind of legerdemain, as Ellis knew so well; sleight of hand, or price, depending on your product . . . and your clientele.

But true magic? Here, now, at the end of the twentieth century, in this brave new world of 100-slot CD players and incessant afternoon talk shows?

I have seen so many things in my long life, most of which I would have thought impossible, had they not taken place right in front of me. From the bank of the Yangtze river, I saw the bright white smoke of an atomic bomb go up over Nagasaki, like a tear in the fabric of the horizon. In Chungking harbor, I saw two grown men stab each other to death over the corpse of a dog because one wanted to bury it, while the other wanted to eat it. And just beyond the Shanghai city limits, I saw Ellis cut that farmer's throat with one quick twist of her wrist, so close to me that the spurt of his severed jugular misted my cheek with red.

But as I grow ever closer to my own personal twilight, the thing I remember most vividly is watching—through the window of a Franco-Vietnamese arms-dealer's car, on my way to a cool white house in Saigon, where I would wait out the final days of the war in relative comfort and safety—as a pair of barefoot coolies pulled the denuded skeleton of Brian Thompson-Greenaway from a culvert full of malaria-laden water. I knew it was him, because even after Wao Ruyen's court had consumed the rest of his pathetic little body, they had left his face nearly untouched—there not being quite enough flesh on a child's skull, apparently, to be worth the extra effort of filleting . . . let alone of cooking.

And I remember, with almost comparable vividness, when—just a year ago—I saw the former warlord Wao, Huang's most respected father, sitting in a Limehouse nightclub with his Number One and Number Two wife at either elbow. Looking half the age he did when I first met him, in that endless last July of 1945, before black science altered our world forever. Before Ellis sold him Brian instead of me, and then fled for the Manchurian border, leaving me to fend for myself in the wake of her departure.

After all this, should the idea of true magic seem so very difficult to swallow? I think not.

No stranger than the empty shell of Hiroshima, cupped around Ground Zero, its citizenry reduced to shadows in the wake of the blast's last terrible glare. And certainly no stranger than the fact that I should think a woman so palpably incapable of loving anyone might nevertheless be capable of loving me, simply because—at the last moment—she suddenly decided not to let a rich criminal regain his youth and prolong his days by eating me alive, in accordance with the ancient and terrible ritual of the Emperor's Old Bones.

* * *

This morning, I told my publicist that I was far too ill to sign any books today—a particularly swift and virulent touch of the twenty-four-hour flu, no doubt. She said she understood completely. An hour later, I sat in Huang's car across the street from the corner store, watching "Mrs Munro" make her slow way down the street to pick up her daily dose of slow, coughing death.

On her way back, I rolled down the car window and yelled: "Lai gen wo ma, wai guai!"

(*Come with me, white ghost!* An insulting little Mandarin phrase, occasionally used by passing Kuomintang jeep drivers to alert certain long-nosed Barbarian smugglers to the possibility that their dealings might soon be interrupted by an approaching group of Japanese soldiers.)

Huang glanced up from his copy of *Rolling Stone's* Hot List, impressed. "Pretty good accent," he commented.

But my eyes were on "Mrs Munro", who had also heard—and stopped in mid-step, swinging her half-blind grey head toward the sound, more as though scenting than scanning. I saw my own face leering back at me in miniature from the lenses of her prescription sunglasses, doubled and distorted by the distance between us. I saw her raise one palm to shade her eyes even further against the sun, the wrinkles across her nose contracting as she squinted her hidden eyes.

And then I saw her slip her glasses off to reveal those eyes: Still slant, still grey. Still empty.

"It's her," I told him.

Huang nodded. "'Fought so. When you want me to do it?"

"Tonight?"

"Whatever y'say, Mr D."

* * *

Very early on the morning before Ellis left me behind, I woke to find her sitting next to me in the red half-darkness of the ship's hold.

"Kid," she said, "I got a little job lined up for you today."

I felt myself go cold. "What kind of job, Ellis?" I asked, faintly—though I already had a fairly good idea. Quietly, she replied:

"The grown-up kind."

"Who?"

"French guy, up from Saigon, with enough jade and rifles to buy us over the border. He's rich, educated; not bad company, either. For a fruit."

"That's reassuring," I muttered, and turned on my side, studying the wall. Behind me, I heard her lighter click open, then catch and spark—felt the faint lick of her breath as she exhaled, transmuting nicotine into smoke and ash. The steady pressure of her attention itched like an insect crawling on my skin: Fiercely concentrated, alien almost to the point of vague disgust, infinitely patient.

"War's on its last legs," she told me. "That's what I keep hearing. You got the Communists comin' up on one side, with maybe the Russians slipping in behind 'em, and the good old U.S. of A. everywhere else. Phillipines are already down for the count, now Tokyo's in bombing range. Pretty soon, our little oufit is gonna be so long gone, we won't even remember what it looked like. My educated opinion? It's sink or swim, and we need all the life-jackets that money can buy." She paused. "You listening to me? Kid?"

I shut my eyes again, marshalling my heart-rate.

"Kid?" Ellis repeated.

Still without answering—or opening my eyes—I pulled the mosquito net aside, and let gravity roll me free of the hammock's sweaty clasp. I was fourteen years old now, white-blonde and deeply tanned from the river-reflected sun; almost her height, even in my permanently bare feet. Looking up, I found I could finally meet her grey gaze head-on.

"'Us'," I said. "'We'. As in you and I?"

"Yeah, sure. You and me."

I nodded at Brian, who lay nearby, deep asleep and snoring. "And what about him?"

Ellis shrugged.

"I don't know, Tim," she said. "*What* about him?"

I looked back down at Brian, who hadn't shifted position, not even when my shadow fell over his face. Idly, I inquired:

"You'll still be there when I get back, won't you, Ellis?"

Outside, through the porthole, I could see that the rising sun had just cracked the horizon; she turned, haloed against it. Blew some more smoke. Asking:

"Why the hell wouldn't I be?"

"I don't know. But you wouldn't use my being away on this job as a good excuse to leave me behind, though—would you?"

She looked at me. Exhaled again. And said, evenly:

"You know, Tim, I'm gettin' pretty goddamn sick of you asking me that question. So gimme one good reason not to, or let it lie."

Lightly, quickly—too quickly even for my own well-honed sense of self-preservation to prevent me—I laid my hands on either side of her face and pulled her to me, hard. Our breath met, mingled, in sudden intimacy;

hers tasted of equal parts tobacco and surprise. My daring had brought me just close enough to smell her own personal scent, under the shell of everyday decay we all stank of: A cool, intoxicating rush of non-fragrance, firm and acrid as an unearthed tuber. It burned my nose.

"We should always stay together," I said, "because I *love* you, Ellis."

I crushed my mouth down on hers, forcing it open. I stuck my tongue inside her mouth as far as it would go and ran it around, just like the mayor of that first tiny port village had once done with me. I fastened my teeth deep into the inner flesh of her lower lip, and bit down until I felt her knees give way with the shock of it. Felt myself rear up, hard and jerking, against her soft underbelly. Felt *her* feel it.

It was the first and only time I ever saw her eyes widen in anything but anger.

With barely a moment's pause, she punched me right in the face, so hard I felt my jaw crack. I fell at her feet, coughing blood.

"*Eh—!*" I began, amazed. But her eyes froze me in mid-syllable—so grey, so cold.

"Get it straight, tai pan," she said, "'cause I'm only gonna say it once. I don't buy. I *sell.*"

Then she kicked me in the stomach with one steel-toed army boot, and leant over me as I lay there, gasping and hugging myself tight—my chest contracting, eyes dimming. Her eyes pouring over me like liquid ice. Like sleet. Swelling her voice like some great Arctic river, as she spoke the last words I ever heard her say:

"So don't you even *try* to play me like a trick, and think I'll let you get away with it."

* * *

Was Ellis evil? Am I? I've never thought so, though earlier this week I did give one of those legendary American Welfare mothers $25,000 in cash to sell me her least-loved child. He's in the next room right now, playing Nintendo. Huang is watching him. I think he likes Huang. He probably likes me, for that matter. We are the first English people he has ever met, and our accents fascinate him. Last night, we ordered in pizza; he ate until he was sick, then ate more, and fell asleep in front of an HBO basketball game. If I let him stay with me another week, he might become sated enough to convince himself he loves me.

The master chef at the Precious Dragon Shrine tells me that the Emperor's Old Bones bestows upon its consumer as much life-force as the consumed would have eventually gone through, had he or she been permitted to live out the rest of their days unchecked—and since the child I bought claims to be roughly ten years old (a highly significant age, in retrospect), this translates to perhaps an additional sixty years of life for every person who participates, whether the dish is eaten alone or shared. Which only makes sense, really: It's an act of magic, after all.

And this is good news for me, since the relative experiential gap between a man in his upper twenties and a woman in her upper thirties—especially compared to that between a boy of fourteen and a woman of twenty-eight—is almost insignificant.

Looking back, I don't know if I've ever loved anyone but Ellis—if I'm even capable of loving anyone else. But finally, after all these wasted years, I do know what I want. And who.

And how to get them both.

It's a terrible thing I'm doing, and an even worse thing I'm going to do. But when it's done, I'll have what I want, and everything else—all doubts, all fears, all piddling, queasy little notions of goodness, and decency, and basic human kinship—all that useless lot can just go hang, and twist and rot in the wind while they're at it. I've lived much too long with my own unsatisfied desire to simply hold my aching parts—whatever best applies, be it stomach or otherwise—and congratulate myself on my forbearance anymore. I'm not mad, or sick, or even yearning after a long-lost love that I can never regain, and never really had in the first place. I'm just hungry, and I want to *eat*.

And morality . . . has nothing to do with it.

Because if there's one single thing you taught me, Ellis—one lesson I've retained throughout every twist and turn of this snaky thing I call my life—it's that hunger has no moral structure.

* * *

Huang came back late this morning, limping and cursing, after a brief detour to the office of an understanding doctor who his father keeps on international retainer. I am obscurely pleased to discover that Ellis can still defend herself; even after Huang's first roundhouse put her on the pavement, she still somehow managed to slip her razor open without him noticing, then slide it shallowly across the back of his Achilles tendon. More painful than debilitating, but rather well done nevertheless, for a woman who can no longer wear shoes which require her to tie her own laces.

I am almost as pleased, however, to hear that nothing Ellis may have done actually succeeded in preventing Huang from completing his mission—and beating her, with methodical skill, to within an inch of her corrupt and dreadful old life.

I have already told my publicist that I witnessed the whole awful scene, and asked her to find out which hospital poor Mrs Munro has been taken to. I myself, meanwhile, will drive the boy to the kitchen of the Precious Dragon Shrine restaurant, where I am sure the master chef and his staff will do their best to keep him entertained until later tonight. Huang has lent him his pocket Gameboy, which should help.

Ah. That must be the phone now, ringing.

* * *

The woman in bed 37 of the Morleigh Memorial Hospital's charity wing, one of the few left operating in St. Louis—in America, possibly—opens her swollen left eye a crack, just far enough to reveal a slit of red-tinged white and a wandering, dilated pupil, barely rimmed in grey.

"Hello, Ellis," I say.

I sit by her bedside, as I have done for the last six hours. The screens enshrouding us from the rest of the ward, with its rustlings and moans, reduce all movement outside this tiny area to a play of flickering shadows—much like the visions one might glimpse in passing through a double haze of fever and mosquito net, after suffering a violent shock to one's fragile sense of physical and moral integrity.

. . . and oh, how the ghost of you clings . . .

She clears her throat, wetly. Tells me, without even a flicker of hesitation:

"Nuh . . . Ellis. Muh num iss . . . Munro."

But: She peers up at me, straining to lift her bruise-stung lids. I wait, patiently.

"Tuh—"

"That's a good start."

I see her bare broken teeth at my patronizing tone, perhaps reflexively. Pause. And then, after a long moment:

"Tim."

215

"Good show, Ellis. Got it in one."

Movement at the bottom of the bed: Huang, stepping through the gap between the screens. Ellis sees him, and stiffens. I nod in his direction, without turning.

"I believe you and Huang have already met," I say. "Mr Wao Huang, that is; you'll remember his father, the former warlord Wao Ruyen. He certainly remembers you—and with some gratitude, or so he told me."

Huang takes his customary place at my elbow. Ellis' eyes move with him, helplessly—and I recall how my own eyes used to follow her about in a similarly fascinated manner, breathless and attentive on her briefest word, her smallest motion.

"I see you can still take quite a beating, Ellis," I observe, lightly. "Unfortunately for you, however, it's not going to be quite so easy to recover from this particular melee as it once was, is it? Old age, and all that." To Hunag: "Have the doctors reached any conclusion yet? Regarding Mrs Munro's long-term prognosis?"

"Wouldn't say as 'ow there was one, tai pan."

"Well, yes. Quite."

I glance back, only to find that Ellis' eyes have turned to me at last. And I can read them so clearly, now—like clean, black text through grey rice-paper, lit from behind by a cold and colorless flame. No distance. No mystery at all.

When her mouth opens again, I know exactly what word she's struggling to shape.

"Duh . . . deal?"

Oh, yes.

I rise, slowly, as Huang pulls the chair back for me. Some statements, I find, need room in which to be delivered properly—or perhaps I'm simply being facetious. My writer's over-developed sense of the dramatic, working double-time.

I wrote this speech out last night, and rehearsed it several times in front of the bathroom mirror. I wonder if it sounds rehearsed. Does calculated artifice fall into the same general category as outright deception? If so, Ellis ought to be able to hear it in my voice. But I don't suppose she's really apt to be listening for such fine distinctions, given the stress of this mutually culminative moment.

"I won't say you've nothing I want, Ellis, even now. But what I really want—what I've always wanted—is to be the seller, for once, and not the sold. To be the only one who has what you want desparately, and to set my price wherever I think it fair."

Adding, with the arch of a significant brow: "—or *know* it to be unfair."

I study her battered face. The bruises form a new mask, impenetrable as any of the others she's worn. The irony is palpable: Just as Ellis' nature abhors emotional accessibility, so nature—seemingly—reshapes itself at will to keep her motivations securely hidden.

"I've arranged for a meal," I tell her. "The menu consists of a single dish, one with which I believe we're both equally familiar. The name of that dish is the Emperor's Old Bones, and my staff will begin to cook it whenever I give the word. Now, you and I may share this meal, or we may not. We may regain our youth, and double our lives, and be together for at least as long as we've been apart—or we may not. But I promise you this, Ellis: No matter what *I* eventually end up doing, the extent of *your* participation in the matter will be exactly defined by how much you are willing to pay me for the privilege."

I gesture to Huang, who slips a pack of cigarettes from his coat pocket. I tap one out. I light it, take a drag. Savor the sensation.

Ellis just watches.

"So here's the deal, then: If you promise to be very, very nice to me—and never, ever leave me again—for the rest of our extremely long partnership—"

I pause. Blow out the smoke. Wait.

And conclude, finally:

"—then you can eat first."

I offer Ellis the cigarette, slowly. Slowly, she takes it from me, holding it delicately between two splinted fingers. She raises it to her torn and grimacing mouth. Inhales. Exhales those familiar twin plumes of smoke, expertly, through her crushed and broken nose. Is that a tear at the corner of her eye, or just an upwelling of rheum? Or neither?

"Juss like . . . ahways," she says.

And gives me an awful parody of my own smile. Which I—return. With interest.

* * *

Later, as Huang helps Ellis out of bed and into the hospital's service elevator, I sit in the car, waiting. I take out my cellular phone. The master chef of the Precious Dragon Shrine restaurant answers on the first ring.

"How is . . . the boy?" I ask him.

"Fine, tai pan."

There is a pause, during which I once more hear music filtering in from the other end of the line—the tinny little song of a video game in progress, intermittently punctuated by the clatter of kitchen implement. Laughter, both adult and child.

"Do you wish to cancel your order, tai pan Darbersmere?" the master chef asks me, delicately.

Through the hospital's back doors, I can see the service elevator's lights crawling steadily downward—the floors reeling themselves off, numeral by numeral. Fifth. Fourth. Third.

"Tai pan?"

Second. First.

"No. I do not."

The elevator doors are opening. I can see Huang guiding Ellis out, puppeting her deftly along with her own crutches. Those miraculously-trained hands of his, able to open or salve wounds with equal expertise.

"Then I may begin cooking," the master chef says. Not really meaning it as a question.

Huang holds the door open. Ellis steps through. I listen to the Gameboy's idiot song, and know that I have spent every minute of every day of my life preparing to make this decision, ever since that last morning on the Yangtze. That I have made it so many times already, in fact, that nothing I do or say now can ever stop it from being made. Any more than I can bring back the child Brian Thompson-Greenaway was, before he went up the hill to Wao Ruyen's fortress, hand in stupidly trusting hand with Ellis—or the child I was, before Ellis broke into my parents' house and saved me from one particular fate worse than death, only to show me how many, many others there were to choose from.

Or the child that Ellis must have been, once upon a very distant time, before whatever happened to make her as she now is—then set her loose to move at will through an unsuspecting world, preying on other lost children.

. . . *these foolish things . . . remind me of you.*

"Yes," I say. "You may."

THE NARROW WORLD

And then I did a strange thing, but what I did matters not.
            —*Oscar Wilde*

It's always the same, always different. The moment you make that first cut, even before you open the—item—in question up, there's this faint, red-tinged exhalation: Cotton-soft, indefinite, almost indefinable. Even more than the shudder or the jerk, the last stifled attempt at drawn breath, this is what marks a severance—what proves, beyond a shadow of a doubt, that something which once considered itself alive has been physically deleted from this tangle of contradictory image and sensation we choose to call "reality".

Cut away from, cut loose. Or maybe—cut free.

And this is the first operating rule of magic, whether black, white or red all over: For every incision, an excision. No question without its answer. No action without its price.

Some people fast before a ritual. I don't. Some people wear all white. I wear all black, except for the purple fun-fur trim on my winter coat (which I took so long to find in the first place that I really just couldn't bear to part with it). Some people still say you have to be a psychopath to be able to draw a perfect circle—so I hedge my bets, and carry a surveyor's compass. But I also don't drink, don't smoke, haven't done any drugs but Tylenol since I was a Ryerson undergraduate, getting so bent out of shape I could barely talk straight and practicing Crowleyan "sex magick" with a similarly inclined posse of curricular acquaintances every other weekend.

Effective hierarchical magicians like me are the Flauberts of the Narrow World—neat and orderly in our lives, comme un bourgeois, so that we may be violent and creative in our work. We're not fanatics. There's no particular principle involved, except maybe the principle of Free Enterprise. So we can afford to stay safe . . . and for what they're paying us to do so, our customers kind of prefer it that way.

$3,000 down, tax-free, for a simple supernatural Q & A session, from U of T Business pregrad Doug Whatever to me, Hark Chiu-Wai—Jude Hark, as I'm known down here in Toronto the Good-for-nothing. That's what brought me where I was when all this began: Under the vaulted cathedral arch of the St Clair Ravine Bridge, shivering against the Indian Winter air of early September as I gutted a sedated German Shepherd, in preparation for invoking the obsolete Sumerian god of divination by entrails.

The dog was a bit on the small side, but it was a definite improvement on Doug and his girlfriend's first try—a week back, when they'd actually tried to fob me off with some store-bought puppy. Through long and clever argument, however, I'd finally gotten them to cave in: If you're looking to evoke a deity who speaks through a face made of guts—one who goes by the slightly risible name of Humbaba, to be exact—you'd probably better make sure his mouth is big enough to tell you what you want to hear.

Since I hate dogs anyway—tongue-wagging little affection junkies—treating one like a Christmas chicken was not exactly a traumatic prospect. So I completed the down-stroke, shearing straight through its breastbone, and pushed down hard on either side of its ribcage 'til I heard something crack.

Behind me, the no-doubt-soon-to-be-Mrs Doug made a hacking noise, and shifted her attention to a patch of graffiti on the nearest wall. Doug just kept on staring, maintaining the kind of physical fixity that probably passed for thought in his circles.

"So what, those the . . . innards?" He asked, delicately.

"Those are they," I said, not looking up. Flaying away the membrane between heart and lungs, lifting and separating the subsections of fat between abdomen and bowels . . .

He nodded. "What'cha gonna do with 'em?"

"Watch."

I twisted, cut, twisted again, cut again. Heart on one side, lungs (a riven grey tissue butterfly, torn wing from wing) on the other. Pulled forth the gall bladder and squeezed it empty, using it to smear binding sigils at my north, south, east, west. Shook out another cleansing handful of rock salt, and wrung the bile from my palms.

Doug's girlfriend, having exhausted the wall's literary possibilities, had turned back toward the real action. Hand over mouth, she ventured:

"Um—is that like a hat you can buy, or is that a religion?"

"What?"

"Your hat. Is it, like, religious?"

(The headgear in question being a black brocade cap, close-fitting, topped with a round, greyish satin applique of a Chinese embroidery pattern: Bats and dragons entwined, signifying long life and good luck. The kind of thing my Ma might've picked out for me, were she inclined to do so.)

"Oh, yes," I replied, keeping my eyes firmly on the prize, as I started to unreel the dog's intestines. "Very religious. Has its own church, actually. All hail Jude's hat—bow down, bow down. Happy holiness to the head-gear."

She sniffed, mildly aggrieved at my lack of interest in her respect for my fashion sense.

Said: "Well, excuse me for trying to be polite."

I shot her a small, amused glance. Thinking: Oh, was *that* what you were trying to do?

Ai-yaaa.

The dog had more guts than I'd originally given him credit for. Scooping out the last of them, I started to shape them into a rough, pink face, its features equally blurred with blood and seeping digestive juices.

"You ever hear the four great tenets of hierarchical magic?" I asked her, absently. "'To know, to dare, to will, to be silent.'"

Then, pulling the mouth's corners up into a derisive, toothless grin, and conjuring a big smile of my own: "So why don't you just consider yourself Dr Faustus for a day, and shut the fuck up?"

She gasped. Doug caught himself starting to snicker, and toned that way down, way fast.

"Hey, guy," he said, slipping into Neandertal "protective" mode. "Remember who's footin' the tab here."

"This is a ritual," I pointed out. "Not a conversation."

"Long as I'm payin', buddy, it's whatever I say it is," Doug snapped back.

Thus proving himself exactly the type of typical three "c" client I'd already assumed him to be—callow, classist and cheap. Kind of loser wants McDonald's-level asslicking along with his well-protected probe into the Abyss, plus an itemized list of everything his Daddy's trust-fund money was paying for, and special instructions on how to make the whole venture look like a tax-deductible educational expense.

To Sumer's carrion lord of the pit, He Who Holds The Sceptre Of Ereshkigal, one dog's soul, for services rendered, I thought, shooting Doug a glance, as I finished laying the foundations of Humbaba's features. And: Try writing *that* one off, you spoiled, Gapified snakefucker.

Well, I wax virulent. But these rich boys do get my goat, especially when they want something for nothing, and it just happens to be my something. Though my contempt for them as a breed may well stem from a certain lingering sense-memory of what *I* used to be like, back when I was one.

In the seven years since my rich old Baba Hark first paid my eventually prodigal way from downtown Hong Kong to RTA at Ryerson, I've dealt with elementals, demons, angels and ghosts, all of whom soon proved to be their own particular brand of pain in the ass. The angels I called on spoke a really obscure form of Hebrew; the demons decided my interest in them meant I was automatically laid open to twenty-four-hour-a-day Temptation, which didn't slack off until I had a sigilic declaration of complete neutrality tattooed on either palm. Elementals are surly and uncooperative. Ghosts cling—literally, in some cases. I remember coming to see Carraclough Devize one time (in hospital, as increasingly ever), only to have her stare fixedly over my left shoulder where the spectre of a dead man I'd recently helped to report his own murder still drifted—hand on the gap between the base of my skull and the top of my spine, through which most possessive spirits first enter. And ask, dryly: "So who's your new friend?"

She dabbled in magic too, ex-child medium that she is, just like the rest of us—helped me raise my share of demons, in some vain attempt to exorcize her own. Before the rest of the Black Magic Posse dropped off, that is, and I turned professional. And she decided it was easier acting like she was crazy all the time than it ever was trying to pretend she was entirely sane.

Now I make my living calling on obsolete gods like Our Lord Of Entrails here: They're far more cost-effective, in terms of customer service, since they don't demand reverence, just simple recognition. The chance to move, however briefly, back from the Wide World into the Narrow one.

Because the Wide World, as Carra herself first told me, is simply where things happen; the Narrow World, hub of all influences, is where things are *made* to happen. Where, if you cast your wards and research your incantations well enough, you can actually grab hold of the intersecting wheels of various dimensions, and spin them—however briefly—in the direction your client wants them to go.

Meanwhile, however—

"Way it strikes me," Doug Whatever went on, "in terms of parts and labor alone, I must be givin' you a thousand bucks every fifteen minutes. And aside from the dead dog, I still don't see anything worth talkin' about."

And: Oh no?

Well . . .

I closed my eyes. Felt cold purple inch down my fingers, nails suddenly alight. My hands gloving themselves with the bleak and shadeless flame of Power. That singing, searing rush—a kindled spark flaring up all at once, straight from my cortex to my groin, leaving nothing in between but the spell still on my lips.

Doug and his girlfriend saw it lap up over my elbows, and stepped back. As they did, a sidelong glance showed me what I wanted to see: Doug transfixed, bull-in-a-stall still and dumb, while Mrs Doug's little blue eyes got even rounder. But she wasn't staring at my sigil-incized palms, or the flickering purple haze connecting them—no, *she* was seeing what Doug's testosterone-drunk brain would have skipped right over, even if he'd been looking in the right direction: The twilit bridge's nearest support girder, just behind me, lapped and drowned in one big shadow that drew every other nearby object's shadow to it . . .

. . . except for where *I* stood.

Snarky Chinese faggot, bloody knife still in hand, smiling up at her under the nonexistent brim of that un-holy hat. With my whole body—burning hands included—suddenly rimmed in a kind of missing halo, a thin edge of blank-bright nothingness. The empty spot where my own shadow should be.

Noticing. Noticing me *notice* her noticing. Trying desperately to put two and two together and just plain getting five, over and over and over.

She wrinkled her brows at me—helpless, clueless. I just pursed my lips, gave her a sassy little wink. Telling them both, one last time:

"I said, *watch*."

And shut my eyes again.

* * *

February 14, 1987. For the gweilo rubes of Toronto, it was time to hand out the chocolate hearts, exchange cards that could make a diabetic go into shock, buy each other gift-bags full of underwear made from atrophied cotton candy. For us, it was just another night out with the Black Magic Posse.

Carra Devize, her pale braids stiff against the light, stray strands outflung in a crackling blue halo. Bruisy words crawling up and down her body as she spun a web of ectoplasm around herself, reel on reel of it, knotted like dirty string in the whitening air. Jen Cudahy, crying. Franz Froese, sweat-slick and deep in full chant trance, puking up names of Power, ecstatic with fear. And me, laughing, so drunk I could barely kneel.

With my left hand, with my bone-hilted hierarchical magician's knife, I cut my shadow from me—one crooked swipe, downward and sideways, pressing so hard I almost took part of my heel off along with it. I heard it give that sigh.

I cut my shadow from me, without a second thought. And then . . .

. . . I threw it away.

* * *

"One for Midnight Madness," I told the girl behind the Bloor's window, slipping her one of Doug Whatever's crisp new twenties; she smiled, and ripped the ticket for me.

I smiled back. There's no harm in it.

Hitting the candy bar, I stocked up an extra-large popcorn, a box of chocolate almonds, and a Cappucino from the cafe upstairs. My Ma always used to tell us not to eat after 12:00 p.m., but the program promised a brand new Shinya Tsukamoto flesh-into-metal monster mosh-fest—and after tonight's job, I was up for as much stimulation as I could stand.

Back down in the ravine, meanwhile, Doug and his girl still stood frozen above the remains of their mutual investment—their blood reverberate with a whispered loop of intimate-form Sumerian, heavily overlaid with mnemonic surtitles: Humbaba's answer to their question. The same question I hadn't wanted to know before they asked it, and certainly didn't care to know now.

I didn't exactly anticipate any repeat business from those two. But for what I'd made tonight, they could both disappear off the edge of the earth, for all I cared.

I took a big swallow of popcorn, licked the butter off my hands. A faint smell of Power still lingered under my nails—like dry ice, like old blood. Like burnt marigolds, seed and petal alike reduced to a fine, pungent ash.

Then the usher opened the doors, and I went in.

* * *

I used to be afraid of a lot of things, back when I was a nice, dutiful little Chinese boy. Dogs. Loud noises. Big, loud dogs that made big, loud noises. Certain concepts. Certain words used to communicate such concepts, like the worst, most unprovable word of all—"eternity".

Secretly, late at night, I would feel the universe spinning loose around me: Boundless, nameless, a vortice of darkness within which my life became less than a speck of dust. The night sky would tilt toward me, yawning. And I would lie there breathless, waiting for the roof to peel away, waiting to lose my grip. To rise and rise forever into that great, inescapable Nothing, to drift until I disappeared—not only as though I no longer was, but as though I had never been.

So I read too much, and saw too many movies, and played too many video-games, and drank too much, and took too many pills, and made my poor Ma worried enough to burn way too much incense in front of way too many pictures of my various Hark ancestors. Anything to distract myself. I took my Baba's feng shui advice, and moved my bedroom furniture around religiously, hoping to deflect the cold current of my neuroses onto somebody else for a while. Why not? He was a professional, after all.

And I was just a frightened child, a frightened prepubescent, a frightened adolescent—a spoiled, stupid, frightened young man with all the rich and varied life experience of a preserved duck egg, nodding and smiling moronically at the next in an endless line of prospective brides trotted out by our trusty family matchmaker, too weak to even hint around what really got my dick hard.

On the screen above me, bald, dark-goggled punks took turns drilling each other through the stomach, as yet another hapless salaryman turned into a pissed-off pile of ambulatory metal shavings. Japanese industrial blared, while blood hit the lens in buckets. I could hear the audience buck-

225

ling under every new blow, riding alternate waves of excitement and revulsion.

And I just sat there, unconcerned; crunching my almonds, watching the carnage. Suddenly realizing I hadn't felt that afraid for a long, long time—or afraid at all, in fact.

Of anything.

* * *

Then somebody came in late; I moved my coat, so he could sit down next to me. A mere peripheral blur of a guy—apparently young, vaguely Asian. Hair to below his shoulders, temples shaved like a samurai's, and the whole mass tied back with one long, thin, braided sidelock—much the way I used to wear it, before Andre down at the Living Hell convinced me to get my current buzz-cut.

I never took my eyes off the action. But I could feel the heat of him all the way through the leg of my good black jeans, cock rearing flush against the seam of my crotch with each successive heartbeat.

The screen was abloom with explosions. A melting, roiling pot of white-hot metal appeared, coalescing, all revved up and ready to pour.

Some pheremonal envelope of musk, slicking his skin, began expanding. Began to slick mine.

More explosions followed.

I felt the uniquely indentifiable stir of his breath—in, out; out, in—against my cheek, and actually caught myself shivering.

Above us, two metal men spun and ran like liquid sun, locked tight together. The credits were beginning to roll. I thought: Snap out of it, Jude.

Run the checklist. Turn around, smile. Ask him his name, if he's got a place.

Tell him you want to taste his sweat, and feel his chest on your back 'til the cows come home.

Then the lights came back up, much more quickly than I'd been expecting them to—I blinked, shocked temporarily blind. Brushed away tears, as my eyes strained to readjust.

And found I'd been cruising an empty seat.

* * *

The next day, I picked Carra up at the Clarke, signed her out and took her for lunch at the College/Yonge Fran's, as promised. She looked frail, so drained the only color in her face came from her freckles. I bought her coffee, and watched her drink it.

"Met this guy at *Tetsuo III*," I said. "Well . . . met is probably too strong a way to put it."

She looked at me over the rim of her glasses, raising one white-blonde smudge of brow. Her eyes were grey today, with that moonstone opacity which meant she was not only drugged, but also consciously trying not to read my mind—so whatever they had her on couldn't really be working all that well.

"I thought you were taken," she said.

I snorted. "Ed? He says I broke his heart."

"I don't doubt it."

I shrugged. I could never quite picture anyone's soft little musclebox as brittle enough to break, myself; it's an image that smacks of drama, and Ed (though sweet) is not exactly the world's most dramatic guy. But be that as it may.

"Dumb gweilo told me I had something missing," I told her, laughing. "You fucking believe that?"

Now it was her turn to shrug.

"Well, you do, Jude," she replied, reasonably enough. Adding, as she took another sip: "I personally find it quite . . . restful."

* * *

Carra Devize, my one and only incursion into enemy territory—lured by the web that haloes her, the shining, clinging psychic filaments of her Gift. The quenchless hum of her innate glory. Most people want to find someone who'll touch their hearts, enter them at some intimate point and lodge there, mainlining instinct back and forth, in a haze of utter sympathy. And Carra, of course—congenitally incapable of any other kind of real human contact—just wants to be alone; enforced proximity, emotional or otherwise, only serves to make her nauseous. So she bears my enduring, inappropriate love for her like some unhealed internal injury, with painful patience. Which is why I try not trouble her with it, any more often than I have to.

That calamitous December of 1989, when I knew the Hark family money tree had finally dried up for good—after I came out, a half-semester into my first year at RTA, and the relatives I was staying with informed my ultra-trad Baba that he had a rebellious faggot son to disinherit—I moved in with Carra for some melted mass of time or so, into the rotting Annex town-house she then shared with her mother Geillis, known as Gala: Gala Carraclough Devize, after whose family Carra was named. We'd sit around the kitchen in our bare feet, the TV our only light, casting each other's horoscopes and drinking peach liqueur until we passed out, as Gala moved restlessly around upstairs, knocking on the floor with her cane whenever she wanted Carra to come up. I never saw her face, never heard her voice; I guess it was sort of like being Carra, for a while. In that I was living with at least one ghost.

And this went on until one particular night, she turned to me and said, abruptly: "So maybe I'm like that chick, that Tarot-reading chick from *Live And Let Die*. What do you think?"

"Jane Seymour."

"Was it?" We both tried to remember, then gave up. "Well?"

"Have sex, and the powers go away?"

"It's the one thing I never tried."

In a way, we were both virgins; I think it's also pretty safe to say we were probably both also thinking of somebody else. But when I finally came, I could feel her sifting me, riding my orgasm from the inside out, instead of having one of her own.

The next time I saw her, I'd been supporting myself for over a month. And she still had an I.V. jack stuck in the crook of her elbow, anchored with fresh hospital tape.

* * *

There were a couple of movies playing that Carra was interested in, so we ended up at the Carlton—but none of their 2:00-ish shows got out early enough for her to be able to keep her 6:00 curfew.

"So what happens if we stay out later?" I asked, idly.

Another shrug. "Nothing much. Except they might put me back on suicide watch."

That pale grey day, and her grey gaze. The plastic I.D. bracelet riding up on one thin-skinned wrist, barely covering a shallow red thread of fresh scar tissue where she'd tried to scrub some phantom's love-note from her flesh with a not-so-safety razor. No reason not to wear long sleeves, cold as it was. But she just wouldn't. She wouldn't give her ghosts the satisfaction.

I looked away. Looked at anything else. Which she couldn't help but notice, of course.

Being psychic.

"This guy you met," she said, studying the curb, as we stood waiting for the light to change. "He made an impression."

"Could be," I allowed. "Why? Something I should know about?"

She still didn't look up. Picking and choosing. When you see so much, all at once, it must be very confusing to have to concentrate on any one particular sliver of the probable—to decide whether it's here already, or already gone, or still yet to be. Her eyebrows crept together, tentative smears of light behind her lenses, as she played with her braid, raveling and unraveling its tail.

" . . . something," she repeated, finally.

We started across, only to be barely missed by a fellow traveller from the Pacific Rim in a honking great blue Buick, who apparently hadn't yet learned enough of North American driving customs to quite work the phrase "pedestrian always has the right of way" into his vocabulary. I caught Carra's arm and spun, screaming Cantonese imprecations at his tail-lights; he yelled something back, most of it lost beneath his faulty muffler's bray. My palms itched, fingers eager to knit a basic entropic sigil—to spell out the arcane words that would test whether or not his brakes worked as well as his mouth, when given just the right amount of push on a sudden skid.

I felt Carra's hand touch mine, gently.

"Leave it," she said. "It'll come when it comes, for him. And believe me—it's coming."

"Dogfucker thinks he's still in Kowloon," I muttered. Which actually made her laugh.

* * *

But we got back just a minute or two later than my watch claimed we would, and the nurse was already there—waiting for us, for her, behind a big, scratched wall of bulletproof glass.

Needle in hand.

* * *

After which I went straight home, through this neat and pretty city I now call my own—even though, having long since defaulted on my student visa, I am actually not supposed to be anywhere near it, let alone living in it. Straight home to (surprise!) Chinatown, just below Spadina and Dundas, off an unnamed little alleyway behind the now-defunct Kau Soong Clouds In Rain softcore porno theatre, whose empty storefront is usually occupied by either a clutch of little old local ladies selling baskets full of bok choi or a daily-changing roster of F.O.B. hustlers hocking anything from imitation Swiss watches to illegally-copied Anime videotapes.

Next door, facing Spadina, the flanking totem dragons of Empress' Noodle grinned their welcome. I slipped between them, into the fragrant domain of Grandmother Yau Yan-er, who claims to be the oldest Chinese vampire in Toronto.

"Jude-ah!" she called out from the back, as I came through the door. "Sit. Wait." I heard the mah-jong tiles click and scatter under her hands. It was her legendary Wednesday night game, played with a triad of less long-lived hsi-hsue-kuei for a captive audience of cowed and attentive ghosts, involving much stylish cheating and billions of stolen yuan—garnished, on occasion, with a discreet selection of aspiring human retainers willing to bet their blood, their memories or their sworn service on a chance at eternal life.

Grandmother Yau's operation has been open since 1904, in one form or another. She's an old-school kind of monster: Lotus feet, nine inch nails, the whole silk bolt. One of her ghosts brought me tea, which I nursed until she called her bet, won the hand with a Red Dragon kept up her sleeve, and glided over.

"Big sister," I said, dipping my head.

"Jude-ah, you're insulting," she scolded, in Mandarin-accented Cantonese. "Why don't you come see me? It's obvious, bad liars and tale-tellers have got you in their grip. They have slandered my reputation and made even fearless men like you afraid of me."

"Not so. You know I'd gladly pay a thousand taels of jade just to kiss you, if I thought I'd get my tongue back afterwards."

"Oh, I'm too old for you," she replied, blithely. "But you'll see—I have the best mei-po in Toronto, a hardworking ghost contracted to me for ninety-nine hundred years. Good deal, ah? Smarter than those British foreign devils were with Hong Kong. We will talk together, she and I, and get you fixed up before I get bored enough to finally let myself die, with a good Chinese marriage to a good Chinese . . . "

She let her voice trail away, carefully, before she might have to assign an actual gender-specific pronoun to this mythical "good Chinese"—person.

"I don't think I could afford your mei-po's fees," I pointed out, tucking into my freshly-arrived plate of Sticky Rice With Shrimp And Seasonal Green. To which she just smiled, thinly—patted my wrist with one clawed hand—and went back to her game, leaving me to the rest of my meal.

A fresh ghost brought me more tea, bowing. I bowed back, and sipped it, thinking about Toronto.

Hong Kong was everything my Ryerson fuck-buddies ever thought it would be—loud, bright, fast, unforgiving. When I was five years old, my au pair took me out without calling the bodyguards first; a quarter-hour later, I buried my face in her skirt as some low-level Triad thug beat a man to pulp right in front of us, armed only with a big, spiky, stinky fruit called a dhurrian. Believe me, the experience left an impression.

In Toronto, the streets are level, the use of firearms strictly controlled, and swearing aloud is enough to draw stares. Abusive maniacs camp out on every corner, and passersby step right over them—quickly, quietly, without rancor or interest. It's a place so clean that U.S. movie crews have to import or manufacture enough garbage to make it pass for New York; it's also North America's largest centre for consensual S & M activity. But if you stop any person on the street, they'll tell you they think living here is nothing special—nice, though a little boring.

The truth is, Toronto is a crossroads where the dead congregate. The city goes about its seasonal business, bland and blind, politely ignoring the hungry skins of dead people stalking up and down its frozen main arteries: Vampires, ghouls, revenants, ghosts, wraiths, zombies, even a select few mage's golems cobbled haphazardly together from whatever inanimate objects came to hand. There's enough excess appetite here to power a world-eating competition. And you don't have to be a magician or a medium to recognize it, either.

"Dead want more time," Carra told me, long after yet another drunken midnight, back in her mother's house—both of us too sloshed to even remember what a definite article *was*, let alone try using it correctly. "'S what they always say. Time, recognition, remembrance . . . "

Trailing off, taking another slug. Then fixing me, with one

blood-threaded eye. And half-growling, half-projecting—so soundlessly loud she made my temples throb with phantom pain—

"Want blood, too. *Our* blood. Yours . . . mine . . . "

. . . but don't mean we gotta give it to 'em, just 'cause they ASK.

The longer I stay in this city, the more I see it works like a corpse inside a corpse inside a corpse—the kind of puzzle you can only solve by letting it rot. Once it's gone all soft, you can come back and give it a poke, see what sticks out. Until then, you just have to hold your nose.

About an hour later, I was almost to the door when Grandmother Yau materialized again, at my elbow. Laying her brocade sleeve over my arm, she said, softly:

"Jude-ah, before you leave, I must tell you that I see you twice. You here, drinking my tea. You somewhere else, doing something else. I see you dimly, as though through a Yin mirror—split, but not yet cut apart. Caught in a mesh of darkness."

I frowned.

"This thing you see," I asked, carefully. "Is it . . . dangerous?"

She smiled a little wider, and withdrew the authoritative weight of her sleeve. I saw the red light of the paper lanterns gild her upper fangs.

"Hard to tell without knowing more, don't you think?" She said. "But there are many kinds of danger, Hark Chiu-wai-ah."

* * *

Off Spadina again, and down the alley, fumbling for my key. Upstairs, the clutch of loud weekend hash-smokers I call my neighbors had apparently decided to spend tonight out on the town, for which I was duly grateful. Locking the door to my apartment—and renewing the protective sigils warding its frame—I took my bone-hilted knife from its sheath around my neck, under my Nine Inch Nails t-shirt, and wrapped it in a Buddhist rosary of mule-bone skulls and haematite beads, murmuring a brief prayer of reconsecration.

My machine held a fresh crop of messages from Ed, both hopeful and hateful.

Poor lonely little gweilo boy, I thought, briefly. *No rice for you tonight.*

Then I lit some incense (sage), peeled a few bills from the wad of twenties Doug Whatever had given me, and burned them as makeshift Hell Money in front of an old Polaroid of my grandmother—the only ancestor I care to worship anymore, these faithless Canadian days.

Own nothing, owe nothing. Pray to nothing. Pay nothing. No loyalties, no scruples. And make sure nothing ever means more to you than any other nothing you can name, or think of.

These are my rules, all of which I learned from Carra Devize, along with the fluid surprise of what it feels like to be gripped by vaginal muscles—the few, accurate, infinitely bitter philosophical lessons which she, psychic savant that she is, can only ever teach, never follow.

Magicians demand the impossible, routinely. Without even knowing it, they have begun to work backwards against the flow of all things: Contra mundi. A price follows. Miracles cannot be had without being paid for. It's the illogic of a child who asks WHY must what is be? Why do I have to be just a boy, just a girl? Why is the sky blue? Why can't I fly, if I want to? Why did Mommy have to die? Why do *I* have to die?

We call what we don't understand magic, in order to explain why we *can't* control it; we name whatever we find, usually after ourselves—because, by naming something, you come to own it.

Thus rules are discovered, and quantified, and broken. So that, when there are enough new rules, magic can become far less an Art . . . than a science.

And it's so *easy*, that's the truly frightening thing. You do it without thinking, the first time. Do it without knowing just what you've done, 'till—long—after.

Frightening for most. But not for me . . . and not for Carra, either.

Once.

* * *

I was lying in bed, almost asleep, when the phone rang. I grabbed for it, promptly knocking a jar full of various complimentary bar and nightclub matchbooks off my night-stand.

"Wei?" I snapped, before I could stop myself. Then: "I mean—who is this?"

A pause. Breathing.

"Jude?"

"Franz?"

Froese.

And here's the really interesting part—apparently, he thought he was returning my call.

"Why would I call you, Franz?"

"I thought maybe you heard something more."

"More than what?"

With a slight edge of impatience: "About *Jen*."

The Jen in question being Jen Cudahy, fellow Black Magic Posse member, of lachrymose memory—a languid, funereal calla lily of a girl with purple hair and black vinyl underwear, who spent her spare periods writing execrable sestinas with titles like "My Despair, Mon Espoir" and "When Shadows Creep". She'd worked her way through RTA as a dominatrix, pulling down about $500 per session to let judges and vice cops clean her bathroom floor with their tongues. The last time I'd seen her, over eighteen months prior, she was running a lucrative new dodge built around what she called "vampire sex shows"—a rotating roster of nude, bored teenage Goths jacking open their veins, pumping out a couple of cc's for the drones, and then fingerpainting each other. Frottage optional. She asked me what I thought, and I told her it struck me as wasteful. But she assured me it was the quickest way she currently knew to invoke the not-so-dead god Moolah.

Franz had loved Jen for what probably only seemed like forever to outside observers, mostly from afar—interspersed, here and there, with a few painful passages of actual physical intimacy. They'd met while both attending the same Alternative high school, where they'd barricade themselves into the students' lounge, drop acid and have long conversations about which of them was de-evolving faster.

"Okay," I said, carefully. "I'll bite. What about Jen?"

"She says she's possessed."

I raised an eyebrow. "And this is different . . . how?"

Way back in 1987, shortly before I cut my shadow away—or maybe shortly after (I'm not sure, since I was pretty well continuously intoxicated at that point)—Jen petitioned for entrance to the Black Magic Posse. She'd been hanging around on the fringes, watching and listening quietly as Carra, Franz and I first planned, then dissected, our weekly adventures in the various Mantic Sciences. I was all for it; the more the merrier, not to mention the drunker. Franz was violently opposed. And Carra didn't care too much, one way or the other—her dominating attitude then, regarding almost any subject you could name, being remarkably similar to the way mine is, now.

Jen quickly showed a certain flair for the little stuff. She tranced out easily, far more so than Franz, who usually had to chant himself incoherent in order to gain access to his own unconscious. This made her an almost perfect scryer, able to map our possible future difficulties through careful study of either the palpable (the way a wax candle split and fell as it melted—Carromancy) or impalpable (the way that shadows scattered and reknit when exposed to a moving source of light—Sciomancy).

But when it came to anything a bit more concrete, it would be time to call in the founding generation: Franz, with his painstaking research and gift for dead languages; Carra, with her post-electroshock halo of rampant energy, her untold years of channelling experience, her barely-controlled psychometric Gift; me, the devout amateur, with my gleeful willingness to do whatever it took. My big mouth and my total lack of fear, artificial though it might have been—at that point—

—and my bone-hilted knife.

"It's bad, Jude. She needs an exorcism."

"Try therapy," I suggested, idly slipping my earrings back in. "It's cheaper."

There was a tiny, accusatory pause.

"I would've thought you'd feel just a little responsible," he said, at last. "Considering she's been this way ever since you and Carra let her help raise that demon of yours . . . "

"Fleer? He's a mosquito with horns. Barely a postal clerk, in Hell's hierarchy."

" . . . without drawing a proper circle first."

I bridled. "The circle was fine; my wards held. They always hold. Carra even threw her the wand, when she saw Jen'd stepped over the outer rim—Jen was just too shit-scared to use it. So whatever trauma she may have talked herself into getting is her business."

"It's pretty hard to use a wand when you're rolling around on the floor, barking!"

"So? She stopped."

Another pause. "Well, she's started again," Franz said, quietly.

I swung my legs over the side of the bed and retrieved my watch from the night-stand, squinting at it. Not even three; most of my favorite hang-outs would still be open, once I'd disposed of this conversation.

Which—knowing Franz—might well be easier said than done.

"Gee, Franz," I said, lightly, "when you told me you never wanted to see me again, I kind of thought you meant all of me. Up to and including the able-to-exorcise-your-crazy-ex-girlfriend part."

"Cut the shit, you Cantonese voodoo faggot," he snapped.

"Kiss my crack, Mennonite Man," I snapped back. "For ten years, you cross the street every time you see me coming—but now I've suddenly got something you want, that makes me your new best friend? We partied, Franz. We hung around. The drugs were good, but I'm not sure how that qualifies you to guilt me into mowing your lawn, let alone into doing an expensive and elaborate ritual on behalf of someone I barely even liked, just because she happens to get your nuts in an uproar."

"But . . . you . . . " His voice trailed away for a minute. Then, accusingly again: "You already said if I found out what was wrong with her, what it was going to take to make her better—you'd do it. I didn't even know about any of this, until *you* called and told me!"

I snorted. "Oh, uh huh."

"Why would I lie?"

I shrugged. "Why wouldn't you?"

Obviously, we had reached some kind of impasse. I studied my nails, and listened while Franz tried—not too successfully—to control his breathing long enough to have the last word.

"If you change your mind again," he said, finally, "I'm at my mother's. You know the number."

Then he hung up.

* * *

Inevitably, talking to Franz sent my mind skittering back to the aftermath of Valentine's Day, 1987: A five a.m. Golden Griddle "breakfast" with the Black Magic Posse, Carra sipping her coffee and watching—with some slight amusement—while Franz blurted out:"But it was your *soul*, Jude."

"Metaphorically, maybe. So?"

"So now you're just half a person. And not the *good* half, either."

At which I really just had to laugh out loud, right in his morose, lapsed-Mennonite face. Such Goddamn drama, all because I'd made the same basic sacrifice a thousand other magicians have made to gain control over their Art: Nothing more serious than cutting off the top joint of your finger, or putting out an eye, except for not being nearly as aesthetically repugnant or physically impractical.

"And that's why you'll always be a mediocre magician, Franz," I replied. "Because you can't do what it takes to go the distance."

"I have *never* been 'mediocre'. I'm better than you ever were—"

"You used to be. Back when Carra first introduced us. But now *I'm* better, and I'm *getting* better, all the time. While *you*, my friend . . . are exactly as good . . . as you're ever going to get."

Simple, really. My fear held me back, so I got rid of it. My so-called "friends" *wanted* to hold me back—the ones still human enough to be jealous of my growing Power, at least. So . . .

. . . thanks for the advice, Franz, old pal. And fuck you very much.

* * *

Sleep no longer an option, I hauled my ass out of bed, ready to pull my pants up and hit the street (so I could find myself a nicely hard-bodied reason to pull them down again, no doubt). That guy from the theatre, maybe; hot clutch of something at my sternum at the very thought, moving from throat to belly to zipper beneath. Itching. *Twisting.*

If only I knew his name, that was. Or could even remember more than the barest bright impression of his shadowed face . . .

But just as I grabbed for my coat, a thought suddenly struck me: How hard could it really be to find my nameless number-one crush of the moment, if I put some—effort—into it?

The idea itself becoming a kind of beginning, potent and portentious, lazy flick of a match over mental sandpaper. Synaptic sizzle.

Beneath my bathroom sink is a cupboard full of cleaning products and extra toilet paper; behind these objects, well-hidden from any prying eyes, is a KISS lunchbox Carra gave me for my twenty-fourth birthday. Made In Taiwan stamp, cheap clasp, augmented with a length of bicycle lock chain.

And behind that—

A glass key made by a friend of mine, who usually specializes in custom-blown bongs. A letter from the Seventh Circle, written with a dead girl's hand. The ringing brass quill from a seraph's pin-feather. A small, green bottle full of saffron. A box of red chalk.

If you want to raise a little Hell—or Heaven—then you're going to need just the right tools. Luckily, I've spent years of my life learning exactly which ones are right for my particular purposes. And paying, subtly, for the privilege of ownership, once I finally found them.

I took my little tin box of tricks back into the living room, where I gathered up a few more select items, and arranged them around me one by one:

TV remote on my left, small hand-mirror on my right, box at Due North. Chalk and compass in one hand, bone-hilted knife in the other. I flipped on the TV—already cued up to my favorite spot on one of my favorite porno tapes—sat back, and drew yet another perfect circle around myself. Made a few extra notations, here and there, just inside the circle's rim: The signs of Venus, Inanna, Ishtar, Astarte, Aphrodite. As many of the ancient significators of desire personified as I could remember, off the top of my increasingly aroused head. Words and images to help me focus—names of power to lend me their strength.

More magician's rules: As long as you're not looking to change anything irrevocably—cause real hate or true love, make somebody die, bring somebody back to life—you can do it all on your own. For minor glamours, for self-protection, willpower is enough.

For larger stuff, however, you need help.

Going by these standards, it's always tricky doing a negative spell—unless you make sure it's on someone else's behalf, so you have no direct stake in its outcome. Making the rebound factor fall entirely back on them.

Obviously, it takes a special kind of detachment to pull this off. But ever since I cut my shadow away, I truly do seem to have a knack for not caring enough . . . about *anything* . . . to get hurt.

Besides, love—true or otherwise—was the last thing on my mind.

As I wrote, a red dusting of chalk spread out across my hand, grinding itself into the lines of my palm. Shrugging off my shirt, I brushed the excess off down my chest, onto my abdomen. Five scarlet fingers, pointing towards my groin.

Up onscreen, an explicit flesh-toned tangle was busily pixilating itself into soft focus through sheer force of back-and-forth action. I turned the mirror to catch it, then zapped the TV quickly off, wrapping my chosen lust-icon up tight in a black silk scarf I keep handy for such occasions. Then I leant the mirror against my forehead and repeated the time-honored formula to myself, aloud:

"Listen! Oh, now you have drawn near to hearkening—your spit, I take it, I eat it; your body, I take it, I eat it; your flesh, I take it, I eat it; your heart, I take it, I eat it. O Ancient Ones, this man's soul has come to rest at the edge of my body. You are to lay hold to it, and never to let it go, until I indicate otherwise. Bind him with black threads and let him roam restless, never thinking upon any other place or person."

The spells don't change. They never change. And that's because, quite frankly—

"Bring him to me, and me to him. Bring us both together."

—they never really *have* to.

Already, I felt myself stirring, sleepily. Jerking awake. Arching to meet those five red fingers halfway.

Purple no-halo raising the hairs on the backs of my forearms, then slipping down to slime my palms with eerie phosphorescence; my wards holding fast, as ever, against the gathering funnel of Power forming outside the circle's rim. My Art wrapping 'round me like a cold static coccoon, sparking and twinging. A dull scribble of bio-electricity, followed by a wash of gooseflesh. Nothing natural. All as it should be.

Until: Something, somewhere, snapped.

The mirror cracked across, images emptied. The funnel suddenly slack as a rubber band, then blown away in a single breath-slim stain—dispersed like ectoplasm against a strung thread, or brains on a brick wall. Just gone, baby, gone.

Which was odd, granted—annoying, definitely; left alone and aroused once more, laid open for any port in a hormonal storm. Even sort of intriguing, for all that I wasn't exactly all that interested in being *intrigued* right now, this very minute. I mean, damn.

But no, I wasn't scared. Not even then. Why should I be?

I sat back on my heels, suddenly remembering how I'd once met my former aunt on the street once, just after Pride, arm still in Ed's, my tongue still rummaging around in the dark of his mouth. How she'd clicked her teeth at me, spat on the sidewalk between us, and called me a banana. How Ed had blanched, then turned red; how I'd just laughed, amazed she even knew the term.

And how I couldn't understand, later on, why he was still so upset—about the fact that I hadn't been upset at all.

Because that's how things go, when you're shadowless: How trouble slides away from you, finding no purchase on your immaculate incompleteness. How the only thing you can hear, most days and nights, is the bright and seductive call of your own Power—your Art, your Practice. How it lures and pulls you, draws you like a static charge, singing: Follow, follow, follow.

And how I do, inevitably—without fail—even at the cost of anything and everything in my way. Like the lack of a shadow follows a black hole sun.

This is probably worth looking at, sometime, I thought. Got the words wrong, maybe, one of the symbols; have to do a little research, re-consecrate my tools, re-examine my methods. All that.

(Sometime.)

But . . .

. . . not tonight.

* * *

An hour later, I swerved up Church Street, heading straight for the Khyber. Wednesday was Fetish Night, and though nothing I had on was particularly appropriate, I knew a brief flirtation with Vic the bouncer would probably get me in anyway. The street glittered, febrile with windchill, unfolding itself in a series of pointilescent flashes: Bar doorways leaking black light and Abba; a muraled restaurant wall sugared with frost; parks and alleyways choked with unseasonably-dressed chain-smokers, shivering and snide, almost too cold to cruise.

Past the bar and out through the musically segregated dance-floor (the Smiths vs. Traci Lords, standing room only), I finally found my old RTA party partner Gil Wycliffe—now head of creative design for Quadrant Leather—strapped face-down over a vaulting horse in one of the club's back rooms, getting his bare ass beaten red and raw by some all-purpose Daddy in a Sam Browne belt and a fetching pair of studded vinyl chaps. The paddle being used looked like one of Gil's own creations; it had a crack like a long-range rifle-shot, and left a diamond-shaped pattern of welts behind that made his buttocks glow as patchily as underdone steaks.

I must admit that I've never quite understood the appeal of sadomasochism, for all that "they"—those traditionally unspecified (though probably Caucasian) arbiters of societal lore—would probably like to credit me with some kind of genetic yearning toward pain and suffering for fun and pleasure, just because the whole concept supposedly originated in the Mysterious East: The Delight Of The Razor, the Death Of The Thousand And One Cuts. All that stale old Sax Rohmer/James Bond bullshit.

Then again, I guess there's no particular reason anyone else really has to "get" it, unless they *are* a masochist. Or a sadist.

The Daddy paused for a half-second between licks, catching my eye in open invitation; I signed disinterest, leaned back against the wall to wait this little scene out, let my gaze wander.

And there he was.

First a mere lithe flicker between gyrating bodies, then a half-remem-bered set of lines and angles, gilded with mounting heat: Vague reflections off a high, flat cheekbone, a wryly gentle mouth, a bent and pliant neck. That whole lambent outline—so neat, so trim, so invitingly indefinite. It was my Bloor mystery man himself, swaying out there at the very heart of the crowd. Head back, body loose. Shaking and burning in the strobelights' glare.

Oh, *waaah*.

Every inch of me sprang awake at the sight, skin suddenly acrawl with possibilities.

The way he stood. The way he moved. The sheer, oddly familiar glamour of him was an almost physical thing, even to the cut and cling of his all-black outfit—though I couldn't have described its components if you'd asked me to, I somehow knew I might as well have picked them out myself.

I *know* this man, I thought, slowly, sounding the paradox through in my mind. Even though I do *not* know this man.

But I *wanted* to know this man.

Lit from within by sudden desire, I closed my eyes and bit down hard on my lower lip, tasting his flesh as sharply as though it were my own.

Movement stirred by my elbow—Gil, upright once more, reverently stroking his own well-punished cheeks. He winced and grinned, drowsily ecstastic, blissed out on an already-peaking surge of endorphins.

Turning, I screamed, over the beat: "WHO'S THE DUDE?"

He raised a brow. *"TONY HU?"*

Definitely not.

"I *KNOW* WHO TONY HU IS, GIL."

"THEN WHY'D YOU *ASK*?" he screamed back, shrugging.

Obviously, not a night for subtlety. I waved goodbye and stepped quickly off, resolved to take matters firmly by the balls. I wove my way back across the dance-floor, eyes kept firmly on the prize: Mr Hunk Of The Millennium's retreating back, bright with subtle muscle; the clean flex and coil of his golden spine, calling to me even more clearly with every footfall.

He was a walking slice of pure aura, a streak of sexual magnetism, and I followed him as far and as quickly as I could—up the ramp and into the washroom at the head of the stairs, just past the coat-check stand, not the large one with the built-in shower stalls (so useful for Jock Nights and Wet

Diaper Contests) but the small one with the barred windows, built to cater to those few customers whose bladders had become temporarily more important to them than their genitals.

The place had no back door, not even an alcove to hide in. But when I finally got there, I found the place empty except for a man crouched half on his knees by the far wall, wiping his mouth and wavering back and forth above a urinal full of fresh vomit.

Annoyed by the force of my own disappointment, I hissed through my teeth and kicked the back of the washroom door. The sound made the man look up, woozily.

"Jude," he said. "It *is* you. Right?"

I narrowed my eyes. Shrugged.

"You should know," I replied. Adding: "Ed."

* * *

He said he'd planned to spend the night waiting for me, but that the Khyber's buy one drink, get another one of equal or lesser value free policy had begun to take its toll pretty early on. I agreed that he certainly seemed in no shape to get himself home alone.

As for what followed, I've definitely had worse—from the same source, too. He didn't puke again, either, which is always a big plus.

That night—wrapped in Ed's arms, breathing his beer-flavored breath—I dreamed of Carra hanging between heaven and earth with one foot on cliff, the other in air, like the Tarot's holy Fool. I dreamed she looked at me with her empty eyes, and asked: What did you *do* to yourself, Jude? Oh, Jude. What did you *do*?

And I woke, shivering, with a whisper caught somewhere in the back of my throat—nothing but three short words to show for all my arcane knowledge, in the end, when questioned so directly. Just *I*, and *don't*, and *know*.

But thinking, resentfully, at almost the same time: I mean, you're the psychic, right? So . . .

. . . you tell *me*.

* * *

The next morning, Ed came out of the kitchen with coffees and Danishes in hand, only to find me hunting around for my pants; he stopped in his tracks, striking a pose of anguished surprise so flawless I had to stop myself—from laughing.

"You heartless little bastard," he said.

I sighed.

"We broke up, Ed," I reminded him, gently. "Your idea, as I recall."

"So why'd you even call me, then—if you were just planning to suck and run?"

"I didn't."

"You fucking well *did.*"

I glanced up from my search, suddenly interested—this conversation was beginning to sound familiar, in more ways than one. Shades of Franz, so sure I was the one who'd called him about Jen. So definite in his belief that I'd actually told him I would help her out with the latest in her series of recurrent supernatural/psychological problems . . . and for free, no less.

"You called last night, when I was studying for Trig. Said you'd been thinking about us. Said you'd be down at the Khyber anyway, so show up, and you'd find me."

"Last night."

"Oh, Jude, enough with this bullshit. You're telling me what, it just slipped your mind?" He grabbed his desk phone, stabbed for the star key and brandished it my way. "How about that?"

I squinted at the display. "That says 'unknown caller'," I pointed out.

Ed dropped the phone, angrily. "Look, fuck you, okay? It was you."

With or without evidence, there was something interesting going on here. A call from somebody who claims to be me being received once is a misunderstanding, maybe a coincidence. But twice? In the same night?

By two different people?

I see you twice, Grandmother Yau had said. And Carra, weighing her words:

. . . *something.*

My pants proved to be wadded up and shoved under the bed, right next to Ed's cowboy boots. I shook them out, pulled them back on, buttoned the fly. Ed, meanwhile, kept right on with his time-honored tirade, hitting all the usual high spots: My lack of interest, my lack of loyalty. My lack, out of bed, of anything that might be termed normal emotional affect. My *lack*, in general.

Adding, quieter: "And you never loved me, either. Fuck, you never even really wanted me to love *you.*"

"Did I ever say I *did*?"

"Yes."

Coat already half done up, I looked at him again, frankly amazed. Unable to stop myself from blurting—

"—and you *believed* me?"

* * *

Heartless, I found myself repeating—a good half-hour later—as I fought my way east through the College Street wind tunnel, back from Ed's apart- ment. *Heart-lost. Heard last. Hardglass.* Then, smiling slightly: *Hard-ASS*.

The word itself disintegrating under close examination, melting apart on my mental tongue. Like it was ever supposed to mean anything much—aside from Ed's latest take on the established him/me party line: "I used to quote-quote 'love' you, but now I quote-quote 'hate' you, and here's yet another lame excuse why."

Annoyed to realize I was still thinking about it, I shrugged the whole mess away in one brief move, so hard and quick it actually hurt.

Chi-shien gweilo! I thought. What would I want with a heart? You don't need a heart to do magic.

Which is true. You don't.

No more than you need a shadow.

* * *

A sharp left turn, then Church Street again: Going down, this time. My Docs struck hard against the cracked concrete, again and again—each new stride sending up aftershocks that made my ankles spark with pain, as though that shrugged-away mess were somehow boomeranging back to haunt me with its ever-increasing twinge. And because I couldn't moderate myself, couldn't control either my speed or my boots' impact, the ache soon reached my chest—after a couple of blocks—and lodged there, throbbing.

Rhythm becoming thought, thought becoming memory; memory, which tends to shuck itself, to peel away. You get older, look back through a child's tunnel vision, and realize you never knew the whole that tied the details together. You were just along for the ride, moving from experience to experience, a flat spectacle, some kind of guideless tour. You

244

remember—or think you remember—what happened, but not where, or why. What you did, but not with who. Details fade. People's names get lost in the white noise.

Reluctantly, therefore—for the second time in as many days—I found myself thinking about that shell of a thing I'd once been, back before the big split: That fresh-faced, fresh-scrubbed, fresh-off-the-boat Chink twink with his fifteen pairs of matching penny-loafers and his drawer-full of grey silk ties. And just as smiley-face quiet, as neat and polite, as veddy, veddy, Brit-inflectedly *restrained* as he'd always been, the homegrown HK golden boy mask still firmly in place, even without a Ba and Ma immediately on hand to do his patented straight-Asian-male dance for anymore . . .

Up 'till he'd met Carra, at least. 'Till she'd sat down beside him in study hall, her sleeves pushed up to show the desperate phantom scribble circling one wrist like a ringworm surfacing for air; looked right through him like his head was made of glass, seen all his ugly, hidden parts at once, and shown him exactly how wrong he'd always been about the nature he struggled to keep in check at all costs, the fears—formless and otherwise—he'd fought against tooth and nail all his relatively brief, bland, blind little life.

How restraint wasn't about powerlessness in the face of such terrors at all, but rather about being afraid of your own power. Its reality, its strength. Its endless range of unchecked possibilities, the good, the bad—

—and the indifferent.

I remember how freeing it felt to not "have" to watch myself all the time, at long last; nobody else was going to do it for me, and why should they? My first impulse, in every situation—as I well knew—was always to the angry, the selfish, the petty. I tried to be kind, mainly because I'd been so rigidly inculcated with the general Taoist/Christian principle that doing so was always the "right" thing *to* do. But even when I managed a good deed here and there, I knew it to be just so much hypocrisy, nothing more. *It was the least I could do, so I did it.*

Parental love is a matchless thing; if it weren't for that, most of us wouldn't have a pot to piss in, affectionately speaking. But even at its most irreplacable, it's still pretty cheap. Any ape loves their children; spiders lie still while theirs crawl around inside them, happy to let them eat their guts.

The only reason anybody unrelated is ever nice to anyone else, meanwhile, is as a sort of pre-emptive emotional strike—to prevent themselves from being treated as badly, potentially, as they might have treated other people. Which makes love only the lie two brains on spines tell each other, the lie that says: "You exist, because I love you. You exist, because you can see yourself in my eyes."

So we blunder from hope to hope, hollowed and searching. All of us equally incomplete.

And after all these years, still the sting comes, the liquid pressure in the chest and nose, the migraine-forerunner frown. Phantom pain. The ghost without the murder.

But what the fuck? That's all it is, ever. You want to be loved. You tell other people you love them, in order to trick them into loving you back. And after a while, it's true. You feel the pull, the ache.

The vibrato, voice keening skyward. The wet edge. Every word a whine. Weak, weak, weak, weak, weak.

When I say "you", of course, I mean "me". This is because everything is about me. To me. Why not? I'm the only me I have.

Truth is, none of us deserve anything. We get what we get.

And the best you can ever hope for . . . is to train yourself not to care.

Ahead, Ryerson loomed; residence row, with a Second Cup on either side of the street and competing hookers on every corner, shivering aslant on their sagging vinyl boot-heels.

I paused at Gould, waiting for a slow light, and put one itch-etched palm to my chest—telling myself it was to chart the ache's progress, rather than to keep myself from jarring the light's signal free with a sudden burst of excess entropic energy. Felt the charge building in my bones, begging for expression. For expulsion.

Some opportunity to turn this—whatever—I felt myself tentatively beginning to feel safely outward, without risk of repercussion. To evict the unwanted visitor, wash myself clean and empty and ready for use again, like any good craftsman's basic set of tools; make myself just an implement once more, immune to the temptations of personal desire.

What had I cut myself in half *for*, in the first place, if not for that? Scarred my heel, halved my soul, driven Franz and Jen one way and Carra the other, busted the Black Magic Posse back down to its dysfunctional roots so I could be this arcane study group's sole graduating student, its unofficial last man standing. And all to immunize myself to stress and fear and lack of focus—to free myself from every law but that of gravity, while still making sure I could probably break that one too, if I just put my back into it. Dictator For Life of a one-person country, my own private Hierarchical Idaho.

Because if the effect wore *off*, however eventually . . . well, hell; that would mean none of the above had really been worth the effort. At all.

I hissed through my suddenly half-clogged nose at the very idea, but nothing happened. The ache remained.

And grew.

But: Something *will* present itself, I forced myself to decide, more in certainty than conjecture. The way it always does.

And sure enough—soon enough—

—something did.

Just past Ryerson proper and into the shadow of St Mike's, moving through that dead stretch of pawnbrokers' shops and photographic supply warehouses. I glance-scanned the row of live DV hand-helds mounted in Henry's window, and caught his lambent shade flickering fast from screen to screen to screen: Him from the theatre, from the Khyber. That particular guy. He Who Remained Nameless, for now.

But not, I promised myself, for much longer.

I was already turning, instinctively, even as I formed the concept—half-way 'round where I stood before I even had a chance to recognize more than the line of his shoulder, the swing of his hair, the side-long flash of what *might* be an eye: A mirror-image glance, an answering recognition. And stepping straight into the path of some ineptly tattooed young lout coccooned in a crowd of the same, Ry High jocks or proto-Engineers out for a beer before curfew, with gay-bashing one of the options passing vaguely through what they collectively called a brain. Who called out, equally automatic, as I elbowed by him:

"Hey, faggot!"

An insult I'd heard before, of course, far too many to count easily—not to mention one for which I currently had both no time and exactly zero interest, within context. So I tried to channel the old Jude, who'd always been so wonderfully diffident and accommodating in the face of fools, especially whenever violence threatened; dodge past with a half-ducked head and an apologetic, "no speakee Engarish, asshore" kind of half-smile, teeth grit and pride kept strictly quashed, as long as it got me finally face to face with my mystery man at last . . .

Except that Mr Hetboy Supreme and his buddies didn't actually move, which meant I couldn't do much but hold my ground, still smiling. And when I took another look, the guy, my quarry, that ever-elusive, unimagin-ably attractive *him*—*he* was long gone, of course. Anyway.

And the ache was back.

"Faggot," the doofus said again—like he'd always wanted a chance to really sound it out aloud, syllable by un-PC syllable. And I just nodded again, my fingers knitting fast behind me; weaving hidden sigils in that empty place where my shadow used to be, feeling them perfect them-selves without even having to check that I was doing it right.

Immaculate. Effortless. Like signing your name in the dark.

"Something I can help you with?" I asked. Adding, for extra emphasis: "Gentlemen."

One of them sniggered.

"Well, yes," said the one with the big mouth, all mock-obsequious. "See, the guys and me were just thinkin' . . . "

Unlikely.

" . . . about how just seein' you come swishin' along here made us wanna, kinda—y'know—fuck you—"

Before he could finish his little game of verbal connect-the-dots, I'd already upgraded my smile to a—wide, nasty—grin.

"Over?" I suggested, coolly. "Or was it . . . up? The ass?"

More sniggers, not all of them directed at me. "You wish," my aspiring basher-to-be snapped back, a bit too quick for his own comfort.

I shrugged, bringing my hands forward. Rubbed my palms together, deliberately. Saw them all shiver and step back, as one, as the skin ignited—and winked, letting a spark of the same cheerless color flare in the pupil's heart of either flat black eye. Allowing it to grow, to spread. To kiss both lids, and gild my lashes with purple flame.

And oh, but the ache was chest-high and higher now, jumping my neck to lodge behind my face: A hammer in my head, a hundred-watt bulb thrown mid-skull. Like a halo in reverse.

"Not particularly," I replied.

Basher-boy's buddies broke and ran as one, pack-minded to the last. But I had already crooked a burning finger at him, riveting him to the spot, a skewer of force run through every limb. Using them like strings, I walked him—a reluctant puppet—to the nearest alley. Paused behind a clutch of trash-cans, popped my fly to let it all hang out. And leaned back against the wall, waiting.

"Down," I told him. "Now."

He knelt, staring up. I stroked his jaw.

"Open up," I said, sweetly.

And kept right on smiling, even after his formerly sneering lips hit the neatly-trimmed hair on my pubic ridge—right up until my sac swung free against his rigid, yet helplessly working, chin. I wasn't thinking of him, of course, but at least I wasn't thinking of that *guy* anymore—or myself, either. When I felt my orgasm at last, I came so hard I would have thought I was levitating, if I didn't already know what that feels like: Off like a rocket, all in one choking gush. I held his head until I was done.

Then I stepped back, him still down on his knees in front of me, leaving him just enough room to pivot and puke everything I'd just given him back up on the asphalt beneath our feet.

My ache, conveniently enough, went along with it.

"You think you're going to do something about this," I told him, as I ordered my cuffs and tucked my shirt back in. "Not that you'd ever tell your buddies, of course. But you're sitting there right now, thinking: 'One day I'm gonna catch him in an alley, and he'll have to eat through a straw for a month.'"

Closing my coat, I squatted down beside him, continuing: "But the thing is . . . even now, even with me right in front of you, you can't really remember what I look like. And it's getting worse. An hour from now, any given gay guy you meet might have been the one that did this to you. Am I right?" I leant a little towards him, and felt him just stop himself from shying away; that little jerk in his breath, like a slaughterhouse calf just before the bolt slams home. "Can't tell, can you?" I asked, quietly.

He didn't answer.

"And do you know what that means?" I went on, sitting back on my heels. "It means that the next time you see somebody coming down Church Street, and you want to say hello—I think you're going to modify your tone a little. Lower your eyes, maybe. Not make any snap judgements. And definitely . . . under any circumstances at all . . . not call this person by insulting names. Because you never know." I paused. "And you never will, either."

Leaning forward again, I let my voice go cold. And whispered, right in his ear:

"So be polite, little ghost. From now on, just be very—very—polite."

* * *

By the time I got home, one quick whiff was enough to tell me my neighbors were not only back, but already smoking up a storm. No '80's nostalgia dancemix filtering up through the floorboards as yet, though—so between the relative earliness of the hour and the obvious intensity of their hash-induced stupor, I figured I had about an hour before their proximity made it difficult to give the ritual I had in mind my fullest possible attention.

Because, morally repulsive as my pre-emptive strike on the Engineer might have been—even from my own (admittedly prejudiced) point of view—the plain fact was, it had done the trick. Back in that alley, the emotional cramp temporarily hampering my ability to plan ahead had flowed out of me, borne on a blissful surge of bodily fluids. And inspiration had taken its place.

So I picked up the phone, and discovered—somewhat to my own amusement—that I really *could* remember Franz's mother's number, after all.

"You're actually going to help?" He repeated, obviously amazed.

"Why not? Might be kicks."

"Yeah, right. For who?"

"Does it matter?"

Planning it out, even as we fenced: use a two-ring circle system, with Jen sequestered in the inner, Franz and I in the outer. Proceed from Franz's assumption that Fleer was the demon in question, until otherwise proven; force him to vacate by offering him another rabbit-hole to jump down, one far more attractive to him than Jen's could ever be . . .

Making the connection, then, mildly startled by the ruthless depths of my own deviousness. And observing, to myself: Now, *that's* not nice.

But I knew I'd have to try it, anyway.

I gave Franz a detailed list of what I'd need, only to be utterly unsurprised when he immediately balked at both its length and its—fairly expensive—specificity.

"Why the hell don't you ever practice straight-up Chinese magic, anyway?" he demanded. "Needles, herbs, all that good, *cheap* stuff . . . "

"Same reason you don't raise any Mennonite demons, I guess."

He invited me to suck his dick. I gave an evil smile.

"Oh, Franz," I said, gently. "How do you know I never did?"

Next step was getting all the appointment-book bullshit dealt with: Setting a time, date and place, with Jen's address making the top of my list in terms of crucial missing information. According to Franz, she'd been living in some Annex hole in the ground for most of the last five years, vampire sex shows and all—though not an actual hole, mind you, or the actual ground. But only because that kind of logistical whimsy would have been *way* too interesting a concept, for either of them.

"And what are *you* planning on bringing to the party?" He asked, grumpily. To which I replied, airily:

" . . . I'll think of something."

* * *

Which is how I came, a mere three hours later, to be sitting side by side with Carra in the Clarke's inaccurately-labelled Green Room—her slump-shouldered and staring at her scars against the grey-painted wall, me trying (and failing) to stop my feet from tapping impatiently on the scuffed grey linoleum floor. We were virtually alone, aside from one nurse stationed on the door, whose eyes kept straying back to the static-spitting TV in the corner as though it exercised some sort of magnetic attraction on her, and a dusty prayer-plant whose leaves seemed permanently fused together by the utter lack of natural light.

"I need a reading," I told Carra, briskly.

Toneless: "You know I can't do that anymore, Jude."

"I know you *don't*."

"Same difference."

It seemed clear she probably sensed ulterior motives beneath my visit, even though she knew herself to be always my court of last resort, when faced with any inexplicable run of synchronicity. But she didn't seem particularly interested in probing further, probably because this just happened to be one of those mornings when she wasn't much into seeing people; not live ones, anyway.

"Look," I said, "somebody's been doing stuff, and taking my name in vain while they do it. Sleeping with Ed, even after I already kicked him to the curb. Volunteering my services to Franz, even after I already told *him* to take a hike." I paused. "I even tried to do a spell, on that guy—the one from the movie?" As she nodded: "Well, *that* was all screwed up somehow, too. Like, just . . . weird."

"Your magic was weird," she repeated, evenly.

"Abnormally so."

She looked up, brushing her bangs away. "Told you there was something about that guy," she said, with just a sliver of her old, evilly detached, Ryerson-era grin.

I snapped my fingers. "Oh yeah, I remember now—you did, didn't you? Just never told me what."

"How should I know?"

"You read minds, Carra," I reminded her.

"Not well. Not on short notice."

"Also bullshit."

She turned to her hands again, examining each finger's gift-spotted quick in turn, each ragged edge of nail. Finally: "Well, anyways . . . it's not like I'm the only one who's told you that."

"Grandmother Yau did say she saw me twice," I agreed, slowly.

A snort. "I'm surprised she could even see you *once*."

"Why?"

"For the same reason I can hardly see you, Jude. You're only half there. Got no shadow, remember?"

Hair back in her eyes, eyes back on her palms—scanning their creases like if she only studied them hard enough, she thought she could will herself a whole new history. Then wrinkling her forehead and sniffing, a kind of combined wince/flinch, before demanding—appropos of nothing much, far as I could tell—

"God. Can you smell that, or what?"

"What?"

"*That*, Jude."

Ah, yes: *that*.

Guess not.

Yet—oh, what WAS that stupid knocking inside my chest, that soft, intermittent scratch building steadily at the back of my throat? Like I was sickening for something; a cold, a fever . . . some brief reflection of the Carra I'd once known, poking out—here and there—from under her hovering Haldol high.

I knew I could still remember exactly what it was, though, if only I let myself. That was the worst of it. Not the innate hurt of Carra's ongoing tragedy—this doomed, hubristic sprawl from darkness to darkness, hospital to halfway house and back again. Carra's endless struggle for the right to her own independent consciousness, pitted as she was against an equally endless, desperate procession of needy phantoms, to whom

252

possession was so much more than nine tenths of the law.

"The biggest mistake you can ever make," she told me, once, "is to ever let them know you see them at all. Because it gets around, Jude. It really gets around."

(Really.)

Remembering how she'd once taught me almost everything I know, calmly and carefully—everything that matters, anyway. Everything that's helped me learn everything I've learned since. How she broke all the rules of "traditional" mediumship and laid herself willingly open to anything her Talent brought her way, playing moth, then flame, then moth again. After which, one lost day—a day she's never spoken of, even to me—she somehow decided that the best idea would be for her to burn on, unchecked, 'till she burned herself out completely.

How she'd spent almost all her time since the Ryerson Graduation Ball struggling—however inefficiently—to get her humanity "back", even though that particular impossible dream has always formed the real root of her insanity. And how I pitied her for it—pitied her, revered her, resented her. How I held her in increasingly black, bitter contempt, anger and resentment over it, all because she'd wasted five long years trying to commit the unforgivable sin of leaving me behind.

No, I knew the whole situation a little too well to mourn over, at this point; almost as well as Carra did, in fact, and you didn't see her crying. She held her ground instead, with grace and strength, until the encroaching tide threatened to pull her under. And then she took a little Thorazine vacation, letting the Clarke's free drugs tune the constant internal whisper of her disembodied suitors' complaints down to a dull roar. Putting herself somewhere else, neatly and efficiently, so the dead could have their way with her awhile—and all on the off-chance that they might thus be satisfied enough, unlikely as it might seem, to finally leave her alone.

What I felt wasn't empathy. It was annoyance. I had had things to talk about with Carra, business to attend to. And she had made herself—quite deliberately—unreachable.

Besides which: Feeling sorry for Carra, genuinely sorry . . . well, that'd be far too normal for *me*, wouldn't it? To feel my chest squeeze hot and close over Carra's insoluble pain, just because she was my oldest Canadian acquaintance, my mentor and my muse. My best, my truest, friend.

My one. And my only.

(A memory loop of Ed's voice intervening here, thick and blurry: "Tell you what, Jude—why don't you surprise me: Name the last time you felt anything. For somebody other than yourself, I mean.")

And when was it we had that conversation, exactly? Two hours ago? Two months?

Two years, maybe. Not that it mattered a single flying fuck.

Ai-yaaah. So inappropriate. So selfish. So, very—

"Still walking around out there, like any other ghost," Carra continued, musingly. "Looking like you, acting . . . *sort* of like you . . . "

—*me*.

"So," I said, slowly. "What you're telling me is—this guy I've been after, for the last couple of days—"

"*He's* your shadow."

And: Ohhhh.

Well, that explained a *lot*.

Rubbing a hand across my lips, then stroking it absently back over my hair. And thinking, all the while: Could be true; why not? I mean—who did that guy remind me of, anyway, if *not* myself? Certainly explained the attraction.

Running after myself, yearning after myself. Working *magic* on myself.

Man, I always *knew* I was a narcissist.

All the lesser parts of me: Weak where I was potent, slippery where I was direct, silent where I was vocal, acquiescent where I was anything but. Myself, reflected backwards and upside-down in a weirdly flattering Yin mirror, just like Grandmother Yau said.

Caught in a mesh of darkness.

"My 'evil twin'," I suggested, facetiously.

She shrugged. "Kind of depends on your definition." Then: "Christ! What *is* that smell?"

In other words: If *he's* the evil one—

—then what's that supposed to make *you*?

I shook my head yet again, flicking the idea away—such a smooth-ass move, and one that really does get easier and easier, the more diligently you practice it. Then propelled myself upwards and outwards, brisky brushing the room's dust from my clothes, like I was simultaneously scrubbing myself free of her aura's leaking, purple-brown, depression-and-defeat-inflected stain. Saying:

"Well, anyway—gotta go. Things to do, rituals to research, shopping lists to compile. Exorcisms don't come cheap, you know."

" . . . don't."

"Why the hell not?"

Hesitant: "I mean, it's just. Not. Not, uh . . . "

(. . . safe.)

Riiiiight.

'Cause that was the big concern, these days: Staying safe, at all costs. Even when the best way to make sure *I* stayed safe, if it really concerned her so much, would be to sign herself out of this shithole—the way we all knew she could, at a moment's fucking notice—and come help out. Instead of just sitting there all smug with dead people's handwriting crawling up and down her arms like some legible rash and the air around her starting to thicken like a rind, to crackle like a badly-grounded electric fence . . .

Bitch, I thought, before I could stop myself. And saw her flinch again, as the impact of my projected insult bruised her cortex from the inside-out; saw blood drip from one nostril, as she blinked away a film of tears.

I shut my eyes to block it all out, feeling that *ache* squirm inside me, twisting in on itself. Knotting tight. Feeling it ripple with fine, poison-packed spines, all of them spewing a froth of negativity that threatened to send my few lingering deposits of tenderness, sorrow and affection flowing away at a touch, leaving nothing behind but emptiness, and rot, and rage.

If I *let* it, that is. Which I wasn't about to.

Not when I still had even the faintest lingering chance of getting what I wanted.

"Listen," I began, carefully. "We both know the main reason you put the Posse together in the first place was because it was the only way you could blow off steam, stop devoting all your energy to just protecting yourself . . . "

Leave it open as sin and let the ghosts rush in at will: Babble and float, vomit ectoplasm and sprout word-bruises like hickey chains, laugh like a loon and know no one was actually going to treat you like one for doing it.

Good times, baby. Good, good times.

"But now the lid's back on all the time, because you're afraid to let it come off, under any circumstances. And the steam's still building. And pretty soon it's going to blow either way, and when it does it'll hurt somebody, which'd be okay if it was just you. Except that it probably won't be."

Carra cast her eyes at me, warily. There was an image lurking somewhere in her downcast gaze, half-veiled by lash and post-meds pupil dilation: Past, present, maybe even future. It took all my remaining self-restraint not to tweeze it forward with a secret gesture, catch it between my own lids, and blink it large enough to scry. But that would be impolite. We were friends, after all, me and her.

And: Like that actually *means* anything, some ungrateful, traitor part of me whispered—right against the figurative drum of my mental inner ear.

"You know," she said, finally, "if you hadn't caught me on an off-day . . . that probably would have worked."

Adding, a moment later—

"And speaking of reading minds—you think I don't know what you're planning, by the way? An open medium, a vessel with no shields; couldn't ask for a better demon-trap, not if you ordered it from Acme Better Homes & Banishments. I walk in, Fleer jumps me, you cast him out and toss him right back through the Rift again—and what the hell, huh? Because I'm *used* to having squatters in *my* head."

"So what—would you have agreed if I'd said it straight out?" I shot back, reasonably enough. "But c'mon, admit it: Be a fuck of a lot more interesting than just hiding in here, where you're no use to anybody."

"I'm sick of being 'of use'. I've been 'of use' since I was born. And now—now *you* want to use me; Jesus, Jude. Is that what 'friends' do to each other, these days?"

I shrugged. Well, when you put it *that* way . . .

Softly: "I'll always be your friend, Carra."

She shook her head. "That other part of you, sure. But you . . . you've changed."

Shadow-coveting vibe just pumping off of me by now, no doubt—extruding at her through my pores, like Denis Leary-level cigarette smoke at a hyper-allergenic: Sloppy-drunk with wanting him, distracted with seeking him, enraged with not finding him. Forgotten emotions colliding like neurons, giving off heat and light and horror. Making me feel different to her, all complicated and intrusive, instead of the calming psychic dead-spot whose absence she'd gotten all too used to basking in. Making me feel just like . . .

. . . everybody else.

"I never change," I said. Contradicting myself, almost immediately: "And anyway, should I have just stayed the way I was: That fool, that weak child? Too scared of everything, including himself, to *do* anything *about* anything?"

"I liked him."

So simple, so plaintive. Her barely-audible voice like an echo of that dream I'd had the night before, the one where I'd seen her hanging between earth and air. Asking me: What did you *do* to yourself, Jude? What did you *do*?

You know what I did, I started to say, but froze mid-word. Because just then—at the very same time—I finally caught a hint of something unnatural in the air around us: Some phantom stink skittering from corner to corner like a rancid pool-ball, drawing an explosive puff of dust from the centre of the prayer-plant's calcified Cry To Heaven. Making the nurse look up, sniffing.

Carra hacked, hands flying to her nose; her fingers came away wet, stained with equal parts coughed-out snot and thick, fresh blood.

"Fuck," she said, amazed. "That *smell*—"

—it's *you*.

And she began to rise.

The nurse's eyes widened, fixing; she made a funny little "eeep"-y noise, and scuttled back against the wall. To her right, static ate the TV's signal entirely, turning All My Children into Nothing But Snow. I took a reteative half-step myself, fingers flashing purple: Wards, activate! Ghosts, disperse!

Thinking—projecting—even as my flared nostrils stung in sympathy: Oh, baby, don't. Please, do *not*. Do not *do* this to *me* . . .

Carra's heels hooked the seat of her chair, knocking it backwards with the force of their upswing; she gasped, blood-tinted mucus-drip already stretching into hair-fine tendrils that streamed out wide on either side, wreathing her like impromptu mummy-wrap. The chair fell, skipping once, like a badly-thrown beach-rock.

Rising to stick and hang there in the centre of the room, her heels holding five steady inches above the floor. Head flung back. Ectoplasm pouring from her nose and mouth. While, all around, a psychically-charged dust devil scraped the walls like some cartoon tornado-in-a-can, its tightening funnel composed equally of frustrated alien willpower and whatever small, inanimate objects happened to be closest by: Plastic cutlery, scraps of paper. Hair and thread and crumbs. Garbage of every description.

A babble of ghostly voices filling her throat, making her jaw's underside bulge like a frog's. Messages scrawling up and down her exposed limbs as the restless dead took fresh delight in making her their unwilling megaphone, their stiff and uncooperative human notepad.

She looked down at me, cushioned behind my pad of defensive Power, and let the corners of her mouth give an awful rictus-twitch. And as her glasses lifted free—apparently unnoticed—to join the rest of the swirl, I saw ectoplasmic lenses slide across her eyes like cataracts, blindness taking hold in a milky, tidal, unstoppable ebb and flow.

Forcing her lips further apart, as the tendons in her neck grated and popped. Wrenching a word here and there from the torrent inside her, and forcing herself to observe:

"Not . . . ever . . . ything. Is . . . ab . . . out. *you*. Jude."

Believe it—

—or not.

* * *

And I, as usual, chose to choose . . . not.

* * *

The primary aim of magicians is to gather knowledge, because knowledge—as everyone finds out fairly early, from Schoolhouse Rock on—is power. To that end, we often conjure demons, who we use and dismiss in the same offhand way most people grab the right implement from their kitchen drawer: Fork, cheese-knife, slotted spoon; salt, pepper, sulphur. Keep to the recipe, clean your plate, then walk away quickly once the meal is done.

But even if we pursue this culinary analogy to its most pedantic conclusion, cooking with demons is a bit like trying to run a restaurant specializing in dishes as likely to kill you as they are to nourish you: Deathcap mushroom pasta with a side of ergot-infested rye bread, followed by the all-Fugu special. They're cruel and unpredictable, mysterious and restless, icily malignant—far less potent than the actual Fallen who spawned them, yet far more fearful than simple elementals of fire, air, water, earth, or the mysterious realms which lie beneath it. Like the dead, demons come when called—or even when not—and envy us our flesh; like the dead, you must feed them blood before they consent to give their names or do your bidding.

Psellus called them lucifugum, those who Fly The Light. I call them a pain in the ass, especially when you're not entirely sure what *else* to call them.

On the streetcar-ride from College/Yonge to Bathurst/College, I chewed my lip and flipped through my copy of the Grimoire Lemegeton, which lists the names and powers of seventy-two different demons, along with their various functions.

Eleven lesser demons procure the love of women, or (if your time is tight) make lust-objects of either sex show themselves naked. Four can transport people safely from place to place, or change them into other shapes, or gift them with high worldly position, cunning, courage, wit and eloquence. Three produce illusions: Of running water, of musical instruments playing, of birds in flight. One can make you invisible, another turn base metals into gold. Two torment their victims with running sores. One, surprisingly, teaches ethics; I don't get a whole lot of requests for that one, strangely enough.

Glasyalabolas, who teaches all arts and sciences, yet incites to murder and bloodshed. Raum, who reconciles enemies, when he's not destroying cities. Flauros, who can either burn your foes alive, or discourse on divinity. Or Fleer himself, indifferently good or bad, who "will do the work of the operator."

If it actually *was* Fleer inside Jen, that is. If, if, if.

Practicing the usual injunctions under my breath, while simultaneously trying to decide between potential protective sigils: Verbum Caro Factorem Est, your basic Quadrangelic conjuration, maybe even the ultimate old-school reliability of Solomon's Triangle—upper point to the north, Anexhexeton to the east, Tetragrammaton to the west, Primematum anchoring. Telling your nameless quarry, as you etch the lines around yourself:

"I conjure and command thee, O spirit N., by Him who spake and it was done; Asar Un-Nefer, Myself Made Perfect, the Bornless One, Ineffable. Come peaceably, visibly, and without delay. Come, fulfil my desires and persist unto the end in accordance to my will. Zazas, Zazas, Nasatanada, Zazas: Exit this vessel as and when I command, or be thrown through the Gate from whence ye came."

The streetcar slid to a halt, Franz visible on the platform ahead—looking worried, as ever. A shopping bag in either hand testified to his having already filled out my list. Which was good; proved he wanted Jen "cured" enough to throw in from his own pocket, at least.

And: I've *done* this, I thought. Lots of times. I can do it again, Carra or not—and what the fuck had I really thought I needed Carra for, anyway? As she'd (sort of) pointed out, herself.

Easy. Peasy. Easy-peasy.

But none of the above turned out to matter very much at all, really. In the end.

* * *

Stepped off the streetcar at six or so. By midnight I was back at Grandmother Yau's, sucking back a plate of Glass Noodle Cashew Chicken and washing it back with lots and lots of tea, so much I could practically feel my bladder tensing yet another notch with each additional swig. Starting to itch, and twinge, and . . . ache.

(Ache.)

"So, Jude-ah," came a soft, Mandarin-accented voice from just behind my shoulder. "Seeing you seem sad, I wonder: How does your liver feel? Is the general of your body's army sickening, tonight?"

And: Tonight, tonight, I found myself musing. What *was* tonight, at the Khyber? Oh, right . . . open bar. No bullshit restrictions. I could wear that tank-top I'd been saving, the really low-cut one.

Wick-ed.

Grandmother Yau reached in, touching her gilded middle claw to my ear, brief and deft; I jumped at its sting, collecting myself, as she reminded me—

"I am not used to being ignored, little brother."

Automatically: "Ten thousand pardons, big sister."

She slit her green-tinged eyes, shrewdly. "One will do." Then, waving the nearest ghost over to top up my teapot: "My spies tell me you had business, further east. Is it completed?"

And waaah, but there were so very many ways to answer that particular question, weren't there? Though I, typically, chose the easiest.

"Wei," I said, nodding. "Very complete."

"The possessed girl, ah? Your friend."

That's right.

My friend Jen, laying there on the tatty green carpet of her basement apartment; my other friend Franz, leaning over her. Shaking her—a few times, gently at first, then harder. Slapping her face once. Doing it again.

Watching her continue to lie there, impassively limp. Then looking back at me, a growing disbelief writ plain across his too-pale, freckled face—me, standing still inside my circle, with no expression at all on mine. Watching him watch.

She's not breathing, Jude.

Well, no.

Jude. I think . . . I think she's dead.

Well—yes.

"Turns out," I told Grandmother Yau, "she wasn't actually possessed, after all."

"No?"

"No."

Ai-yaaah.

Because: I'd taken Franz's word, and Franz had taken Jen's—but she'd lied to us both, obviously, or been so screwed up that even she hadn't *really* known where those voices in her skull were coming from. So I'd come running, prepared to kick some non-corporeal butt, and funnelled the whole charge of my Power into her at once, cranked up to demon-expelling level.

But if there's no demon to be *put* to flight, that kind of full-bore metaphysical shock attack can't help but turn out somewhat like sticking a fork in a light socket, or vice versa. If that's even possible.

Franz again, in Jen's apartment, turning on me with his eyes all aburn. Reminding me, shakily: *YOU said you could HELP.*

If she was possessed, yes.

Then why is she dead, Jude?

Because . . . she wasn't.

You—said—

I shrugged. *Whoopsie.*

He lunged for me. I let off a force-burst that threw him backwards five feet, cracking his spine like a whip.

You don't EVER lay hands on me, I said, quietly. *Not ever. Unless I want you to.*

He sat there, hugging his beloved corpse with charred-white palms, crying in at least two kinds of pain. And snarled back: *Like I'd want to touch you with some other guy's dick and some third fucker pushing, you son of a fucking bitch.*

(Yeah, whatever.)

Fact was, though, if Franz hadn't been so cowardly and credulous in the first place—if he hadn't wanted an instant black magic miracle, instead of having the guts to just take her to a mental hospital, the way most normal people do when their girlfriends start telling them they hear voices—then Jen might still be alive.

Emphasis on the might.

I can call demons. I can bind angels. I can raise the dead, for a while. But just like Franz himself had observed, more than once, I can't actually *cure* anybody—can't heal them of cancer, leprosy, M.S., old age, mental illness or color-blindness to save my fucking life. Not unless they *want* me to. Not unless they *let* me.

The other way? That's called a miracle, and my last name ain't Christ.

Franz, crying out, tears thick as blood in his strangled voice: *You PROM-ISED me, you fuck! You fucking PROMISED me!*

Followed, in my memory, by a quick mental hit of Carra, half the city away: Still floating, still wreathed. And think: If I *could* do something for people like that, you moron, don't you think I WOULD?

She *wants* to be nuts, though. Long and the short of it. Just like, on some level, Jen wanted to die.

But hell, what was Franz going to do about it, one way or another? *Shun* me?

I took a fresh bite of noodle while the ancient Chinese spectre I'd come to think of as Grandmother's right-hand ghost flitted by, pausing to murmur in her ear for a moment before fading away through the nearest lacquer screen. And when she looked at me, she had something I'd never seen before lurking in the corners of her impenetrable gaze. If I'd had to hazard a guess, I might even have said it looked a lot like—well—

—surprise.

"Someone," she said, at last, "is at the Maitre D's station. Asking for you, Jude-ah."

Glancing sidelong, so I'd be forced to follow the path of her gaze over to where . . . *he* waited: He, it. Me.

My shadow.

My shadow, highlighted against the Empress' Noodle's thick, red velvet drapes like a sliver of lambent bronze—head down, shyly, with its hair in its eyes and its hands in its pockets. My shadow, come at last after all my fruitless seeking, just waiting for its better half to take control, wrap it tight, gather it in and make it—finally—whole again.

Waiting, patiently. Quiet and acquiescent. Waiting, waiting . . .

. . . for me.

I met Grandmother Yau's gaze again, and found her normally impassive face gone somehow far more rigid than usual: Green-veined porcelain, a funerary mask trimmed in milky jade.

"The Yin mirror reflects only one way, Chiu-wai-ah," she said, at last. "It is a dark path, always. And slippery."

I nodded, suddenly possessed by a weird spurt of glee. Replying, off-hand: "Mei shi, big sister; not to worry, never mind. Do you think I don't know enough to be careful?"

To which she merely bowed her head, slightly. Asking—

"What will you do, then?"

And I—couldn't stop myself from smiling, as the answer came sliding synapse-fast to the very tip of my tongue, kept restrained only by a lifetime's residual weight of "social graces". Thinking: Oh, I? Go home, naturally. Go home, dim the lights, light some incense—

—and *fuck* myself.

* * *

So soft in my arms, not that I'd ever thought of myself as *soft*. I pushed it back against the apartment door with its wrists pinned above its head, nuzzling and nipping, quizzing it in Cantonese, Manadarin, ineffectual Vietnamese—only to have it offer exactly nothing in reply, while simultaneously maintaining an unbroken stare of pure, dumb adoration from beneath its artfully lowered lashes.

Which was okay by me; more than okay, really. Seeing I'd already had it pretty much up to here with guys who talked.

Feeling the shadow's proximity, its very presence, prickle the hairs on the back of my neck like a presenitiment of oncoming sheet-lightning against empty black sky: All plus to my mostly minus, yang to my yin, nice guy to my toxic shit. And wanting it *back*, right here and now; feeling the core-deep urge to penetrate, to own, to repossess those long-missing parts of me in one hard push, come what fucking might.

Groin to groin and breath to breath, two half-hearts beating as one, two severances sealing fast. Unbreakable.

Down on the bed, then, with its heels on my shoulders: Key sliding home, lock springing open. Rearing erect, burning bright with flickering purple flame, allll over. And seeing myself abruptly outlined in black against the wall above my headboard at that ecstatic moment of (re)joining, like some Polaroid flash's bruisy after-image: My inverse reflection. My missing shadow, slipping inside *me* as I slipped inside *it*, enshadowing me once more.

Ten years' worth of trauma deferred, all crashing down on me at once. Showing me first-hand, explicitly, how nature abhors a—moral, human, walking—vacuum.

* * *

And now it's later, oh *so* much, with rain all over my bedroom floor and beads of wood already rising like sodden cicatrices everywhere I dare to look. Rain on my hair, rain in my eyes—only natural, given that the window's still open. But I can't stand up, can't force a step, not even to shut it. I just squat here and listen to my heart, eyes glued to that ectoplasmic husk the shadow left devolving on my bed: A shed skinfull of musk and lies, rotting. All that's left of my lovely double, my literal self-infatuation.

I've done the protective circle around myself five times now, at least—in magic marker, in chalk, in my own shit. Tomorrow I think I'll re-do it in blood, just to get it over with; can't keep on picking at these ideas forever, without something starting to fester. And we don't want *that*, do we?

(Really.)

Because the sad truth is this: My wards hold, like they always hold; the circle works, like all my magic works. But what it doesn't do, even after all my years of sheer, hard, devoted work—all my Craft and study, not to mention practice—

—is *help.*

Once upon a time—when I was drunk, and young, and stupid beyond belief—I cut my shadow, my *soul*, away from me in some desperate, adolescent bid to separate myself from my own mortality. And since then, I guess I haven't really been much good for anybody but myself. I bound up my weakness and threw it away, not realizing that weakness is what lets you bend under unbearable pressure.

And if you can't bend . . . you break.

My evil twin, I hear my own arrogant voice suggest to Carra, mockingly—and with a sudden, stunning surge of self-hatred, I find I want to hunt that voice down and slap it silly. To roll and roar on the floor at my own willfully deluded stupidity.

Half a person, Franz chimes in, meanwhile, from deeper in my memory's ugly little gift-box. *And not even the GOOD half.*

No. Because *it* was the good half. And me, I, I'm—just—

—all that's left.

My shadow. The part of me that might have been, if only I'd let it stay. My curdled conscience. Until it touched me, I didn't remember what it was I'd been so afraid of. But now I can't think about anything else.

Except . . . how very, very badly, no matter what the cost . . .

. . . I want for it to touch me again.

Thinking: Is this *me?* Can this possibly be *me,* Jude Hark Chiu-Wai? *Me?*

Me.

Me, and no fucking body else.

Thinking, finally: But this won't kill me. Not even this. Much as I might like it to.

And maybe I'll be a better person for it, a better magician, if I can just make it through the next few nights without killing myself like Jen, or going crazy as Carra. But that's pretty cold comfort, at best.

Sobbing, retching. All one big weakness—one open, weeping sore. And thinking, helpless: *Carra, oh Carra. Grandmother Yau. Franz. Ed. Someone.*

ANYone.

But I've burnt all my boats, funeral-style. And I can't remember—exactly, yet—how to swim.

The Wide World converges on me now, dark and sparkling, and I just crouch here beneath it with my hands over my face: Weeping, moaning, too paralytic-terrified even to shield myself from its glory. Left all alone at last with the vision and the void—crushed flat, without a hope of reprieve, under the endless weight of a dark and whirling universe.

Ripe and riven. Unforgiven. Caught forever, non-citizen that I am, in that typically Canadian moment just before you start to freeze.

Keeping my sanity, my balance.

Keeping to the straight and Narrow.

AFTERWORD

DISCLAIMER:

Those of you who read the afterword to my last collection, **KISSING CARRION**, will remember the drill. For those of you who haven't, meanwhile—

What follows is far less a classic post-manuscript analysis of the ins and outs of my particular creative process than a (hopefully) amusing "interview", done tapeworm-style—myself with myself, by myself. Those of you truly intrigued by the contortions my mind goes through while intermittently birthing 7,000 to 15,000 words onto the computer's screen may find this informative, if potentially disillusioning.

To the rest, meanwhile, I say thank you and goodnight, pausing only to bow deeply; you've just read half my entire literary output, a good fifteen years' worth of metaphorical blood, sweat and unfulfilled spiritual longing—I'll make sure to search the crowd for your face sometime soon, at the launch-party for my first novel. (And if you're interested in reading the other half of my ouevre, meanwhile, please do remember that copies of **KISSING CARRION** are still available for order through the Prime Books website, amongst other places.)

So. Now that's that's done, on to the really hard part . . .

Q: "This stuff seems far more on the dark fantastic side of the literary blanket than the gritty, urban stuff in **KISSING CARRION**."

A: Is that a question? But yes. This is where I started. You can see it best in stuff like "The Land Beyond The Forest" (first published in THE VAMPIRE'S CRYPT #10, ed. Margaret L. Carter) and "A Single Shadow Make" (first published in TECHNO MYTHS, Obelesk Press, ed. S.G. Johnson), the first story I ever had accepted for (unpaid) publication; as you might expect for initial efforts, they're both variants on familiar templates—Dracula (albeit the chick version, with a fair debt probably owed to the romantic fantasy writings of Tanith Lee and the historical fantasy writings of Chelsea Quinn Yarbro) vs. Frankenstein (the big gay version, with an equally fair debt owed to my shaky memories of Sting in THE BRIDE and Keanu Reeves in DANGEROUS LIAISONS).

"Flare" (first published in DANGEROUS WOMEN, Obelesk Press, ed. S.G. Johnson) also goes in there, as a sort of Vertigo graphic novel-style revisionist super(anti)hero(ine) piece; it certainly uses a lot of the imagistic/internal narrative tropes I've since brazenly continued to plunder the collective works of Alan Moore, Neil Gaiman and Garth Ennis for, over the years. I also wrote the earliest version of it back in high school, where it later won me an honorable mention in some sort of pan-Toronto Board of Education competition—it came with the chance to go to dinner at the top of the Sutton Place hotel, where I also unwittingly insulted Australian novelist Janette Turner Hospital by calling her native province, Queensland, "South Africa with a CROCODILE DUNDEE accent".

It's funny: In the KISSING CARRION Afterword, I briefly touched on the fact that while I started out writing science fiction, I quickly threw it over for horror, where my shaky grasp of science wouldn't get quite so much of a spotlight. But there was another reason, too: Horror seemed more "real" to me, more rooted in a world I could understand, emotions I could share, etc. This may have been due to the fact that the most popular type horror I read while growing up was the type of "name-brand horror" pioneered by Stephen King and Peter Straub, set in specific, almost journalistically-detailed North American neighbor-hoods where fact and fiction lay cheek-by-jowl—vide the fact that 'Salem's Lot, even though you couldn't locate it on a map of Maine, was always referenced as being just a little ways off from Bangor, which you could. This juxtaposition rendered scariness inevitable, because it removed the audience's automatic defense reflexes: The fake made the real seem "real-er", just as the real made the fake seem not only possible, but plausible. Everybody won.

Unfortunately, however, there was a side-effect: Horror stories not squarely located in the here and now began to be seen as making their potential audience work far too hard for its entertainment value. You could sort of get away with it in books like IT or FLOATING DRAGON, which went slippy-sliding back and forth through different time-periods but kept to the same area—but something like THE TALISMAN (Straub and King, two shots of scare for the price of one!) or King's THE EYES OF THE DRAGON and the Gunslinger series were considerably dicier. Which is why, to my mind, the dorks who are passionate about LORD OF THE RINGS and the dorks who are passionate about Sam Raimi's THE EVIL DEAD movies haven't tended to hang out at exactly the same conventions, up 'till recently.

What changed? Well, in fact, horror and fantasy have always had deep fingers in each other's chocolate and peanut butter, from Drac and Frank on: Part of Bram Stoker's "masterwork"'s eternal appeal is not just that he casually rifled Romanian history for a freak with an evocative name to defame and boiled the myriad conflicting vampire myths gathered from across Europe down into one set of rough guidelines (which other people almost immediately started to break—"catches fire in sunlight", anyone?—but lay that by), but that he also used all that state-of-the-art Victorian technology, social and sociological minutiae to back his story up. Reading an epistolary novel like DRACULA, with its mildly voyeuristic/boring mishmash of diary entries, letters, railroad timetables, book excerpts and newspaper article fragments, gives you the same slightly ill frisson as rifling through somebody else's desk-drawers, or (the way I often used to, during my babysitting years) looking under somebody's bed to find out not only where they keep their porn, but exactly what kind of porn they keep. It's the literary equivalent of "reality" TV, and even the earliest version of this docudramatic collage—FRANKENSTEIN, or the short stories of Edgar Allen Poe, with their breathless first-person confessional vibe—have the same vague intimations of automatic validity: Hey, buddy wouldn't say this shit if it wasn't true, on some level, right? Would he?

Here at the century's beginning, however, the pattern seems to have come full circle; "truth"-based fear is now the provenance of visual story-telling media, taking off from/leading into the wonderfully incestuous real-vs.-fake debates surrounding films like THE BLAIR WITCH PROJECT or RINGU. Is one medium inherently "realer" than another? Is something more likely to be "true" simply because it doesn't seem artificially husbanded? See Joe Berlinger's much/unfairly-maligned **BOOK OF SHADOWS: BLAIR WITCH II** for a sly take-down of that particular fallacy: "Video doesn't lie, man!" Oh yeah? How so, and why not? Like one Cinema Verite pioneer says, in Peter Wintonick's wonderful documentary **DEFINING THE MOMENT**, "it's only a lie if you don't like it"—ie, if the story being told isn't one you're interested in believing. And supposed raw authenticity vs. all-too-obvious artificiality ain't gonna help you with that one bit.

And wow, but we've come a fair old ways away from just discussing my fantastic juvenillia now, haven't we? Still, I'll end by asserting my belief that we're well due for a new epistolary horror novel soon, since the dark fantastic on paper has apparently become firmly reserved for all the poetic layering of internal and external voice, sensual input et al which movie scripts must regularly pare away in order to preserve their faithfulness to the stark onscreen image—a tabloid scare for a tabloid generation. Hell, I might even step in and fill that breach myself, one of these days . . .

Q: "God also seems to show up in a lot of these stories."

A: Yes, surprisingly—God, or the lack thereof.

In a review of my first collection, **KISSING CARRION**, Paula Guran of DarkEcho said that my characters inhabit a Godless universe, which I don't think is entirely true. On the one hand, I certainly wasn't raised with any religion to speak of; my Mom introduced me to the Bible via a book of Old Testament stories for kids, the same way she gave me Greek and Norse mythology by way of the D'Aullaires. No special emphasis was ever placed on Christianity as a system of belief—I knew about as much about Joseph and Jezebel as I did about Zeus, Thor, or various other deities, heroes and monsters from around the rest of the world. So as a result, I grew up with a heart that loves the mystic, vs. a brain which distrusts it on empirical principle—I feel the yearning, just like everybody else, but I'm from the (metaphorical) show-me state. And one day, I guess, I'll get either a nice or a very nasty surprise, on that front . . . again, just like everybody else.

Heh heh heh heh.

But more than anything, what my lack of grounding faith has left me with is the conviction that it's just as foolish to take ideas on faith as it is to reject them out of hand: Even science breaks down, the further away from palpable measurement things become. What's at the centre of a gluon? Will, or can, anybody ever know for sure? Far from being Godless, I see my universe as full of an endless, unproven possibility which might be as easily seen as despairing or hopeful, or both at once: A place in which no one is assured of the existence, presence or approval of God, yet no one is actively denied that, either.

Except, perhaps, by themselves.

Q: "And history, too. Why do you find the challenge of writing period pieces so inspirational?"

A: The simple answer to a complex query: I study history for its patterns, for the way things fit together, because part of what I tend to focus on about anything inevitably seems to concentrate on its interconnective qualities—the forest vs. the trees, leaves vs. roots, words vs. meanings, and so on. On top of that, though, there's also the inherent exoticism factor—the attraction of the alien, whether you're talking about mere sensual conundrums like what things must have felt like or smelled like during a different time, or something a little more difficult to get across: What people believed and why, the limitations of human knowledge and understanding, the rationalizations they made for their own actions, let alone for the universe's. 'Cause I'm all about the motivations, yo.

And then, not so surprisingly, there's the sheer grue of it all. Human beings really have done some amazingly dreadful stuff to each other, over the years—which certainly isn't news, I know, but bear with me; this is, horribly enough, often where my interests in anything tend to concentrate. Yet it's not all just mere voyeurism: I truly do believe that writing about what hasn't happened to me—and, hopefully, never will—helps me understand how it could have happened, in the first place. In other words, it makes me think . . . which, to my mind, is always useful.

Thus, pieces like "Nigredo" (previously unpublished), "Ring Of Fire" (first Published in PALACE CORBIE #6, Merrimack Books, ed. Wayne Edwards), "Year Zero" (first published in THE MAMMOTH BOOK OF VAMPIRE STORIES BY WOMEN, Robinson, ed. Stephen Jones), "Sent Down" (previously unpublished) and "The Emperor's Old Bones" (winner of International Horror Guild Award for Best Short Fiction of

1999, first published in **NORTHERN FRIGHTS** #5, Mosaic Press, ed. Don Hutchison). They've all got little kernels of steal-what-you-can-and-make-it-yours at the heart of them, like everything else I (or any other writer, to be really, really sollipsisticly inclusive) tend to write: For "Nigredo" it's the TV miniseries **UPRISING**, the first film about the Warsaw Ghetto that—to my mind—outfitted its freedom-fighters with genuine human faces rather than martyrs' masks, which is also why Kotzeleh always looks like Leelee Sobieski whenever I picture her stalking through the rest of her endless night. For "Ring of Fire", meanwhile, it's Paul Scott's Raj Quartet and **THE JEWEL IN THE CROWN**, cut with bits of Peter Brook's adaptation of **THE MAHABHARATA** and the seductive vocal rhythms of Rudyard Kipling's Jungle Book stories; "British people go crazy in such interesting ways," I remember telling a friend once, after a screening of **LAWRENCE OF ARABIA**, and this story neatly encapsulates many of my (no doubt biased) ideas about why that craziness always seems to involve going to another country and telling the people there how best to run their own shit.

"Year Zero"? That evolved from a longstanding double obsession with Baroness Orczy's **THE SCARLET PIMPERNEL** and **DANGEROUS LIAISONS** once more, with ten years' research on the French revolution chucked in for good measure. "Sent Down" is another side of the "British as crazy white folks" coin, here the colonized rather than the colonizers, a blatant **HEART OF DARKNESS** riff pitting civilized Romans against savage pseudo-Picts; all hail to Pauline Gedge for planting the seed with her novel **THE EAGLE AND THE RAVEN**, long long ago.

And then there's "The Emperor's Old Bones", my IHG Award-winning monster-piece, which everybody I know was rather amazed I didn't build my first collection around: Yes, it got its start with J.G. Ballard's and Steven Spielberg's versions of **EMPIRE OF THE SUN**, respectively, and no, I've never pretended otherwise. But I will take a moment here to thoroughly debunk the idea that I reference Peter Greenaway's name because I was thinking of **THE COOK, THE THIEF, HIS WIFE AND HER LOVER**—mystic longevity achieved through ritual cannibalism's been around a hell of a lot longer than that, as a concept. Ask the Chinese.

Q: "But don't you think it's a little dicey, appropriating other people's cultural voices the way you do in pieces like these?"

A: I've been thinking a lot about that lately, probably because putting this book together meant digging fairly deep through the extremely obsessive, highly influential alchemist's refuse-pile I like to call my subconscious—more so even than last time, when I cobbled KISSING CARRION into publically acceptable shape. That's because while KISSING CARRION's theme was "simple" dark, urban creep and slime of a sort all too distressingly easy to extrapolate from my own experiences, THE WORM IN EVERY HEART's leaning is firmly towards the fantastic rather than the realistic, and the exotic rather than the familiar; the detritus of a thousand hours misspent skimming non-fiction for inspirational nuggets, those few shaky grains of research which form the grit from which I've spun this particular string of black, bloody pearls.

But the fact that Martin Scorsese's GANGS OF NEW YORK is my favorite film should tell you something, in context—I like my history the way I like my melodrama, big and bloody, with lots of tabloid spice to shore up the painstakingly accurate detail. And that means that by blithely discarding or ignoring whatever didn't support my various theses, along the way, I've no doubt opened myself up to a thousand charges of demeaning or insulting all those I'm not and never will be, "stealing" their various voices to support my nasty tales: Gay Torontonian magicians of Hong Kong descent, Warsaw Ghetto uprising survivors, mythological Indian demons, aging British "speculative fiction" writers with an occasional bent towards black magick, etc.

To all the people who may see themselves in my characters, therefore, I apologize in advance for seeming to claim/exploit your pain or plunder a part of your heritage. Granted, I am white as a sack of sheets and Canadian as a sack of maple leaves (for all I was born in England), but world conquest has never been my aim, not even on a pen-to-page level. I just get these things in my head, all shiny and swollen and blood-encrusted: Gold and scarlet, with prayers to gods both forgotten and un- singing teasingly through my veins, leaving shadows on my CAT-scans and blank spots on my x-rays. Which is why, for the sake of my health—not to mention the health of those around me—they really do just have to come out, eventually; better here than through the barrel of an Uzi, I guess.

Still, though. How can I possibly justify the constant juxtaposition of human and inhuman horror, of using real tragedies—revolutions, massacres, the Holocaust itself—to throw various mythical daemons into relief? Am I piggybacking my prose on the suffering of others, and isn't there something profane about that—something blasphemous, even in this very secular world we live in?

I remember interviewing documentarian Errol Morris about his film **MR DEATH: THE RISE AND FALL OF FRED A. LEUCHTER, JNR.**, back when I was still a film critic. It's an amazing portrait of a man who went from being a self-taught electric chair redesigner (he wanted to make execution a more humane process) to a Holocaust-denying pariah in just a few, hideously easy steps. His stubborn deification of "scientific" detachment sent him to Auschwitz, where he took a hammer to its walls and stuffed bits of masonry he chipped off into his socks so he could smuggle them back to the States and test them, hoping to debunk the validity of the "six million killed" figure.

Morris said that what he found particularly offensive and naive about Leuchter's actions was that if you drew a map of human misery, Auschwitz would be dead centre. And I can still see myself nodding sagely—but even then, I didn't really believe it. Because we close these events off like pockets, and I understand why we do, but to some extent this habit just perpetuates our overall human bent towards justifying genocide: We say "the worst has already happened", and overlook something equally horrible happening right in front of us. On the one hand, it's great to be able to put pain into perspective—to say "well at least this isn't as bad as X". But when we use that exact method to dismiss other people's pain, we're back in the same old same old, the red rut we've been plowing since Sumer, when every other man in a conquered city routinely had his flayed skin hung from the walls.

1940's Germany was a "civilized" nation, an organized nation, and thus they set a standard which ideologically-justified murderers all over the world continue to kill up to. Stalin's gulags, China's Cultural Revolution, Rwanda, the Balkans, Pol Pot's killing fields—tribal hatreds crossed with cold-blood political scapegoating, plus modern technological methodry. Does the very innate brutality of Bosnian rape camps make them somehow less evil than herding children quickly and efficiently into gas chambers? These fine gradations can't help but be barely meaningful: Evil, like shit, don't come in degrees, and recognizing it on sight when other people do it will never innoculate you against your own inherent tendency toward demonizing whatever—or whoever—you happen to disapprove of.

That's the best lesson I ever learned, way back in City Alternative School's interdisciplinary Holocauset course—the plain fact that my pain doesn't trump your pain, no matter what: Never will, and never should. That nothing in history should ever be declared so sacred it can't be examined, even creatively, poetically, fantastically.

So: Will history really teach us nothing? Ask Sting, man. Ask yourself. I've got no answers—or maybe I do, and these are them.

Say, that's kind of . . . scary.

Q: "So which of these experiences actually come closest to your own?"

A: "By The Mark" (previously unpublished) and "The Kindly Ones" (previously unpublished). One's a not-exactly-love letter to the area of Toronto I spent my tween years in, as well as the people I spent them with—the ones who might best remember me as that girl who strangled a fellow student for saying her drawing of a whale looked like a tadpole, or threatened (in medically-accurate detail) to give someone else who was teasing her a lobotomy with a geometry compass. Or just "that fucking weirdo". The other is a thinly-veiled slander against my maternal grandmother, and I like to think it pretty much speaks for itself. Which is why I'm not going to discuss it in any sort of detail . . . here, or anywhere else.

That being said, no one ever molested me—not even the creepy boyfriend of my mother's housemate who originally told me that "you started licking me" story (uck!)—and my mother's still alive. I lie for a living, folks. Hope you enjoy the result.

Q: "Still with the sex, though, I notice."

A: (Smiles) Yes. That's right.

Those who've read the KISSING CARRION Afterword will, I hope, recall my rather snide breakdown of the 1990s' "erotic horror" era—but you know, I'm just as happy to have been thus asskicked into cultivating my ability to write frankly about people putting their parts into other people's parts, because (horrors!) the plain fact is, I enjoy it. Not all the time, mind you, and not with every story; I'm still amazed that Showtime's erotic horror anthology TV series ended up optioning some of the stories they did, since some of them—like "Fly-By-Night" (first published in THE VAMPIRE'S CRYPT #8, ed. Margaret L. Carter) and "The Guided Tour"(first published in THE VAMPIRE'S CRYPT #9, ed. Margaret

L. Carter), for example—not only had no sex in them to begin with, but didn't exactly benefit from having sex shoehorned into them.

'Course, with "The Guided Tour", it was pretty much a "they changed everything but the title, and then they changed the title" scenario from the get-go. Years later, I still receive occasional mail from fans of the HUNGER episode "Wrath Of God" who've looked up my story, only to be very surprised; better take it up with HUNGER executive producers the Scott brothers and/or episode director Russell Mulcahy for further details on that one, ladies and gents. And "Fly-By-Night" was basically rewritten both on set and in the editing suite, as is often the wont with TV—they got considerably more than they bargained for during the filming of one particular sequence, so they used it. And having seen the result, I've got to admit that I might well have made the same call myself.

I was far happier with the adaptation of "Bottle Of Smoke"(first published in DEMON SEX, Masquerade Books, ed. Amarantha Knight), but then again, why wouldn't I be? I wrote the thing. I do, however, remember being incredibly amused by how much of my scriptwriting duties essentially boiled down to taking out all the hot Lesbian action which had caused this piece to be optioned in the first place: Apparently, my little genie-in-a-bottle as ultimate masturbational aid parable (I once described it to one friend as "Paul Bowles' THE SHELTERING SKY meets Michael Ondaatje's THE ENGLISH PATIENT, but all in one house, and there's a whole lot of girl-on-girl") was too explicit for THE HUNGER, baby! That's gotta be some sort of achievement.

Q: "Yeah, I guess. And now?"

A: Remember how I said I was working on a first novel? Well, make that "novels". And like a lot of other writers contemplating making this very important step, I'm bringing the 'verse I've painstakingly cobbled together throughout all these stories along with me, in one way or another: Two of the novels take off from "The Narrow World", in one way or another. Characters from "The Emperor's Old Bones" have shown up here and there. There's also a backing structure on which I may hang several new stories, to create a Scheherazade/Tanith Lee-esque secret history of the world—and the city of Toronto—as a burgeoning misery vector. Those who know me will understand what I'm hinting around by making these starements, but hopefully even those who don't will find at least one or two of them intriguing. That's the plan.

It occurs to me, however, that I should probably warn those who liked **KISSING CARRION** more than they liked **THE WORM IN EVERY HEART** that several of these projects will turn one way or the other, contain elements of one slant or the other, etc. Because between the two of them, like I said when we first began this little hoe-down, they pretty much encapsulate not only the last fifteen years of my working life, but everything I've ever been . . . and continue to be . . . interested in. These two collections are me, straight up and twisted: All my tropes, all my patterns, the full evilly-tinted spectrum of my many, many, many obsessions.

Ah, obsession. I've been thinking a lot about that factor lately too, especially as it pertains to my writing: This engine of passionate interest which continually drives me to grab what moves me and cannibalize it for spare parts, then build something new from its bones. And when it spills over into paying work, that's admirable, but when it spills over into anything else—fan fiction, for example, the usually-denigrated flipside of that self-same spring—it's not; self-indulgent at best, border-line-illegal at worst.

People often congratulate me on being able to channel my interests in "useful" pursuits, an idea I've been somewhat shamefacedly perpetuating myself, as though all the more directly-influenced writing I've already done vis a vis these subjects were a slightly dirty not-exactly-secret. As though even when all I do with it is simply post it in my blog, it's the virtual equivalent of what the cat keeps doing to me every time I incautiously lie down and try to get some sleep: Jump up, thrust his hindquarters in my face and squeal imperiously, like "Hey, look! It's my ass! What do you mean you don't want to see my ass? It's MY ASS!"

And maybe that's true. Maybe at this point in my life, continuing to enthuse over various movies or what have you like some haphazard cultural garburator and writing about the result is like exposing myself in public, an eccentricity that's bound to get me negative/tabloid attention. Maybe it's annoying to my peers and fans in the same way that I tend to find the forays of other writers whose stuff I've admired at one point or another into areas I have absolutely no interest in annoying: Pop music fandon = crack! Yaoi/anime = crack! Poppy Z. Brite writing about cooking or Sam Raimi making movies about baseball or Stephen King going back to those damn Gunslinger books = crack! What kind of crack have y'all been smoking, that you're not content to simply stick with the stuff which attracted my attention to you in the first place?

But: Everybody's crack is crack, equally—all-consuming, inaccessible, impossible to totally understand from an outsider's perspective. There's no crack that anyone can really argue you into accepting as "non-crack". Me being the queen of Fandoms Of One, I already know this far better than anybody else; all we can do is look in, disconnect, then surf on. So if you can't understand why the next thing you see from me may or may not be motivated by wanting to turn my strident interest in the Five Points section of 1860's New York into something which won't have Martin Scorsese's fingerprints all over it, though it will have all the gross supernatural stuff you've come to expect from me tooling around its edges, then feel free to do, and do—I won't hold it agin' ya. It's MY crack, see? It's MY ASS! Look, or don't—like it, or don't; don't matter to me, shouldn't matter to you. And all that jazz.

But if you are along for the rest of the ride no matter what the destination might turn out to be, or even if you've only gone along with with me thus far, then bless you. You are what keeps me sane, and I mean that very sincerely.

So: Goodnight and thank you, whoever. Enjoy the book(s). And I'll see you again . . .

. . . as soon as I possibly can.

Made in the USA
Lexington, KY
19 August 2014